THE ACADEMY

A Joe Traynor Novel-Book #8

BY DANIEL J. BARRETT

A Black Opal Books Publication

GENRE: Mystery,

This is a work of fiction. Names, places, characters and incidents are either the product of the author's imagination or are used fictitiously, and any resemblance to any actual persons, living or dead, businesses, organizations, events or locales is entirely coincidental. All trademarks, service marks, registered trademarks, and registered service marks are the property of their respective owners and are used herein for identification purposes only. The publisher does not have any control over or assume any responsibility for author or third-party websites or their contents.

THE ACADEMY
Copyright © 2023 by Daniel J. Barrett
Cover Design by Transformational Concepts
All cover art copyright ©2023
All Rights Reserved
Print ISBN: 978-1-960050-06-9
Publication: July 2023

All rights reserved under the International and Pan-American Copyright Conventions. No part of this book may be reproduced or transmitted in any form or by any means, electronic or mechanical, including photocopying, recording, or by any information storage and retrieval system, without permission in writing from the publisher.

WARNING: The unauthorized reproduction or distribution of this copyrighted work is illegal. Criminal copyright infringement, including infringement without monetary gain, is investigated by the FBI and is punishable by up to 5 years in federal prison and a fine of $250,000. Anyone pirating our eBooks will be prosecuted to the fullest extent of the law and may be liable for each individual download resulting therefrom.

ABOUT THE PRINT VERSION: If you purchased a print version of this book without a cover, you should be aware that the book is stolen property. It was reported as "unsold and destroyed" to the publisher, and neither the author nor the publisher has received any payment for this "stripped book."

IF YOU FIND AN EBOOK OR PRINT VERSION OF THIS BOOK BEING SOLD OR SHARED ILLEGALLY, PLEASE REPORT IT TO: skh@blackopalbooks.com

Published by Black Opal Books http://www.blackopalbooks.com

Books by Daniel J. Barrett

Conch Town Girl Series
Joe and Julie Traynor
Conch Town Girl
Can't Sing or Dance
Taking Care of Your Own
Never Say Never
Death But No Taxes
The Academy

Jack Manning and Mary Evans
You Don't Know Jack
Second Chances

Chapter 1

The phone rang at their home in Tavernier. Joe picked up and said, "Hello, may I help you?"

"Hi Joe, it's Jake," said Rear Admiral Barnes. "We're certainly going to miss you, Call me when you and your family get up to the Academy and get settled. I'd like to come up for a tour and help you get welcomed properly. Are you all packed and ready to go?" he asked.

"Yes, sir. We're all packed and ready to go. It snowed up in New London last night. I hear they got five inches which isn't much from my time in the northeast," said Joe.

Joe continued, "We have a Coast Guard cargo plane hauling all our belongings and dropping them off at our new home, right off campus. As you know, there isn't any officer housing on campus so we were lucky to get a place just vacated by another transferred officer. It has three bedrooms and two baths and is two blocks from campus and the hospital. We'll fly directly into the Groton, Connecticut's Groton-New London Airport, which is about three miles from the Academy. I remember when I first arrived at the Academy as a student almost fifteen years ago that I came up by ship from Miami. That first trip wasn't real pleasant and I don't think I slept for ten minutes. This seems a lot better," Joe said and laughed.

"I guess you made progress then," said the Rear Admiral.

"I guess you could say that. They said it would take about a week to get everything settled. In the meantime, as you know, there's a Suites Hotel only a few blocks away from campus that will provide us a makeshift home until everything arrives. We'll eat our meals in the cafeteria when we can."

Joe went on, "Julie's delivery is due any day and it's been hectic to say the least. Santa came for Christmas and we thought there would be another delivery but it looks like it will be up in New London. She'll be delivering at the Coast Guard Academy Hospital, right down the street. It's a two-minute walk to the hospital from 31 Mohegan Avenue Parkway to 15 Mohegan Avenue Parkway. You can see the hospital from our suite at the hotel. Hopefully, we'll be in our new home before the delivery. I have to put the crib together. They're already aware that she will be delivering within the next week or two at most. Thank God that Tillie, Julie's grandmother, will come with us and stay for a month or two until Julie is ready to be on her own."

"Joe, stay in touch. If there's anything you need let me know. The Rear Admiral and Superintendent of the Academy, Rear Admiral Kelly, said he is looking forward to your arrival. I know that you've been back and forth over the last year getting familiar with the administration and staff as well as the students but this is a new chapter and a complete change in your life."

Rear Admiral Barnes added, "You may not know this but Bill Kelly and I graduated together from the Academy in 1987. We took different paths. He moved through the education side of the service while I wanted action, just like you. I think we're two peas in a pod. He and I are very good friends and I told him all about you. Over the last year, he has called me and said he was very impressed by you personally and impressed by your experience, education and grasp for what matters. He knew all about your time during the crisis in New Orleans during Katrina and your time in Haiti. He was quite impressed. He had been made aware of you for quite some time, way before even meeting you when you visited the Academy, I may add," said Jake. "Just remember, I'm Jake to you and he will always be addressed as Rear Admiral Kelly."

"Got it," said Joe. "I promise I won't make that mistake."

They ended the call and Joe was getting nervous. His whole world and his family's world were about to dramatically change. Julie was fine with the move and the Northeast because she spent five years in Providence, Rhode Island getting her bachelor's and master's Degree of Fine Arts from Brown University. Brown is only an hour away by car from the Coast Guard Academy. She was thinking of teaching or spending time as a visiting author at Brown until she received a call one day from the Dean of Education from Connecticut College in New London. The college is one block away from their new home in New London. She told the Dean about her pregnancy and pending delivery date so they would meet when she was settled and had the baby.

The Dean was well aware of Julie Chapman's credentials from Brown University and her impact on young women throughout the nation with her trilogy called *A Girl's Story* and her new series from Disney based on those three editions. The Dean said she would be honored if she would consider a position or relationship with the college when she arrived. She said she would be pleased to meet with her but obviously there would be a delay due to circumstances. Connecticut College is one of the finest liberal arts colleges in the country, ranked 50th and among the most expensive in the nation.

Both Joe and Julie agreed that as soon as they get there, after moving into their new home, their first priority would be to have Bella start the second grade in her New London elementary school, mid-semester from her old school in Key Largo. It will be quite a change for her so they'll have to pay special attention. When Bella gets nervous, she reverts back to Spanish so it may prove a challenge. Bella just missed attending the Coast Guard Child Development Center right on campus that serves kids ages six-months to five years old. Julie is qualified to home school her but she's having a baby and home schooling for a while may prove difficult at best. That's why Tillie is staying with them for a month or two until Julie gets back on her feet and into a daily routine. Julie felt she needed Tillie now as much as she did back when she was eight years old when her mother died. Julie didn't know what she would do without her grandmother. Hopefully, everything will all work out in the near future.

Joe needed to say goodbye to all his college friends and associates at The College of the Florida Keys before departing to Connecticut. He had served right up to Christmas time at the college, almost a year to the day when he was first appointed as Interim President, taking the place of Dr. Morgan Hennessey who left to become Provost at Barry University in Miami. Joe left the college in good stead. Joan Talbot was promoted to Lieutenant and took over Joe's old job as head of the military wing of the college. She was still in the service and would retire within the next two years. She really needed to stay to run the $5 million dollar Trust recruitment effort at the college, set up by Mary Evans. They were about halfway through with excellent results. Money combined with talent and experience was a winning combination. The college board wanted Mary Evans to become the new President of The College of the Florida Keys but she was not ready for this position. She was moving back and forth from Troy, New York to Key West in Florida and needed to spend time in both regions so the presidency was out. She thought maybe in the future but was just starting to get back to normal after her being kidnapped by three members of the Nationalist Alliance, a Florida white supremacy group. Joe Traynor saved her life and showed her that she needed to be aware of her circumstances at all times, regardless of how hard it was. Being showered with $480.0 million dollars in lottery winnings coupled with her husband, Jack Manning's $330.0 million dollars, proved to be too much of a target for groups like this and endangered her life every day. So, Mary offered to be on a selection committee to help hire a new president of the college and they found what they thought could be a very good match to where the college was moving through an intense strategic plan.

The College of the Florida Keys selected a woman, Dr. Nancy Shapiro, as the next president of the college. She was 50 years old, the exact same age as Mary. She was divorced but had two grown children residing in Washington, D.C. During her interview period, she stated that she loved Washington, D.C. but needed a change in her life and this position offered her the perfect opportunity for growth and experience.

Dr. Shapiro has her undergraduate degrees from George Washington University in Washington, D.C. and her Ph.D. in education from Georgetown. Nancy comes from a multinational background. Her father is Jewish and a Washington, D.C. attorney and her mother, also grew up in Washington, D.C. and was born in the Dominican Republic, arriving in the United States when she was five years old. She is fluent in Spanish, a woman, and an excellent choice for this position. Both Joe and Mary thought she was more than qualified and as Mary said, other than her money, more qualified than her. Joe and Mary got a good laugh out of it but would never repeat it to anyone. They held a very unique bond coming from the same place, the same Catholic schools in Troy, New York and now the same Ph.D.'s from Barry University. Mary was a multimillionaire and Joe was heading to the Coast Guard Academy to fulfill a dream he had when he first entered the Coast Guard at age eighteen years old as a dropout from MIT.

They had a small party for Joe at the college and everyone in town showed up. What was accomplished over the last few years was amazing. Starting with Joe and Morgan's plan, coupled with Mary's original twenty million dollars to build a state-of-the-art technology center, proved wildly successful. It proved so successful that even after the first year during a pandemic, Morgan Hennessey was offered the position of Provost at Barry University, moving Joe Traynor into the Interim President position. The contracts coming out of the technology center paid all the facility bills so Mary's money went directly into cutting-edge technology and support for students. It also jumpstarted careers into the Coast Guard for minority students and women of color. Those students who graduated and went to work for the college in the technology center were making over fifty thousand dollars a year with benefits.

The economic impact on the community was substantial and they moved from being a weak organization to the leader of the pack in south Florida and the Florida Keys. Student enrollment was up over twenty-five percent from a few years ago and continuing to climb. Joe thought it was nice to hand off a successful tenure to someone else who was probably even more qualified than either he or Mary. Of course, you can't replace the money that was pumped in but that's for another day and another person to achieve.

Joe and Julie offered their house to Tillie in Tavernier but she didn't want to move from Key Largo even if it's only a few miles away. She was happy in her garden apartment and was close to her friend, Ed Lansing. She would only be gone for a month or two up north to New London to help Julie with the new baby and with Bella. So, Joe and Julie put their house, 107 High Street in Tavernier, on the market and it sold within a week. It's only four blocks from Coral Shores High School, within a block of the ocean, and close to the main highway into the Keys. They paid $385,000.00 three years ago and the taxes are very low. This house is in a federal-government-designated area with a minimal risk and is an "X Zone" and the FEMA flood insurance, although expensive, was the cheapest of all flood insurance at less than $1,500.00 a year. They made out well. The new owners paid $485,000.00 in cash. Less the 5% commission, they made $75,000.00 on their investment added to the original $30,000.00 they had put down. That money would go right into a certificate of deposit to keep for when they needed to buy another house.

Joe and Julie also had a trust fund set up by Mary Evans for one million dollars for their children's education and for Tillie's care if and when she would need it. Julie was still receiving substantial royalties from her books and from Disney Studios for her new series. Joe was rather curious about his new salary and was it enough for him alone to cover the bills up north. It was. Starting salary for a new Captain in the Coast Guard started at one hundred and fifty thousand dollars a year, plus housing. That wasn't too bad a deal considering where he started as a new eighteen-year-old recruit making twenty thousand dollars a year to start, almost 19 years ago. He was out of the service for a few years receiving his MBA from Rensselaer Polytechnic Institute and working for a nonprofit in Albany, New York. When he got back in the service, it was flawless and they even counted his time that he left as part of deal to get him back into the Coast Guard. Joe could actually retire at thirty-nine years old with twenty years of service. However, that was the furthest thing from his mind. He thought he might just make a career of the Coast Guard, especially since he now has this assignment as Assistant Superintendent of the Coast Guard Academy.

Joe, Julie, Tillie, and Bella finally arrived at New London, Connecticut to start this new chapter in their lives. Even though Tillie wasn't staying permanently, it would still change her daily routine that she thoroughly enjoyed, stopping every day to give Bella a hug at the bus stop or having her stay at her apartment and then having either Joe or Julie pick her up. She would miss that. Joe and Julie were both used to the great northeast, winter and all but they worried about Bella. She seemed to enjoy visiting Troy last year for Christmas and seeing snow for the first time. They hoped she would continue to enjoy new surroundings. As soon as they arrived, they were treated like rock stars and shown to their temporary suite. As soon as all their belongings were put in place, they would move into a real home near the campus. They were able to sell most of their furniture and give Tillie several items that she wanted. Joan Talbot took a few items for sentimental reasons, making the journey to New London a little easier for everyone. Julie left her car with Tillie and Joe only drove a Coast Guard vehicle.

At Julie's party, there wasn't a dry eye in the place. She was in this school district every day from kindergarten through graduation and then came back to work at Coral Shores High School after graduation with her Master's in Fine Arts from Brown University. She walked to school every day after getting Bella onto the bus to head to the same elementary school that Julie attended many years ago when she met Joe as an eleven-year-old, in 5th grade. He was brand new in the Coast Guard at eighteen, just going on nineteen. *She thought that was quite a walk down sentimental lane.*

Chapter 2

The move went smoothly. Boxes were unpacked with supervision by Julie and Tillie. Joe put the baby crib together but they would use a bassinet for the first month or two so Tillie could have her own room as well as Bella. It was closing in on the second week of January. It was cold but not by New London standards. It was thirty-two degrees, freezing by every calculation, but the wind was calm and there were only a few inches of snow on the ground making driving in the area okay. Both Joe and Julie would have to remember how to drive in this weather. It has been quite a long time living in the Florida Keys that would make you forget about the slipping and sliding on a daily basis throughout the winter.

"Joe?"

"Yes," said Joe. "Are you okay?"

"What time is it?" she asked.

Joe turned to look at the alarm clock on the end table by the bed. "It's 3:30 in the morning," he said.

"Joe?" she said again.

"What? Are you okay?" he asked.

"Joe, my water just broke. I think I've been having

contractions for about a half an hour or so. I'm glad I put the rubber mat over the mattress. I could have ruined it."

"Are we going to the hospital?" Joe asked cautiously.

"Can you quietly wake Tillie so she can help me sponge off and get dressed? I'll need about twenty minutes. Go start the car. I think I'm only a few centimeters dilated but I don't want to take a chance. I know we're only a few blocks away but I don't really want to walk," she said. "Tillie can stay with Bella until the morning and they both can come over. I'm sure I'm dilated. Don't know how much but I think I'm ready."

Tillie got up quickly. She thought this would be the week that Julie would be delivering. Julie's go-bag was all packed and she gingerly washed up with Tillie's help and got dressed. She went to Bella's room and gave her a quick kiss on the forehead and Joe helped her to the car. Julie gave Tillie a hug and a quick kiss and told her to be at the hospital as soon as Bella woke up. She could skip school today. It was a big day for all of them.

Joe was nervous and it showed. He had a big smile on his face and said, "This is it, Julie. This is what we've been waiting for. I think Bella will be thrilled whatever we have. I know Tillie is thrilled."

It took Joe about four minutes to drive up to the emergency room entrance and open the door for Julie. He had called the hospital on the way and they were waiting for them at the door with a wheelchair. Joe didn't believe it to be true but the staff were well aware of who the Traynors are in this close knit Coast Guard community. Joe always acted as a normal human being and was polite to everyone, most of the time unless they were in a combat situation so he didn't realize what a big deal everyone made of this delivery. Evidently, it was the first delivery of an Assistant Superintendent and his wife since the wing opened.

Joe went with her as soon as he parked the car out of the way of the emergency room entrance. He walked in with jeans, an L. L. Bean shirt, boots, and a jacket. If they didn't know who he was, his appearance would not have given it away. So, they arrived about 4:00 a.m. with no one around. It turned into 8:00 a.m. when everyone on the day shift began arriving. Tillie was already there in the waiting room with Bella, who was eating a banana and drinking chocolate milk. Tillie thought it would take her mind off of it. And she sipped her coffee. Finally, around 8:45 a.m., Joe came out with the doctor and they were all smiles.

"Bella, you have a new little sister," said Joe. Tillie was all smiles. "How big?" she asked.

The doctor said, "She weighs seven pounds and ten ounces and is twenty inches in length. She's perfect."

"Yeah," said Tillie and Bella together. "Can we see her?" asked Bella.

"We have to wait for the nurses to clean her up and then we can go to her room to see the baby, but only for a few minutes, Bella," said Joe.

"That's fine," she said, all smiles.

About a half hour later both Bella and Tillie were shown to Julie's room. The baby was in Julie's arms. Julie was exhausted. It took longer than she thought but had heard horror stories of how long some went so she was grateful. Joe was beaming. Bella went up to the baby and kissed her on the forehead and smiled. Tillie was still in awe. It was her second great-grandchild, counting Bella, even though she raised Julie as her daughter not her granddaughter.

"Do you have a name picked out?" said Tillie.

Joe turned and nodded to Julie who said, "Tillie, we are naming her Ann after my mother but Ann Marie Traynor.

The Marie is your middle name and Joe's mother's first name. His mother was Marie Bridget O'Malley, a fine Irish name if there ever was one. No offense Tillie but I didn't have the heart to name her Matilda, you know?" She laughed. "We will call her Annie just like you called my Mom."

Tillie started to cry but those were happy tears. How far they have come she thought. They have come all the way from being dirt poor in the Florida Keys to this. It was a dream come true for Tillie.

"By the way," Joe said. "I checked with the Catholic Chaplain, who is also the Pastor of our new parish, and Annie can be baptized at the Coast Guard Memorial Chapel next month at the 9:00 a.m. Mass. I have to call everyone but Tillie you know you and Tanya are the Godmothers and Pete is the Godfather, so you will have to at least stay for the baptism," he smiled and laughed.

"I'm not going anywhere for a while, Joe. You can't get rid of me that easily," she said.

Tillie took Bella home and made her lunch. She would take her to her school for the afternoon and then pick her up and they would walk back to the hospital together. Julie would only be there until 5:00 p.m. the next day and then would be released. Thank God the weather held out so they could get both Julie and Annie home safely. A few blocks away seemed like a mountain to climb with everything going on. Joe had to meet with his Superintendent and then would make all the calls. He assumed that his father, brother and sister-in-law, Tanya, would come over in a day or two just for a day trip to see the baby. It was nice only being a few hours away instead of fifteen hundred miles.

"Come on in, Joe," said Rear Admiral Kelly. "I understand congratulations are in order."

"Yes, sir. Ann Marie Traynor was born at 8:45 a.m.

today at the Coast Guard Hospital right here. She weighs seven pounds and ten ounces and is twenty inches long, tall for a girl, I understand. We'll call her Annie."

"Great name. I did a little research on the Irish. Evidently the Kellys and the Traynors, in Ireland are related in Counties Meath and Mayo."

"Yes, sir. I believe that's true according to my father at least."

"Well, welcome to the Kelly family," he said.

Joe thought that was unusual after Jake gave him the lowdown on calling him sir and how rigid he was. *Maybe he changed, Joe thought.*

"I also understand that you and my good friend Jake Barnes are very close."

"Well, sir. I have worked under Rear Admiral Barnes since I was eighteen years old when I joined the Coast Guard. I'm now thirty-seven, so that's half my life I guess."

"Don't get me wrong it's just that Jake highly recommended you and I had to see for myself what you were all about. As Jake said, he went into the service for the action and I went in for the education but we both did fine. Joe, I looked into your Coast Guard career and I am very impressed. You speak fluently Russian, Chechen, Spanish and are now learning Chinese. When you first came back to the service to take care of Julie and her grandmother, you were working at a nonprofit in Albany. You took down a major Mexican cartel and shot four gangbangers including the son of the general of the Mexican Mafia and he wound up in the custody of the CIA. You also received, as a Warrant Officer, from the President of the United States, presented by the FBI, the Coast Guard Commendation Medal with a Ribbon. It is the highest award issued for heroism, not involving combat with an enemy outside the country, by the United States Coast Guard. Joe, that's a hell of an accomplishment."

"Thank you, sir." Joe said.

"I think you bring a different perspective to the Academy, Joe. You started as an eighteen-year-old recruit out of MIT, to getting your Ph.D. recently and coming here as second in command of the Coast Guard Academy. What I would like to see is for you is to take what you have learned from your leadership Ph.D. but even better from your experience and tell us here what we can do better."

"I would like that sir. I would like to attend classes from the first year through the fourth year. I'm not a Narc but the world is changing. I want to see more minorities represented here not just because it's the right thing to do, we need their language skills to find out exactly, on a daily basis, what terrorists and criminals are planning. I don't think we have that now and it's a critical piece that seems to be missing. Remember, I've been floating around here for the better part of a year before I became full time."

"I also wanted to commend you on breaking up the kidnapping case for your friend Mary Evans. How the hell did you think about putting GPS clips onto her shoes and convincing her it was necessary. Most rich people would have balked," Rear Admiral Kelly said.

"I explained, I yelled, I begged and pleaded with both her and her husband that it was necessary. They are both extremely bright people. It's not the rich part. They didn't inherit it and expect people to lavish them. Mary's an ex-nun and Jack is just an average nice guy, who became very smart as he spent his money on worthy causes. In fact, they received, combined, $810.0 million dollars before taxes and are doing remarkable things," Joe said.

"I understand that perfectly. As a matter of fact, I understand that you learned, after the fact, that Mary has donated ten million dollars to the Academy in honor of the Miami Seventh Coast Guard District with you and only you to decide what to do with the money. I would say that's a ton of gratitude for what you did for her," said Kelly. "Jake told me the real reason we are getting the money and without you, it wouldn't be coming here. So thanks, Captain," he said and smiled. *Captain not Joe, he thought Jake was right.*

"I'm sure, sir, everyone here can figure out what to do with the ten million dollars. I would hope a lot goes to recruiting minorities and women and promoting them to officers in the very near future," said Joe.

"Joe, you better head out. I understand you're heading to the hospital. Let's continue this conversation. I just wanted to let you know that we understand where you're coming from and will support new cutting-edge ideas to make the Academy that much better. By the way, we also know all about your brilliant, beautiful wife. The president of Connecticut College called me yesterday to lobby her to be part of their English department. As you know, they are very exclusive but your wife is a prize they are after with her national reputation as an author and Brown graduate. Let's talk more at the end of the week. I know you're busy so go and thanks for being here," said Read Admiral Kelly.

"Thank you, sir, for your understanding. It's appreciated." With that, Joe left and headed for the hospital. He had called Tillie and told her they could meet in the cafeteria to have dinner and then see Julie and the baby. He asked her how Bella was reacting and she said fine but she seems to need a little more attention from everyone as we get back into the groove. He agreed. On the way, he called his father and brother and they said they would come over in two days, not stay but wanted to see the baby and Julie. They would definitely be there for the baptism coming up.

That night, Joe put his feet up on the hassock and had a beer in his hands. He was looking at his iPad, trying to figure out where all the buildings on campus were located. He was supposed to meet the Board of Trustees next week and give a presentation on his almost nineteen-year career with highlights but wasn't sure what to say. Almost everything he did, he was either undercover or under orders from the Coast Guard, the FBI and Homeland Security. Carrying all three credentials meant that at any given time he could tell anyone whom he represented at that moment and get away with it. Now, he was second in command at the Coast Guard Academy. He wasn't sure if he would ever get that freedom back to perform at his peak. He already missed the action. He didn't think he was an action junkie but he probably was. He just tried to stay low key about it for everyone's sake.

Joe's major accomplishments were based on his ability to never panic in tight situations. He prided himself on that. When Mary was kidnapped, everyone around her panicked and didn't know what to do. Immediately, his training kicked in and he went for his iPhone to get the app that tracked Mary's location. That probably saved her life because it was only a short while later that he found her and his team rescued her without any harm, other than being drugged. There was major harm to two of the four kidnappers but that was for another day. He wondered if he could teach a course to first year cadets on developing immediate responses for difficult situations, especially when those situations are presented to them in different languages.

Chapter 3

It was Saturday and Julie had been home for a few days. Little Annie seemed to be sleeping okay and Julie was getting her rest as well. Tillie was the full-time caretaker at this point since Joe's duties seemed to have not stopped since they landed in New London. Bella seemed to like her new school. It was only a few blocks away so Tillie walked her there for the first few days and then Bella wanted to be on her own. Being the new kid and being walked to school in second grade seemed to make Bella a little nervous. So, Tillie relented and saw her to the door and followed her down to the corner. From there it was only a few minutes walk to the front door to her school. At 2:30 p.m., when she got out of school, Tillie would wait on the porch, sipping a cup of coffee to see that she made it home all right. It seemed to be working and Bella was much happier. It was January and a little warm for the month so Tillie was not complaining. Right now it was seventy-eight degrees in Key Largo and the sun was shining. She was torn. She wanted to be home but wouldn't miss this time with Julie, the baby, and Bella for the world.

Joe's father, brother, and wife, made it to New London

in two and a half hours with a stop on the Mass Pike. It's one hundred and sixty-five miles door-to-door. Joe greeted them on the front porch and gave a hug to Tanya, his new sister-in-law. He shook hands with his brother and father. They stopped hugging when Joe was starting his freshman year at Catholic High in Troy, after a few of his female classmates saw him getting a hug from his father and smiled at him without saying a word. That was it. That was the last official hug. He was sure there were some in between then and now but they didn't count, he thought.

"Do you know you're exactly fourteen miles from the Mohegan Sun, directly due north? With traffic, it can't be more than twenty minutes away. We need to keep that in mind next time we come down. We could have stayed over and lost all Annie's gift money," he said and laughed.

"How much could that amount to?" said Joe with a smirk.

They walked in and saw Julie holding Annie in a new rocking chair, new to them that Tillie picked up this week at an antique store in town. Where they lived was right next to the Academy and a mile from downtown. They dropped the chair off to her yesterday afternoon and Julie loved it. Tanya reached out to give Julie a hug and kissed Annie on the forehead.

"May I?" she asked.

Julie got up from the chair and Tanya sat down and reached out for the baby. "Oh what a beautiful little girl you are, Annie," she said. She stared at Pete and nodded to him and said, "Next?"

Pete didn't know what to say. Hell he waited until his late thirties to get married and now Tanya wanted a baby. Joe thought it finally hit him that time catches up with everyone.

Joe said, "Dad, that would be a great idea for Pete and

Tanya to be next, don't you?"

John picked up on the ball busting very quickly. He was a quick study and didn't miss a beat. "You know, for the longest time I wanted grandchildren and so did your mother. Thanks for picking up speed," he said. "Pete, you're next."

"By the way, Julie and Joe, thank you for giving Annie the middle name of Marie. I know that's Tillie's middle name but it was my wife's first name. Marie Bridget O'Malley was her full name when I met her and added the Traynor to her name. Tillie you must be proud as well?"

"I am. I'm also proud that both Tanya and I will serve as Godmothers and Pete as Godfather. I couldn't be happier. I'll be staying here until after the baptism next month and then heading back to Key Largo. I won't miss the cold that's for sure but I'll certainly miss these little ones.

Bella came out of her room with her iPad and smiled at John, Pete, and Tanya. She went over and gave them a hug that made Joe feel great. They asked her how she felt about being a big sister and she said great. She said, "Mommy, can I hold Annie now?"

"Sure, take Tanya's seat and I'll hand the baby to you but very gently." Once again, Julie showed her how to hold the baby's head and body in her arms. Bella was beaming and she looked so grown up. They would be very careful to let her know that she was as much their very own daughter as was Annie. It was a balancing act for her to remind Bella about her own mother who passed away and her Hispanic heritage that they wanted her to embrace. Thank God that Joe was fluent in Spanish and that Julie was getting there. It would be harder up in New London than it was down in the Florida Keys, where Spanish was spoken every day by thousands of transplanted Cubans living there.

It was closing in on 5:00 p.m. so John was getting anxious to start heading home. He didn't like driving in the dark so Pete would do the honors. They had pizza and wings for dinner from a place right in town. They were getting used to ordering out because of their busy schedules. At least the take-out places were getting used to their address. Joe knew, coming from a college town in Troy, New York, that a lot of restaurants wouldn't deliver around colleges because of the hassle of trying to collect while standing at the door of a large dorm. It was great that they actually had a nice house that they were renting and got lucky when the other officer was suddenly transferred out due to his expertise in Arabic and Farsi, the languages of Iraq, Iran, Afghanistan, and Saudi Arabia. Evidently something was brewing and he was rushed to headquarters in Washington, D.C. His loss was Joe's gain but Joe would never be surprised if it happened to him. It has happened to him in the past, many times. Maybe being second in command here would mean they wouldn't move him unless there was a national crisis, and he means a very big national crisis.

Joe said goodbye to his family. John said that what they might do for the baptism is to stay right at the Mohican Sun in Uncasville and make it a three-day weekend. Joe had invited Mary Evans and Jack Manning as well so they could all come down together. Mary and Jack still had their bodyguards in John Jefferson and Fred Tucker, two retired FBI agents who have been with them since Jack first hit the lottery several years ago. They are especially more careful now after Mary was kidnapped by white supremacists in Florida. If they were there it might not have ever happened but they would never know. They were vigilant to say the least.

It was Wednesday and the Board of Trustees was having their monthly meeting and Joe was invited to attend for a meet and greet and explain his background to those assembled. Little did Joe know that Rear Admiral Barnes was to be there as an invited guest and a potential board member for someone who was retiring in the spring. A Board of Trustees exercises oversight of the Coast Guard Academy. The Assistant Commandant for Human Resources, Linda Jones, chairs the Board. Members consist of active duty and civilian employees of the Coast Guard, Coast Guard Reserve, and Coast Guard Auxiliary. Special representatives are assigned from time to time. That's why Rear Admiral Barnes is attending this meeting. The Board's role consists of advising the Superintendent, advocacy, strategic planning and alignment, and ensuring the safety and wellbeing of the cadets, faculty and staff. Currently there are nineteen board members, not counting Rear Admiral Barnes.

After the meeting began, and old business was discussed, the Assistant Commandant introduced Captain Joseph Traynor, Ph.D. as the new Assistant Superintendent of the Coast Guard Academy. Rear Admiral Barnes simply smiled and sat back and watched Joe do his thing. Joe began to introduce himself as he looked around the room. He was thirty-seven years old and many of the faces at the table were well into their fifties at least. He thought they probably wondered how Joe Traynor got to where he got with only eighteen years of service. Joe started to give his background, starting from his short time at MIT right up to getting his Ph.D. just last Christmas at Barry University. He explained his role as an active team member taking down the bad guys over many years while at the same time moving up the ladder due to receiving his degree from the Coast Guard Academy,

Rensselaer Polytechnic Institute and then, Barry University. Joe thought it was funny but he never took a language course in college. He took several Berlitz style courses over the years but he said he learned on the job from his fellow enlisted men including Mark Silva, his best friend and Lieutenant in the Coast Guard assigned to District 7 in Miami.

Laura Chavez, Captain, and stationed at the Academy attempted to take his thunder by asking him a very extensive question in Spanish. Joe immediately replied and asked her if her dialect was Mexican or Costa Rica because they were slightly the same. He then said that the Cuban and South American speech patterns were vastly different and that not all Spanish speakers were the same and had the same idioms. He told the story in English about a young man going to college in the south and made a big mistake in front of the class. One of the young female students said, "Well, bless his heart." He took it as a kindness when in fact it was a put down. He said when his wife said it was "fine," that meant exactly the opposite. All the women at the table smiled and seemed to enjoy Joe's conversation. Next, an obvious member of the Board with a Russian background, Dr. Ivan Petrov, ask him in Russian a similar style question and Joe answered in both Russian and Chechen. Dr. Petrov didn't know Chechen but did pick up a few words.

Joe was only one of a few multi-lingual officers in the Coast Guard, predominately Russian, Chechen and Spanish, now in the process of learning Chinese. His Chinese acumen is what started his interest in what came out of Wuhan, China and developed into a world wide pandemic, killing over five million people in a year. He interpreted the intelligence intercepts as best he could for his own team, his Rear Admiral and some in Washington.

After these two small confrontations, Joe made the same presentation that he made down at The College of the Florida Keys last fall, which was attended by Rear Admiral Barnes and tons of dignitaries and corporate executives. Joe put on a video that he developed over the last year, as Interim President of The College of the Florida Keys, that showed the vulnerability of the technology systems in the United States and how fragile and unsafe these systems are. He brought up speeches from various countries including Russia, Venezuela and China and served as the interpreter for each of the three speakers in their own languages.

After his presentation, several Board members came up to him to congratulate him on his appointment and on his presentation. They all agreed that they have never had a presentation by a Coast Guard officer that hit so many details of what they were now looking at for strategic planning purposes. Joe didn't go into great detail about his ideals of what the Academy should be but he did emphasize the recruitment of young men and women of color and Hispanic background to meet the challenges of 2022. He said he reviewed the language requirements at the Coast Guard and he felt that they should look more deeply into an entirely different approach. They should be recruiting cadets that already were firmly entrenched in another language so they could hit the ground running with what they learned at the Academy.

Before the Board broke up, Rear Admiral Barnes asked if he could speak. He was granted time so he went into detail about Joe Traynor's background, expertise and training that would never show up on a piece of paper including taking down four gangbangers in Albany belonging to the Mexican Mafia including the son of the Mafia general. He also went into Joe's quick thinking by saving a woman who was kidnapped by simply tying GPS tags to her shoes. He also reminded them that at the previous board meeting that he did not attend, they discussed a ten-million-dollar donation to the Coast Guard Academy that was to be administered by Joe Traynor at the request of the donor. At that point, it was clear to the Board that Joe Traynor had the support of all his superior officers here at the Academy as well as in Washington, D.C. and in the Miami 7th District. Joe Traynor's last stop was not at the Academy and this was vividly pointed out. Joe thanked everyone and received a strong approval with clapping at the end of the meeting. Now, Joe hoped that the rocket ship that he appeared to be on wouldn't crash and burn during immediate take off. He hoped to gain support not just through the administration but from the cadets themselves. He would show up at all kinds of events and sit and simply talk to the cadets of what being a cadet meant to Joe and still does. It was like he was running for an office he never wanted. So, he would make the best of it. He misses his friends. He misses the action. Jake hit it right on the head. He needs to fix what he can and then move on to situations that need his expertise more. The world is becoming a very dangerous place. He hoped that Bella and Annie would have a chance at a meaningful life. He wasn't so sure at this point.

Chapter 4

The baptism of Ann Marie Traynor would take place right after the Sunday, 9:00 a.m. Mass in three weeks at the Coast Guard Memorial Chapel, right on the west side of the campus. It was two blocks from their new home. The Pastor, Father Henry DiMarco, at their new parish in town, would be doing the baptism at the chapel. He was also the Catholic Chaplain at the Academy. As soon as Joe and Julie arrived in New London, Tillie stopped by the parish office and signed them all up as parishioners. She commented that in Key West, Florida, they had the same name for a parish except it was also nominated as a Basilica. Their new parish ironically was St. Mary Star of the Sea and only a little more than a mile from their home. What thrilled Tillie was the fact that it had a large Hispanic population in the parish and there were two Masses, the first at 9:30 a.m. on Sunday in English, and the second at noon in Spanish. This would help Bella acclimate even more into the local parish community.

Joe and Julie wanted to invite everyone that was important to them for the baptism. When they adopted

Bella, Joe and Julie were unsure if Bella had been baptized. Juanita Lopez, Bella's mother, was a single mother who escaped from Cuba and rescued on the shores of the Florida Keys. She died of a brain tumor at thirty years old and before dying, Juanita begged Julie to take Bella as her own daughter. Julie didn't need to be begged and neither did Joe. Bella was born shortly after Juanita landed from Cuba at eight months pregnant and adopted by Joe and Julie when she had just turned five and was in Kindergarten at the Key Largo elementary school where both Julie and Juanita worked.

After Joe and Julie's wedding and the funeral for Juanita, they put in adoption papers for Bella and then had her baptized at their Catholic Church, St. Justin Martyr in Key Largo. The only attendees were Tillie, standing in as her Godmother and Mark Silva as Godfather with his wife, Louise. Now, most invited guests were from Florida but Joe and Julie wanted to offer an invitation to show what these people meant to them. They did not expect them all to come because of the distance and other family obligations as well as the cost of the trip.

When they received back acceptances, they would book several rooms at the Holiday Inn right in town at their own expense. They would start obviously with the Godparents, Tanya with Pete and Joe's father, John, and Tillie, who would stay for the ceremony. They also would invite Mary Evans and Jack Manning from Troy, New York and Skip and Linda Lennon from Key West and obviously, Rear Admiral Jake Barnes and his wife, Becky. Joe thought it was funny that Mary Evans never did change her name to Mary Manning. He might ask her about that. They also invited Audrey and Mike Kenny, good friends from the Keys who helped them with the adoption of Bella. They would also invite Joan and Jeff Talbot and Lucy. Lucy was at the University of Miami but not that far from home. Nick and Jane Swanson would also get an invitation but Nick was a long hauler for Covid-19 so they didn't expect them to come. Julie's best friend, Maddy White, couldn't make it with her husband, Jim, since Maddy's mother was due for immediate surgery.

Joe had personally called Sean O'Neil but he was away with the Coast Guard Academy basketball team and wouldn't be back for a week. They needed to catch up. Sean was married to Samantha, Sam, and had two kids. He was a Coast Guard Academy lifer and had been at the Academy almost twenty years ago. Last year, when Joe had been in and out of the Academy for meetings before coming full time, he met with Sean and Samantha. He stayed at their house a few times as well. Sean O'Neil was originally from Boston and met Joe the same day they both joined the Coast Guard in Malden, Massachusetts, just outside of Boston. They went together for basic training and were friends ever since. Sean went to Albany to be with Joe when he took down the Mexican Mafia son and they both had each other's back forever, just like Jack Forest and Mark Silva. Sean's best gift was his athletic ability. He was All State in basketball in Massachusetts in high school and had several Division I and II offers from Holy Cross and Assumption College. He was tired of school so he joined the Coast Guard before ever attending college, and after boot camp and a few meaningless assignments, the coach at the Coast Guard Academy offered Sean a spot on the team if he came to the Academy. The Academy is Division III but it didn't matter to Sean who got a full ride and a Master's degree out of basketball at the Academy. He has been there ever since and is now the Associate Athletic Director and Chair for Health and Physical Education at the Academy.

Sean's wife, Sam, met Sean while she was a student at Connecticut College, right across the street. They have been married for nine years and have a daughter, Emily, age seven and a son, Josh, who is four years old. Sam has been a full-time mother and a part-time Teacher's Aide right at the elementary school where Bella and Emma are now attending. The nice thing is, that Emily is also seven and in the same grade as Bella. They have different teachers but have classrooms right next to each other. Julie thought it would be nice if Bella could make a special friendship with Emily. It would go a long way to help the family settle in.

Kidding with Sean, Joe told him he still had three years of baseball eligibility left since he only pitched for MIT for one semester. Joe had a tremendous pickoff move to first base as a lefthander because he walked so many batters that he needed to perfect it. One of the saves Joe had at MIT was against the Coast Guard Academy. Joe came into the game in the bottom of the last inning with a runner on first and third, with two outs and MIT leading 7-6. Joe picked off the runner on his first throw to first base to end the game. The box score was unusual because Joe got a save without any official pitches thrown to home plate. Sean loved that statistic and always remembered it.

Winding up the invitees, Joe and Julie weren't sure if they could make it but they wanted to invite Claire and Brian Murphy from Orlando. Claire was Tom Jones's daughter, Joe's first official drill sergeant and long time friend, and now Claire is a special friend to Julie as she works directly for Marshall Tillman, the president of Disney World's Hollywood Studio. Claire is the liaison in charge of Julie's books translated to the television screen. Of course, Jack Forest, as single as ever, would be here as well. Mike McGreevy, who came from Seattle, was sent an invitation but quit the service several years ago and was captain of an ocean liner, ten months of the year. At least they will send him an invitation, if he ever gets it.

Julie got back responses almost immediately. She was shocked at how many said yes. She called each one and told them that they already booked rooms for them and all they had to do was go to the front desk and everything was taken care of. After all, Joe and Julie were handed one million dollars from Mary a short while ago. Money was not an issue.

Three weeks later, everyone showed up on time and gathered at the Chapel for the Mass and baptism that would follow. The baptism started immediately after 9:30 Mass at the Chapel. It went quite smoothly and Annie cried when the water was dropped on her poor little head and brought tears to Julie's eyes and Tillie's as well. The guys sort of just smiled a little. After the baptism, there was a breakfast buffet set up, catered by Joe and Julie, right in the adjacent hall next to the chapel. Everyone appeared happy and glad to be there.

Many had not seen each other in quite a while, even before the Covid-19 pandemic. It was like homecoming for a lot of them. At one time or another, all of Joe's Coast Guard friends wound up at the Academy for one reason or another, mostly for training or language classes to help combat crime and terrorism. Having Joe at the Academy now seemed like full circle for many of them. Rear Admiral Barnes and his wife, Becky, came over and hugged Julie and the baby as well as Tillie and Bella. It was nice that they showed up. They didn't have to and it meant the world to Joe. Having his best friends there as well as the new friends they both made over recent years also felt like home to them. Joe wasn't sure how long he would be at the Academy but when he was told that he was the first Assistant Superintendent to have a baptism in the Chapel, he smiled and thought that was pretty great. Julie felt the same way.

Joe cornered Mary Evans at the end of the buffet and asked if she and Jack would mind staying through Monday to meet the Superintendent of the Academy, Rear Admiral Bill Kelly. Joe told her that Jake told him to always make sure he called him Rear Admiral Kelly not Bill. Mary caught on quickly and said she would do the same. Joe's father, brother and Tanya were staying at the Mohican Sun, only fourteen miles north of the Academy. They would stay there Sunday night, gamble, and then head out Monday. Most of the guests wanted to stay a day or two as well to get a full tour of the Coast Guard Academy and would fly out late Monday or early on Tuesday. Joe had meetings and Julie was obviously tied up with the baby so Joe got Sean O'Neil to give a grand tour all day Monday and they would have lunch in the cafeteria and then fly out of the New London Airport that night. All had reservations for the same flight into Miami and then others would fly back home from there or simply drive.

Mary and Jack were at the Mohican as well and Pete drove them down to Joe's house to walk over for the meeting with the Rear Admiral. Joe would drive them back to the Mohican Sun and they would go back with Pete, John and Tanya to head home. They leased an oversize van in Troy so they all could go together. It worked out fine. Mary and Jack arrived at 9:00 a.m. at Joe's and they walked over to the Rear Admiral's office in the administration building. After the meeting, they would meet everyone for lunch in the cafeteria and then head out from there. The meeting was at 10:00 a.m. and lunch was for 12:30 p.m., giving them sufficient time to meet with the Superintendent.

They walked up the landing to Rear Admiral Kelly's office and were greeted by his assistant Ensign Meg Olsen. "Good morning, Captain," said Meg and smiled.

Joe said, "Ensign, let me introduce you to Mary Evans and Jack Manning. We have a meeting with the Rear Admiral at 10:00 a.m."

"Yes, sir. He is finishing up a meeting and will be with you shortly. Mondays are a little busy around here. At least our football team beat the Merchant Marine team 28 to 7 on Saturday. It's not been a good year at 3-7 but we're starting a lot of freshmen so next year, watch out," she said and laughed. "I understand you were tied up this weekend too. Congratulations," she said.

"Thanks," he said. "Annie is doing well as are my three bosses, in order of Tillie, Julie and Bella and now Annie. I'm outnumbered just like our football team," he said.

"I can't wait for baseball season. It's my favorite sport. I like to brag that my only semester at MIT, in my freshman year, I got the save here at the Coast Guard Academy 7-6 by picking off the runner in the bottom of the last inning. I told Sean O'Neil that I still have three years left of eligibility." He laughed. She did too.

"Maybe, you can pull some strings and be the oldest living reliever in the history of the Coast Guard Academy," Meg said.

"I'll take it but I don't like the 'oldest' part," said Joe.

On that note, Meg ushered in Mary and Jack followed by Joe.

"Good morning, Joe. Isn't that a news show or something?" Rear Admiral Kelly said.

"I believe it is, sir. This is Mary Evans and Jack Manning, sir."

"Nice to meet you. Please have a seat. We brought in coffee, tea and bottled water, and bagels and cream cheese if you haven't eaten yet," he said.

The Rear Admiral got up and asked Mary and Jack how they wanted their coffee. Joe got his own and a bagel and cream cheese. He learned long ago when out on an assignment to eat when you can and sleep when you can because it may be a while before it happens again.

"Ms. Evans, I just want to thank you for your very nice gift to the Coast Guard Academy in honor of the 7th District in Miami under Rear Admiral Barnes. It is appreciated. We understand that Captain Traynor and a team of Coast Guard members broke up your kidnapping now in the Florida Keys. It was a very nice gesture on your part to reward the Academy for their efforts. They were honored by the way." Kelly said.

"It is said that you can't put a price tag on happiness but I can tell you if you have the money, you certainly can. I gifted ten million dollars to the Academy with the condition that Captain Traynor is in charge of the distribution of funds. May I make a few suggestions?" she asked.

"By all means," he said. There was a knock on the door and to their surprise it was Rear Admiral Barnes walking into the meeting. Rear Admiral Kelly had set it up for him to attend without their knowledge as a surprise. They were also surprised to learn that Jake Barnes would be the next Board of Trustees member upon the retirement of one of the members. Jake told Joe in confidence previously. Jake had no intention of ever being the Superintendent of the Coast Guard Academy to supervise all the daily activities and functions. That wasn't his thing. His was to structure strategic planning that was effective and worked and was innovative. That's why he was so happy with Joe. Joe needed no supervision to act effectively. He knew that the day Joe was asked by him why he shot the gangbangers on

I-95 and Joe replied that if he were dead he would be unable to explain why he shot them. Jake found that to be outstanding logic in the face of immediate danger. He never questioned Joe after that. When he saved Mary Evans, he knew he would catch up to him and Joe would explain why he immediately acted to save her life regardless of impediments placed in front of him. *Jake still marveled at the logic of placing GPS clips onto Mary Evan's shoes wherever she went. What a simple, effective, solution that saved her life, he thought.*

Mary went through what she and Jack have accomplished with their lottery winnings and how she has effectively change Coast Guard recruitment of minorities and women, especially women of color. She explained Joe's role as first the Vice President for The College of the Florida Keys and then as Interim President and for the role played by Joan Talbot in securing bright young women who needed a hand up and a career in the Coast Guard. As she was finishing, Rear Admiral Barnes gave his perspective as the commander of the 7th Division in Miami. He thought their efforts brought the Coast Guard into the 21st Century with faces that represented all the populations in the United States. He also emphasized Joe's language skills as a major necessity to be terrorists at their own game. He also wanted to see more enlisted men at the Academy giving hands-on instruction in daily procedures that kept them from harm while taking down the bad guys. He said the worst thing that could happen to a new graduate and Coast Guard officer was to have limited language skills and no experience doing what they do every day. They needed mentoring from the people doing the job. Being bright is great as long as it's comingled with everyday experience.

Rear Admiral Kelly agreed with this philosophy but

until now, he didn't have anyone with the capability to provide that experience. Jake told him they did now and Mary said, "If you need more money, just ask. I can't be any plainer than that."

Jack Manning, quiet up until now said, "This is Mary's project but whatever Mary wants to do with you, I'll match her 100% until I run out of money. Rear Admiral Kelly, I don't know if you understand our philosophy but we are giving away a majority of our lottery winnings over the next five years to projects we believe in, that have a payback either monetary or social that effectively changes the way we work in the United States and beyond. These are lessons learned and we are willing to pay for both successes and failures if the intent of the failure was to learn something and make it better," he said.

"Joe, I am now starting to understand your value as well as Mary, Jack and Rear Admiral Barnes understand your value. Can we come up with a plan or a strategy or whatever you want to call it and put a price tag on it to discuss and move forward?" said Kelly.

"Yes, sir. I'll start today but I would like to be a coach on the baseball team this spring if possible," said Joe and meant it.

"Done," said the Rear Admiral.

It was close to 12:15 p.m. with just enough time to meet the rest of the guests for lunch in the cafeteria. Then everyone would head out to his or her own activities.

As they walked over, Rear Admiral Barnes asked Mary if she was pleased with the meeting. She said she was but wanted to make sure everyone was still on the same page. She likened it to the priests down in Key West who were happy to get the money to fix their facilities but only wanted to do it their own way and leave the nun's building the way it was. That wasn't good enough with Mary and she made it very clear that it was going to be her way since it was her money. She asked Joe if he was okay with what she said and he said no problem. He did say he didn't know Rear Admiral Kelly very well but felt over time he would show him success and not have to explain why they failed. Jake told him in front of Mary and Jack that if it didn't work out here, he always had a home at the 7th District under his command. He didn't think that would be necessary. Joe was learning on the quick and though he could catch up on the academic side just like he did on the action side of why the Coast Guard was actually put into place, to serve and protect at all costs to all Americans.

At the baptism reception, Joe caught up with Joan, Jeff, and Lucy Talbot. Lucy asked him if he had time could he talk to her about the Academy. Of course, Joe said yes. Julie would love nothing better than to have Lucy right around the corner from them up in New London. Julie was Lucy's first babysitter, friend, then Girl's cross-country coach guiding her to All Florida status and a full scholarship to the University of Miami.

Chapter 5

After lunch in the cafeteria, Joe walked the grounds with Lucy and they sat in the bleachers around the Coast Guard athletic fields including baseball, softball, football, and track. Cross-country started in the facility but wound up in the streets of New London with friends and family standing by the curb cheering them on. The women's cross-country team was practicing, doing stretches and exercises for next year's meets in the Division III NEWMAC conference. They were ranked 8th nationally in 2021 with everyone doing well but they didn't have that exceptional runner that could put them over the top.

The head coach, Ethan Brown, spotted Joe and Lucy sitting in the bleachers and came over to say hello. Joe had met the coaches during his first week after a tour by his friend, Sean O'Neil. Coach Brown said, "If I'm not mistaken, you're Captain Joe Traynor, our new Assistant Superintendent. Am I right, sir?"

Lucy never heard Joe ever called sir or Captain and was quite taken back by the deference shown to him by the coach.

"Yes, Coach Brown, I'm Joe Traynor. Good to see you again. We briefly met when Sean gave me a tour. I'm a big fan of all sports. I attended the Coast Guard Academy sometime after I was a noncom for almost ten years. I got my bachelor's from here and then my MBA at Rensselaer Polytechnic Institute when I got out. Got back in again quickly and just got my Ph.D. from Barry University down in Miami. By the way, this is Lucy Talbot. I watched her grow up and my wife, Julie, was her babysitter and cross-country coach at Coral Shores High School in Tavernier, Florida. She was both academic and first team All Florida cross-country last year. She just started her first year at the University of Miami, obviously a major Division I university, nationally."

"Nice to meet you, sir," said Lucy, picking up on Joe's responses.

"Nice to meet you as well," said Coach Brown. "What are you doing up here, Lucy?"

"My family was attending Annie's baptism yesterday at your chapel. It's a lovely place," she said. "Annie is his newborn daughter," she added.

"I was just walking her around. To be frank, I was trying to get her to come here to the Coast Guard Academy as a transfer student. She's allowed to work out with the team at Miami but was redshirted as a freshman because of Covid-19. Nearly everyone came back for their senior year and the coach didn't want them to not complete their four years so as good as Lucy is, she sits. At least she never lost her eligibility and now can get a master's degree under scholarship as well if she wants," said Joe.

"You know, Lucy. I've heard of you. I know your mother from training classes. She's now a lieutenant assigned to Islamorada and a college down in the Keys. I remember she told me about you. I did look you up and saw your times. No wonder you were All Florida. Your times are better than our best runners on this team right now. I don't want to interfere with your choices for college because Miami is very prestigious but if you're not running, you're not running. I'm sure that with your mother's position, Captain Traynor's recommendation and a few others, you could be running with us for four years at the Academy. I'll bet you would do very well at the Division III Championships, next year in Austin, Texas. Just a thought. We're eighth nationally in Division III right now and could be near the top if you came here. Just remember when they pick the Olympians, they don't just look at schools or competition, they look at your time and conditions. That's what counts. You could run in the 2024 Olympics in the women's 10,000 meters or cross-country if approved as a Coast Guard Academy student, as a third year member with another year to go for the NCAAs. If you want more information, please call me anytime," he said.

He gave her his cell phone number and card. He shook Joe's hand and thanked him for coming by to see the facilities. Both he and Joe knew what Joe was doing. Lucy did not. Joe smiled. He can't do any more than this. What's the saying, "You can lead a horse to water but you can't make her drink."

"What do you think of the Academy, Lucy?" Joe asked on the way back to meet her parents.

"It's really nice. It's probably more than I expected. It's not the University of Miami but what is? This place is beautiful and I could see myself here next fall. Just saying that's all. Thanks for the walk," she said. "That was quite a coincidence meeting the actual coach for the Coast Guard Academy women's cross country team, Captain Traynor," she said and laughed.

"Guilty as charged, Lucy. You know our feeling about you, especially Julie's. She would be your mother away from home just like Tillie and your mom were for me when I was only eighteen years old and in the Florida Keys, away from home for the first time. If you stay at Miami, I can see why but this could open you to an entire new career that you never thought possible. I couldn't imagine better role models than your mother or Julie," he said.

"I know what you mean. What's the saying, 'Your parents seem to get smarter as you get older,'" said Lucy. "I'll let you know, Joe. I can still call you Joe when we're with family, right?"

"Yes, just like I call Rear Admiral Barnes by his first name, Jake," he said. "But as I was told by Jake, Rear Admiral Kelly will always be sir, or Rear Admiral Kelly. Amazing how those things stick in your mind."

They made it back as everyone was starting to get ready to leave. Little Annie was sound asleep and Bella was getting anxious. She was very happy to now have a friend in Emma and Julie and Sam made plans for them to get together the following week after school. Joe could pick up Bella at 6:00 p.m. when he was leaving for home or better yet, Julie would travel over to the O'Neil's and meet Joe for dinner at the O'Neil's house. That made more sense. Tillie would be heading home and they had to be on the same page to now take care of two children instead of one. Julie was also anxious to talk to the Dean at Connecticut College and weigh her options compared to Brown University come springtime. Joe knew who the breadwinner was in his family. It was Julie. She made more last year selling her books than Joe made in the Coast Guard. Of course, it didn't seem to matter since Mary Evans gave them a trust fund.

Tillie was leaving for Florida by herself. She stayed

another week and would fly out of the New London Airport on a Coast Guard jet that was landing in Miami. She would be met at the military wing at the Miami International Airport and would be met by Jane Swanson, who would drive her down to Key Largo. She would stay overnight and head back the next morning. Nick was doing much better and was back to work as a neurologist on a part-time basis. He couldn't do surgery yet until he was cleared of the after effects of Covid-19 but he was well on his way. Joe, Julie, Bella and the baby, Annie, took Tillie to the airport for the direct flight to Miami. There wasn't a dry eye in the SUV. Julie had not been away from her Grandmother since she was eight years old except for her college days at Brown in Providence Rhode Island.

Tillie wanted to be home in Florida but was completely torn. Hopefully, Tillie would be around for a long time. Joe didn't think his stay at the Academy would be more than five years. If Lucy came on board, they would love to see her graduate from the Academy while he was second in command, and maybe even first depending on Rear Admiral Kelly's retirement status. Joe wanted to hand Lucy her diploma from the Academy. He would ask Joan and Julie to do the honors while he stood there to make it official.

He thought, *if dreams can only come true*. Of course, he also wanted to pitch at least one game for the Coast Guard Academy as a reliever in a scrimmage game, one that didn't count in the record. He wanted one more pickoff and his life would be complete as he smiled at the thought. He thought, if there wasn't anyone on first or second, he might just walk the batter to see if he still had it. Picking off an eighteen-year-old would make his career complete. What a dream. Of course having the Coast Guard Academy win the NCAA baseball championship would also be right up the top as well.

Tillie called late. They had arrived on time and landed safely at the Miami International Airport. Jane was a little confused as to where to pick her up but made it to the military side to see Tillie's plane land and taxi right over to where she was standing. Tillie got out and gave her a hug. They carried her bags to Jane's car and headed south. Eighty miles to Key Largo wasn't bad at night. Jane got on the phone with Tillie and said Tillie was fine. It took a little over an hour to get to Key Largo and Tillie's apartment.

Tillie's friend, Ed Lansing, met them at the apartment. He found the hidden key and made sure that Tillie's refrigerator was filled. He picked up groceries at the Publix Supermarket at the Tradewinds Plaza, only a mile away from Tillie's place. He seemed to know his way around. When Tillie got out of the vehicle, she gave Ed a hug. Being older, Tillie was unsure as to how she should show her emotions in front of Jane. At the hug, Jane turned and got the bags out of the car so as not to interrupt their moment. Jane guessed it had been some time since they have seen each other. Ed stayed for one beer and went home. Both Tillie and Jane were tired so they went to bed within the hour of arriving. Tillie made Jane breakfast and she headed out. It was clear to her that Tillie and Ed were some kind of a couple but unsure what that even meant any more. If asked by Joe or Julie, she would simply say Tillie seemed fine but obviously missed them already.

Chapter 6

The telephone rang and Julie picked it up. "Traynor residence. May I help you?" Julie asked.

"Yes, Mrs. Traynor. It's Rear Admiral Kelly. May I please speak to your husband?"

"Of course, sir. Let me go get him. He's just about to leave the house for work."

"Hello, Rear Admiral. It's Captain Traynor speaking," Joe said. Joe was quite quizzical because he never got a call at home before, especially at 7:30 in the morning.

"Joe, we have a real problem. We have a special Board of Trustees meeting at 8:30 a.m. this morning. I think we can use your knowledge and background. I don't want to say any more at this point. It is truly an emergency," he said.

"I'm leaving now, sir. I'll be there in fifteen minutes," said Joe as he kissed Julie and ran out the door. He told her they had an emergency on the way out and he would call her as soon as he could, if he could.

Julie's been down this path before and it made her anxious but she knew this was what Joe did for a living. He got in the middle of some very bad situations and usually helped everyone get out of trouble. She had no idea what was happening this morning that would make Rear Admiral Kelly distraught as Joe kind of alluded to. The last time this happened was when Joe got the call that Mary Evans was missing and subsequently kidnapped. He never panics or at least he never appears to be in panic mode. He did what he always did under pressure. He got Mary back safe and sound and never worried about the consequences of his immediate actions. He performed at a high level to save lives and that was his only concern in the moment.

Joe ran from his house down the two blocks to the Academy and then ran into the campus and up the stairs to the Rear Admiral's office. It was twelve minutes flat since the phone call. Ensign Meg Olsen saw him running up the stairs and immediately opened the door to the Rear Admiral's boardroom. She turned and did a thumb's up meaning thanks for beating the land speed record to get here. As he took a seat at the conference table, he saw the Rear Admiral walk in with five of the nineteen board members. Evidently, the rest would be on a very secure phone call. Joe thought this must be big to mobilize everyone this quickly.

Rear Admiral Kelly began the meeting by thanking everyone at the table and on the line for their quick response to what appeared to be a crisis. He said, "At 7:00 a.m. this morning, I received an email from an unknown sender stating that there was a bomb placed on the Academy campus grounds. The email demanded five million dollars to unarm the bomb and gave the Rear Admiral until 7:30 p.m. that night or the campus would be significantly damaged beyond repair. He said he would call again at 3:00 pm and 7:00 p.m. and if the cash were not received by 7:30 p.m., the bomb would be discharged. He said he would email again and give further instructions on where to go with the money and to have a good day."

The Rear Admiral added that they have received numerous calls from outsiders but those threats were never followed up and were usually sent to close down a building or stop an event but nothing of this caliber. He asked the Board of Trustees what they thought they should do at this point. None of them seemed to have an opinion on the next steps as Joe simply sat there and listened intently at what was happening. Rear Admiral Kelly turned to Joe and said, "Joe, have you had experience with these kinds of situations?"

"Yes, sir. I have. Do you need me to quickly outline a plan on how to address this situation?" Joe asked.

Rear Admiral Kelly said, "Do any of the Board have any suggestions or should we let Captain Traynor speak freely and make suggestions?" The Board told him to let Joe speak and see if he had an immediate plan.

Joe started the discussion. "First, sir, I need a copy of the email that was sent to you this morning. We have the best hackers in the world working for the Coast Guard under Jack Forest in the intelligence division down in Virginia. He will stay on top of it until we find out who sent the email. Second, if there are bombs placed on the campus in one or multiple locations, then it had to be done within the last few days. Also, the bomb cannot be on a timer because the blackmailer can't know exactly when and if the money is coming. If he says its for 7:30 p.m. tonight regardless of the outcome of getting the cash, then we have roughly ten hours to stop it. It sounds like it's tied to a cell phone because then he can release the bomb at any time with a call."

Joe went on, "The biggest problem we have is that the Academy is an open campus. I went to YouTube yesterday to see videos on the Coast Guard Academy, and it stated that over seven thousand visitors already showed up to visit the campus. We need to check all the cars on campus right now that do not have a Coast Guard Academy parking sticker. Those that do not have stickers have to be checked for the license plate and owner of the vehicle. Also, we need to check all vehicles coming into and going out of the campus that have single men driving with no other passengers. This is not a family guy but could be a guy who even with a passenger could get in and do harm. Again, I think if there is a bomb, then it would be set off with a cell phone not a timer, so the terrorist, and that's what the person is, can hit the call button anytime he or she wants. It's 99% a man as I know from experience."

"Joe, thank you, that's a great start. Can you start the ball rolling? Do you think I need to find five million dollars in cash?"

"No matter what, just let him know that the money will be there on time but you need to go through channels to get the funds so it looks like you're cooperating. I believe this is a domestic group in Connecticut or in the immediate area or they would have asked for a wire transfer. If this is an internal problem to the Academy, we will find out. If it is external then it could be a lone wolf but I doubt it. It sounds like we're funding an organization. It could be foreign entities but I think it may be domestic in nature, hence the need for cash. I don't know if you're aware of how many white supremacist groups there are in the state of Connecticut alone. In the kidnapping of Mary Evans, it was the Nationalist Alliance white supremacists. We took care of them, never to be heard from again," Joe said. "Also, to find these individuals, we need to call in the FBI who has jurisdiction. I carry credentials, probably unknown to most of the Board of Trustees, as a Coast Guard Captain, an FBI Special Agent and a member of

Homeland Security. I have used all three credentials at one time or another to fix a problem and this is a major problem," said Joe.

All of the Board of Trustees voted and gave Joe the go ahead and see if he could resolve this emergency. They might have thought it was a lot but to Joe, it was what he was built for, active duty. He still wondered if moving to the Coast Guard Academy was the right move for him and his family. Evidently, the Academy needed him most right now.

The meeting broke up and Joe spent a few minutes with Rear Admiral Kelly. "Thank you, Joe," said the Rear Admiral. "I now understand how effective you can be during very trying times. What do you need from me right now?"

"I need every car on campus checked out that it is a Coast Guard vehicle, a vehicle owned by staff or students, or a car without a parking sticker. We need to concentrate on the non-sticker cars for now. A bomb could be left in the trunk near any of the major buildings, not dissimilar to the McVeigh bombing in Oklahoma City. That was domestic terrorism at its finest. I really don't think a foreign agent or terrorists could have made it to this campus without incident. At least that's what I hope."

"I'm on it, Joe. It shouldn't take more than an hour. I'll get our security team to write down every car, license and if it has a sticker."

"If it doesn't have a sticker, call me and we'll investigate," said Joe. "In the meantime, I'll get Jack Forest on the phone. Right now send him from your computer, your email to ForestJVA@USCG.com. I'm calling him now."

Kelly nodded his head and walked briskly to his office. He said the cars would be rechecked, starting in ten minutes. He also said as soon as they found a car without a sticker, they would look at the video of cars coming in and going out of the campus. If a car came in and didn't go out, then that might be a major clue. Then, Joe would check with the FBI and state motor vehicle department.

"Jack, it's Joe."

"Joe, I just saw you. I barely got home from the baptism. It was a great baptism, reception, and congratulations. Makes me almost want to get married and have kids," he said and laughed.

"Sure, Jack. I have an emergency and you need to drop everything. The Rear Admiral got an email at 7:00 a.m. telling him there has been a bomb or bombs placed on campus and demanded five million dollars. I think it's domestic white supremacists. After Mary's rescue, I've been reading up on it and Connecticut, believe it or not, has five major white supremacist groups. I'll send you the information. I need the email traced back to the sender. I have a feeling that the demand for money will be here in New London or close and the bomber must be near the Academy within range of a cell tower."

"Joe, the Rear Admiral's email just got here. Just looking at it, this is no ordinary email. It looks like it's bounced all over the world before it got here. And by here, I mean at the Rear Admirals computer. Is his email listed on the site?"

"Yes, unfortunately. All of them are and that must change ASAP. Also, it's an open campus and anyone can drive through during daylight hours. I don't think they could sneak in a bomb at night. It has a lot of security at night just not so much during the day and that will change too," said Joe.

"Let me go and do my thing, Joe," said Jack. "Call me every half hour." He hung up.

Joe went outside and met the security team. Everyone was armed with an iPad and ready to go to count cars. There were twenty men and women assigned to the task and each had their own section. It was over an hour before someone got back to Joe to let him know that five cars were not registered for parking and had no sticker. One even had a Coast Guard Academy sticker in the back car window, obviously purchased at the campus bookstore. Joe took the list of five cars and went to look at each one. He sent the information to Jack Forest who would look up the license plate and match the model and hopefully the owner. It took Jack less than twenty minutes breaking into various state sites and found a 2010 Toyota Corolla four-door sedan that was reported stolen last Saturday from Hartford, Connecticut.

Immediately, Joe's eyes lit up and he had already called Tom Matthews in Albany and Paul Philips in Miami to contact the Special Agent in the Boston region. They both got to the Special Agent in Charge and said there was a field office in New London, simply due to the fact that both the Navy Submarine Base and the Coast Guard Academy were right there. The Special Agent was Kim Matz and she was called and given Joe's cell phone number. She called Joe and Joe asked her for a team of investigators to come over and check out a car that appeared stolen and on campus for no reason. She was there within fifteen minutes.

Joe met her by the front gate and hopped in her car and they drove down to where the car was parked, right outside the field house where every cadet went every day. It could be a disaster. Her team showed up and they were reluctant to open the car so they used infrared to see what was inside. There were two large containers in the trunk. They looked like gas tanks for a Weber gas grill. Joe asked if the stolen car could be moved and they thought it was a possibility because as Joe explained the bomb, if it were a bomb, probably would go off with a cellphone call not by jarring the containers. From the infrared video the containers looked secure. The FBI had their own tow trucks and they said they were on their way down from Providence, about an hour away. They waited by the front gate and watched as the tow truck drivers, fully suited up with bomb protection came onto the campus and gingerly hauled the car off campus. Once they got the car opened using a robot, and if nothing exploded, they would remove the bombs and then go over the car for DNA or anything leading to the bomber.

Hopefully, getting the car off the campus solved one problem. Jack Forest was in constant contact with Joe. He told him the car was stolen from the west side of Hartford on Saturday night so the car had to show up no earlier than sometime Sunday as the baptism for Annie was going on. It made Joe think how dangerous this could have been and wiped out a good portion of the campus, the cadets, and his own family. He still had to worry that there weren't more bombs so he needed to wait to see if there was any DNA evidence associated with the stolen car.

Jack called Joe and said he got a break on the trail for the email sent to Rear Admiral Kelly. The initial email was sent from Liberty Global in Great Britain and had bounced from Belgium, the Netherlands, Ireland, Poland, and Switzerland subsequently ending at Xfinity with headquarters in Philadelphia. From Philadelphia, the sender was traced to Xfinity in Hartford, Connecticut to an internet user identified as Frederick Elliott, at 51 Grant Street in Hartford Connecticut, located on the west side of Hartford and only 59 miles to the Academy. Frederick Elliott is a renter at the property and was 42 years old, single, white, and six foot tall according to his Connecticut licensee. He has one conviction for felony assault and two misdemeanors for petty larceny and resisting arrest. He has served two years in the Connecticut state prison at Cheshire Correctional Institution for the felony. Jack added that it appears but he wasn't certain without more information that Elliott became indoctrinated while in prison and hung out with the white supremacist gang known as the Sovereign Citizens of Connecticut. The "sovereign citizen" movement is a network of groups and individuals who have adopted a right wing, essentially anarchist ideology that has its origins in the beliefs of a group called the Posse Comitatus, which first emerged in the 1970s. Often those people who have suffered financial or other personal reverses are most susceptible to the lure of extreme antigovernment ideology. This has proven true for many of Connecticut's anti- government extremists.

Joe hoped that DNA from the Toyota Corolla could be traced back to Frederick Elliott. In any case, he and the FBI were heading to Hartford to take down Mr. Elliott and anyone else in his house. They immediately got a warrant from a judge in New London. He had Elliott's picture from Jack and that's all he needed. They would deal with the white supremacy connection at a later date. They needed to get Elliott's cell phone and see if there was an app on it that would send a message to the pressure cooker bombs and to see if there were any more bombs in place.

It was now 4:30 p.m. Joe and the FBI agents in New London would be met by the Hartford Police Department a few blocks away at a grocery store parking lot before heading to Grant Street around 5:30 p.m. It would be dark by the time they got there and would provide the cover they needed. Before leaving for Hartford, Joe stopped by his house, grabbed a sandwich and told Julie what they found. She was nervous about what could have been just like Joe. It was no different than other situations that Joe had been in charge of. She prayed to God he would be okay but understood that many lives were on the line.

At 3:00 p.m. Joe had showed up at the Rear Admiral's office in full tactical gear. He gave Rear Admiral Kelly the full explanation but told him since this was now an FBI investigation, he couldn't tell him anything more. Although Kelly protested, he understood that Joe was now in full swing as an FBI Special Agent not Captain in the Coast Guard. Kelly was relieved but still worried about the Academy. The email from the bomber came in at exactly 3:00 p.m. and the Rear Admiral replied that the money would be there at the time required.

Joe told the Rear Admiral he was worried as well but he thought this would resolve the issue for today and everyone would be safe. He did say that they needed to sit down and thoroughly review safety and security at the Coast Guard Academy. To say the least, Rear Admiral Kelly was in awe of Joe Traynor and how he stepped up. He asked him what would happen to the perpetrators and Joe simply said they would be permanently gone and left it at that. Joe smiled and simply said, "The CIA will take over from there and then I'll explain to you how it works in real life."

Chapter 7

It was getting close to 3:30 p.m. and Joe hopped into the FBI vehicle with Kim Matz. They wanted to be in Hartford no later than 4:30 p.m. Joe was there when the Rear Admiral received the email from the bomber exactly at 3:00 p.m. and he responded that the cash was being received at the Academy by 7:00 p.m. and he would wait for further instructions on where he wanted it dropped. He responded that no bank in New London had that much in cash so it was coming from their Boston Coast Guard office by armored truck all in fifties as requested. After the email was answered, Joe headed out and the Rear Admiral shook his hand and wished him good luck.

As they were driving, Special Agent Matz said, "Now explain to me how you have three credentials for the Coast Guard, the FBI and Homeland Security and are the new Assistant Superintendent at the Coast Guard Academy. How does that work exactly?" Kim asked.

For the next half hour, Joe explained his background and how he was able to pinpoint what the issues were and how to address those issues quickly. After stopping by to see Julie, they left the Academy and took Mohegan Avenue to Briggs Street and I-95 Frontage Road to I-95 South. They followed 1-95 South and CT-9N to CT-71N/New Britain Avenue in West Hartford. They took Exit 40 from I-84E and drove quickly past 51 Grant Street. There were two cars in the driveway and two parked on the lawn by the road. Best guess was there were at least four individuals in the house. Couldn't guess more accurately without slowing down and being noticed in the area.

They met up six blocks away at the Price Chopper on New Britain Avenue, where they met several members of the Hartford Police Department in plain vehicles. Special Agent Matz pointed out three of her fellow FBI agents as well. They got out of Matz's vehicle and shook hands with the group. The house at 51 Grant Street was six blocks away so they needed to get a little closer. Joe went online and found the Family Dollar only a block away. So, they would all leave separately and at different times, within minutes of each other. Joe didn't have the benefit of Joan Talbot's drones or infrared equipment but they didn't have to worry about the safety of a kidnap victim. They believed everyone located in this house, at this time, had something to do with planting the bomb. Mr. Elliott was single so they were hoping that there were no women or children in the house. They really had to weigh that against the possibility that there were others bombs on the Academy campus other than those found in the Toyota Corolla.

They were all prepared at 5:15 p.m. They parked in the Family Dollar lot and some parked on the side of the road where spots were available. Their plan was to walk to the 51 Grant Street location and surround the house. Their first attempt at capture would be at 5:30 p.m. on the dot with flash-bang grenades being thrown through the windows front and back and them breaking down the doors. The element of surprise would hopefully carry the day. At exactly 5:30 p.m. Joe said over his cell phone, which was fully connected to each person in the take down crew, "one, two, three, GO!"

The element of surprise worked well. There were four individuals rolling around the floor with their hands holding their ears due to trauma caused by the flash-bang grenades. Mr. Elliott tried to move and grab a cell phone on the coffee table but Joe was quicker and grabbed it inches from Elliott's hands. These four individuals were in shock. The officers lined all four up against the living room wall and searched them for weapons. Three had guns and two had knives. Mr. Elliott had neither and was staring at Joe Traynor.

"What's this about? We have rights you know," said Elliott.

The others started to say the same things over and over. The FBI special agents started an immediate search of the house, which was small, about 1,200 square feet. In the back bedroom, one of the agents found a large bag of roofing nails and another bag of ball bearings. They tagged the bags and would compare them to the bomb if they were able to take it apart and not explode. They would also compare all DNA from these four guys to any samples found in the car or around where the car was parked. When Joe got back to campus, he would spend hours looking at video of these four individuals to see if they came and went from the Academy. Joe showed Elliott the Judge's warrant and he knew that it was over.

Joe said to the four of them, "The first one who tells us if there are any more bombs placed at the Coast Guard Academy, will receive either a lighter sentence or no sentence depending on the information given." All four looked at each other and one guy simply nodded and they took him into a back room where he told them that there is two more bombs placed in the laundry room at the Academy field house. Joe immediately called the Rear Admiral and told him to get the FBI agents and the bomb squad over to the field house immediately to remove or disarm the two remaining bombs from the laundry room. Joe told him to clear the facility immediately. It was now a little after 6:00 p.m. and they still had an hour and a half before the bombs were supposed to go off. Hopefully, a cell phone and not a timer would trigger the bombs. Joe went back into the living room and went through Elliott's cell phone. It was obvious that Elliott didn't use his cell phone to send the emails so they needed to get any burner phones in the building. The guy they took into the back room told them they had four burner phones, one in each car in case they had to leave quickly and send the call to trigger the bomb as they were leaving.

Joe grabbed the keys to all four cars and the team went through each one. One of the FBI Special Agents was a technology expert that they brought along just for this reason. He checked all four phones and found the same app on each one. He took the phones in an evidence bag and immediately left to where the Toyota Corolla was taken, near the water outside of New London and away from everyone.

During this entire time, Joe had made a call to his good friend Mike Hanley down in Miami. Mike was head of the CIA in that region. Even though they cannot act within the confines of the United States waters, Mike had a unique perspective of what that actually meant. He called his CIA buddy up in the New England region that covered right up to Canada and all the international waters down to Virginia. Mike said to bring the four terrorists to the Boston FBI headquarters and he would take it from there.

Joe told him all about the Connecticut white supremacist group that he believed these four belonged to. Mike said he was unaware of all the groups in Connecticut but would make himself aware. Mike took care of the Nationalist Alliance member and his mother after the kidnapping of Mary Evans. *It was good to have such fine friends,* Joe thought.

Joe waited around until 7:00 p.m. to see if any emails came to the Rear Admiral. None had come. The bomb crew that took the Toyota Corolla down to the water's edge managed to get the doors opened by having the robot cut a hole in the driver side window and hit the button on the side of the door. Then, the robot opened the door while everyone stayed as far back as possible. They programmed the robot to hit the trunk lid button and the rear truck opened. As they crawled closer, they saw two pressure cookers wrapped up in several blankets. The Special Agent with the burner phones arrived and played with one of the apps and saw the button to cancel the app and removed it from the phone. As soon as that happened, he tried the phone for other apps and nothing happened to the bombs. It was now clear that the bombs were not disarmed but could not be activated with the cell phone. So, the bomb crew got closer and were able to unhinge the pressure cookers while dropping out all the nails and ball bearings to the ground. The C4 placement was removed and carefully stored in a lined bomb box. They brought the box over by the river's edge and exploded the C4 that remained.

At that point there was great relief from everyone involved. They needed to wait for the other two bombs in the laundry room at the Field House but they expected the same results. Within the hour, the other FBI agents made it to the bomb removal site and performed the same tasks.

With no cellphone app, there would be no explosion but they always had to be careful because someone's life was on the line.

Fred Elliott and his three compatriots were removed and transported to the Boston FBI office. Joe wasn't sure if they would ever be heard from again. But he knew that something had to be done to break up the Sovereign Citizens of Connecticut. That would be for another day and not for him personally. He was quite sure that Mike Hanley would know exactly what to do with the four members now in hand and by the time he got done, he would send Joe specifics on what further action was needed.

Joe and Kim Matz were on their way back to New London. They stopped quickly at McDonald's on the way and ate in the car on the way home. Joe really liked Kim and thought she handled herself very well and very professionally. She was the only woman in the group but she held her own and Joe kiddingly asked her if she would like to transfer over to the Coast Guard. She kidded back and laughed and said why couldn't she get all three qualifications just like him so she could move around as well. He said he would mention it to the higher ups when he got a chance. He invited her over for dinner with Julie and the kids and she took him up on it for the following Sunday. She was thirty-two, two years older than Julie, and married for five years. She and her husband lived in New London, in a condo near downtown and in walking distance of Joe's house. They didn't have any kids but hoped to one day. Joe said he knew the feeling and to ask Julie all about it. She dropped Joe off at his house so he could see Julie and the kids before heading back to see the Rear Admiral and staff.

"Joe, are you okay?" asked Julie.

"I'm fine. I'm better than fine. There were two more

bombs in the field house. Thank God we got there and turned one of the terrorists around by offering the first one a deal. It didn't take long after that. There still could be a problem about the Connecticut terrorist group but that can wait. I need to get to the Rear Admiral's office. It close to 9:00 p.m. and they're waiting for me."

"Go, Joe. Call me as soon as you leave the office on your way back. I'll have sandwiches ready for you. You must be hungry."

"Kim Matz and I had McDonald's on the way back so I'm okay for now but I will be hungry in a while. By the way, I invited Kim and her husband to dinner Sunday to hang out. I think you'll like her, Julie. She is very sharp and very nice. Don't worry about dinner, I'll get pizza and wings so we can watch football."

"Let's see, football or take down terrorists? Pizza and wings? All have the same weight, huh?" she laughed.

Joe gave her a big kiss and headed out the door. It was cold tonight so he pulled his coat closed and put his hat on. He never wore gloves so he put his hands in his pocket and Julie locked the door. He walked the two blocks to the Academy and wondered what the hell just happened? He had been here only a few months and boy did he see changes that needed to be made to protect the cadets, the staff and families walking in and out of the place. Before he could change the cadets into something different reflecting the year 2022, he needed to make sure they were safe, secure, and knew how to protect themselves. *Hell, scrap his plans, he needed to move quickly on safety and security issues, now.*

Joe walked through the front door of the administration building and up the stairs to the Rear Admiral's office. As he walked into the boardroom, everyone there, that had been there all day, broke out in complete bedlam. They started clapping, including the Rear Admiral. Ensign Meg Olson starting singing, "Joe's our man, if he can't do it, no one can, YEAH."

Joe turned red from ear to ear and simply said thanks. The Rear Admiral came over and shook his hand and said, "Joe, you did more in one day to protect our cadets than I did since I've been here. We are all eternally grateful to you and those who went with you to take them down. We understand all the bombs have been found and disarmed and four terrorists are on their way to the Boston FBI. Is that right, Joe?"

"It is, sir. But tomorrow, we need a clean sweep of this campus from door to door and look in every cubby hole we find and then we all need to do a better job of protecting our cadets, sir."

"We all totally agree, Joe. I have no idea how you started this morning and came to the conclusions you did, almost immediately and got us out of extreme danger. I heard you were a man of action but this really takes the cake. Thank you. Thank you. Thank you, from all of us," he said. "You need to go home and rest. It's been a full day already. I'll see you tomorrow around noon. Take the morning off. You deserve it."

They walked out together and the Rear Admiral said, "Joe you really saved the day and I won't forget it. By the way if people start looking at you kind of funny, the word is already out about Joe Traynor our very own national hero. This is coming from the cadets not us. The male cadets are calling you the 'Real Deal' and the females are calling you affectionately, the 'Bomb.'" He laughed. "Never had a military rock star on campus before, Joe. By the way I called your friend, Jake, and told him what you did and all he said was 'I'm not surprised'. I also spoke individually with each member of the Board of Trustees and Captain Laura Chavez, who tried to slam you at the board meeting in Spanish, felt quite inadequate compared to the 'Bomb.' Yes, she heard the scuttlebutt from the cadets since she's on campus here every day. I'm sure she won't 'screw' with you anymore, Joe," the Rear Admiral said and smiled. "Good night, 'Real Deal.'"

Joe waved back at the Rear Admiral and headed home. It was almost 11:00 p.m. He hoped Julie was still up. He was still feeling the high you get from a takedown like this. Maybe, since it turned out okay, he could get things done. Sometimes, the shit hits the fan and taking chances are seen as a flaw but not today, not tonight. Everyone is happy to say the least.

Chapter 8

Joe woke up around 9:30 a.m. Evidently, he'd been running on pure adrenalin since yesterday. Julie was nursing Annie as he walked into the living room. Bella left for school almost two hours ago.

"Any calls?" asked Joe.

"There were calls about your warranty on a car you owned ten years ago and two others from Verizon and VISA wanting to raise your credit limit," she smiled and laughed.

"Why do we have a landline anyway?" Joe asked.

"As you explained it to me when we had it installed, the phone was basically free due to bundling whatever that is," she said.

"I guess free isn't so free is it? No calls from the Rear Admiral?"

"No. You seem disappointed, Joe."

"I guess when he said take the day off he meant it and meant no calls for which I am actually grateful. After breakfast, why don't we walk up to see the Connecticut College campus and then walk over to the Academy to see what's going on," he asked.

"Sounds like a plan. It's not that cold out so I'll bundle Annie into the carriage and she should be warm enough. Maybe we can walk up to Bella's school as well and wave to her if we see her? What do you think?" she asked.

They left after breakfast around 11:20 a.m. Bella had lunch around 11:40 a.m. so they might just see her outside in the playground for a few minutes. It was brisk outside but they were once again getting used to the winter weather in the northeast. It only took about fifteen minutes to get to Bella's school first. As they walked by the school, they noticed that the second graders were coming out the side door. Bella was with Emma O'Neil. That made Julie and Joe very happy. Bella saw them and waved and blew a kiss to Annie. Emma waved as well and they ran over to the swing set and waited their turns. Julie smiled at Joe and nodded. They waved again and headed over to the college campus. It was a beautiful place, only blocks from their house. Julie thought maybe she could feel comfortable at this well-respected liberal arts college. She was now in a routine and could go see the Dean about a potential position or a visiting author contract. She just about gave up on the idea of going to Brown University several times a week. It was an hour drive each way and she just didn't have that kind of time when she could do just as well right around the corner. They walked around and went into the cafeteria and each had a donut and coffee. They would have a late lunch when they got back home.

It was closing in on 1:00 p.m. and Annie was sound asleep in her carriage. They walked over to the Academy and as they started into the campus at the main gate, the sentry looked at Joe and saluted. He said, "We're glad you're here, sir. Congratulations."

Joe smiled and didn't know what to say. Julie looked at him and thought they must think or know that what Joe did yesterday was a very big deal. They walked down the sidewalk and they couldn't go twenty feet without someone, a Coast Guard member, administrator, or cadet, saluting Joe and thanking him for saving their campus and their lives.

Joe said, "I hope this ends soon. I can't imagine carrying this burden with me over the next several years."

They walked down to the field house and around the open playing fields and then back to the Rear Admiral's office. Joe picked up Annie and left the carriage outside. He thought they didn't have to worry about anyone stealing the carriage from Joe or his wife after all this.

They walked up the stairs and to Meg Olson's desk and Joe introduced her to Julie and Annie. Meg asked if she could hold the baby and Joe handed Annie to her. Meg was all over her and cooing and kissing her forehead. Julie laughed. The Rear Admiral heard the noise outside his office and opened the door and smiled. "Welcome Traynors," he said and introduced himself to Julie and grabbed Annie's little fingers and smiled. "She's beautiful, Julie. She looks just like you," he said.

"Well that's certainly a good thing," she said. I don't want her looking like the 'Bomb,' you know," and she smiled. The Rear Admiral smirked and could see why Julie was as attractive as he heard about her. She had brains too, he thought.

A few of the office staff came over to shake Joe's hand and to be introduced to Julie and little Annie. They all asked him what they were doing there after yesterday and Julie said they were just out for a walk to Bella's school and to Connecticut College. No one at the Academy really knew the story of how Bella became their daughter but it was clear that Julie was way too young to have a seven year old and to have accomplished all she has accomplished by now. Someone asked about Bella and they spoke for a while and Julie informed them that Bella came to them after her mother died of a brain tumor at a very young age. She explained that Bella's mother and Julie worked at the Key Largo elementary school and she asked Julie to have Bella become their daughter upon her death. Right after the wedding and the funeral for Bella's mother, they adopted Bella. She said her only issue now was when she became excited she reverted back to Spanish. Julie explained that she was learning Spanish as quickly as she could but Joe was fluent and was helping her along the way. They asked them to please bring Bella over to see them when they could. Everyone was quite impressed by this new couple that just arrived at the Academy only a few months ago.

Joe and Julie said their goodbye's and bundled up Annie for the trip home. Joe originally thought it was a wasted day but now he knew that they needed to spend more time together as a family since they were in a new area and a brand new life. As they were walking home, they saw Bella walking down the street heading for home. Boy, how she has grown and changed. They wanted her and Annie to be as close as Julie and Tillie were. Julie waved to Bella as she came into sight. Bella ran over and hugged Julie and grabbed the baby's little hand. Joe bent down and hugged Bella and they walked hand in hand back to their house. It was getting late in the afternoon so Joe went and got a pizza in town and stopped at the market to get some beer. He was back in the northeast so his favorite beer, *Sam Adams*, was in every store. His favorite was *Octoberfest* so when they arrived, he started to check out the stores to see if they carried it. He didn't need to stock up on it like he did down in Tavernier, Florida when they got Joe a few cases ordered special for him. Back at the house, they ate their pizza and Joe helped Bella with her homework while Julie gave Annie a bath and got her ready for bed. Joe and Bella spoke in Spanish in conversation but they always spoke English when Joe helped her with her homework so she would understand the teacher's language the next day. Not only did Joe need to bring Bella's English up to speed but now he had to explain the difference between a New England accent and someone living in Florida. The words were the same but the ear heard them differently. *English is by far the most confusing language,* thought Joe. *How can you have a to, two and too pronounced exactly the same with three different spellings and three different meanings?*

Annie went to bed shortly followed by Bella. Julie read Bella to sleep like always and came down to the living room around 8:30 p.m. so she could watch the rest of the *Voice,* Julie's favorite television show. Joe sat in his chair with a bottle of beer on the stand next to him and was reading the newspapers online on his iPad. The *Hartford Courant, The Day* from New London, and the *West Hartford News* had virtually nothing about the events that took place the previous night in West Hartford. No one picked up any news about a bomb on the campus of the Coast Guard Academy. That made Joe very happy. The less the news, the less questions that had to be answered. As he reached for his beer, Joe's cellphone rang. He picked it up on the second ring as Julie looked at him to go away so she could watch her favorite show. He said "sorry," picked up the phone and his beer and went into the kitchen and answered it at the kitchen table.

"Is the 'Bomb' there?" asked Jake. "Or can I speak to the 'Real Deal?'" and laughed.

"Jesus, not you too," said Joe. "Please make it go away," he added.

"I thought you were going to keep a very low profile until you got the lay of the land up there in academia?" said the Rear Admiral. "What did it take two months or less?"

"Less. How are you, sir?" Joe asked.

"As Dave Ramsey says every day, 'Better than I deserve,'" said Jake. "All kidding aside, congratulations. That was one hell of a quick catch. Solved a bombing at the Academy in less than ten hours. That must be a record of sorts. Not only did I hear from Kelly but a few of my friends in Washington, D.C. called me today to tell me all about it. They were the ones who heard the scuttlebutt about your new superhero names," he said and laughed.

"Make it go away or I'll never hear the end. By the way Mike Hanley's close friend in Boston, picked up the four compatriots and they are now residing on a boat outside the United States territorial waters as I have been informed. But I know nothing about it. I think we will know a great deal about white supremacy in the very near future," said Joe.

"Is any of that legal, Joe?" asked Jake.

"I'm afraid to ask. All I know is they are no longer in the state of Connecticut and every Coast Guard bomb squad member and local FBI member are going over the campus with a fine tooth comb. I also heard that the Navy Submarine Base down the river will be getting the same inspection next," said Joe.

"Joe, I know I'm heading to the Academy as a future board member but many of us have been well aware of the shortcomings in safety and security at that facility for some time. It's not Bill's fault but he is strictly by the book and has a very limited imagination on how the Academy should move forward. That also has been discussed at the highest level. However, I do not want to see you staying there for year after year wasting your qualifications. I want you to fix whatever is deemed wrong and then come back to Florida or move on to something else. You do not have the patience to sit and wait for change to happen. It has always been clear that the person who comes in to make major changes, and accomplishes that goal and gets everything moving in the right direction, is not the person to run the operation on a daily basis. It would kill your creativity and drive. You need to keep moving throughout your career, whatever that is," said Rear Admiral Barnes.

"I'll keep that in mind, sir. But, I have a lot to do to get to a point where I'm comfortable in the number two position at the Academy. I can learn a lot from Rear Admiral Kelly and I want to. I also want to be the Assistant Coach for the Baseball team this spring. Can that be accomplished?" Joe smirked.

"Are you any good at baseball, Joe? We don't want a losing team you know just to make you happy," Jake said and laughed.

"You better check my record for MIT beating the Coast Guard Academy nineteen years ago, sir. I never had to throw home as a reliever. We were ahead 7-6 with two outs and a man on first and third. My first throw was to first base, picking off the runner, and ending the game. The Coast Guard Academy got beat that day 7-6 by the mighty Joe Traynor's All-Stars," he said and laughed.

"That's good to know, Joe. But what have you done for us lately? Oh, that's right, you closed the campus for a day," Jake said.

"Thank you for your support, sir. Just remember pitchers and catchers start Tuesday, March 1st. The first game at home is Sunday, March 20th versus Clark University from Worchester. You're invited to see how the pitching has improved from year to year," said Joe. "I already have Bella and Annie and Sean O'Neil's daughter, Emma, fitted for their Coast Guard Academy baseball uniforms and hats as the first female batgirls in team history, numbers 1, 2 and 3."

"So this equal opportunity thing you been pushing travels all the way to the baseball team?" asked Jake.

"All the way and beyond. I think all three could be in the starting infield as soon as they arrive at eighteen years old. We'll have to wait for Annie to become first team NCAA Division III All American after Bella and Emma opened the gate for her, after they were nominated first, of course," said Joe.

"Well you can't say you don't have it all well planned out, you pain in the ass, Joe," said Jake. He was laughing and said, "If you're serious, I'm sure they'll let you coach or you'll bring a discrimination law suit up based on your age and infirmity. Goodbye Joe, stay in touch."

"Will do and thanks for the call. It is always appreciated," said Joe.

Joe walked back into the living room and Julie asked him who called. He told her Jake and to start getting the measurements for the three girls for their baseball uniforms, numbers 1, 2 and 3, with their names on the back of the uniform and the word BAT GIRL in bold letters. Julie just shook her head and said, "Are you serious?"

"As a heart attack," he said and sat down with a new beer and smiled.

Chapter 9

It was a new week. The weekend was relaxing. Kim Matz and her husband, Eric, came over to watch football at Joe and Julie's house. Julie relented and they had pizza and wings once again but Julie put together fresh salads for her and Kim. She made fresh garlic bread with a marinara dipping sauce and fresh mozzarella. The more she thought about it, she was as bad as Joe was. She laughed. Julie liked Kim and her husband, Eric. Although Kim was an FBI Special Agent, Eric was a CPA with an office in town specializing in corporate taxes. He was easy going and not like any CPA they have ever met. Eric was as down to earth as Kim was and they got along famously. They had no pretense and were relatively the same age as Julie. They had no children so there was no competition as to what child needed to do what whenever. They could get a babysitter and walk to Kim and Eric's house for a quiet night out or head down two blocks to some very nice restaurants. Then, they could walk home and were within minutes of their house in case of an emergency. The hospital was right down the street. Connecticut College was nearby and Joe was minutes from his office.

As far as location, they really had it made. Bella's school was across the street from Connecticut College so Bella walked every day unless the weather was bad and Julie could bring her or pick her up. Joe didn't even need a vehicle. If he had to go somewhere, he could bum a ride or take one of the fleet cars. Julie's car was in the driveway right next to their house. She would have liked to have a garage but you can't always get what you want, as the saying goes. For their short time being here, things were falling into place and into a routine that they could handle. Both Joe and Julie were very worried about how the move from Tavernier, Florida to New London, Connecticut would affect Bella but she seemed to be doing fine. She had her moments like most seven-year-old girls but Julie was on top of it.

What Julie missed the most was obviously her grandmother, Tillie. They spoke to each other most nights but that was a lot different than seeing her in person four or five times a week. Back in Key Largo, Tillie made sure Bella was on the bus or had her come to her apartment when Julie needed time for errands and work. Julie missed the closeness and wondered if they would ever get that back. At least Tillie said she was fine. She hoped Tillie was okay but she was good at keeping up a happy front so no one worried about her. As a grandmother, Tillie was only forty when Julie was born. Then she was a full-time mother at forty-eight after her daughter and Julie's mother died. Now, Julie was twenty-nine and Tillie was sixty-nine, closing in on seventy. Tillie never had a chance to grow into whatever she wanted to be. She was always a mother first, since she was twenty-two years old. Julie had a tear in her eye and had to stop worrying about her grandmother. At least Tillie had Ed Lansing in her life and he was a very good man who cared a great deal about Tillie. There were no plans for Tillie getting married. It just wasn't in the cards and Ed lost his wife a few years ago and they both seemed content to enjoy themselves now, today, and not worry about what if. Being in New London gave Julie a lot of time to think about the future, which could be both good and bad. She was worried that Joe would be called upon for bigger and bigger things especially after solving the bombs planted on the Academy grounds. This was Joe's calling and Julie knew this about him since she was at a very young age. They had a good life and she couldn't ask for more.

Joe finally got around to going to his assigned office, which was just down the hallway from Rear Admiral Kelly. The boardroom was only a few doors down. He didn't like being in a fishbowl so he got out of his office as much as he could. No one really noticed or said anything but he was sure it would be brought up eventually. As Jake pointed out, Joe was not an operations person. He was a change agent and needed to fix things for the better. He needed to appoint the right people who were geared to run operations efficiently. That wasn't in Joe's nature.

Joe sat at his desk and looked out the window. He could barely see the Chapel where Annie was baptized but saw the steeple, the tallest spiral on the campus. The only pictures he had were of Julie, Bella, and Tillie last winter down in Tavernier with the sun shining on a bright seventy-degree day. He missed the Florida weather but was starting to get accustomed to the northeast, once again. After all, he lived in upstate New York for the first eighteen years of his life. They hadn't framed Annie's baptism pictures yet and he would need to put that on his credenza along with the others.

Joe didn't want an assigned assistant and asked Rear

Admiral Kelly if every once in a while he could utilize Meg Olsen for assistance. He'd never had a secretary or administrative assistant and he didn't want to start now. He was perfectly capable of writing his own reports and he was computer savvy to say the least. Joe was very big on daily checklists of things to do. He made excel sheets with daily activities and only worked two weeks out. If he didn't finish a job this week, then he would simply move it to the next week if it were important. By Friday, Joe always had a clean desk. If something were important, he would move it until it got done. If it were not, he would simply throw it in the garbage and have the bag shredded so no one could see what his plans were unless he wanted them to be part of it. Joe didn't think he was paranoid but he knew, no matter where you were, someone always wanted to know what you were doing at any given time. Now, he wanted to concentrate on the safety and security of the cadets first and then everyone else on campus.

Joe started his spreadsheet with one line item at a time. He wanted to meet with the assigned security team for the Coast Guard Academy. He wanted to see their emergency management plan and what procedures were in place for an immediate shutdown of the facilities. When the bombs were on campus, the Rear Admiral and the Board of Trustees called him in to handle it when in fact, there should have been a team in place to do that exact thing. There wasn't as he found out during the day's activities that they were flying by the seat of their pants. It was run like a small New England college, which it was, but it was also a military facility and should have been better protected. Joe needed to know and soon if the staffing was inadequate or if the planning was inadequate or both. He had a feeling it was both. He had so many other thoughts about how to bring this campus up to 21st century standards but those thoughts had to wait until today's issues were addressed and solved. It was getting later in the day as he was reviewing all the staff in all the departments at the Academy and was trying to figure out who reported to whom and why. What was the chain of command at the lower and middle levels?

It was obvious at the top. The Rear Admiral is the chief administrator and Joe as Assistant Superintendent. There was a Provost, the same as at Barry University. The Provost is a member of the Rear Admiral's cabinet and potential replacement when the Superintendent retires, if this was only a college but it isn't. It is also a military facility and all that connotes. The Provost is the chief academic officer of the Academy and has responsibility for all academic and budgetary affairs. The Provost collaborates with the Superintendent in setting overall academic priorities and allocates funds to carry these priorities forward. It was a big job and Joe wanted to work with the Provost and be on the same page.

However, his job is not just academic. His job is to ensure that these cadets are mentally prepared upon graduation to take on very dangerous issues of the day to keep America safe as well as be in charge of their daily safety and security. So, first, Joe would ask the security head to come in with his immediate boss, whomever that was. It was not clear from any report outlining administrative responsibilities. Joe would sit with the Superintendent as soon as possible to reconcile duties and responsibilities.

Before Joe would meet with the security team and whomever the boss was, Joe wanted to make sure that he still had the power of the purse over Mary Evan's ten-million-dollar bequest to the Coast Guard Academy. He wanted her to clarify if she had any priorities for the funds especially in the areas of minority and women recruitment, especially women of color. Right now, Joe was more concerned with their safety and security. He did not want to recruit anyone if the Academy couldn't keep him or her safe. He decided to call Mary first before he held any meetings.

"Hello, Mary Evans speaking," she said.

"Mary, it's Joe Traynor. Am I interrupting anything?" he asked.

"No, just sheer boredom. Tell me how exciting Troy, New York is in the wintertime, Joe," she laughed. "Can you believe how dark it is at 4:30 p.m. in the afternoon? This is ridiculous. It makes you want to head home and tuck yourself in and sleep until daylight savings time. It's March 13th this year, right? We lose an hour's sleep. That will be fine by me," Mary said.

"Can I ask you a question about the ten-million-dollar donation to the Academy?" he asked.

"Absolutely, you have the authority over what is to be done with the funds. Is that your question?" she asked.

"Sort of," he said. "Let me tell you what just happened and what is going on and then you'll understand my reasoning," Joe said. He went on to tell her about the bombing and how he and a team of Hartford cops and FBI agents took down a white supremacist team that had placed four bombs on the campus at the Academy. He told her about the lack of planning and had just done extensive reading on what would be necessary to bring the Academy up to speed to secure the safety and security of everyone on campus. He mentioned a real program developed by the United States Military Academy at West Point and how they generously give away their program to other military institutions and colleges. He said he made a few calls and talked to their Assistant Superintendent who put Joe in touch with the assigned development team responsible for the full implementation of the program. He also said that it could cost almost three million dollars to implement, install, train staff, and manage over the next four years. Joe said he didn't feel comfortable recruiting anyone to the Coast Guard Academy if he couldn't ensure his or her safety and security.

Mary spoke and said, "Joe, we have already been informed about your heroic efforts in removing the bombs from campus. I know you like to downplay your involvement but Jake Barnes told us of your efforts and you have only been there a few months," she said. "He called me to update us on the spending down in the Keys for the recruitment and training at The College of the Florida Keys. The new president is fulfilling all the required obligations and contracts and the Coast Guard has another seventy-five recruits from the program that joined the service. They are fully trained in technology and have received all their certifications and are on their way to boot camp for the full Coast Guard experience," she said.

She went on, "Joe, you can use the money for whatever you want. All we need are invoices from vendors and other out of pocket expenses so we can pay the bills immediately upon your approval. We can wire transfer any amount at any time upon approval. You certainly can use three million dollars of the ten million dollars allocated for this purpose. Is that okay?" she asked.

"Better than okay. Thank you. I see Rear Admiral Kelly starting to leave his office so I need to grab him. Can I call you tomorrow and let you know what happens next?" he asked.

"Yes, do. I'll talk to you tomorrow. Bye, Joe."

"Rear Admiral Kelly, can I speak to you for a moment?" Joe asked.

"Sure. I have ten minutes to meet my wife or I'll blame you," he said and laughed.

Joe told him that he talked to Mary Evans and quickly told him about the West Point safety and security state-of-the-art program and how he would like to investigate utilizing the program at the Coast Guard Academy. He also asked who was in charge of safety and security. The Rear Admiral told him that they usually just report directly to him since it's not about academics or it would go through the Provost. He asked Joe if he wanted that duty and if he did, he certainly would approve it with the blessing of the Board of Trustees. He said that after his heroics, and he did call it heroics, he didn't see anyone refusing to let Joe take care of these issuers. Joe told him that Mary Evans approved an initial three million dollars to start the program installation and he said it was up to him according to Mary. However, Joe said he didn't want to usurp his authority or step on toes but he would if he had to. The Rear Admiral said he could pretty much do what he wants and it will be approved. Joe thanked him and told him to say hello to his wife and have a good night. *That wasn't too hard,* he thought.

The meeting was set up for 10:00 a.m. the next day. Joe would finish his notes at home tonight and be prepared for tomorrow's meeting. You never knew whose feathers you would ruffle from day to day. It was nice knowing that the Rear Admiral already approved his semi-plan of action and that he had the money to make it happen. *That really didn't happen often in real life,* he thought.

Chapter 10

Lieutenant Dave Simon, Director of Safety and Security for the Coast Guard Academy, has been the director for the last four years. Just like Joe Traynor, he has worked himself up to this position since joining the Coast Guard at age twenty-three. He graduated from Dean College outside Boston, in Franklin, Massachusetts near Gillette Stadium, home to the New England Patriots. There, he received an associate's degree and then received his bachelor's degree from Regents University in Criminal Justice, a military friendly top ten school, located in Virginia Beach, Virginia. He got his bachelor's degree, just like Joe did while on active duty. He moved to the officer's track, as a Petty Officer Third Class.

Lieutenant Simon has a full-time staff of twenty-four officers, which is split into three rotating shifts of eight each, serving over five days. On the weekends, there is a lot more activity down at the field house and various arenas depending on the season such as soccer, baseball, track, football, and other sports. Sixty percent of the roughly 1,069 cadets participate in varsity sports at the

Division III level, twelve in Men's and ten in Women's and three co-educational teams. The Coast Guard Academy also participates at the Division I level in its core mission of sailing, rifle, and pistol. For weekend security, a separate part-time team of sixteen men and women, eight on Saturday and eight on Sunday covers these events. Two are assigned to the visitor's booth at the incoming gate while the rest roam the grounds on foot or in specially marked SUVs, clearly identified as Coast Guard Academy Security.

Dave Simon met Joe at his office at 10 a.m. He seemed to be as punctual as Joe. They introduced themselves to each other even though they met briefly during the bomb incident. Dave stayed on campus and was instrumental in securing the two pressure cooker bombs that were located in the laundry room at the field house. He was there when they gingerly removed both bombs utilizing the robot sent in for that purpose. At that time, they were unsure if they had all the bombs planted until Joe had secured the four phones that had the app to trigger the mechanisms. Once removed, they were disarmed. At the time, not really knowing the pecking order of the security team at the Academy, Joe had made it known that he was grateful that they put their lives on the line for the benefit of the Academy. At the same time, Joe wanted to ensure that it didn't happen again but he knew that was impossible. If someone or some organization wanted to cause harm anywhere in the world, it could happen regardless of caution. However, Joe was of the belief that you did everything you could to make it harder and harder to gain access and have it happen. With that in mind, Joe kept an open mind as to the reliability of the head of security and the security team for the Academy.

Dave formally introduced himself to Joe and vice versa.

Joe thought it would be a good idea to get out of his office and start walking the campus. No matter what, Joe didn't want prying eyes on the conversations he was about to have with Lieutenant Simon. They walked out of the building and strolled over to the cafeteria for a cup of coffee. Once again, on the way, several cadets and a few professors thanked Joe for his efforts in saving the Academy. He felt rather sheepish in front of the man that was supposedly in charge of these kinds of crisis. Joe simply nodded and said thank you and nodded to Dave as to say no big deal and it will be over soon. They entered the cafeteria, got their coffee and went over to a window table so they could look out on the campus and they talked.

Dave said, "Sir, I am ashamed to tell you that I allowed this to happen. It was clearly my fault and my responsibility for not noticing what you picked up immediately and ran with. For that. I will never forgive myself and if necessary, I will resign my commission as Lieutenant. I do not want to be responsible for the death of even one cadet due to my incompetence."

"Thank you for that self-observation," Joe said. "But it is unnecessary. I don't know how this could have been prevented with the current state of your security systems now in place. And, as we speak, and get to know each other, please simply call me Joe. I have a very difficult time responding to sir, or Captain or anything other than simply, Joe. If we are in a meeting and you know how to read the room, call me sir then and only then. I am very close to Rear Admiral Barnes as you probably already know. We are on first name basis since I worked for him since I was eighteen-years-old as a new recruit. He told me to always call Rear Admiral Kelly the title he obviously admires and wants. I always call him sir or Rear Admiral or Rear Admiral Kelly, wherever and whenever I am in his presence. Enough," said Joe.

"Thank you, Joe. I do feel responsible but are you saying that we don't have adequate coverage for this facility?" he asked.

"That's exactly what I'm saying. You may have twenty-four sets of eyes on this campus at all times but you can't see through the trunk of a car unless you open it and even then you might not know what you're looking at, at any given time." Joe went on, "Let me update you about my background and then you can do the same. I have read some very fine things about you. We both started the same way and maybe took different routes to get here. But, we are here together.

"I am the beneficiary of a ten-million-dollar gift from a donor to improve the Academy in any way I deem appropriate with the Rear Admiral's approval as well as the Board of Trustees. They all know about it and know I am looking high and low to fix what I understand to be either antiquated or out of balance with the 21st century. I called the donor last night for clarification and the donor told me I could start to improve safety and security at the Academy by using three million dollars to start with to bring this facility up to, equal to and to even surpass the U.S. Military Academy at West Point. The donor lives in upstate New York and is very aware of West Point."

"Really?" said Dave. "No shit!"

"No shit is right," said Joe. "My wife, Julie, calls me on my 'No Shit' line all the time. Someday I'll tell you how we met the donor in Key West at Sloppy Joe's Bar and the term 'No Shit' popped up a few times," Joe smiled and laughed. "We'll get along fine."

Dave was three years older than Joe. He had just turned forty this year. Dave remarked that he was unaware of what Joe had accomplished over his career until Joe solved the bomb issues. It seemed that everyone started to download "Joe Traynor" on the internet and they found some very fascinating incidents when pulled together. Dave said, "You speak Spanish, Russian, Chechen and are now learning Chinese and you just got your Ph.D. from Barry University in Miami?"

"I did, just last Christmas. I was also, for one year, the Interim President of The College of the Florida Keys, before coming here. At the same time, I had been back and forth from the Academy many times over that one year period learning as much as I could before coming here as Assistant Superintendent. I know a lot of people think I leap frogged over some fine candidates and maybe I did and maybe there was good reason for it. Like you, I bring the vision of a lowly enlisted man, not from an immediate officer's perspective, just because I graduated from the Coast Guard Academy and immediately became an officer. By the way, do you know that I am a graduate of the Coast Guard Academy as well?" Joe asked.

Dave said, "No, I didn't." He added, "You are quite a surprise, Joe. And a breath of fresh air."

Joe became a little quieter and said, "I hope our conversations today and in the future will remain confidential. I know how to avoid backlash and I'm really good at making up various stories to see which come back, letting me know whom I can trust."

"I will give you my word," said Dave.

At that point, Joe handed Dave a bunch of reading material on how he wanted to address safety and security at the Academy and how he was thinking about spending an initial three million dollars to start the ball rolling. Joe mentioned that he wanted to go to West Point with Dave and meet the officers who were in the development stages for new high technology-based security systems. West

Point officers said they were willing to share all they had to make the Coast Guard Academy secure. Joe added that the U.S. Military Academy, in West Point, N.Y., has begun using wireless networks in its classrooms, but only after conducting extensive research on security hazards and waiting two years for fast wireless technology to become available. West Point officials believe the wireless network they now have is secure, unlike most wireless networks on college campuses. But to secure the network, West Point had to pay some $625,000, about five times what the network itself cost.

Most colleges have dealt with the threat of casual attackers by providing, at a minimum, secure Web pages for students' course work. But West Point officials say they had to pay for a higher degree of security because their campus network, which is connected to the Defense Department's network, is a more likely target of deliberate attackers. Joe said the Coast Guard Academy also is connected to the Defense Department network and Dave said he was aware but was not competent in advanced technology. Joe told him that he was tech-savvy but not at the nerd level so they both needed to get up to speed to put into place all the bells and whistles needed. Joe said if it cost more than three million dollars, he would ask for more and didn't think he would be turned down. Joe told Dave that the ultimate goal is to get worldly candidates on campus that were fluent in other languages, were street smart and book smart and had creativity to meet the challenges they now faced.

Joe and Dave appeared to be on the same page. Dave asked Joe specifically how he knew what to do exactly when told about the ransom note and the demand for money or the bombs would go off. Joe explained the kinds of crisis that he had been involved in including earthquakes in Haiti, Katrina in New Orleans, the takedown of the Mexican Mafia, the breaking up of the Dixie Mafia in Nashville, the Columbian cocaine conspiracy that involved Coast Guard officers, and the trafficking of young girls right in Miami. He also mentioned breaking up the Russian mafia in Miami as well, while deporting the leader to an unknown CIA site. He said that, although dangerous, and could have killed a lot of cadets, that this bombing incident was homegrown and didn't have the outreaching strength since they were white nationalists and supremacists in Connecticut. He said that asking for cash in this day and age was tantamount to capture. If they were sophisticated, they would have had the money wired to ten different countries in ten minutes, never to be seen again. However, desperation on their part made them as dangerous as any Chechen takedown he encountered as he told him about the Boston Marathon wannabe in Orlando.

Joe told Dave that the next step was for Joe to meet with the Rear Admiral and discuss next steps. He would outline what he wanted to do to bring security up to speed on campus and what staffing and funding he would need over the next four years to accomplish all these goals. He would remind the Rear Admiral that his funding didn't come from the annual budget so that the Provost didn't need to approve purchases. He would make sure that the Provost was always informed of course because down the road, Joe wanted changes to the academic curriculum.

He didn't want fluency in foreign languages and the recruitment of minorities who spoke those languages to be placed at the tail end of the academic backbone of the Academy. Joe wanted language majors, which currently didn't exist to actually be on a par with all the engineering and scientific course work now offered. In fact, 60% of the cadets graduated with a science-based degree. Joe thought that was great back in the 20th century when they built bridges and boats and weapons but now if there were a World War III it wouldn't be bombing as much as taking out power systems, computer failure, technology failure, and atomic bombs.

The Coast Guard and all the other service academies need to bring in speakers of other languages to understand what they are up against. They needed to understand the culture as much as understanding the weaponry they would use. Intercepting messages from foreign adversaries were even more important, especially with the understanding of cultural differences, religions, morality, and other social factors that could cause an international incident as much as the Russians taking over Ukraine. They needed to know about it months or years before it happens. Joe wanted to see these changes made before he would move on to the actual everyday planning for crisis that he was hoping to build against.

Chapter 11

As Joe and Dave were walking around the campus, Joe asked him, "I can see how the car got in here with the pressure cooker bombs in the trunk but how the hell did they manage to get two others into the laundry room at the field house?"

"I've been wondering the same thing," said Dave. "We have cameras at every entrance at the field house and at all the other buildings as well. If they went in the front door of the field house, that's one thing. But how did they get into the laundry room which should always be locked?"

"Are there cameras inside the building and especially in all the hallways?" Joe asked.

"Yes. Do you have time right now?" asked Dave. "Let's go to the security office and pull up all the cameras from Friday through Sunday night. As you said, you thought the bombs were probably set in place over the weekend. Let's look at the Toyota Corolla that we found that was stolen and see if there were any other cars in line at that time. Maybe the people in the car were the lookouts for the others entering the field house."

"They were parked close enough to the Field House so

that could be a possibility," said Joe.

They went to the security office, located two doors down from the field house, right in the middle of the campus. As they walked in, Joe looked around. There were two officers in the small building, both looking at cameras from across the campus. They were tied right into the front gate as well, so in addition to the guards at the gate looking at incoming traffic, they could as well, in real time. There was a combination break room and additional office that held all the video equipment. Dave fired up the video from the weekend, starting Friday early morning. There were continuous loops so all the film could be seen at the same time. There was just normal traffic going in and out with food trucks dropping off product at the cafeteria and others bringing supplies to the various offices. There were three mail deliveries and pickups every day. Dave said they saw the same post office employees daily but truckers came and went. They rolled through the video and finally found the Toyota Corolla at 12:35 p.m. coming through the front gate on Sunday, the same day as Annie's baptism. The car stopped and there were two individuals in the car. The driver could be seen and his picture showed it to be one of the other three individuals picked up with Fred Elliott. Joe noticed him right away. "Got one," he said.

"That takes care of who drove the car," said Joe. "We don't need to know who the passenger was. We'll find out eventually. Now we need to follow and see if they took anything out of the car and brought it into the field house," said Joe.

Just as Joe mentioned it, a FedEx delivery truck came right after the Toyota Corolla. The driver quickly flashed the guard his delivery invoice to be dropped off at the field house. It was an official FedEx truck and the guard reviewed the paperwork and told him to drive through.

Low and behold, as the driver spoke to the guard, Joe thought the driver looked familiar. It was in fact, Fred Elliott, driving the vehicle.

Joe said, "Bingo. Do you see that driver, Dave? It's the bomber that we picked up. It's Fred Elliott. What the hell is he doing with a FedEx truck? I need to make some calls immediately."

Joe called the main FedEx facility in Hartford and gave the manager the truck number and license plate number. The manager said that the truck was supposed to be in the parking lot and not scheduled until the following day. Joe asked the manager if they knew a Fred Elliott. He said they did. He said he was a part time driver for FedEx at the 130 Old County Circle warehouse in Windsor Locks, Connecticut, which is actually Hartford and right next to the Bradley International Airport. It was the main warehouse for FedEx in the region. That's where that truck was parked. Joe thanked him and turned to Dave.

"Looks like we now know how the bombs got into the field House but how the hell did they get into the laundry room?" he asked.

At that point, they turned their attention to the field house since they now knew almost the exact time when the delivery was made. They went back to the video to pick up the parking lot and saw the Toyota Corolla parked near the facility at 12:45 p.m. The FedEx truck was right behind them and then pulled up to the front of the field house and the driver had two boxes, one under each arm. Someone opened the door for him and he thanked the cadet. From there, Joe and Dave picked him up walking the hallway down to the laundry room. He tried the door and it was locked. One of the custodians saw him in the hallway and asked him if he needed help.

He said his delivery of the two boxes was to the laundry

room manager but the door was locked. The custodian simply went over to the door and used his master key to open the door. Fred Elliott simply walked in and placed the boxes by the wall nearest the door, one on top of the other. He thanked the custodian and told him to have a nice day. Elliott simply said goodbye, walked out the front door and opened the back of the truck. The two guys driving the stolen Toyota Corolla jumped into the back of the truck and Fred Elliott closed the door and took off. He waved to the guard in the guardhouse and mouthed, "Thanks."

Dave turned to Joe and said, "That's really embarrassing." He added, "I'd talk to the custodian but he's not the problem. The problem began at the front gate and went downhill from there. I won't even try to think about why they didn't check the truck on the way out to see if they stole a cannon or two. What the hell? Joe, I am so sorry," said Dave.

Joe looked at Dave and all he could do was laugh. "Dave I wouldn't show this video to Helen Keller. Even she would pick up the lunacy that went on. These cadets are our most precious assets and this is how we take care of them? I really don't want to show the Rear Admiral because someone will wind up in Juneau, Alaska counting whales while wiping oil spilled off of seals. Jesus, what a clusterfuck this is," he said.

"Joe, go ahead. Do what you have to do. Please don't cover up for me. Just following all the safety and security rules put into place in 1980, doesn't seem to pick up anyone who has an IQ over 80," he said.

"Let's figure out immediately what changes we need," said Joe. "People are not to come in and out of this facility without proper ID or have their vehicles registered. I don't care if the vehicles are personal or commercial. Everyone shows IDs every day from now on. We do need the video to send to the FBI as evidence of what happened here. I don't think it will matter because the four Musketeers we caught are well on their way to a CIA security facility. I will call Mike Hanley and let him handle the embarrassment for us. I owe him and he owes me. I'll also talk to Kim Matz and take her through what happened here. I'll also invite her to come with us when we head to West Point to start the process of completely upgrading all our safety and security systems."

"Thanks, Joe. I don't know you at all but I certainly respect what you have done previously and I am very grateful about how you will handle this situation. I can learn a lot and I am sincerely sorry. If you weren't here, I can only imagine what could have happened," said Dave.

They shook hands and Joe headed back to his office. He has never seen such a lapse in security in his entire life. If all that just happened on one of his previous assignments, he and his crew would probably be dead by now. He needed to talk to someone but it wasn't going to be Rear Admiral William Kelly first. He needed some guidance from Jake Barnes. He trusted his good sense and appropriate solutions for solving everyday situations without throwing people under the bus. Today could have been Dave's last day with the Coast Guard, period. It could still happen but Joe thought he deserved a second chance.

That night, Joe called Jake at his home down in Miami. Jake's wife, Becky, picked up and after small talk, she knew that Joe had something very specific on his mind and needed to talk to Jake right away. "He'll be right with you, Joe," she said.

"Hi, Joe. What's up?" asked Jake.

"It's kind of official and I need some guidance from you if that's all right?" said Joe.

"No problem. I hope I can help," said Jake.

Joe went over what he had found out about the bombs on campus at the Academy. He didn't come right out and call it total incompetency but he alluded to it. He said it's not just the officer in charge, Dave Simon, but there was a complete breakdown in safety and security as far as he could tell from the top down. The safety and security plan currently in place was from the 1970s when there was very little terrorism or need to worry about an Academy in the northeast. He said obviously that everything is different in the year 2022 and changes had to be made immediately. Joe wanted to know how Rear Admiral Kelly would take it if he came right out and told him what he found out and what was needed to correct the situation for now. Every day things change he said and they had to be on their toes to survive. He told him that Mary Evans gave him the go ahead to spend at least three million dollars to fix the problem and if he needed more out of the ten-million-dollar donation to the Academy then that was at his discretion. Joe told him that he had to make a presentation to the Board of Trustees next week and asked if he was invited.

"I wasn't invited but I can be," he said. "I'm not officially on the Board until the Trustee that I'm replacing is gone and that won't be until the spring at least."

"I don't want to have Dave Simon fired because quite frankly he's in a tough spot. He has next to nothing for a budget and his officers are trained to watch buildings not terrorism. If I can gently point this out and offer to beef up the security budget and lead with that, do you think it will fly without ruffling any feathers? As you know, sir. I don't care about creating hard feelings if it protects those we are entrusted to protect, namely the cadets and staff at the Academy."

"Joe that might be a good idea. You're in the driver seat

right now and they owe you big time for stopping a multiple bombing on campus. Whatever you suggest would fly as far as I'm concerned. I can be there next week. I'll let them know that I would like a tour while I'm up for a meeting in the Boston area. They may suspect something else but that's too bad. What do you think?" asked Rear Admiral Barnes.

"I think that would make me feel better," said Joe. "In the meantime, I'm putting together a complete upgrade for safety and security at the Academy based on new innovative methods developed at the think tank at West Point. Dave, Kim Matz from the FBI and I will be heading there in a few weeks to go through a complete breakdown of their systems and participate in a mock attack on West Point to see how it's handled. I will make that part of my presentation and maybe some Trustees will also want to attend," said Joe.

"That sounds very smart, Joe," said Jake. "I'll call you when I get up there and maybe we can go to lunch. Maybe I'll ask Bill Kelly to join us off campus and bounce a few things off of him. He's a good guy. Maybe he's behind the times a little but I know he has the cadets in his heart and will do anything to make sure they are protected. I'll see you next week," said Jake.

"Thank you, sir. I needed this. Once again, fools rush in where wise men fear to tread is the old saying," said Joe.

"There's another old saying about an old bull and a young bull on the top of the hill looking over the herd. I won't repeat it here, though," Jake said and laughed.

"Yes, sir. I got it. Thanks." And with that, they ended the call. Joe needed to be a little more patient as he was just advised but not to the point of not ruffling feathers. Jake reminded him of his best assets and he was grateful.

Joe set up a meeting with Rear Admiral Kelly for the

day after next. He told him that the topic was very important and if he would clear two hours of time he would be grateful. The Rear Admiral said "fine."

Joe and the Rear Admiral met at 10:00 a.m. like usual. The Rear Admiral liked to get in around 8:00 a.m. and have his coffee, read the papers, go online, answer emails and sign reports first thing in the morning. Then, at 10:00 a.m. or after, he would schedule face-to-face meetings with staff and others.

Joe was in earlier at 7:00 a.m. He walked the campus first just to keep the visuals of what happened in his head. Joe was left-handed and had what used to be called a photographic memory. Now, after much study, what Joe had was recalibrated to be "total recall." Joe remembers everything that has ever happened to him, both good and bad. He remembers within close proximity, the day, around the time and exactly who said what, to whom, and everything in between. He did this through what he thought was left-handed visualization. He had basically immediate total recall. So, by walking around for an hour, he completely visualized every step that he thought happened and what he actually saw happen on the video.

From there, he knew what had to be done, even if he didn't know if there were tools to prevent it from happening again. He assumed what he was thinking had been thought of before by people smarter than him. He laughed to himself about the only new things ever invented were the pet rock and the hula-hoop. They weren't actually new just marketed and packaged for mass consumption. He needed to package someone else's cutting-edge technology and do a technology transfer to the Coast Guard Academy. The systems were being rapidly developed and he wanted it known to the military, regardless of branch, that he wanted to be in on the new advances. Marketing 101 he called it. It worked at The College of the Florida Keys and in his other assignments so it should work here or at least it moves them closer than they were to being safe and secure.

Joe walked into the Rear Admiral's office at exactly 10:00 a.m. Joe thought about his presentation to the Rear Admiral and what was expected of him in his new position at the Academy. Joe thought to himself how he would feel if he were only given half the truth about a situation just so the staff would be protected. Joe didn't think it would be fair to Rear Admiral Kelly if he didn't tell him exactly what he found out. However, he would immediately defend Dave Simon and hope to move forward with technology that would help save the day.

"Joe, welcome. From the look on your face, I see you are troubled. What is it?" Rear Admiral Kelly asked.

"Sir, I need to inform you of what happened exactly concerning the bombing on campus. I don't want to sugarcoat it but after my explanation, I hope you will understand and listen to my solution which I believe is well thought out and I can back it up," said Joe.

"Joe, please go ahead. I have cancelled all my meetings until you are completely done. There is nothing more important to me or the Academy than the safety and security of our cadets."

"I'm really glad you feel that way, sir," said Joe. Then, Joe went through all the day's activities and the follow up with Dave Simon as they walked the campus a few days after the incident. Joe fully explained how they were able to identify Fred Elliott as the terrorist through the email by Jack Forest down in Virginia. He described in detail the takedown of the four white supremacists in West Hartford. He explained how the FBI handled the arrests and how those men were taken to Boston and handed over to the

CIA. He explained that those four terrorists, even the one he promised immunity, it was a lie, would be taken offshore and never see the justice system. That was an eye opener for the Rear Admiral. He asked Joe if he had done this preciously and Joe said yes with the head of the Russia mafia in Miami and the white supremacists in Big Pine Key, those who survived and not shot dead on the spot.

"Joe, I am surprised but not surprised by what you are telling me, especially about how terrorists are handled. You are thirty-seven years old and I'm a lot older than that. What you have done in the Coast Guard is really hard to explain to those not in the know. I have heard rumors about you and your team down in Florida but most think it's a myth. It's not. Calling you the 'Real Deal' is not an exaggeration," Kelly said.

"Sir, I haven't even gotten to the good parts yet," he said and smiled.

The Rear Admiral nodded and Joe continued. He told him how they simply sat and watched the video from Friday through Sunday afternoon. Joe used the line than even Helen Keller could have gotten there but obviously maybe not in time before the bombs went off. That was Joe's saving grace. He got there and got the bombs off campus and disarmed in time. He told him that they followed the FedEx truck in right after the Toyota Corolla and how Elliott simply sauntered through the front door and had a custodian open the laundry room so Elliott could place the bombs inside the door. The laundry room was near the front door that would harm anyone coming in but was right under the grandstands immediately above and there was a Division III basketball game that went off at the same time with tons of fans immediately sitting above the bombs in the laundry room.

"The custodian helped the bomber by opening the door

for him? Wow," he said.

"Remember, it wasn't for the bomber, it was for the FedEx delivery guy struggling with a box under each arm making his way into the field house. Even a cadet opened the front door for him," Joe was now smiling. "I looked it up, Sir. It's called a 'clusterfuck' of major proportions, a term first used in 1969. And guess what, no one here in any capacity could be blamed because there are no safety rules and regulations that I can find for this campus. Guests, parents, cadets, officers, staff, alumni and any and all delivery people just come and go as they please with a nod from the guard at the main gate. This is a completely open campus that needs to be closed until we get it fixed. Sure, there has been little or no problems on campus other than those found at any college with the age group being served. It seems that the security staff is only here to protect the cadets from one another, period and that needs to change. We need to make sure every cadet understands that they live on a military site and need to be vigilant especially now with terrorist attacks everywhere on a daily basis. Maybe Covid-19 shut this campus down for a while but it is now fully open to everyone. Sir, I don't mean to be disparaging to you or your staff. I simply want this problem fixed and I have been given permission by Mary Evans, the donor, to do everything and anything we need to do to fix it," said Joe.

"You know, Joe. I have never met anyone as direct as you in all my time in the Coast Guard. You appear unafraid of rank or consequences for telling people what they need to hear. Thank you. Normally, I would never let a subordinate tell me what you've just told me but I needed to hear it and I think you really don't give a crap about my feelings. Is that about right, Joe?"

"I wouldn't quite put it that way, sir. But you are

correct. Someone's feelings and the potential death of a cadet are not even on the same plane, sir," said Joe.

"I totally agree with you. Can you present this to the Board of Trustees next Wednesday?" the Rear Admiral asked.

They went through Joe's plans for the Academy utilizing the new state-of-the-art West Point technology advancements, one by one. Joe started with wearable devices for each cadet for contact tracing as well as for anyone working at the Academy, regardless of position. The devices were small and would allow everyone to be immediately alerted in case of any major crisis. It would also allow for them to have an immediate GPS code identifying exactly where they were at all times. It was devised by West Point and Joe was told that after a week's time, no one would ever even know they had the device pinned to their clothing. Joe understood this completely after saving Mary Evans from kidnappers only because of GPS tabs secured to her shoes. Joe went over the four examples of how technology is helping to make college campuses more secure with smarter identification and access, with easier intelligence sharing with others, with digitized surveillance and tech-enabled theft prevention. The common thread with all these upgrades is improved communication throughout the Academy and with its partners including Connecticut College across the street, the Naval Submarine Base down the river and other military installations. Joe explained that the first three million dollars would go toward multi-channel emergency notification systems, anonymous alert apps for reporting problems, disaster readiness online orientations directly to the cadets' cell phones, social media platforms integration, and therapy online for those suffering from trauma at any time that could cause a major problem like a shooting on campus. It would also include a new database for support groups and causes for after tragic events occurred.

"Joe, when the hell did you get the time to read up on all this and contact West Point?" asked Kelly.

"Well, I've been thinking about it for a while but as soon as the bombs came into view, I knew it was needed now not later so all I did for the last few days was read, read, and read more. That's when I called the West Point think tank and got invited to participate in their next mock crisis on campus," said Joe.

They finished their meeting around 1:00 p.m., unheard of up to now for someone to get that much attention from Rear Admiral Kelly. Kelly asked Joe if he'd like to join him for lunch in the cafeteria and Joe obviously said yes. They walked down and into the building. There were a lot of saluting and smiles to go around. The officers had their own dining hall but the Rear Admiral simply picked up a tray and stood in line with the other cadets. Joe started to like Bill Kelly a lot more every day. He really did have the students' best interests at heart. Joe was sure that this would get around as well. At lunch, they talked about baseball. Kelly was a Red Sox fan and Joe was a diehard Yankee fan. Where they were in New London was right on the border for each team so there were as many fans of both teams. Joe told him that he pitched at MIT before going into the Coast Guard and he told Kelly that if he had time and he would like to make time to work this spring with the baseball team if the Rear Admiral would mind. Joe kiddingly but not kiddingly told him that both his daughters and Sean O'Neil's daughter, Emma, had already been fitted for Coast Guard Academy baseball uniforms with their names and BAT GIRL printed on the back. He told Kelly that was the selling point to become a part time assistant baseball coach for probably home games only.

"Joe, you are something else. At least you have your priorities right. You have a beautiful, brilliant wife, two daughters and a career. How the hell can you be a Yankee fan?" he asked.

"You know, I didn't know my brother was a Red Sox fan until 2004 when he called me at midnight to tell me how proud he was of the Red Sox winning after being down 3-0 in the championship. It was funny how he never brought it up before. You know I hate frontrunners," he said and smirked. "Go Yanks."

"I'll leave it at that. However, if I find out that you changed their uniforms for pinstripes, you will be fired on the spot," Kelly laughed.

"May be worth it," Joe said.

"Smartass and Irish too. Who would have thought," said Kelly.

Joe thought that this meeting kind of broke the ice for both the Rear Admiral and for Joe as well. Up to then, they both tried to figure out the other's motivation and feelings toward the Coast Guard and especially to the Academy. The Rear Admiral figured out that Joe was all in, and regardless of the time or place, Joe would always try to do his best and make his opinion known regardless of consequences. Jake Barnes told Kelly this when they first spoke and now Kelly truly believed it. Joe felt the same way walking back to the office.

Chapter 12

I t was the following Wednesday and time for the Board of Trustees meeting. Joe was fully prepared to go through exactly what happened. It wasn't just a bomb scare, it was four real bombs placed strategically to kill and make a statement. It was about the five million dollars to put into the coffers of the local white supremacists' group but Joe was sure that they would have set off the bombs anyway even if they got the ransom demands met. If the incident got out, it would mean even more bragging rights for the terrorists. Joe wanted to make sure this would hopefully be the last incident on his watch.

Joe arrived a little early, placing his coat and hat on his rack inside his office door. It was about 8:30 a.m. and the meeting was for 10:00 a.m. Joe felt good about the presentation he would make. He was prepared and the kicker was that the Coast Guard Academy wouldn't have to pay a dime for all the new multi-million dollar improvements that Joe was going to recommend. At least he had that going for him. He also had Rear Admiral Kelly's initial approval to set up the meeting at West Point and research the hardware, software and other equipment that would be required and a timeline for installation. Joe was shooting to have everything needed installed no later than July first this year. That would give him almost four months to install and then training would begin immediately and they would be fully installed and ready to go when the fall semester began. At least there would be one new class coming in and they could start fresh with that group.

Board members started to come into the building, grabbing coffee and Danish before the meeting. Rear Admiral Barnes appeared at Joe's office door and said, "Hello Captain. How are you doing this fine day?" He smiled and winked at Joe. *He made it at Joe's request.*

"I'm doing fine, Sir. We can't wait for the official first day of spring. Pitchers and catchers are already in spring training. Baseball is on its way," he smiled. "I'm surprised to see you, Sir. I thought you'd be down in sunny Miami and not up here in this winter wonderland."

Just so he would be overheard a little, Rear Admiral Barnes said, "I had a meeting up in Boston at Harvard with the recruiters for the Coast Guard and a group of potential recruits. Remember when we started recruiting women of color and Latinos, we wanted language majors as well and one of the best places to do that is at Harvard. The meeting went well. I don't know if anyone will join but the publicity alone is worth its weight in gold." Barnes looked around quickly and noticed a few Board members trying to overhear the conversation. "Since I was in the neighborhood, Rear Admiral Kelly asked me to sit in on your presentation today."

"That's great, Sir. We will begin in a few minutes. I better hit the head. It might be a long meeting," Joe said and smirked.

Barnes whispered, "I can only imagine what you are

about to say. I wouldn't miss it for the world. Just remember when they try to get rid of you for insubordination, you always have a place with us in Miami." Jake smiled and smirked and put his hand over his mouth to contain himself as he walked toward the men's room.

Once again, The Assistant Commandant for Human Resources, Linda Jones, who chairs the Board of Trustee meetings, started the meeting with a roll call of all the members. All were present and they recognized Rear Admiral Barnes as an invited guest. In front of each member was a copy of today's agenda. It was short and sweet and had Captain Joseph Traynor as the only presenter at the meeting. Rear Admiral Kelly spoke immediately after Ms. Jones opening remarks and explained why this meeting was being held. He mentioned that the meeting was very confidential and no one was to release any information about what Captain Traynor was to discuss. He made it very clear that the future of the Academy was at stake.

Joe began. He started the presentation with the first call he received from Rear Admiral Kelly and how he wound up at an impromptu board meeting only an hour later where he was given permission to go ahead and find the bomber or bombers with only an email address to start with. He explained the entire process to the board. He had a white board presentation prepared and he had actual video footage including the takedown in West Hartford, Connecticut. The part he wanted to downplay at this point was following the FedEx truck and the Toyota Corolla into the campus. He simply said that after the arrest of the four individuals and handed over to the FBI, he never mentioned their CIA fate. He also mentioned that he was able to proceed so quickly was simply because he carried credentials as Captain in the Coast Guard, credentials as Special Agent with the FBI and above all, clandestine credentials with Homeland Security. At that point, several board members were looking at each other thinking, *"Who the hell is this guy at thirty-seven years old?"* Joe was so precise in his presentation that there was simply no room for misunderstanding.

Finally, after the arrests and taking possession of the cell phones with the bomb app and the removal of all the bombs themselves, Joe told them how they discovered how they got onto campus in the first place. Joe rolled the video as it followed the Toyota Corolla and then the FedEx truck as it rolled down to the Field House where a custodian simply opened the laundry room door so he could place the bombs inside. He then showed the two men hopping into the back of the FedEx truck and the driver mouthing the words "Thank You" to the guard at the main gate. At that point, before discussing next steps, Joe asked if anyone had any questions.

Joe thought that maybe some of his steps went over a few of the Board of Trustees members' heads. The man retiring and being replaced by Rear Admiral Barnes said, "So who's getting fired for this? Somebody should be fired for this total incompetence. We need to replace these people immediately before it happens again."

Joe simply looked at him. He said, "Sir, who should be fired and for what particular valid reason do we have for firing anyone at this point?"

"First, I'm not blaming you, Captain, but the head of safety and security should go and the custodian and anyone on duty that day at the front gate for letting them in."

"Again, Sir. What policy or procedure did anyone of them violate?"

"They violated the safety and security policy of the

Coast Guard Academy, obviously, Captain," he said with anger in his voice.

"I hate to disagree with you, Sir, but the Academy has no policy or procedures to violate when it comes to terrorism or bombs or major emergency crisis. There is no policy. I looked and I read every document to date. They violated no policy. Do you have a Safety and Security Committee as part of the Board of Trustees?" Joe asked.

"Yes, we do and I'm chairman of that committee," he said.

"Sir, when was your last meeting and did you review and update current policies and procedures, Sir?" asked Joe.

"We met a little over a year ago and we had no problems at that time so there was no need to update anything. Why change it if it isn't broke?" he said.

"I would suggest, Sir, that it isn't broke. I would suggest that it doesn't even exist," Joe said as he looked squarely at each board member and Rear Admiral Kelly.

Rear Admiral Kelly jumped in at this point and said, "Captain, perhaps you can tell us how we intend to fix this situation that we find ourselves in right now. Members of the Board, I have had extensive conversations with Captain Traynor and he is absolutely right, we have no safety and security policy for the Coast Guard Academy. What we have is an illusion at best. We need to immediately develop a 21st century standard across the board, in writing, and shared with every member that we serve including all the cadets, teachers, employees and service men and women stationed here. Joe please tell us how you need to proceed and the timeline and costs involved."

Joe started up with stares from the retiring board member. Evidently, no one has ever been able to shut him up before and everyone at this table knew exactly what happened and now why this gentleman was retiring and being replaced by Rear Admiral Barnes. Joe first said that all improvements to safety and security would be paid for out of a ten-million-dollar donation from the Teresa Trust Fund, a 501C3 nonprofit organization from upstate New York and in the Florida Keys, Joe's last assignment. He said the initial purchase of software, hardware and training would be three million dollars and then close to a half million dollars a year, each year, over the next four years. He also said, he had the authority from the foundation to request more funding if needed. Joe went through his plans to meet with West Point specialists who have developed a state-of-the-art system. He handed out an overview of what the new systems will do, the same overview that he presented to Rear Admiral Kelly in his private meeting.

At the end of his presentation, Joe thanked the board for its patience and asked if there were any more questions. Captain Laura Chavez, the board member who originally tried to give Joe a hard time in Spanish and failed and then became a big fan after Joe stopped the bombing attempt asked a question. She wanted to know if board members could attend the West Point meeting and go through the crisis intervention package that would be set up for their benefit. Joe looked at Kelley and he nodded yes.

Rear Admiral Kelly immediately approved her attendance. Since she was a full-time professor at the Academy, they would have to find coverage for her classes at both the Academy and at Connecticut College where she also taught Spanish, since it wasn't offered at the Academy. Joe thought this might be even a bigger opportunity down the road when he wanted to move language requirements back to the Academy from Connecticut College for advanced speakers only who would begin a career in the intelligence division, just like he did so many years ago.

As the meeting let out, Jake came over and winked at him and said, "Good job, Joe." He then added, "There was very little bloodshed involved but our retiree certainly didn't know what hit him."

Joe smiled and nodded. Captain Laura Chavez came over and shook his hand and asked if they could meet soon to discuss their trip together to West Point with Dave and Kim. He said sure, anytime. She certainly seemed to change her tune. Maybe she figured out that Joe was really a good guy who didn't take a lot of crap from anyone and maybe that's just what the Academy needed at this time.

The next day as Joe was walking to lunch, Dave Simon came up to him and thanked him for saving his job. He told Joe that the scuttlebutt was that he didn't back down one inch from the retired board member and made a fool out of him by being so nice. Joe told him, he tried this new tactic and it seemed to work but he hated it since he wanted to punch the son of a bitch in the mouth. Dave laughed. Joe told Dave that he did what he thought was right but if Dave continued down that primrose path he would have Joe to deal with. Dave was apologetic once again and said he trusted Joe implicitly. They shook hands and talked about heading to West Point. Joe wondered if they could also fit in a meeting with the Merchant Marine Academy in Kings Point, New York, on the Hudson River near New York City. He said they were never thought of in any of these discussions but were supposed to be on the same par as the four major military academies including Army at West Point, the Naval Academy at Annapolis, the Air Force Academy in Colorado Springs, and the Coast Guard Academy in New London, Connecticut. They would decide when they would go visit. The Merchant Marine

Academy needed as much help if not more than the Coast Guard Academy. Joe needed to make some new friends fast.

Chapter **13**

Joe would be away for several days, heading to West Point with Kim Matz, Dave Simon, and a late request to go by Captain Laura Chavez, a professor at the Coast Guard Academy and member of the Board of Trustees. The trip was about one hundred and fifty miles and three hours with a pit stop. They would all meet and then leave the Academy around 8:00 a.m. from Joe and Julie's house on a Tuesday and would be back late Friday afternoon.

Julie would have both children all by herself which wasn't a problem but she also had an appointment on Wednesday to meet the Dean and the President of Connecticut College to discuss possible employment at the college. It wasn't that she wasn't interested but she needed to make sure it wouldn't interfere with her duties as a mother of two daughters. Both daughters had different needs. One was a newborn, Annie, less than four months old and the other, Bella, who needed attention because of her circumstances. Bella didn't need attention so much from being adopted by Joe and Julie. That was going just fine. It was her language difficulties, being brought up to age five, speaking nothing but Spanish, when she arrived at the Key Largo elementary school where Julie became friends with Bella's mother. It was never a question that Julie and Joe would adopt Bella at her mother's request. It was harder for Julie because she was just learning Spanish while Joe was old hat at it. Bella gravitated to Joe more because of this comfort level but Bella surely loved Julie just as much.

Julie decided to call up her best friend in the northeast, Maddy Malone, who was her roommate at Brown University, from the first day at the college through both their master's degrees. Maddy still lives in Reading, Massachusetts, and is married and is still a teacher in the next town's school district, Wakefield. Even though they were a thousand miles apart, they always kept in touch after college. Maddy visited Julie in Key Largo and Julie was in Maddy's wedding as Maid of Honor. Maddy was Julie's Maid of Honor at St. Patrick's Cathedral in New York City. Beside Maddy, Tillie, Julie's grandmother, also served as Matron of Honor at Julie and Joe's wedding. New London was about one hundred and twenty miles southwest of Reading, going down south on I-95. It took a little over two hours depending on the traffic heading right out of Boston. Reading is ten miles north of Boston, where all the major highways converge heading to New Hampshire.

Julie invited Maddy to stay over Tuesday night through Friday so she could see Joe once he got home. Maddy jumped at the chance. Being the same age as Julie, Maddy didn't have children yet but they were considering it. Maddy Malone was now Maddy White. Her husband is Jim White. He was twenty-five when they first met officially. He grew up in Reading and was two years ahead of Maddy in high school. He didn't even know she existed when they were at the Reading High School. He was actually in one of her art classes when she was a sophomore and he was a senior. He needed one class in art that didn't interfere with his baseball spring schedule. They never spoke, they didn't even sit near each other but he remembered her at the conference they both attended. You never know what life brings. Her parents are thrilled to say the least. He is also a teacher but at Reading High School and is the high school baseball coach, which pleased Joe to no end.

Julie still loved Maddy's parents who took her in for the entire summer while she finished her MFA at Brown. She commuted with Maddy every day for the entire summer so Julie could graduate and Maddy only had one semester left. Maddy's father, Arthur T. Malone, Ph.D., was a full professor at Harvard Law School and he served as a town councilman for Reading, Massachusetts, as well. Maddy's mother did not work but certainly had the credentials to do so. Marilyn, her mother, had a master's degree from Boston University and was previously a full-time teacher in Wakefield, the next town over. That's how Maddy fell into her current teaching position at Wakefield. Maddy got her student teaching assignment through her mother, but due to pure luck, she was able to take over an existing 3rd grade class for the teacher going on pregnancy leave. She was assured of another position in the fall, obviously based on how well she performed that spring. They were very impressed with her presentation and advanced educational technology skills and she has been there ever since. Holding an IVY school degree still is impressive especially for an elementary school teacher.

Maddy arrived about 10:00 a.m. on Tuesday. Joe had already left for West Point. She parked in their driveway and met Julie at the door. Although she and Jim were invited to attend the baptism for Annie, they were unable to attend. Maddy's mother Marilyn was not doing well physically. She'd had surgery and was doing better but there were several complications and Maddy didn't feel right leaving her. She's better now, allowing Maddy the chance to see Julie and the kids. Julie had been in that position when Tillie had her accident and was in a coma so she understood completely. The first thing Maddy wanted to do was hold little Annie. Julie had her in the playpen in the living room and picked her up after Maddy sat down on the couch. Julie handed her the baby and Maddy was just mesmerized.

"God, how beautiful she is, Julie," said Maddy. "I think she looks like you but like Joe too. Her nose is Joe's and rest is you," she said.

"Don't tell Joe," said Julie. "He'll get a big head," she laughed.

After handing the baby back to Julie, she brought Annie to her room for her nap. Then, she brought Maddy to the guest room and let her put her things away while she made lunch. Bella wouldn't be home until almost 3:00 p.m. walking directly from school. Julie still waited on the front porch from 2:45 p.m. just so she wouldn't miss her. From there, she would meet Maddy and they bundled up Annie to walk the campus at the Academy. Maddy and Julie had a lot of catching up to do. Maddy just couldn't believe the transformation that Julie made from that soft-spoken southern girl from Key Largo many years ago.

They had dinner and watched the *Voice*, Julie's favorite show. They talked well into the night. Julie explained the dilemma she was in concerning not only taking a position at Connecticut College over going back to Brown University but she was also getting pressure to start a new book by her publisher, Sarah Atwood in New York City.

Her nonfiction trilogy, *A Girl's Story*, starting with *Conch Town Girl*, was wildly successful on a national level, earning her several hundred thousand dollars in royalties and a contract with Disney in Florida and a national award for nonfiction as a new author.

Disney was turning her trilogy into a television series, filmed right at the Hollywood Studios in Disney World. She was very comfortable with that since her and Joe's close friend, Claire Murphy, was her immediate contact to the president, Marshall Tillman, of Disney World's Hollywood Studio. Sarah Atwood, Julie's publisher, said she would come up to see her in the very near future to discuss future plans. Julie also owed a sit-down meeting with her old Dean at Brown University, Gerald Spaulding. Both he and his wife Marilyn attended their wedding in New York City and stayed with the Atwoods, who were close friends. Julie never really had an agent but used the one that Dr. Spaulding recommended at the time. She was perplexed because she could never remember her agent's name. She would ask the Dean for her number to contact her or she would actually prefer to get someone like Jane Swanson, her personal attorney down in Miami to fill that role. It was Jane who actually closed the deal along with Sidney Clyne, her partner. She told Maddy that there was just too much going on but she was trying to keep her head above water.

Just then, Julie said, "You have to see what Joe had made for Annie and Bella and the daughter, Emma, of our good friends, Sean and Samantha O'Neil. I'll be right back."

Julie walked into the room holding three petite Coast Guard Academy baseball uniforms with the numbers 1, 2 and 3 on the back and their names, Bella, Emma, and Annie, and BATGIRL spelled out below their names. "Joe wants to be a part time baseball coach at the Academy and he thought this might win them over," and she laughed.

"Oh my God," said Maddy. "Jim would love these uniforms. Are they really going to be batgirls?" she asked.

"If Joe has his way. He also wants them to be the batgirls for the women's softball team as well so there's no discrimination to get him in hot water. The Rear Admiral said this would be fine but as a Red Sox fan, if Joe changed the uniforms to Yankee pinstripes, he would be fired on the spot," she said.

"That awesome," said Maddy.

Julie told Maddy about her potential next book. It wouldn't be part of the trilogy because she wanted to break out and do something other than what she has been known for. She wanted to turn her hand at semi-fiction, somewhere between an autobiography, nonfiction and fiction, so she could move around and have everyone guess who she was talking about, if not her. Obviously, the main character would now be a young woman, in her early twenties, trying to make it in life while keeping a balance. Maddy was fascinated about Julie's concept and was amazed on how focused she could be in light of all the responsibilities she had now as a young mother, a nationally well-known author, and the wife of the Assistant Superintendent of the Coast Guard Academy, the youngest ever she added.

Maddy was up early to help Julie get Bella off to school. Joe had called early to wish her luck with her meeting at Connecticut College. The meeting was for 11:00 a.m. with a tour and a scheduled lunch with the new Dean, Dr. Erica Jones, the president of the college, Dr. Kate Ballenger and Liz Winter, professor of English and Chair of the English Department. Julie had researched each of their background so she could have some insight to where they possibly stood on her potential employment. The Dean was just recently hired from Brandeis University and had a master's from Harvard Graduate School of Education. She was also African American and Julie could certainly relate as to the struggles of lifting oneself up from poverty. The president has been there since 2014 and had a stellar career and a Ph.D. from Cornell University. Liz Winter, the Chair of the English Department had a Ph.D. from Yale. Julie thought she was in pretty good company. She has an MFA from Brown University and experience working with young adults at the high school level and has been a very successful career counselor as well. However, none of the three individuals she will meet have ever published a very successful book, let alone three nor had a contract from Disney. Julie felt a little unsure and mentioned it to both Joe and Maddy and each told her she had nothing to lose. If they didn't want her, it would be their loss. Dean Spaulding would give her a contract immediately and already said so. Sarah Atwood already confirmed that Julie would receive a very large advance payment of future royalties for the rights to her newest unnamed book and she could also keep the film rights to send to Disney upon completion. Julie thought, *"What do I have to lose? Mary Evans already gave us a trust fund for our children and to help defer any expenses for Tillie's care in the future. I'll play it by ear."*

Julie walked to Connecticut College, leaving about 10:30 a.m. for her 11:00 a.m. meeting and then lunch. She kissed Annie goodbye and hugged Maddy and said, "Wish me luck."

"You don't need luck," said Maddy. "Just be yourself and that should be good enough and if it isn't, you know what Joe would say. I'll leave it at that," as Maddy smiled.

"Something worse than 'No Shit,' I believe," said Julie

as she waved walking down the stairs to the street. She walked the few blocks and went in to the president's office, arriving right around 10:50 a.m., ten minutes early. She didn't want to be too early and not late at all. She learned her lessons in dealing with people who tried to wield their power through intimidation. Joe taught her lessons from a very early age and those lessons stuck with her. He told her if you're not comfortable, to simply thank them and walk away. He also told her to always prepare at least twenty dumb questions that would probably be asked. That way, after preparing, you could answer with confidence and look like your immediate response to the question was a measure of your quick intellect. Joe said it worked every time. He said that spontaneity came with practice.

The president's secretary welcomed Julie and told her that she was expected and she would tell everyone that she was here. Julie sat in a comfortable chair near her desk and started looking at the college academic catalog for the year. She asked the secretary if they had another catalog that she could have and she said certainly, pulling out a desk drawer and handing her the catalog. Julie immediately went to the English Department and started looking at the curriculum. Julie expected nothing more than an initial meet and greet the staff meeting and would have a nice lunch and nothing more. Her expectations were never too high or too low, another life lesson from Joe.

The president of the college opened her office door and came over to greet Julie, as she was engrossed in the catalog. It surprised Julie and she immediately got up from her chair and shook Dr. Ballenger's hand. She escorted her into the boardroom, immediately adjacent to her office. Julie asked her where she should sit and Dr. Ballenger pointed to a chair right next to her. As she removed her coat and hat, Dr. Ballenger reached out and gave the items to her assistant to hang up. As soon as she sat down two other women came into the room and Julie was immediately introduced to the new Dean, Dr. Erica Jones, and Dr. Liz Winter, professor of English and Chair of the English Department. They took seats across from the president and Julie and they both welcomed her to the college. Dr. Ballenger spoke first and said they would like to introduce themselves to her and then go to lunch. From there, they would walk over to the English Department across campus. All three told her they were very excited to meet her and welcomed the opportunity to discuss a possible relationship with her and Connecticut College.

It appeared that the new Dean was not informed that in addition to Julie being a nationally published author that her husband, Captain Joseph Traynor, was also the new Assistant Superintendent of the Coast Guard Academy, right across the street. The Dean then smiled and said now she saw the connection of why Julie Chapman Traynor was now residing in New London, Connecticut. The three administrators all looked at Julie and couldn't believe how young she was and they all had read her trilogy, *A Girl's Story*, and were thrilled that she was there.

The president introduced herself first, giving her education and background and then the other two did the same. They were all academics with inspiring education and administrative experience. They asked Julie if she could give them some of her background. Julie had that memorized and for the next half hour, she told them of everything she has done since she was eight-years old, living with her grandmother, Tillie, in Key Largo, Florida. By the time she finished her shortened autobiography, the three women were basically in awe of Julie. At twenty-nine years old, and the mother of two children, one adopted and one a newborn, she has accomplished more than all three of these women combined. She mentioned that her publisher was pushing her for a fourth book and she had already started her research and thought about topics that would interest young women in their early twenties, who needed direction in their life. It was not a jump from her trilogy to this new stand-alone book, which would cut through nonfiction, fiction and real life and she was ready to start. She said she would write around her current obligations and was interested in Connecticut College as a refuge from which to work. She did mention that Dr. Gerald Spaulding, her old Dean at Brown University wanted her back on campus but with a newborn and a seven year old daughter, she needed to be closer to home, only a few blocks away rather than an hour's drive to Brown each way.

The president of the college was also interested in Joe Traynor. She knew that at thirty-seven years old, he was the youngest Assistant Superintendent of the Coast Guard Academy in history. She also knew he spoke several languages, just got his Ph.D. from Barry University and through the grapevine knew that he, almost singlehandedly, saved the Academy from several bombs planted on campus. Dr. Ballenger was very impressed not only by Julie but also by both her and her husband. Quietly, she would put on a full court press as they say to make Julie comfortable to be part of Connecticut College in almost any capacity that she wanted. She could be a guest national author. She could be a professor in the English Department, perhaps helping students develop their own novels like she did when she was at Brown University in the MFA program.

They went to lunch and dined in the faculty dining facility. Several professors and staff came over to meet

Julie and offered their assistance. The president laughed and told her it was not a setup. She said she never told anyone about you coming for a meeting but evidently it got out. They wanted to meet n award winning nonfiction writer with a massive following at such a young age.

As they walked back to the English Department, Julie noticed several students had copies of her books and they wanted the books autographed. Julie was unprepared to say the least about the reception she had. The nice thing was that Julie knew none of this was preplanned on the part of the three women. She felt relieved and astonished at her reception at the college. Dr. Ballenger asked her to consider various opportunities at the college. She didn't have to answer right away.

They knew she had a full load and had just arrived in New London. They were thinking about coming on board maybe during the summer months and then perhaps develop a class for students to write their own novels. Maybe at the end of the semester, one of the students could be published just like Julie did at Brown University. She would ask Sarah Atwood, her publisher, what she thought of the idea.

On the way back home, after shaking hands with the three women, she thanked them for a very enjoyable day and told them that she would get back to them concerning potential next steps. They knew she didn't need the money. The advance on her next book would be close to what Dr. Ballenger would make in an entire year as president of the college. She opened her front door and was greeted by Bella who just got home. Maddy was holding the baby who immediately reached out for Julie. "How did it go?" asked Maddy. Julie nodded, "fine."

Chapter 14

Joe would call later that night. They got there on time. They had their first meeting with the Colonel in charge of security for the Military Academy at West Point. His job was of the same caliber as Joe's at the Coast Guard Academy. The West Point campus was 16,000 acres in total or twenty-five square miles in size. It is 60% larger than Manhattan at 10,890 acres and bigger than the City of Albany, New York at 21.5 square miles. Hartford, Connecticut is only 18 square miles in area. In other words, the Military Academy at West Point is huge. The Coast Guard Academy is only 103 acres in total in New London, and the Navy Submarine Base right next door is 608 acres in size. Both were still very small in comparison to West Point. However, safety and security was only a small portion of Joe's position description as Assistant Superintendent.

Nonetheless, solving a bombing on this small campus and strengthening security, became a major issue and moved to the top of the list as a priority. To their knowledge, there has never been a bomb placed on a military installation in the United States. There have been multiple shootings and the massacre of 2009 at Fort Hood in Texas by an Army Major and psychiatrist, who killed thirteen people and wounding thirty others. Major Nidal Malik Hasan, thirty-nine years old, armed with a semi-automatic pistol while shouting "Allahu Akbar," was the worst tragedy of its kind. Since June of 1994, there have been multiple shooting incidents including at an Air Force base, at a Naval Systems Command in Arlington, Virginia, and a shooting spree at Fort Bragg in North Carolina, killing one officer and wounding eighteen soldiers. There was a shooting in Little Rock, Arkansas by a self-described Islamic radical killing one and wounding another. The list goes on and on and several more at Fort Hood. However, this current bombing incident at the Academy is the first known bombing attempt in the United States at a military institute or facility. Joe had to repeat that twice because he thought for sure there would be more cases.

That's why Joe and the others were at West Point to go through a complete simulation using the West Point cutting-edge security systems and software. A bombing attempt was an unknown until now. They seemed to have shootings down pat as to what to do but a bombing attempt was very different in the scope and planning. They would go through what a terrorist attack would look like at West Point and the procedures they would use to halt the assault. Then, Joe would be allowed to substitute the actual attack on the Coast Guard Academy and go through a simulation to see how the new software would handle such an event and then compare it to what they actually did, minute by minute. Obviously they stopped the bombs from exploding but considering how limited their security sophistication was, Joe thought maybe he was just lucky. Or, he was right on target in handling the situation. They would go through the process to see where they fell short, if they did, using state-of-the-art algorithms in the simulation process.

Moving through the ranks over the years, Joe was unconcerned about his title or position. He was simply interested in getting the job done whatever he was charged with at the time. Since he would be meeting with Army personnel, Joe actually looked up to see what the equivalency was for being a Captain in the Coast Guard as opposed to the Army, which most people understood. During peacetime, the Coast Guard is part of Homeland Security but during war, the Coast Guard is part of the Navy. As a Captain in the Coast Guard or the Navy, Joe was equal to a full Colonel in the Army. Both were one step below a Brigadier General in the Army and a Rear Admiral Lower Half in the Coast Guard. Joe believed that since both titles were comparable, both jobs should be as well. This Colonel had responsibility for 16,000 acres but Joe had responsibility for all the 1,069 cadets and 130 academic staff, both service men and women on campus, and everything in between that Superintendent handed Joe to manage. Everything meant everything including removing bombs from campus.

They arrived before lunch on Tuesday and went right to the Thayer Hotel, only steps from the campus. In 1829, the West Point Hotel was built near the Plain on Trophy Point. The West Point Hotel served the Academy for over a century, hosting a long list of dignitaries such as Robert E. Lee, U. S. Grant, Stonewall Jackson, General Sherman, Washington Irving, and Allan Poe. The hotel's history is tied most famously to one of West Point's most famous graduates, General Douglas MacArthur. During General Douglas MacArthur's time as a cadet, his mother lived in the West Point Hotel. When Brigadier General Douglas MacArthur returned from World War I to become the Superintendent of West Point, he started a major expansion program of the buildings.

The new Thayer Hotel was one of these expansion projects and the Thayer Hotel officially opened May 27, 1926 with 225 rooms. General MacArthur would return to West Point and stay in the hotel in 1962 for one final time to give his noted "Duty, Honor, Country" speech to the cadets as he received the Thayer Award. Joe and his three partners were immensely impressed as they walked to their rooms, looking around at the history right at their fingertips. After packing and lunch, they hopped back into Joe's vehicle and went to the West Point Security Office DPTMS at 621 Wilson Road, a few miles away at the south end of the campus. After parking in the visitor's lot, they walked to the front door and rang the bell. Security at West Point was far more restrictive than at the Coast Guard Academy and to each of the four individuals, it became quite obvious.

On the wall, right next to the door is the sign that states, "Emergency management contributes to the protection of West Point by coordinating and integrating activities necessary to build, sustain, and improve the community's capability to prevent, mitigate and protect against, respond to, and recover from threatened or actual natural, technological, and human-caused hazards." In addition, a sign read, "Visitors with DoD identification, please proceed to any of the entrance gates." Joe was considered a "Qualified Escort," since he carried credentials from Homeland Security. Qualified escorts are Department of Defense identification card holders, which included Captain Joseph Traynor. This includes Common Access Card holders (Military, Civilian Government employees and contractors) or Teslin identification (synthetic paper material) cardholders (Retirees, their spouses, and Military dependents.) A qualified escort must accompany each individual he or she is escorting and can only escort up to fifteen individuals. Joe was responsible for his associates.

Captain Chavez kept looking at Joe as if to say, *"Who the hell are you really? You can't be just a Captain in the Coast Guard."*

Joe looked at her and smiled. "Are you okay? You look a little unsettled," he said.

Chavez said, "After all this, can I ask you a few questions concerning your background? I am kind of overwhelmed at the kind of influence you carry. We are both Captains in the Coast Guard. All this influence is certainly more than I would expect from a Captain in the Coast Guard. I know you've done a lot in your career but I'm simply fascinated. In the few months you've been at the Academy, I have never seen such a change in everyone."

"I'll be glad to. I don't think I carry any more weight than anyone else but I have been in a lot of close encounters and have managed to escape unscathed. Maybe that's it?" he said.

Colonel Keenan Smith, head of security for West Point, met them at the reception area after they checked in. He introduced himself to everyone and showed them to his "war room" as he called it. He handed them schedules for today, Wednesday and Thursday with a short meeting Friday morning, ending at 11:00 a.m. so they could make it home for the weekend. Today, he would simply give his overview of West Point and introduce them to the new state-of-the-art technology systems that served to protect everyone on the campus. He also mentioned if they are trying to get you they can if you're not vigilant.

Colonel Smith went on to describe West Point by saying that the West Point student body numbers approximately 4,300. In addition to the Corps of Cadets,

West Point is home to approximately 1,200 active duty soldiers and approximately 3,000 family members. Supporting the mission of the Academy is a civilian workforce of approximately 5,000 personnel. The United States Military Academy at West Point graduates approximately 1,000 new officers annually, which represents approximately twenty-five percent of 2nd lieutenants required by the Army each year. The Coast Guard Academy had only 1,069 Cadets, in total, with limited personnel of 120 academic instructors and staff, and everyone except the cadets lives off campus. The Coast Guard Academy was so much more open and run like a college rather than a military base.

The main reason for the high technology security is that West Point is a major think tank for modern warfare and the development of means and methods for securing the country's safety and security. The security has to be airtight to manage all that was housed on this campus. Joe had to weigh this with his campus that had limited research and no families living inside the Academy grounds. However, the processes and technology had to be the same because both campuses were connected to the Department of Defense. Joe thought this would be a very interesting week.

Around 5:00 p.m. they left for the evening. They had to be back by 9:00 a.m. to start the terrorist attack simulation that would last all day. They would start with an armed conflict, then proceed to an internal event like the tragic event at Fort Hood and proceed to potential bombings within the confines of West Point. The following day, they would take what they learned and apply it to their own actual situation, which just happened. They would attempt to see if they could develop new approaches utilizing the new simulation and what might be possible using the new system that would be installed shortly at the Coast Guard Academy.

After cleaning up, they all met at Patton's Tavern at the hotel. It was opened Sunday through Wednesday and the main restaurant, MacArthur's Riverview Restaurant, was only open Thursday through Saturday. Breakfast was served everyday Monday through Saturday. Joe was just as happy not going out for a big meal. They could reserve that for their last night, Thursday, and the restaurant overlooked the majestic Hudson River. He only remembers seeing West Point from the train heading to New York City from Albany looking from the east side to across the river to the west side on the Hudson River. The view is simply stunning.

Tonight, at Patton's Tavern, they could have a few beers, eat pizza, wings, or a light dinner, and talk over the day's activities. Joe needed to call home so he wouldn't stay out late. He was just glad that Maddy was there with Julie. He did want to find out how she made out at the meeting with Connecticut College. He needed to have his own meeting with the president of the college within a week or two as well to see if he could sit in on language classes, especially in Captain Chavez's Spanish class. He really wanted to understand what she was teaching the student Cadets. There were huge differences between what was said on a wire pickup from drug cartel members who were speakers with limited education, and what was being taught at the college level. Some of the people he arrested wouldn't understand a word spoken by Captain Chavez. Spanish was becoming Spanglish with half the words in English and the other either Creole or Native South American Indian dialects. Joe's Spanish was influenced with Mexican idioms but he understood many different Spanish dialects. He wanted to discuss this with Dr.

Chavez.

At dinner, on Tuesday night, Joe shared his background with Dave Simon, Laura Chavez, and Kim Matz. They sat in a booth way in the back of the pub and there were hardly any diners in the room. Joe brought his IDs with him to pass along to the three guests. He explained his role using his Coast Guard Captain credentials, his FBI Special Agent credentials and his Homeland Security documents. He went through a lot of his investigations and explained why he needed the various covers in order to make an arrest or stop a situation from continuing. He explained that a kidnapping was federal and involved the FBI. When he took down the Columbians, he needed the CIA involvement and his FBI credentials to pass the foreign nationalists on to the CIA. The Dixie Mafia up in Nashville required his using the Homeland Security so he could connect to the DEA and ATF (Alcohol, Tobacco, and Firearms and Explosives Bureau). The explosives part was covered by Homeland Security in the Academy bombing incident and then was handed off to the CIA as a terrorist event. The four arrestees in Hartford were taken to Boston by the FBI, handed over to Homeland Security and ATF, and then on to the CIA, where as terrorists they were shipped to an unknown facility. He said the four would be found eventually and then tried and convicted but not until they gave up everything on the Sovereign Citizens of Connecticut. All three looked at Joe as if to say, *How can you be so sure? How do you know this? Is this legal?*

Joe saw the look and said, "I didn't make this up. This is what actually happens. Yes, there are a lot of gray areas that we find ourselves in but it is always approved by the judicial system before we act. We didn't have time in Hartford but I guarantee you that there is complete documentation by now with a legal warrant for everything that happened."

Laura Chavez had already started to look at Joe in a different light. In fact his actions saved countless lives at the Academy that day. She'd tried to snow him with an elaborate question at the first Board of Trustees meeting in Spanish and he wasn't even fazed. She spoke to him in Spanish at the dinner and he answered back as if it was his primary language. He even told her some jokes he heard in Spanish and that is the true test of language ability, the ability to tell jokes and laugh in another language. Kim and Dave were both smiling trying to see if they could understand what they were saying. For fun, Joe broke into Russian, then Chechen and then a few sentences in Chinese. He asked Laura how she was doing and laughed. She smiled and said she gave up. She would have no more interrogations of Joe from now on.

Joe became serious and asked Laura if she would mind if he could attend her Spanish classes. He said he wanted to do the same for Russian and Chinese. Connecticut College didn't teach Chechen but it was only an offshoot of Russian anyway. He told her he would be meeting with the president of Connecticut College in a few weeks and asked her if she would like to attend. She had never been asked before and jumped at the chance. This trip seemed to work out quite well on several levels. When they got back, he would meet with the Superintendent and explain exactly what they encountered here at West Point and the benefits for the Coast Guard Academy. He also would mention his passion for language acquisition to benefit the Coast Guard and use as a recruiting tool for minorities and speakers of other languages, other than English.

Out of the blue, Kim asked Joe how her meeting went with Connecticut College. Neither Dave nor Laura knew of Julie's background. She still wrote under Julie Chapman and that would change with her next book. Kim knew all about it since she met Julie when Kim and her husband went to their house to watch football on a Sunday.

Laura looked at Joe and said, "Julie Chapman, the national award-winning author, is your wife, Julie? I would have never connected the two," she said.

Dave just listened. He would have to ask his wife about her since he never read anything except security magazines.

"Yes," Joe said. "Julie Chapman is my wife and the author of *Conch Town Girl* and the trilogy, *A Girl's Story*. She is also in the development stage for a series on the Disney channel from the Hollywood Studios in Disney World in Orlando."

"Joe, you are just full of surprises," said Laura. "What's she doing at Connecticut College?"

"I'm not sure but I am told through the grapevine that they want her to be an Author in Residence and a professor in the English Department. She is a graduate from Brown University with an MFA in English Literature and her old Dean wants her to do the same thing at Brown. She met this week with the president, the Dean and the head of the English Department. I assume it went well but it happened today at lunch so I haven't heard anything. I have to call her and see how she made out."

After dinner, Joe headed to his room to call Julie and see how the kids were doing and to ask about her meeting. Maddy picked up the phone and said that Julie would be right down and that she was putting Bella and Annie to bed for the night. Julie got on the phone and told Joe all about the meeting and that it went well and she had to decide what she wanted to do. She said it was based on what her publisher wanted her to do to complete her next book. Julie said, Sarah Atwood, her publisher and her editor would come up to New London next week for a visit. Julie said she was bringing a check, payable to Julie Chapman Traynor, for two hundred thousand dollars as an advance. She also said that her old Dean at Brown, Gerald Spaulding would also be at the meeting. They would meet at their house and then head to a nice restaurant in town for the meeting. Since Maddy had to leave late Friday, she asked Joe to babysit that afternoon and he said anytime she made two hundred thousand dollars, he would be more than happy to babysit. He laughed and she did too as they hung up.

Wednesday and Thursday were very intense going through the various simulated attacks on West Point from both an outside and inside perspective. They were taught to use the new technology tools available and became quite comfortable in raising questions and making suggestions so they could tailor the processes to the much smaller Coast Guard Academy. The simulation for a campus bombing went pretty well. What Joe had done to clear out the bombs and capture the four individuals was almost textbook when they finished. In fact, the software never picked up Joe's ability to offer a pass to the first man to give up the other two bomb locations. Up to that point, the simulation only decided that there were two bombs and that they were found and removed from campus and that was the end of the incident. After Joe added the addendum of his offer did the software pick up the possibility of additional bombs planted on campus. It went from zero after finding the two in the car to 82% that there were more bombs on campus. That in itself, made Joe extremely pleased. Only Kim knew what Joe did because she was right there. She knew the offer was bogus as well as Joe but the individual did not. Joe felt bad but not that bad. He did tell the FBI agents to pass it along, in writing, that he was the only one to cooperate. It could mean a few years off his sentence, if they ever got to a trial, which didn't seem likely. Both Dave and Laura asked Joe how he knew how to do that without a blip and he said he's done that before on many an occasion. A lie to a suspect to save lives immediately didn't affect Joe in the least. He would worry about that afterwards, after everyone was safe. He told them that if it made a difference he only lied to the suspect as an FBI Special Agent and then as a Homeland Security officer, never as a Coast Guard member. Joe smiled and laughed and so did they. Always blame it on the other service he told them.

Chapter 15

After Joe's phone call, Julie and Maddy sat down to watch one of her all-time favorite movies, *Finding Forrester*. The movie came out in 2000, when Julie was eight-years old. Now at twenty-nine, she couldn't count the number of times she's seen the movie. It starred Sean Connery as William Forrester, a recluse author, with a book as famous as *Catcher in the Rye*, and as a professor, he only wrote the one book and lived on the royalties forever. The other stars included Rob Brown, who was an African-American kid from the Bronx with no acting experience or credentials. F. Murray Abraham, a well-known actor, played the mean, obnoxious professor, Robert Crawford.

The professor was actually a real person, named Robert Crawford, a history teacher at Philip Exeter Academy in Andover, Massachusetts, just north of Boston. Julie could never understand why Professor Crawford would allow his name to be used for such an awful character. The point of the movie, to Julia, was that a poor black kid from the Bronx, after being mentored by Mr. Forrester, could get recognition for his talents and become someone. In the end, after Mr. Forrester died, he left everything to Jamal Wallace, played by Rob Brown. Julie watched the movie as an eight-year-old and then wanted to be a writer, which affected her ever since. Julie, being a poor girl living in poverty in the Florida Keys, was very much like Jamal Wallace, pulling herself up and rising to the top through Tillie's love, Joe's help, and a passion for learning. Her trilogy reflected all that she went through to become a major national author and a Brown University MFA graduate.

Both Julie and Maddy always cried at the end of the movie. In one of Matt Damon's first movie roles, he played a very young attorney, who had to tell Jamal that William died and left everything to him. Every time she watched the movie, Julie said, "Boy, this gets to me. Talk about his life and mine being very similar." And every time Maddy watched with her, she would simply shake her head and be amazed at how far Julie had come from that dinky little house down in Key Largo. Of course, Maddy never wanted for anything but a sister and now Julie provided that role. Both were very happy.

On the way back from West Point, they stopped when they got out of New York into Danbury, Connecticut for a quick lunch at the Windmill Diner Restaurant, right off I-84E. It was about an hour from when they left and would have about an hour and a half left to get back to New London. Joe wanted to get home but the ladies wanted salads. He ordered a burger and fries and Dave had the same. Forty-five minutes later they started to head back to New London. Joe bought a few bottles of water to go to have for the trip. Kim had some snacks left over from her room so she passed around the chips.

They began talking once again about the West Point experience. They all agreed that it opened their eyes as to what could really happen if they weren't prepared. Laura said she definitely wanted to be on the Safety and Security Committee at the Academy. She would be more prepared than the retiring head of the committee. Unless Jake Barnes wanted to be on that committee and the head of the committee, once he came on board as a member of the Trustees Board, then Captain Laura Chavez could be a perfect fit.

On the way home, Joe explained exactly what the initial three million dollars would buy in terms of securing the facility. He definitely wanted to invest in everyone receiving proximity loggers that would be worn on each individual's clothing to inform everyone of any major disaster. He especially wanted the loggers, no different than the GPS chips on Mary Evans shoes, to pinpoint where people were and have the loggers flash, meaning head to a certain location, when set off. This was a downfall when the first bombs were discovered. They didn't know if this was all of the bombs and didn't know where to send people in case of an emergency. With the rest of the systems in place, they would immediately know a safe location, set up for that purpose. In addition, all cars and vehicles registered on campus would have GPS access ability. No other vehicles would be allowed on campus except to park in one specific lot designated for visitors only. Delivery trucks would have other features and a full scan of the truck before entering the premises. If anyone parked in a secured area, the cars without a device would generate a loud piercing sound in the spot where they parked. Each parking spot in a designated area would be wired to make sure that only properly registered vehicles parked there. At least this was a first major step in stopping individuals from coming on to the campus with wrongful intent.

They made it to New London a little before 3:00 p.m. Joe parked his vehicle next to Maddy's. Dave and Laura walked over to get to Joe's, so they would walk back to campus. Kim parked by the side of the road in front of Joe's house. She drove because she was meeting her husband in town and needed to pick him up. They said their goodbyes and all made arrangements to meet with Joe on Monday morning around 9:00 a.m. He wanted then to attend his meeting with Rear Admiral Kelly to discuss what they learned the same day at 11:00 a.m. He had all weekend to put together a small slide show for his benefit. If accepted, he could use the same presentation at the next Board of Trustees meeting, the following Thursday.

As promised, Joe took Julie, Maddy, Bella, and Annie to dinner in downtown New London at 5:30 p.m. at *On The Waterfront Restaurant and Bar*. It takes less than ten minutes and is three miles south of their house. Julie made the reservations a little early so it wouldn't be too crowded. This was their first attempt at taking Annie out to a restaurant in her infant car seat. The restaurant wasn't busy at that time so they got a table next to a window overlooking the Thames River. The food was an excellent mix of Italian, seafood, steak and Mediterranean. Joe got the Baked Fisherman's Platter and both ladies got the fresh scallops. The seafood couldn't be any fresher than that caught that day right at the dock. Annie was satisfied with her bottle and then fell fast asleep, for which they were all grateful. Bella had a soda with an umbrella in it, which made her night complete. She loved seafood and had the children's fish and chips and chocolate cake for dessert. Bella seemed to be in her own world, which made the night for Julie even better. It had been a long three days without Joe even though Maddy was with her. Everything seemed to be happening all at once and she was starting to feel the pressure. Next week she would meet with her publisher at her home and then decide if she wanted to work at a college or not. These were all positives that were happening to her but certain decisions were in fact life changing.

As they were finishing dinner, Rear Admiral Kelly and his wife, Ellen, walked into the restaurant. Joe got up and approached the Rear Admiral and his wife as they were walking in after being relieved of their coats. Joe said hello and immediately Kelly introduced him to his wife, Ellen. "How did you know about this place?" said the Rear Admiral.

"I didn't. Julie made the reservations. She spoke to Sean O'Neil's wife, Samantha, and she highly recommended it," he said.

"I forgot that you and Sean were buddies, coming up together right out of Malden. Massachusetts, right?"

"Right, you are, Sir," said Joe. "How did you remember that?" he asked.

"I have no idea but I think I was looking at your background last week and it popped up how you and Sean joined together and went to boot camp together." He said, "Sean was one hell of a basketball player for us. We went to the Division III tournament every year he played," said the Rear Admiral.

"Let me introduce you to Julie and her best friend, Maddy. They were roommates at Brown for five years, both finishing their masters. Bella is playing with her dessert and Annie is sound asleep, thank God," said Joe.

They walked over to the table and Joe made the introductions. Ellen said, "You were roommates at Brown, I understand?" she said.

Julie answered, "Yes, we were, well over a hundred years ago," and smiled.

Ellen said, "You have certainly aged well," and laughed. "What was that movie when the older woman said, 'I'll have what she's having?' I can't remember," said Ellen.

"When Harry Met Sally?" said Maddy.

"That's it. I have to watch it again," said Ellen.

"We just finished *Finding Forrester*. It gets me every time," said Julie.

"Love that movie, too. We'll have to get together sometime and trade DVDs. I have a few hundred," said Ellen.

"I'm right behind you, Ellen," said Julie and smiled.

"By the way, congratulations on your obvious success as an author. Joe's not the only rising star, I hear," she said. "Our daughter, Grace, is a junior at Connecticut College and has heard through the grapevine that you might be teaching there next year. That would be great. I would love to sit in on a class with you," said Ellen.

"Well, I'm not sure. I have an offer from Brown but with two young children, being closer to home is more practical and both schools are excellent. I'll let you know," said Julie.

Rear Admiral Kelly shook Joe's hand and they went to their table. Joe got the bill and paid and started to bundle up Bella and picked up Annie to carry to the car in her infant seat. All in all, it was a very nice evening. One of the best they have had in some time. Julie said, "Ellen, seems to be a very nice woman. Have you met her, Joe?"

"No, this is the first time. She seems to like you a lot. I'll bet she does invite you to lunch sometime. It would be nice to make new friends. You seem to have a very easy time of it."

Maddy headed out for home early Saturday morning. They promised not to be strangers and to get together more regularly. Maddy invited Joe and kids to come up to Wakefield for a weekend when her husband's baseball team had a spring game. Joe thought that would be great as long as it didn't interfere with his plans to be a coach at the Academy. Sean O'Neil called Joe about 8:00 p.m. Friday night and asked him if he and Bella wanted to play catch with Sean and Emma in the field house. It was really so Joe could see the men's baseball team start their spring practice. Which was only two weeks, long before their first game late in March. Joe couldn't believe spring was coming. He was so busy, all his days ran in to each other but he wanted to make time for this is his true passion, baseball.

Joe took Julie, Bella, and Annie shopping the week before at the Waterford Commons Mall, only a few miles from them. Julie shopped for clothes for her and the baby and Joe took Bella to Dick's Sporting Goods. He started looking at baseball gloves but he had his own. He still had his Catholic High baseball uniform with "Crusaders" spelled out and Catholic High on the away jersey. He kept his MIT uniform, number 19, as well, including his hat. Hell, Joe had his Little League hat and uniform, his Lansingburgh Independent League and his South Troy Dodgers uniform and hat for his two years playing American Legion baseball. He was offered baseball scholarships to The College of Saint Rose in Albany, a Division II college and a partial scholarship to Siena College, a Division I program.

He was all area Capital Region as a left-handed pitcher his senior year at Catholic High. When he got his full academic scholarship as mathematics major to MIT, the Massachusetts Institute of Technology in Cambridge, Massachusetts, that's where he decided to attend. He did well at MIT and pitched well enough to earn him honors in his first fall semester, playing Division III. They played thirty games and Joe was 4-1 with three saves. At the end of the semester, he decided that he had enough school for a while and went and joined the Coast Guard as an eighteen-year-old. He tested so well in basic training that he was placed in the Intelligence Division and the rest is history as they say.

They left for the Academy, walking hand in hand with Joe holding his old MIT gym bag with the gloves, balls, and a bat. While at Dick's, Joe saw a few young women who obviously were into sports. He walked over to the young ladies holding Bella's hand and asked them what she needed to start playing softball at age seven. The two girls melted and grabbed Bella's hand and brought her over to the softball equipment aisle. They said they played softball for the Waterford High School girl's varsity and their team was pretty good. Joe asked them their schedule so he could bring Bella to a game to see them play. He told them he was stationed at the Coast Guard Academy but didn't spell out what or who he was. They were both juniors and he asked if they were going to college and they said they were but not sure exactly where. He asked if they applied to the Coast Guard Academy. They said no. He gave them each his card and said he would be glad to give them a tour. He was still in his recruiting mode to get young women into the service. Bella walked out with a glove that actually fit her hand. She was of average size but had long fingers like a pianist. She got one size larger than she needed but would grow quickly. She got a bat that fit her and they got several different types of softballs, depending on if they played T-Ball or regular softball. She got a baseball hat that said, Waterford Softball, in honor of her new friends. It was nice of Dick's to offer local team hats to honor their community. Bella couldn't carry everything so Joe brought the stuff to the car and they walked back and met Julie and Annie at the food court where they had lunch. Joe had as much fun as Bella. He couldn't wait to show her the ropes.

They met Sean and Emma and the girls, like young girls do, hugged and went to have a catch. Nether had a clue what to do as Joe looked at Sean and laughed. "So long ago and so far away," he said. As they went over to show the girls how to catch, Sean waved to the baseball coach. Sean was the Assistant Athletic Director and all-star basketball player for the Bears. Brian Casey, at age 34, was the new head baseball coach at the Academy, moving up from an assistant position at the beginning of the year. He was well qualified as the recruiter and pitching coach at William and Mary and was very young. He helped the "Tribe" at William and Mary record five straight thirty win seasons. Joe was in awe of his baseball prowess. After speaking for a while it was clear that both had a passion for baseball. Brian had heard rumors about Joe Traynor and his saving the Academy from disaster only weeks earlier but he didn't know Joe or know of Joe's love for baseball. Joe had mentioned it to Rear Admiral Kelly but wanted no help from him about coaching. They spoke for a while and Joe gave him his baseball background and told him his first encounter at playing for MIT at the Academy and how he got a save without throwing a pitch to home plate. Brian thought that was great. He asked him if Andy Pettitte was his hero and he said of course and smiled.

"When you walk a lot of batters, as left-handers tend to do, you watch Andy Pettitte like a hawk, to nail down his pickoff move or your dead," said Joe.

"We have the luxury of having three left-handers on our pitching staff and no official pitching coach other than me, but I'm right-handed. Only two will go to games while the other one will be on a taxi squad. If you can show them exactly how to do that move, I'll move him up in a heartbeat," he said.

"Done deal," said Joe. "I have to spend time with Emma and Bella. They are going to the Olympics for 2032 or 2036 depending on where they go to college," said Joe with a smirk.

"At least you have your priorities straight," said Brian with a huge grin. "I'll call you to see what your schedule is. We practice indoor for two weeks and then out on the field as soon as the first game of the season. As you know, since you pitched fall ball for MIT, the spring is even shorter and colder." Joe nodded and he and Sean went over to the girls where they had a catch and let them hit for an hour. They treated Bella and Emma to lunch in the cafeteria and then they were going to stay at Bella's house until Samantha or Sam picked her up around 4:00 p.m. When they walked in, Julie had just gotten off the telephone with Tillie. Tillie wanted to come up for Easter so they started making arrangements. Joe knew he could get her up here on a Coast Guard transport at any time but if she wanted to fly out of Key West or Miami, he was good with that as well.

Chapter 16

As promised, Joe took all day Sunday, after Mass, to develop a presentation to Rear Admiral Kelly on Monday morning, and then if approved, to the Board of Trustees that Thursday. He was meeting Kim, Laura, and Dave at 9:00 a.m. on Monday in his office, before his meeting, to review what he was to present to the Rear Admiral. He thought about it for a while and he thought it would be less confusing if he did the presentation alone while telling the Rear Admiral that it was a team effort with him, a board member, the head of Safety and Security and a Special Agent with the FBI, who was involved in the takedown of the white supremacist with Joe. He would present the written document to him, signed by all the participants at the West Point simulation and dated. He also knew that Laura would be attending the Board of Trustees meeting and could be helpful in addressing any issues since she now has firsthand knowledge of what they would be implementing.

Precisely at 9:00 a.m. everyone met in Joe's office. He pulled together the entire presentation, slide show and video taken at West Point for the actual simulation of the attempted bombing of the Academy. They all agreed on the facts but wanted it to be presented in a more dramatic fashion, starting with the simulation. Laura, who was used to the give and take of the Board, said it would shock them and then wake them up and they would be more receptive of any new suggestions, especially when presented with the actual price tag that would be funded with a contribution by the Teresa Trust Fund. They finished around 10:30 a.m. giving Joe a little time to have some coffee, chitchat about other things and then hit the bathroom. Meetings made him nervous and out of place and then he always had the urge to hit the head. He thought it was caused by nerves but never showed it unless you counted the number of times he went to the bathroom before a major meeting. Joe laughed to himself. *If it gets worse, I'll have to move my office into the men's room*, he thought.

His meeting with the Rear Admiral went quite well and was an eye opener for Kelly. After seeing the simulation and finding out that this was the first of its kind, he was a little shocked. When he found out that the simulation was fine but then stopped and suggested that all the bombs were found. It wasn't until Joe reprogrammed the simulation, to include the fact that he offered clemency to the first individual who would give up any more bomb placements that the simulation picked up that there were more bombs to be found. So, the conclusion of the simulation is that it is only as good as the data fed into the system.

Rear Admiral Kelly said, "Joe, did you really offer clemency to this guy to give up more bombs?"

"Yes, of course. That's what we're trained to do. Not from a Coast Guard point of view, but from top-secret Homeland Security and FBI briefs, we are told to get the information anyway we can. Yes, we are allowed to lie in these circumstances. I didn't mean it but I did put a note with the final CIA staff that stated that this individual saved lives with his confession of two more bombs placed in the field house laundry room."

"Well, I'm amazed and obviously the simulation-based program was unaware of this as well. I'm certainly glad that you're around," he said. "Tell the Board of Trustees exactly what you just told me and watch for their reactions. I'll bet they'll be shocked just like I was," he said.

"They shouldn't be shocked, Sir. This is a new era of terrorism and we have to fight fire with fire if we are to protect our cadets and our country. I hate to tell you this happens every day, day in and day out and there is no stopping it. We have to be ahead of the curve, Sir."

The presentation was approved and Joe informed the other three immediately and they were pleased. Captain Laura Chavez said she couldn't be happier with the results and couldn't wait for the meeting. Joe thought it was a good time to mention to her that he had a plan in mind about language requirements at the Academy and he wanted to bounce off a few ideas with her to get her reaction. He mentioned that he wanted to attend her Spanish classes at Connecticut College to start his plan and then mentioned that he has Hispanic Coast Guard service people that he has worked with and solved crimes with and he wanted to bring them in and show the class what it was like during a takedown involving cartels from Mexico, Columbia and other South American countries.

He also had in mind to bring in his best friend, Mark Silva, a Lieutenant in the Coast Guard, stationed in Miami. He is Joe's best friend and Godfather to Bella. In Spanish, they could discuss how they handled situations before and after arrests and interrogations leading to arrests, all in

Spanish. In addition, he also wanted to bring in Mary Evans's four bodyguards, all Hispanic, stationed in Islamorada. They included Alex Deleon, Mia Santiago, Antonia Andres and Martina Diego. Those three women represented the best of the best women in the service. They were members of an elite strike team and have all served many years in the Coast Guard. They could not only serve as storytellers but as a recruiting tool to get more minority women into the service.

Joe was nervous like always before his Thursday meeting with the Board of Trustees. He didn't need to be since they were all grateful for what he did to save the day from the bombing but Joe was a perfectionist and he knew it. He tried to contain it the best he could but when the meeting approached he became restless. Julie knew when to hold them and when to fold them as they say and she bought him a case of his favorite beer, *Octoberfest* by Sam Adams. *It helped* he thought.

Thursday came around faster than Joe expected. He added several additional ideas to his presentation and it helped to solidify his position, in his own mind. He was ready. He went in early Thursday just to make sure that the video equipment worked with his computer simulation presentation and his slide show was working well. He sat in the boardroom for a while and then got up and had coffee, a Danish and then hit the head. By the time he got back, all the board members started to come in. They were talking to each other, telling stories, and greeting each other like old friends. Rear Admiral Barnes couldn't make this meeting but Joe would update him after asking permission.

Once again, precisely at 11:00 a.m., The Assistant Commandant for Human Resources, Linda Jones, who chairs the Board, started the meeting with a roll call.

Everyone was present including the old retiree who would be leaving in a few short weeks. Rear Admiral Kelly took over as soon as new business started and explained Captain Joe Traynor's role as Assistant Superintendent and then as lead on various assignments including the bombing incident. He offered the Board's congratulations on his role in saving lives at the Academy and then said that Joe had a full presentation on the state of safety and security at the Coast Guard Academy.

Joe set his computer ready to start the simulation of what the West Point program would conclude and then what happened when he added the "get out of jail free card" to one of the perpetrators. He ran the simulation and the immediate conclusion was that all the bombs were accounted for on campus. He then went to phase two and added the incentive piece, which ran a new simulation that picked up the possibility of added bombs to the scenario. It never helped solve the problem other than to continue to the next phase of evacuation and bringing in massive bomb squads and robot equipment. This phase became extremely complicated with Homeland Security, the FBI, DEA, and ATF (Alcohol, Tobacco, and Firearms and Explosives Bureau), and finally the CIA depending on whom the terrorists were, if from outside or inside the United States.

Each board member appeared riveted to the screen and the presentation. It was clear that immediate actions taken by Joe Traynor saved the day and got all the bombs that were planned that day. Then Joe ran a video of the day's activity as a follow up and it showed the Toyota Corolla arriving followed by the FedEx truck and all the subsequent events that followed. Joe then went into all the preventive measures that would now be put into place including the wearing of contact tracing wearable devices by everyone on campus as a first warning system. He went through the vehicle instructions for incoming and outgoing traffic, parking, and infrared technology to ensure the safety and security of everyone on campus. Finally, Joe went over the budget and told them it would be an investment by the Teresa Trust Fund of a minimum of $3.0 million dollars to start and fund over the next four years. If it became more expensive, Joe said he could spend more out of the ten-million-dollar pledge by Mary Evans. He ended on a positive note stating that all the equipment would be ordered immediately, installed within the next few months and all those involved would receive training in time for a new freshman class to start in the fall. He then asked for questions.

Everyone was completely silent. At that point, Captain Laura Chavez spoke up. She said that she attended the West Point conference with Dave Simon, Kim Matz and Captain Traynor. She said she was extremely impressed by the professionalism shown by the team and by the West Point staff. She also mentioned that if Joe didn't offer immunity to the first insurrectionist, according to Kim Matz, lives would have been lost. She said that Joe was excellent under pressure and would guide the Board through the installation process and it would be successful. After that, several members spoke and thanked Joe and the team for their due diligence and they said they were very grateful that they were here at the Academy.

Someone asked Joe if there was anything he wanted or needed while here at the Academy. Joe replies, "After we complete this project, I want our men's baseball team and women's softball teams to have winning records, make the playoffs and go to the Division III championships. That would be my request," he said and laughed.

The Rear Admiral smiled and said, "Joe, wants to be the pitching coach for the baseball team this year. I told him if he even attempts to change their uniforms to pinstripes, he's fired. He's a diehard Yankee fan over here in Connecticut."

"There are just as many Yankee fans here, Sir. As a matter of fact, I looked it up. We are almost as close to Yankee Stadium and the Bronx, at 118.4 miles as we are to Boston's Fenway Park at 109.9 miles. Go Yankees." He added.

"On that note, can we adjourn?" asked the Rear Admiral with a smile and a laugh.

Captain Linda Jones announced that the meeting was adjourned.

As he was gathering his stuff, many of the board members came by to shake Joe's hand. Laura smiled at him and said she would call him about attending her classes at Connecticut College. Joe asked Rear Admiral Kelly if he could forward his presentation to Rear Admiral Barnes down in Miami and he said of course. He said Jake will be taking over the board seat in two weeks, ready for the next board meeting. Rear Admiral Kelly brought Joe to the side after everyone left the room and congratulated him on a job well done. He said those in the know learned about his intervention at the Academy and were all very impressed. He told him it wasn't Jake that mentioned it to the Admiral, he said it was anonymous and was one of the board members who is a close friend of the Admiral in charge of the Coast Guard, at headquarters in Washington, D.C.

Chapter 17

College baseball had very short seasons two years in a row including 2020 and 2021 because of Covid-19. The Academy's record for 2021 was 3-7 and the rest of the games were cancelled. At the height of the pandemic in 2020 they were 4-3, cancelling 28 games. Hopefully for this year, they would play their full schedule of 33 games. However, there would be no trip to Florida for the first week of the season and it would begin in mid-March instead of the first of March, giving the team only two weeks of spring training. The first game at home was Sunday, March 20th versus Clark University from Worchester. They would play a full schedule of nine NEWMAC (New England Women and Men Athletic Conference) games and there'd be a conference tournament at the end, sending the winner to the first round of Division III national baseball tournament in early May. Baseball in New England was a very short season if they didn't schedule games in Florida. In fact graduation from the Academy is May 18th this year which could affect attendance.

The last full season in 2019, the team was 16-19 and

hadn't had a winning record in some time. Hopefully, the new coach from William and Mary would change all that. The Coast Guard Academy didn't redshirt players like many college teams, meaning allowing them to attend a fifth and even sixth year to play and then hopefully graduate. The Academy was not backed up with seniors hoping to play another season. Those seniors had other career choices. They graduated and were now called "Officers" in the United States Coast Guard.

Coach Casey has done a remarkable job of recruiting cadets not only to play baseball but also to attend the Coast Guard Academy. In many ways it was an easy sell. Only Division I and Division II could offer athletic scholarships to its students. Division III did not have that option but attending The Coast Guard Academy, just like West Point, Annapolis or the Air Force Academy, all the cadets received a $500,000.00 equivalent scholarship for room, board and tuition, since they attend a military academy for free. However, after graduation, they owed Uncle Sam four years of their lives to serve in the Coast Guard. It was a pretty good trade-off for many poor students, who would never have had the chance at a college education, especially poor female minority students that Joe was so insistent on recruiting.

What Joe couldn't wait for was when the Coast Guard Academy played MIT at home on Saturday, April 2nd. Since he beat the Academy while playing his one semester at MIT, he wanted the Academy to even the score while he helped get the left-handed pitchers into shape. He wanted all three on the team to perfect the Andy Pettitte pick-off move to first base. You never knew when you needed it from game to game, but in that moment, it came in real handy.

Joe reviewed his schedule with Coach Casey and he

could make himself available for three afternoons a week during the baseball season. He could attend all home games and a few away games that were near the Academy including those in Worcester and Boston and right in New London and the surrounding areas. He would work with all the pitchers at the direction of Coach Casey and then when they felt comfortable with each other, Joe could work a little closer with the team, especially the left-handed pitchers. Starting next week, Joe would follow his schedule religiously. If there were any interference with his duties as Assistant Superintendent, then he would say so and miss a few games if necessary. Since he would be on campus 98% of the time, he could still help with practices. Coach Casey gave Joe a Coast Guard Academy uniform, number 19, his favorite number throughout the years. He couldn't wait to tell Julie. *He was like a kid in the candy store,* he thought.

Julie reminded him that Sarah Atwood was coming to town next Tuesday to meet with her about her potential new book. Her old Dean at Brown University, Gerald Spaulding, was also invited. They would meet at their house and Joe would watch Bella and Annie during the day. Joe asked Julie if they would like to dine in the Officer's dining room and she thought that would be great. Joe would set up a luncheon with a private table near the window overlooking the grounds. It was an impressive sight for anyone who has not been to the Coast Guard Academy. Joe thought that at least he could pull rank on Julie's behalf as the second in command of the Academy. He would tell the Rear Admiral just in case. A word from him to the staff at the facility would certainly improve the service a little. Sarah and her assistant would arrive Tuesday morning from New York City. Joe had inquired about rooms at the hotel in downtown and would reserve three rooms just in case they wanted to stay over for the grand tour. He could then treat them all to dinner at *On The Waterfront Restaurant and Bar*. He would stay home with the kids and Julie could start feeling like an adult again instead of a daycare worker. It was clear. Julie was missing adult interaction and stimulation coming from her academic friends. He couldn't blame her. Joe was surrounded by his colleagues at the Academy, all day long. Julie loved being a mother but she definitely needed a break.

The rest of the week was pretty normal. It was now mid-March and Joe was gearing up for baseball, his meetings with Connecticut College, and attending language classes with Laura Chavez. His time seemed to be planned out by the minute. It was Saturday and he looked at the Waterford girls' softball schedule and the varsity team had a game that afternoon at 1:00 p.m. Joe asked Bella if she would like to see the two girls play that they met at Dick's Sporting Goods at the mall. She jumped at the chance so Julie told her that all of them would go and then have pizza later before coming home. The two girls, Riley Miller and Isla Harris, would be shocked to see Joe and the family pull up to see the game. He was going to have Annie and Bella wear their new Coast Guard Academy batgirl uniforms but didn't think it would be fair without Emma. So, Bella wore her Waterford softball hat that she got at the store.

They pulled up to Waterford High School and walked down to the girls' softball field. Annie was in her stroller fast asleep. Bella had her glove and ball in her hand and her new hat secured to her head. Joe had his new Coast Guard Academy hat on and his warm coat. It was still cold even though spring was on its way. They sat on the first row of the bleachers so Julie could rock the stroller if

Annie woke up. Joe looked up and waved to Riley and Isla. They came over and said hello and gave Bella a hug. They said they would see them after the game. Bella was thrilled. They were playing a team from Bridgeport, who had a better record last year but lost a few girls to graduation. The Waterford team had only two seniors, two juniors, and the rest sophomores and freshman. Riley and Isla were the two juniors.

It was early in the season so there were a lot of mistakes in the early going but both girls seemed to know what they were doing. It wasn't a pitcher's duel with the score at 10-7 going into the last inning trailing. In the bottom of the 7th, Isla dropped a bunt and made it to first. Another girl walked and then Riley hit the longest homerun Joe ever saw for girl's high school softball game. The score was now tied and with two outs, another girl hit a double driving in the winning run 12-11. Bella was screaming. Julie got into the act as well. Julie didn't play softball but was as competitive as hell in cross-country. Joe smiled and said to himself, "Yes!"

At the end of the game, Riley and Isla came over to see them with big smiles. "You need to come to all our games, Bella," they cheered. Riley's parents and Isla's mother came over to introduce themselves. Joe mentioned that he was stationed at the Coast Guard Academy. Riley's mother said she read his card when her daughter got home and said that he was more than just stationed at the Academy. "I'm the assistant baseball coach as well," he said. "I'm also the team recruiter," and laughed.

"You're the Assistant Superintendent, or second in command according to your website. Thank you for coming. We hear you told our daughters that you would give them a tour of the Academy if they wanted. Can they still get in?"

"It's close right now for seniors but they're juniors so there's plenty of time to apply. If they would like a tour and you as well, I can arrange it. After all I'm the assistant superintendent as you know," he said and chuckled.

"No offense, but how old are you? You look like a kid and your wife looks like she just graduated from high school," said Mrs. Harris.

"I'm a very old thirty-seven-year-old," he said and Julie will be hitting the big one next fall. By the way, this is Julie Chapman Traynor, or Julie Chapman as she is known."

"No way," said Mrs. Miller. "Are you Julie Chapman, author of the trilogy, *A Girl's Story*?" she asked.

"Yes, I am," said Julie. Annie started to wake up and she picked her up as Annie yawned and reached for Julie.

"We're honored to meet both of you. Thank you for coming to the game. Wait until I tell my friends. I can tell my friends, right?" asked Isla.

"Of course. You have my card. It's nice to meet you all. Good luck for the season. I have your schedule and we'll come to more games. I want Bella to see how much fun sports can be when done right," Joe said. They waved and headed to the car. Recruitment is still a big tool. The more in the tent the merrier, he was taught. He was sure he'd get a call from either the Harris family or the Millers in the very near future.

They headed back to New London and stopped at Nana's Byrek Pizza on Boston Post Road in Waterford. They're supposed to have the best pizza in town. If Annie started to act up, they could simply pack up the pizza and eat it when they got home. Pizza was a win-win as far as Julie was concerned. It was a very nice, pleasant easy going Saturday. They haven't had too many of those since they got to the Academy. They would sleep in Sunday morning and go to the Spanish Mass at Noon at their church. It would keep Bella's interest when she heard songs in Spanish and then follow along in her prayer book. Bella was now seven, going on eight but Joe and Julie both thought she was growing up too fast. They never got a chance to raise her as an infant like Annie. They were still fortunate to get her early years and then watch her grow into a woman. Julie always said a prayer for Bella's mother, thanking her for bringing Bella to them. It was a blessing.

Sarah Atwood and her assistant arrived around 11:00 a.m. Tuesday morning and Dr. Spaulding came a few minutes later. Dr. Spaulding had a one-hour trip of about sixty miles from Providence. He wouldn't be staying overnight unless there were negotiations that needed to be part of the following day. Julie asked Sarah if she and her assistant wanted to stay over because they had booked rooms for them and then on Wednesday morning, Joe could give them a tour of the Academy. They thought that would be great. Julie almost forgot how close the Atwoods were to the Spauldings. That's why Dr. Spaulding recommended Sarah's publishing house for her first book. Both couples attended the baptism for Annie as well. They couldn't believe how big she had gotten in only a few short months. Annie was all smiles as Sarah picked her up to give her a hug. Dr. Spaulding held her little hand while Sarah held her. He passed on holding her. He said, "the last thing I want to do is drop her. No thanks. I'll give her a kiss instead," he said.

"Chicken," said Sarah and laughed. "The big bad Dean can't hold a baby? Oh my word," said Sarah. Julie just smiled and Sarah handed her back. Joe bundled her up. If they left now, they might catch Bella in the playground at 11:40 a.m. her scheduled lunch time. He said, "If you need anything, just call me on my cell. Everything is set for your luncheon at the Officer's Dining Room. The Rear Admiral made a call and made sure everything was set," said Joe. With that, he waved and walked down the street with Annie in her stroller.

Julie, Sarah, Dr. Spaulding and Sarah's assistant, Catherine left the house and walked to the Academy. They stopped at the front gate and Julie gave the guard her husband's business card and told him they had a luncheon scheduled at the Officer's Dining Room. He nodded and told them to have a pleasant day. It was a short walk, about halfway across campus. As they entered the building, they were greeted by Rear Admiral Kelly. He introduced himself to Julie's associates and walked them to their reserved table right next to the large bay window, overlooking the expanse of the lawn just starting to come into bloom. He told the dining room manager to send the bill to him for his signature. He nodded and said to Julie that he hoped she enjoyed her "alone" time as he called it and laughed. "God knows being around Joe, I'm sure you need a break," he said and laughed. He also told her, knowing that this was her publisher and former Dean at Brown University, that she always had a place at the Academy if she so desired. He said it would occur whenever she wanted. He left it at that and shook her hand.

Julie thanked him profusely and it was evident that her guests were very impressed by what just took place. They all had salads, an appetizer, and a mixed seafood platter, fresh from the docks, every day. New London is at the mouth of the Thames River as you enter the Atlantic Ocean. New London, Connecticut was named in 1658 and incorporated in 1784. The harbor is considered the best deep-water harbor on the Long Island Sound. Julie was having an excellent time. She couldn't remember the last time she saw her Dean and publisher together talking about business. Obviously the last conversation was about Annie's baptism. They never brought up her intentions for her next book.

Julie decided to tell them that she had started her new novel, a stand alone, but based on her age, education, experience, and desires to help young women in the world. She said her working title for her new book is *Matter of Choices*. She went on to say that it was aimed at twenty-year-olds as they went through those ten years, culminated in age thirty, as was now happening to her. She said it was a simple matter of choices that moved her from the death of her mother in the hospital parking lot of the Tavernier parking lot to what she has become. Her choices were informed by her grandmother, by Joe, and by her Dean, as she turned to him and he had a tear in his eye. She then addressed Sarah and told her that she made all the difference in the world by giving her a chance. However, the choices she made along the way that were spelled out in her trilogy, *A Girl's Story,* needed to be followed up with her life now as a wife, a mother, an educator, and a national author and media personality because of her Disney Studio connections. She said she wanted to continue with Sarah as her Publisher and wanted Dean Spaulding involved as well. However, she wanted her personal attorneys, Kristen Sorenson and Jane Swanson to act as her agents in all things. She said she learned a great deal about life in general from both Jack Manning and Mary Evans, and both her attorneys served Jack and Mary extremely well. In fact, Jane was her attorney in the development of her contracts with Disney Studios. She said it was hard to classify her new book, *Matter of Choices*. It is nonfiction based on her life, fiction in many parts, and an obvious autobiography. She didn't know what to call it but said she had it outlined and would give it to both Sarah and the Dean.

Sarah was very pleased. She really didn't know how this would play out. She knew Julie had much more to offer in her books, but when she came forward with Joe to adopt Bella, she knew she wanted to be a mother as well, and that was solidified with Annie's birth. She also wanted to stay in education, which presented other problems. She didn't want to turn down Dean Spaulding's offer of a position at Brown University but her first priority was to her husband and children and that meant staying closer to home at Connecticut College. She explained her reasoning to Dean Spaulding and he told her there was no pressure from him. He would always be there for her.

Sarah reached out and handed Julie an advance check for $250,000.00, payable to Julia Chapman Traynor, more than originally thought. No strings attached she said. They would obviously need a contract signed and she would like to publish the book by Christmas of 2022, just in time for the book-buying season. That meant a deadline no later than October 1st. Julie didn't say anything but she was all ready a third of the way through and it was coming to her chapter by chapter and she already knew the ending, not perfectly but the direction it would culminate in. She thanked Sarah and put the check in her pocketbook. She would deposit it this afternoon at the local bank. They had their Coast Guard Credit Union accounts but she didn't want to advertise her good fortune. As soon as they arrived in New London, she opened both a checking and a savings account so Sarah could wire transfer her quarterly royalty checks. Joe taught her well about business. Keep your cards close to your vest, he always said.

Joe waved to Bella as she came out to the playground area with Emma. He would meet her at the front door as she walked home and they would head over to his office for a while to give Julie some more free time to get ready for dinner. She would pick up Sarah and Catherine at the hotel and drive over to the restaurant. Dean Spaulding said that he was heading home and thanked her for a very pleasant day. He wasn't needed anymore and he had appointments in the morning and couldn't make the tour of the Academy. Julie gave him a hug like a favorite uncle and he appreciated it. She picked up Sarah and Catherine and had a wonderful dinner on the river at *On The Waterfront Restaurant and Bar*. They really caught up this time. Catherine seemed to enjoy being outside of the hustle and bustle of New York City. They had a bottle of wine and Julie was as relaxed as she could remember. Sara and Catherine met Julie at her house around 9:00 a.m. Julie had Annie all wrapped up and ready to go for their tour of the Coast Guard Academy. Finally around noon, Annie was sound asleep and they wound up at Joe's office in the administration building. He said goodbye to Sarah and Catherine and he hoped they had a good time. They both did and said they would love to come back again. He said anytime. Julie loves the company. "The next trip, we can show you around Connecticut College and maybe you could address Julie's class," he said.

Julie said, "How do you know I'm taking the position at Connecticut College?" she asked.

"I just assumed that was your choice and a little bird told me," he said. "You called Tillie first didn't you? She let it slip. She's definitely coming for Easter," he said and smiled.

Chapter 18

After much consideration, Julie called Dr. Kate Ballenger, the president of Connecticut College to let her know her decision. Julie said she would be honored to work with the college and would like to sit down with the Dean, Dr. Erica Jones, and Dr. Liz Winter, Chair of the English Department. She told Dr. Ballenger that her publisher, Sarah Atwood and her assistant, Catherine, came to visit her to discuss her new book. She also mentioned that Dean Spaulding also came because she respected his wisdom and he and his wife were very close friends with the Atwoods. That's how she met Sarah and received her contract for her first book while she was a graduate student at Brown University.

Julie mentioned that Dr. Spaulding was fine with her decision but would want her to come back to Brown once in a while for a presentation to their MFA graduating students as a guest author. Dr. Ballenger saw no issues with that and was pleased that Julie didn't take her friendships lightly. They made arrangements to meet within a few weeks to discuss her potential role. Julie did mention that her new book, *Matter of Choices*, will be released in late fall of 2022, right before the Christmas buying season. Obviously, Dr. Ballenger was well aware of the need to publish when the buying season began.

Dr. Ballenger also mentioned that her husband, Joe, had scheduled a meeting with her this week as an introduction and review of the close association that both institutions enjoyed. She said she was well aware of Captain Traynor's new position at the Coast Guard Academy but was unaware of his extensive background not only in the military but in the field of education as well. She said that Joe sent her his Curriculum Vitae (CV). She said it was very impressive, especially for his age. She didn't know that he has a Ph.D. from Barry University and served as Interim President for The College of the Florida Keys or that he was fluent in Spanish, Russian, Chechen and currently learning Chinese. Julie said it should be a very interesting conversation knowing Joe.

That night she asked Joe why he sent the Curriculum Vitae before he met with Dr. Ballenger. Joe explained that he didn't want to rehash old information. Unlike Julie, who was internationally known as an author, the United States government classifies Joe's successes. He said a Curriculum Vitae was much stronger than a resume. He said that the CV presents a full history of your academic credentials, so the length of the document is variable. In contrast, a resume presents a concise picture of your skills and qualifications for a specific position, so length tends to be shorter and dictated by years of experience (generally 1-2 pages). He continued by saying that CVs are used by individuals seeking fellowships, grants, postdoctoral positions, and teaching/research positions in post-secondary institutions or high-level research positions in industry. Graduate school applications typically request a CV, but in general are looking for a resume that includes any publications and descriptions of research projects. Joe said he can't publish anything other than his doctoral thesis from Barry University. He will explain that to Dr. Ballenger when they meet.

"So you're saying I don't need a CV?" she asked Joe.

"Not at all, unless you would like to become a full professor at a university like Brown. They might require it but it would be like asking James Patterson for his resume. It just won't happen," he said.

"Good to know," Julie said. "Well, good luck tomorrow at the college. I'm sure she'll be very intrigued by the very mysterious Joe Traynor," she said and laughed. "Does she know about the bombs on campus?" she continued.

"I think she has been made aware of the bombing attempt but doesn't know the ramifications for her own institution. I may have to enlighten her about it. I already asked the Rear Admiral for permission for a one-on-one discussion with Dr. Ballenger and he said fine, she should know. We should also look at her safety and security team and see if they are up to par. Remember our students attend Connecticut College every day and we are a main source of income for them. Our students don't pay them to attend their college, the Academy pays them monthly a big chunk of change and we should make sure everyone is safe so we can continue our affiliation," he said.

Joe arrived at Connecticut College in full uniform for his meeting with the college president. He sat in the waiting room outside her office for barely a minute before she came through the door to greet him. She thanked him for coming and said she looked forward to talking to him. She said that his wife is a delight and she is very pleased that she has chosen to be part of Connecticut College. She said they would be working it out with all her other responsibilities including a newborn infant. They walked into the boardroom and he was greeted by the new Dean, Dr. Erica Jones, who was already sitting at the table. It was around 10:00 a.m. so they had coffee and Joe said he had to be back for a meeting at the Academy at 1:00 p.m.

Joe said he simply wanted to introduce himself to them and find out more about the very close relationship both institutions enjoyed. He went over his background and how he wound up as second in command of the Coast Guard Academy at such a very early age. Both the Dean and the president were very much in awe of Joe just as they were of Julie. Joe asked them permission to sit in on their various language courses. He understood that the Academy did not provide language curriculum and it was not a requirement of the Academy for graduation. He spoke plainly that he thought this was very short sighted. He learned Spanish from his best friend and partner in the Coast Guard, Mark Silva, who was of Mexican descent from San Diego. After many years, he learned the subtle differences in Spanish from region to region and even within certain countries. His Mexican Spanish was almost Spanglish due to the many English words that popped up in their discussions. Subtle changes in tone or mannerism informed them more than the actual words. He mentioned a few of his interdictions with the Mexican Mafia, the Columbians, the Haitians, the Russians, and the Chechens. He told them about his desire to recruit minorities and especially women of color and speakers of other languages not only into the Coast Guard but also into the Academy as well. He spoke of his lengthy discussions with Captain Laura Chavez, who is now a friend and confidant, and a member of the Academy Board of Trustees. She is also a professor of Spanish at Connecticut College. Joe wants every Academy student to learn a second language because it is a changing world and getting smaller and smaller. In fact in a few years, the Hispanic population in the United States may be the majority and the Coast Guard Academy needs to prepare for that day.

Both Dr. Ballenger and Dr. Jones were listening to Joe very intently. He wondered if they could discuss potential graduate level courses in languages where the student learner would actually immerse himself or herself into the normal language and daily culture so that their skills became seamless. That's why he wanted to recruit students brought up in a different language. He said that terrorists don't always speak English unless it's domestic terrorism, which is proving to be a much larger problem than imagined. He wanted those who spoke the language on a daily basis to receive the education to bring themselves up academically so they could understand the differences from professional level language to what's heard on the streets so they would know the level of the terrorists they are dealing with before and not after the fact.

Joe then looked at Dr. Ballenger and said he would like to bring her up to speed on a topic of mutual interest. He looked at her and said it was highly classified and wanted to know if Dr. Jones should be here for this discussion. Quite frankly, she didn't know so she was erring on the side of diplomacy and asked Dr. Jones to leave the room for a few minutes. Joe went into a complete breakdown of what happened at the Academy and how they captured the white supremacists in West Hartford. He explained that he found out additional bombs were placed other than what they found through negotiations with one of the perpetrators. He then told her of his simulations at West Point and how they were spending an initial three million dollars on safety and security at the Academy to prevent it from happening again. When he finished, Dr. Ballenger was astonished. She said, "Joe, may I call you Joe?"

"Of course," he said.

"Please call me Kate," she said. "You have just told me more about the Academy in the last hour than I have learned since I've been here. It's one thing to say we are affiliated and work closely together but we need a stronger appreciation of both our needs." She went on, "You have just scared the crap out of me, Joe," she said.

"I'm sorry. I didn't mean to but remember you are sitting across the street from a world class military institution in the Coast Guard Academy and only a mile or two down the street from a United States Navy submarine base with nuclear subs in dock. That's scares the hell out of me as well. Our students, our cadets, go to your college every day, day in and day out. You will be collateral damage if we are attacked once again. We can prevent this by working together. I have thought about it and discussed it with Rear Admiral Kelly, who by the way is a fine officer and a finer man. He told me to do whatever I need to do to strengthen our security both at the Academy and at your college that our cadets attend," he said.

Joe proposed an immediate solution. "Dr. Ballenger, I am the sole judge over a ten-million-dollar contribution from a foundation that gives me full reign over any project I choose. So far, since the bombing incident, I have approved, with Rear Admiral Kelly's blessing a three million dollar upgrade to our Academy to stem the flow of any attempt at harming the Academy. I would like to tie our new system to your safety and security systems and offer to you the same benefits that our cadets receive at the Academy. I can upgrade your software and your training and your procedures so you are able to identify any threats and address them as soon as possible. It does not make the threats go away, however. You need to upgrade your staff to benefit from what I am offering Connecticut College."

"Joe, I don't know how much this costs but I will work with you to see what we can fund," she said.

"I'll tell you what, you be completely honest with me and don't shortchange me and I will dip into our fund and pay for a majority of the costs. So, there is limited cost to you. I can spend up to ten million dollars but I certainly want to bring it to the attention of our benefactors," he said.

"You would do that for us? Really I don't know what to say. You just met us and we get this kind of assistance. I am eternally grateful and I don't know what to say," said Kate.

"Well if my kids are going to be walking around your campus, towed by Julie, I want this place as safe as ours. It's a two-way street though, I definitely want advanced language classes as we discussed and I'll pay for that too. Did I tell you that Julie and I have friends who may be one of the richest on the planet and like giving money away to good causes? Perhaps I'll invite them over here for a visit so you can see what philanthropy really is," he said and smiled.

"You are one enlightening guy, Joe, and the most direct human being I've ever met," she said.

"Takes one to know one as they say," said Joe. He laughed and she gave him a hug.

The Dean was invited back into the room. She brought lunch for all three of them knowing Joe had to leave at 1:00 p.m. They sat and ate and the Dean asked him what his biggest challenge was going to be at the Academy. He said having the left-handed pitchers learn the Andy Pettitte pick-off move to first base.

That surprised Erica and she asked what his involvement was with the baseball team. He said he was the new part time pitching coach and actually pitched against the Coast Guard Academy for MIT when he was a freshman. He said that was a story for another time. Erica said she was well aware of Andy Pettitte's pick-off move since she and her family are lifelong Yankee fans. She said that might be hard to do since he held the record for pickoffs for left-handed pitchers. Joe told her how as a left-handed pitcher he picked off the Coast Guard Academy player at first base when he was at MIT winning the game 7-6. He said that's what he did best since he walked so many batters. They both laughed. Kate didn't seem to have a clue what he was talking about but she was all smiles and felt a great relief about safety and security for the college. She thought, *thank God both Julie and Joe Traynor wound up at their doorstep.*

Joe met Julie at home and told her everything that happened. She thought that was very wise offering them the safety and security package and paying for it out of the fund. She was sure that Joe would probably get anything else he wanted from Kate and Erica from now on. Julie needed to develop a plan of what she would be doing with the college. She would work on it all spring and then have discussions over the summer on exactly what a college curriculum would look like that tied into the development, research, writing and publishing of her new book. She would have Sarah Atwood discuss her process. She would invite Dean Spaulding to discuss his duties as Brown's Dean of the MFA program and how he managed to get the first contract for Julie. She would bring in Jane Swanson, on her own dime, as the attorney to discuss all the legal ramifications involved in publishing and finally she would ask the president of Disney Studios to come up and explain how you take a book, turn it into a screenplay and then into a media production for the movies, television, streaming or cable. She had a lot of work to do.

Joe fed the baby and tucked her in for the night. He read to Bella and they snuggled on the couch. They had breakfast for dinner, which Joe usually wanted when he was bored with food. He had sausage and pancakes with strawberry compote and of course a cold *Octoberfest* Sam Adams beer. He had several. Julie had wine. She asked what wine went with pancakes and he said any box wine would do and laughed. It was a nice, quiet night for a change.

Chapter 19

Joe was sitting at his desk in his office and started to think about how he would approach the three left-handed pitchers to see if he could actually teach them how to do a left-handed pick-off move to first base. First, he wanted to know if mathematically, a pitcher could be fast enough throwing to first base while the runner had a ten-foot lead. He downloaded a bunch of information to see if a pitcher could actually get the ball over to first base without trying to fool the runner. He got out his calculator. It was to the advantage of the pitcher because he knew when he was going to throw the ball over and the runner did not. The runner always watched the pitcher's motion to see if he could pick up any delay when he threw home. If he did, then the runner had the advantage in stealing second base. Then, if he could disrupt the pitcher, he had a good chance of causing the pitcher to balk, meaning he got second base because the pitcher violated the rules throwing to home. However, if the pitcher could fool the runner legally by looking like he was throwing to home, but wasn't, while throwing to first base, the pitcher could pick up a half a second to a second in time, because of the runner's hesitation, allowing the ball to get there before the runner got back to first.

That wasn't good enough, thought Joe. Joe wanted to know precisely how much time a pitcher really had to pick off the runner. What happens if the pitcher throws the ball over at 60 miles an hour and the runner is ten feet off first base. If the runner is only off six feet, and you can obviously tell, don't throw over because you're wasting a pitch and letting the runner know your intention. So at 60 miles per hour, you can travel 60 miles in one hour. That seemed easy to Joe. Subsequently, you can travel one mile at 60 miles per hour or 5,280 feet. The pitcher's mound is exactly 60 feet and six inches from first base. That means at 60 miles per hour, the ball can travel 88 feet in one second. It only has to travel 60 feet 6 inches, so it should take .69 seconds to get there. At 80 miles an hour, the ball will travel to first in .51 seconds. The fastest runner in the league's average speed, stealing second is 90 feet in 3.17 seconds or 28.4 feet per second or 18.93 miles per hour, significantly less than the pitcher's throw over to first. The fastest human being ever, Usain Bolt, runs at nearly 28 miles per hour in the 100-meter sprint.

To get back after a pick off move, the runner only has to get back 10 feet, or about a third of a second. So, if the runner sees the throw to first without hesitation, then he is easily back safe at first. If he hesitates or if his body weight is shifted toward second base, it takes from a half second to a full second to start back to first. Adding the third of second running and the half-second to one second of hesitation, then the runner will be out by two feet. To Joe, that makes a lot of sense.

So how do you fool the runner to make him hesitate and lose precious time trying to get back to first? That was Andy Pettitte's secret and Joe knew exactly how he did it by watching film over and over and over again. Andy Pettitte adhered to the rules but there was no rule that stated that your body weight couldn't be heading home while your left arm was heading to first base. As long as your left foot was on the rubber at all times, in the set stretch position as opposed to the full windup position, and your free right leg didn't come back and break the plane of the pitching rubber (going backwards), you were free to throw to first base after immediately shifting your weight to first and throwing.

However, the right foot and right leg had to be in direct line diagonally to first base. However Andy did it, it worked. A recent pitcher, Johnny Cueto, a left-handed pitcher for the San Francisco Giants, was the only other pitcher to use the same body control technique. Obviously, Andy Pettitte was the all-time career leader in successful pickoff moves. Cueto is second.

Joe downloaded the videos that were online and he could stop and start at will to show the pitchers every precise move and where the runner was during that time period. Joe could also point out his own successful record at MIT, picking off several runners at first during his only semester. Even with only one semester, Joe still held the MIT record with a 4-1 record with three saves and 7 pickoffs. Joe laughed to himself that he still had three years of eligibility left. Maybe he could get a master's degree in something else and accumulate enough credit hours to make him eligible. *That would be really cool* he thought, *maybe in his dreams.*

Lucy Talbot decided to speak to her cross-country coach at the University of Miami. She was now in her second semester at the university and academically she was doing very well, with straight "A's" in all her classes. She was a computer science major and one of the top students in the 5-year Bachelor of Science + Master of Science program in Computer Science. It provides research training for students who wish to work in a computing research lab, or possibly continue to Ph.D. studies. This program is open only to currently enrolled Computer Science undergraduates. Lucy already had eighteen credits of Advanced Placement approved coupled with her fall semester and now spring semester curriculum.

Since she was being redshirted, she decided to add classes so she wouldn't be heavily burdened when she started cross-country in the fall of 2022. She was very upset that she never got a chance to compete last fall, even though her times were as good if not better than her teammates. She was allowed to practice and her work ethic continued to show that she was capable of much more. The problem at the University of Miami is that it is an international university and teams recruit on an international level. As an example, her teammate was from Greece and was a sophomore and had appeared at the South Regional Championships and she recorded the fastest time by a Hurricane at 21.05.96, topping the previous mark of 21:15.5. Lucy's time in practice only, was 20:55.15 and was redshirted because of Covid-19 meaning no student on the team had used any eligibility so no spots were open and may not be open in 2022. This student was still considered a freshman for eligibility purposes. In addition, she was already on Greece's 2024 Olympic team.

Lucy walked over to the sports complex and knocked on her coach's door. He said come in and when he looked at Lucy, he knew something was up. She sat down in the chair in front of his desk and he asked her what was on her mind. She told him that she enjoyed her time at the University of Miami, and really liked the girls on the team, but this was not a good fit for her and she was thinking of transferring for the fall semester. The coach said he didn't realize that she was unhappy and asked her what she wanted him to do about the situation. He said his hands were tied. She was on full scholarship. He also knew that her scholarship included her academic status, which was higher than any girl on the team. He didn't want to lose her and he told her that. He asked her where she would be transferring because he didn't want her to lose her scholarship.

When she told him that she was applying as a transfer student to the Coast Guard Academy in New London, Connecticut, he was floored. She said if accepted, she would be on a 100% scholarship just like all other cadets so financially there was no issue. She said she could also be a member of their Women's cross-country team as early as this summer. If she were accepted, she would have to make up days of leadership training. She could substitute academic credit for time to perform these duties because academically, she was already on track as a full sophomore in her chosen field. In addition, since she was already in a 5-year bachelor and combined master level program, she could transfer that academically to be a two-major student at the Academy and be on target to obtain a Ph.D. as well. She also told him that as a Division III student athlete, she could go to the Division III cross-country championships since the Coast Guard Academy is already ranked 8th from last year, moving up to 5th this year pre-season in the rankings.

The coach appeared to be in shock. He realized that Lucy Talbot was very smart and a highly sought after athlete. He just shook his head knowing that he had made quite a blunder in dealing with Lucy Talbot. Once she told him that it didn't matter what NCAA Division she ran, the only thing that mattered was her time. She said she was told that when trying out for the Olympics for the United States, her time was the most important qualification not what division she ran in. It wasn't like in football where the University of Miami would beat a lower division team 69-0 just to add a win to their total. She would be running head to head with the best in the country regardless and she wanted to try out for the 2024 Olympics and she could do that as an Academy student or as an Academy graduate and officer in the Coast Guard.

She smiled at the coach and said, "You know it might be fun running for the USA against my former teammate from Greece. Head to head I beat her every day in practice. She will be on the Greece team because she already has a place on it. Hopefully, I'll have a place as well."

Lucy knew she took a big chance in talking to the coach at this level. Usually he or she would be resentful but this coach knew he'd screwed up big time and wanted to keep her. He said, "Lucy, all your points are valid and I don't blame you. You were only a freshman and I didn't think about your feelings at all and for that I'm really sorry. One thing I can guarantee is if you want to come back, you can at any time and if you want to get your masters here at Miami and you still have eligibility left, you can do that as well. Will you keep me informed of your decision? You have all the time you want and if you decide to stay, I will be more cognizant of your situation, I promise."

With that, Lucy shook his hand and left the building. She made it back to her dorm room and called Julie first and then her mother. She would talk to Joe about this but she didn't want to put him in the middle of anything or compromise his position. She would also call the head coach of the Academy cross-country team and ask for his endorsement. She would tell him that she didn't want Joe involved but he could certainly use Julie Traynor and even her own mother, Lieutenant June Talbot for references. She already read up on what she needed to do to apply to the Coast Guard Academy as a transfer student and duel major. She didn't have a lot of time because the April deadline was coming up and her final classes at Miami would be ending in April as well. She would need to head home and prepare for a full summer of training by the Coast Guard, called Swab Summer, to make up for her lost time for requirements that she missed as a freshman.

"Julie, Hi. It's Luce," said Lucy. "Can you use a babysitter for Bella and Annie?" she asked and laughed.

"Anytime, anywhere. You owe me anyway for being your babysitter for a lifetime," said Julie.

Lucy wasn't crazy about the name Lucy but hated her given name Lucille even more. Lucille was Joan Talbot's mother name. Just as Julie was grateful not to be named after Tillie or Matilda, she knew that Luce felt the same. Julie was one of only a few people who called her Luce and has called her that for many years as both her original babysitter and as her cross-country coach at Coral Shores High School, where they shared four years together culminating in Luce's being named all Florida first team for girl's cross-country, winding up with a full scholarship to the University of Miami in Coral Gables, Florida, not that far from home.

"Are you trying to tell me something, Luce?" asked Julie.

"I just spoke to my coach at Miami and told him that I was transferring to the Coast Guard Academy as soon as this semester ended," she said.

"Does Joe know?" she asked.

"You and mom are the first two I've told, Julie," she said. "I want to call the coach at the Academy and see what his reaction is. I think it will be positive. However, I only have less than a month to get all my paperwork in including my transcripts from Miami. I have enough credit to actually go into my junior year with the Advanced Placement that you helped me with. I think I can use all the credits for a duel major in Computer Science or Operations Research and Computer Analysis with a duel Government bachelors degree. I could also get a masters at Connecticut College at the same time."

"Do you want me to go down and see the coach? I can head out right now with Annie if you want. Eventually you need to inform Joe. A letter from his commanding officer and the Superintendent of the Academy will go a long way," said Julie.

"Would you mind, Julie. That would be great. I've ordered all my paperwork. I've been working on it for a few weeks and then I was working up the courage to go see my coach. He actually understood and apologized for not giving me the time of day. But, that's what happens at a big school like Miami. You get lost in the shuffle. What finally made him understand is that I want to be in the 2024 Olympics. When I told him that a girl from Greece was getting all the accolades and was already on the Greece Olympic team for 2024 and that I beat her every day in practice, it sealed the deal. He finally figured out that I was no dummy. By the way, I have a 4.0 index for both semesters here."

With that they said goodbye and Julie rushed out the door with Annie. She had one hour and a half to get back to catch Bella coming home from school. She made it to the field house and knocked on the door of the head coach's office. It was off-season so things were slow. He was around a lot but still was in recruiting stage to make sure that the kids he recruited got all their paperwork in on time to be approved for a spot this fall. Ethan Brown answered the knock and Julie introduced herself with Annie in her arms. He asked her to step in and he introduced himself. He seemed to know a lot about Joe Traynor and his author wife, Julie Chapman Traynor. He'd heard about the baptism as well and knew that Joe was unofficially at this point a pitching coach for the men's baseball team. He obviously knew that Joe was the Assistant Superintendent of the Coast Guard Academy.

Julie started the conversation about Lucy Talbot and told him that she preferred Luce, pronounced "loose," instead of Lucy. She told him that Lucy was tired of hearing from adults, "Lucy, I'm home," from Lucille Ball's husband, Ricky Ricardo, in the never-ending series of *I Love Lucy*. The Coach made a note of it and asked for Luce's phone number. Julie said that Luce didn't want Joe to be involved to put him in an awkward position. Coach Brown said, "Awkward position? With Luce, we could win the entire Division III NCAA Championship this fall. There is no limit to her talent if she chooses to excel and I believe she will.

"This is a gift not an awkward position. I'm thrilled and I'm sure the ladies will be thrilled as well. It's different here. We all pull for each other and that's true at all the military academies. Regardless of sports, when they graduate, they are officers in the United States Coast Guard and equal to every other new officer from the Army, Navy, Air Force or Merchant Marines."

"Will you call her?"

"Of course," he said. "I do need to talk to her coach because we cannot be considered 'poaching' other athletes from other universities even if we are different divisions," he said.

Julie smiled, "Here's her coach's phone number. Can

you call him right now?" She said, "Luce told him to expect a call from you." He immediately called the coach and they spoke for several minutes.

Julie had to head out to get Bella when she got home. Coach Brown ended the call and said he was getting a letter of recommendation from her coach at Miami that she was well deserving of a place at the Academy and was an outstanding student, athlete, and person, and as honest as the day is long. He told Coach Brown how she went directly to him and laid out her plans. He said he wished that he had done more to keep her but his negligence cost him a true star.

"I will do everything I can to ensure her admission to the Academy," said Coach Brown.

When she got home and met Bella sitting on the front steps she asked her if she wanted to get ice cream down the street and they went on their merry way.

When they got back, Julie called Joan Talbot and they spoke for almost an hour. Joan had mixed emotions about Lucy going up to Connecticut far from home but she knew she was in good hands and could always count on Joe and Julie to watch over her only daughter. *Now, they would wait to see if she was accepted. She'd have to be or they were nuts, right?* Thought Julie.

Chapter 20

Chapter **20**

Joe looked at Captain Laura Chavez's class schedule at Connecticut College. She taught every day, five days a week. Monday, Wednesday, and Friday, her classes were 50 minutes long. On Tuesday and Thursday, since it was a two-day schedule, classes were one hour and fifteen minutes each, or two and a half hours per week. They decided that Joe should attend one of the advanced classes later in the day, on a Thursday. That way, he could judge the level of Spanish taught in the class and then more importantly, the relevance of the actual Spanish itself.

Would a Spaniard, Mexican, Cuban, and Columbian all conversing in Spanish understand each other perfectly or have difficulty in holding a conversation? The answer is they will until one of them says he is going to do something like the British say go to the "loo" or put something in the "bonnet" for the trunk of a car. An American may not understand the meaning of these words developed exclusively in Great Britain or Australia. When explained, they laugh and say, "Oh, you mean the trunk or the bathroom" and then they would continue.

Joe's biggest problem would be for students

understanding a foreign language in the middle of a drug bust, on a ship, out on the ocean. As some discovered as Spaniards visited Mexico, that they learn to do small changes in style or tone, and then the only difference is the accent, itself. As Mexicans travel in Spain, they are well liked for the politeness but sometimes don't get the best service until they learn to be a little more assertive. The differences can be subtle but major in the moment. As Joe found out speaking Russian, Chechen, Spanish, and Chinese, that even English is spoken differently in the United States, Canada, England, and Australia, and there can be regional dialects even within those countries. Chinese has a slew of dialects as well. Someone living in Alabama might not understand someone from Brooklyn.

For the first step in developing a new language curriculum, Joe wants to see if the Spanish spoken in class could effectively help the cadets understand poor, uneducated individuals coming from Mexico, the Caribbean, Cuba, and Central and South America. These individuals were working for a major cartel dropping off drugs into the United States. Once they were caught, the Coast Guard members needed to understand what they were saying after they were captured. Learning perfect Castilian Spanish from Spain just didn't cut it as Joe knew from these encounters.

He would take copious notes and rehash what he was thinking with Laura. Maybe he could take the Coast Guard students into a special class by themselves and teach them the basics they need to know at the street level. He could bring in a few of his Coast Guard friends, who were Hispanic, and dealt with this on a daily basis. If you go to Miami, and a lot of the cadets will upon graduation, they will find that over 50% of the population in Miami are foreign born and 80% Hispanic with a growing Russian and Haitian population, who spoke Creole French. It was a never-ending challenge to keep up with this new America.

Before the class on Thursday afternoon, starting at 3:00 p.m. and ending at 4:15 p.m., Joe stopped at the Connecticut College president's office to let her know that he was attending Captain Chavez's advanced Spanish class that day. He asked Kate Ballenger if she would like to go with him to the class. She said it's been a while but she would be delighted to attend as long as Dr. Chavez approved her attendance. Joe called her on the spot and she said that it would be fine but to sit in the back of the class with Kate. The classroom was in a theater-like setting in the round with seats climbing higher and higher. Her class had almost thirty students at the advanced level. Joe was simply dressed in a sport coat over khakis, a blue shirt, and no tie. He had on his comfortable shoes. Kate had her power outfit on after just attending a finance meeting with several board members.

As they walked down the hall to the classroom, Kate said, "Joe, how are you going to approach the class if they start asking you questions like, "Why are you here, etc?"

Joe said, "I will simply answer any questions they have. I'll bet a lot of the students are cadets from the Academy," he said.

Kate said, "As a matter of fact, I checked the attendance sheet before we left and at least half of the students are third- and fourth-year cadets at the Academy. I can't wait to see your interaction with them. The scuttlebutt is that you were the Academy's savior a short while ago. I wonder what they will think when you start talking to them?"

"I have no idea. This is something I've wanted to do for sometime. I don't know if you are as familiar with my background as you may think. I am fluent in three languages besides English, working on Chinese as we speak. However, my language skills are more geared to action while on duty than academics. I really want to see how the students present themselves if called on."

"I can see your point. I didn't realize you had that many languages under your belt. Maybe you can wind up teaching here as well as Julie."

"I doubt it. I would do it without a book. I would immerse them in a language as soon as they entered the door. I would teach them to listen first before speaking. This is a skill lost especially in English."

They entered the classroom and climbed the stairs to the right, going up several rows until they hit the back of the classroom. Professor Chavez closed the door and went to the front of the room. She went into her normal teaching routine for the first half hour. It was a lively give and take and Joe thought these students were well-prepared and obviously interested in the topic. At the end of the half hour, Dr. Chavez told the students, in Spanish, that they had two guests in the back of the room. She introduced the college President and then introduced Joe as Captain Joseph Traynor, Assistant Superintendent of the Academy. There was polite applause for both individuals. At that point, Laura asked Joe to come down in the front of the class and explain why he and the President were auditing the class. The students, both cadets and civilians, were very attentive to this obviously young Captain. He explained, in Spanish, his background and how he wound up at the Academy. He asked the students if they had any questions. One cadet simply asked how he became so proficient in Spanish and Joe explained that it was a lifetime of learning since he was 18 years old, as a new Coast Guard member attending training with his now best friend, a member of Mexican descent from San Diego. He explained how they interacted until he no longer had to think about language skills, as it became second nature to him. He then told him that he is now fluent in Russian, Chechen, and learning Chinese. Students asked him why and he simply said, America is changing. If you don't change then America will suffer. Until this year's domestic terrorism came to the forefront, it was foreign terrorism that took away all the attention and for that they needed speakers of other languages. Those in the highest command needed knowledge of their adversaries and the extreme cultural differences that divided them.

Joe swiftly, over the next 45 minutes, went over the differences even within the various Spanish communities, both domestic as well as in Mexico, the Caribbean, and Central and South America. Joe explained some of the duties he had to perform to protect the country and the students appeared riveted. Kate continued to sit at in the back of the class and was mesmerized by Joe's interaction with the students. He answered every question without hesitation. He told several jokes in Spanish that reflected the various Hispanic communities. He outlined the differences in nuances, tone, and perception and education levels of those with whom he had interacted.

Finally, the bell rang and class was dismissed. Since it was the last class of the day, a lot of the students hung around to meet Joe after class. He shook hands with everyone and brought down Kate for introductions as well. He explained that he was very impressed by Connecticut College and wanted to tighten their ties even more. He did say that he would be interested in developing a graduate level course or even an advanced course that would teach students street-smart Spanish as he called it. It was Spanglish but more than this it was the language of the people these graduates would be dealing with, especially the cadets.

After everyone left, Joe turned to Kate and Laura and asked both of them how he did. He never taught a class before, especially in this kind of setting. Both said it was refreshing to hear from a leader, on exactly how he felt and thought. Kate asked Joe if he would mind meeting with several language professors, including Laura, to have a sit down and talk about the real-world implications of what these students were being taught. Joe knew that this conversation would get back to Rear Admiral Kelly and that was fine. He wanted feedback at every level. He also wanted to move fast because he was unsure if this current job would last for more than a few years. Like most change agents, Joe knew that once the change was made, others had to come in to run it on a daily operational basis. This was not the change agent's job.

As they were walking back to the Academy, Laura said, "Joe, every day you surprise me. I had no idea of the depth of your knowledge of Coast Guard duties and especially how you deal with them on a daily basis. As you were discussing Mexican slang and introduced jokes using that dialect, I was actually amazed. You could see the students looking pretty dumbfounded and didn't know what you said in Spanish because they never heard those words said in that way." She added, "I need to bring myself up to speed especially after what you said about desperately needing street-Spanish to catch the bad guys. I never once thought about it that way. You have certainly enlightened me. I would like, with your permission, to present this discussion to the Board of Trustees and see where it takes us."

"You don't need my permission but thank you for asking. This is one reason why I wanted to come to the

Academy. I want cadets to know what they are dealing with before something bad hits them and they don't understand or know what to do in an emergency situation. They are young but at the age of third and fourth year cadets, I was fully immersed in Spanish taking down drug lords in South Florida on a daily basis. I saw more danger by age twenty-four than most of these cadets will see as an officer over their entire career."

"I believe it, Joe. By the way, Dr. Ballenger was wide eyed when you were speaking. I don't think she could have been more impressed. She said something about your wife, Julie having nothing over you. What did she mean by that?" asked Laura.

Evidently Laura didn't know anything about Julie's background and her status as a national author. Laura just shook her head and said she would like to meet her sometime if that was all right. Joe told her to pick up her books in the college library, either at the Academy or at Connecticut College. He said Julie's books are in just about every library in the country. He said she approved that because her audience mostly included those poor girls who couldn't afford books but read everything the local library had to offer.

By the time Joe made it home, Julie said that Kate called him and wanted to thank him for a very interesting concept today. Julie also mentioned that she wanted to sit down with her again and review a few issues she needed clearing up, especially with her new book pending. Kate mentioned that it would be nice to have lunch next week with both of them. Then, she wanted both to meet the Board of Trustees at Connecticut College. Kate said it was a feather in her cap to present them both at the same time. Julie thanked her and said she would pass the message on to Joe. Kate said that she had already told the board about

Joe's offer to update all their security systems and tie it to the Coast Guard Academy with a grant from a foundation for which he had control and final say over funds approved.

Chapter 21

In Joe's weekly meeting with Rear Admiral Kelly, Joe mentioned that he wanted to take a tour of the Naval Submarine Base, located right across the Thames River, on the east side. It is located about two miles away and is connected by the Gold Star Memorial Bridge. The base is situated on 680 acres, about six times larger than the Coast Guard Academy, and has over one hundred and sixty major facilities. It's also home to fifteen nuclear submarines. Joe said that was enough to get anyone's attention. While the installation's history dates back to 1868, Naval Submarine Base New London was designated the Navy's first, permanent continental submarine base in June 1916. It serves as home to more than seventy tenant commands and sixteen attack submarines. Joe was very sure that with this much firepower under one roof, they probably had the most sophisticated security system in the entire Navy. Joe thought that was probably why the Coast Guard Academy was targeted rather than the Naval Submarine Base. He really wanted to see their safety and security setup to see how it matched up with the new system being installed at the Academy.

The Rear Admiral has met the commanding officer, Captain Larry Curtis, on a few occasions. Captain Curtis has a very similar record to the Rear Admiral with thirty-seven years of service with this being his last assignment before retirement. Just like Joe, Captain Curtis spent nine years in the enlisted ranks and in 1994, he was accepted into the Enlisted Commissioning Program and attended North Carolina State University, receiving his bachelor's degree in computer science and commissioned in 1997, three years after entering the program.

Joe thought that Captain Curtis's background was very similar to his, except Joe continued upward and at a much earlier age received his Ph.D., and is now the same rank as Captain Curtis. Joe thought he would get along fine with him. The Rear Admiral asked his assistant, Ensign Meg Olson, to set up an appointment for both the Rear Admiral and Joe to visit and take a tour of the facility. The Rear Admiral had taken a tour previously but it was several years ago and the base has increased substantially since that time.

The Rear Admiral and Joe pulled up to the front gate at the New London Submarine Base. They handed their ID's to the two guards at the gate. It was quite clear that from this point forward the security at this base looked to be superior to what the Coast Guard Academy had and Joe wanted to see if their new system would equal that of the submarine base. He was afraid it wouldn't be as effective but he thought that his facility was a university not a nuclear base. He had to let people into his complex. However, he knew that changes had to be made and he didn't have to let everyone who wanted to come in, do so. Team buses, parents, visitors, tours for potential students, and deliveries all had to be considered.

The submarine base did not have these kinds of

activities. They also had ten times the manpower in their security force simply because of the nature of their command. The submarine base had seventy commands on campus, 6,500 military personnel, more than 300 drilling reservists, 12,000 family members, 1,000 civilian employees, more than 1,000 civilian contractors, and more than 15,000 additional military personnel in and out of the facilities on campus annually. The total population of New London Connecticut is 26,550 in 2021. So, almost 45% of the population was right at this submarine base. The children attended local schools and many lived off campus as well. Between the Coast Guard Academy and the New London Submarine Base, this was a military town.

They were led to Captain Curtis's office and they exchanged pleasantries. They would take a quick tour in a golf cart and would wind up for lunch at the main cafeteria. Captain Curtis told both Joe and the Rear Admiral that he knew about the bombing incident and congratulated them on resolving the issue without destruction or loss of life. Captain Curtis told them about a recent incident where a truck deliveryman was stopped at the gate and taken into custody because of his lack of identification and discovered criminal record. Up until then, they have had no major external problems with people trying to enter the facility for clandestine reasons. However, he said, he still had the problems that any ordinary police department would have with domestic abuse, drug abuse and disorderly conduct, petty theft and a few more serious charges. He told them that you would think that they would be on their best behavior being surrounded by nuclear submarines but he smiled and said just like the comedian mentioned about his own son, "You can't fix stupid."

Joe was very impressed with Captain Cutis and his team. They exchanged cards and both he and the Rear

Admiral invited Captain Curtis and his security team to visit the Academy and give their honest appraisal of the new systems being installed based on the technology transfer from West Point. Captain Curtis said that he studied those systems and thought the systems would be more than adequate, in fact, he said that he uses several of those components, especially when reviewing incoming traffic and infrared diagnostics to ensure that what came in matched the paperwork and that nothing left any facility that was not matched electronically. Every individual entering or leaving had tracking devices assigned to the person and the vehicle.

They had a nice lunch and Joe thanked the Captain for his hospitality. Captain Curtis also wanted Joe to come back and explain in detail what they did to stop the bombing attack, without any input at the time. He said that Joe's instincts carried the day and led to the arrest of the domestic terrorists. Before Joe could even say it was a team effort, the Rear Admiral agreed with Captain Curtis and said they would have been in deep crap if Joe didn't step forward and solve the bombing. He told Captain Curtis to ask Joe what happened to the four arrestees because he was still trying to wrap his head around the fact that they were handed off quickly from Joe and the Hartford police, to the FBI and then driven to Boston into the arms of the CIA, to be placed in secure custody until they were thoroughly interrogated.

Evidently Joe and Captain Curtis were on the same page. Captain Curtis had issues previously with internal personnel. Within hours, the individual wound up with the CIA offshore from Miami. They wanted to prevent another Fort Hood incident where the officer gunned down his fellow members in a terrorist attack on the base. Captain Curtis explained in detail how he found out about the individual he had arrested and had immediately had him placed into the arms of the FBI for the handoff. It seemed that Joe and Captain Curtis were cut from the same cloth. Joe made a new friend immediately.

That afternoon, Joe found himself in the field house during baseball practice. As he told the coach, he could make practices every day but could only attend home games or away games where he could get back to campus quickly in case of an emergency. Laughing, he told the coach that this Assistant Superintendent position was getting in the way of his true calling as a pitching coach. The three left-handed pitchers were sitting with Joe in the coach's office and watching video of Andy Pettitte's pickoff move to first base. None of the three lefties knew anything about the undocumented science of pitching as a left-hander. Joe had told them his history as a lefthander including problems with everyday life including handles on refrigerator doors, scissors, and other activities that right-handers took for granted.

In a way, he said it was a blessing in certain sports. Left-handed tennis players had the advantage over right-handed opponents because there were so few of them. When a right-hander hit the ball back, in a volley, to what they believed was the opponent's backhand, the player was actually hitting the ball to the left-hander's strength, the forehand. Many commented that their opponent had the best backhand they ever saw but they were mistaken. The same with pitching, the population was only 10% left-handed. A baseball team was lucky to have two left-handers on a team out of 25 players. This team had three and Joe wanted all three to be successful.

They watched film for an hour and then went outside to the pitcher's mound. He took to the mound and had one player behind home plate, one leading off first base, and a first baseman. Joe had gone through the calculations and timing to throw to first base. He explained the moves required to get the ball over to first, attempting to deceive the runner at first but not break the rules and cause a balk. After a half hour, the three lefties started to understand what Joe was talking about. Each in turn tried the pickoff move. One was quicker than the other two so Joe had him explain what he did to the other two lefties so it came from a peer not a coach. He told them to continue to study the tape every day and especially before a game. As he said, you never knew when a team would be put into a spot where they needed an out to end a game or stop a rally. Other than striking out the batter at home, which was very difficult to do at this level, it was the surprise move that could change the outcome.

Joe recruited a few other players from the field house and had the pitchers simply pitch, one after the other to the regular teammates. After only a few batters, you could see the change in attitude and concentration from the pitchers. Joe had the runners move out six feet, then ten feet and then fifteen feet. Anyone could pick off a runner at fifteen feet but that usually meant that the runner was going to attempt to steal second. So, Joe showed them how to immediately throw the ball over and then have the first baseman throw to second for the out.

Coach Casey was watching the entire time that Joe was working with the team. He was very impressed at how Joe explained everything that he was thinking in detail, in an orderly fashion. He saw immediate progress and attention to everything that Joe was pointing out. Perhaps they were paying attention because Joe was the Assistant Superintendent of the Academy and not just a coach. But, Coach Casey didn't think so. Joe left that office as soon as he got to the diamond and he was simply Coach Traynor.

He was now simply a pitching coach for the Coast Guard Academy baseball team. Joe felt good about that.

As they were finishing up, Julie walked up to the field with Bella and Annie in her stroller. They waved to Joe and he went over and gave all of them a hug. He told Julie that they would be done in a few minutes and he would walk back with them. It was a beautiful day. It was mid-March and getting warmer every day. Their first home game was on Sunday, March 20th against Clark University from Worcester, Massachusetts, not that far from the Academy. The game he really wanted to see was against MIT, Saturday, April 2nd at home. He wondered if the old MIT coach actually remembered him from his one semester so many years ago. He couldn't wait to dress up the three girls in their Batgirl uniforms. He had to be careful since he was one of the top administrators. He would bring them to the women's first softball team home game and let them sit in the stands with him simply as an administrator and fan. He thought Julie would definitely approve that as a first step before bringing them to the baseball field.

The women's softball team's first home game was also against Clark University but on Saturday, March 15th, the day before the baseball home opener. It was a 1:00 p.m. start, so they hurried up and went directly to the softball field where they met the O'Neil's with Emma in her full dress Bat Girl uniform. They all sat together as friends and cheered on the team. This was old hat for Bella who already saw the Waterford high school girl's team win. She was hooked and Joe was thrilled. The softball coach came up to them and thanked them for their attendance and asked Joe if the two older girls could sit with them in the dugout for part of the game. Julie thought that was great especially after seeing smiles on Bella and Emma's faces.

They sat for the first few innings but got restless as seven-year-olds tended to do so they went back and sat with their parents and had some snacks and drinks, watching to the end of the game. Julie asked the O'Neil's over for pizza after the game and they made a day of it. The ladies won 10-5.

Sunday came and they went to early Mass so Joe could be down with the team by noon. It also had a 1:00 p.m. start. Joe was nervous. He had never coached a game before. He sat in the dugout with Coach Casey and all they talked about was baseball. Joe was in seventh heaven as they say. This team was very well coached. They didn't need any left-handed relievers for the game. It was already 14-3 by the end of the fourth inning and the Coast Guard was on fire. Three home runs, two were back-to-back. Coach Casey knows what he's doing. From William and Mary to here, it's starting to rub off, Joe thought. The little girls had their pictures taken by the fans who thought they were so cute. Joe never asked for them to be Bat Girls but Coach Casey picked up on it and asked Bella and Emma if they would help out between innings by picking up all the discarded bats and equipment and putting the articles into the dugout. He winked at Joe and he smiled with a thanks. Joe wondered if they would ever need his left-handed crew. He would hang in there just like he did when he pitched at MIT. He waited and waited and then proved himself to the coach. He was trusted in tough situations. He needed to convey that to his lefties. They were freshmen or first year cadets and had to wait their turn just like everyone else. The Rear Admiral showed up with his wife, Ellen, just like at yesterday's women's game. It was a good start to both their seasons. Joe was glad that the administrators were not just the administrators but were part of the daily lives of these cadets. Meg Olson waved to

Joe and Julie and gave a thumbs up. She attended every game. He saw Laura Chavez at both games as well. He was very happy to have her as a friend. Things could have gone very wrong in the beginning after her devious move but she came around and he now counted her as a friend who wanted to make the Academy better as well.

Chapter 22

It was late one night and Joe was starting to outline his week coming up. He had a meeting with the Rear Admiral. He wanted to attend a few classes at Connecticut College. He would meet again with Captain Chavez's advanced Spanish class to discuss a possible outside class project. He and Laura had already discussed the potential value to both Connecticut College and the Academy. The project would be a simulation of a takedown of a cartel in south Florida. It would include speakers of Spanish at all levels. Joe would take the place of the uneducated drug mule being interrogated. They would immediately see the difference from what they were learning in class compared to what would be in front of them in a year or two after they were commissioned and serving in south Florida. They needed to be prepared.

Joe also wanted to meet the professor for Russian. He wanted to know if the professor spoke Chechen as well. If not, perhaps he could review the differences. To Joe it was as simple as a person from Birmingham, Alabama talking to someone living in upstate New York. To the professor it may be totally different. Joe learned languages on an everyday basis. When he hit the classroom for formal training and education, he was already prepared to learn. Again, to Joe, it was like someone who learned to play guitar after being self-taught and then later on, receiving guitar lessons from a professional. The guitar player could play very well, if talented, but may not know progression from chord to chord but could pick it up quickly with the right instructor.

Julie also was having lunch with Rear Admiral Kelly's wife, Ellen, at Connecticut College. She would meet their daughter, Grace, and discuss literature and books and her upcoming book release and new class at the college. After lunch, she would drop by the president's office. Julie had several ideas on how to develop a real hands-on course that would bring a student from the initial stages of thinking about writing a book to actually learn the complete process ending up with a published book by the time the student graduated from Connecticut College with a bachelor's degree in English. Julie also wanted to target young women of color and other speakers of other languages to develop literature and books related to their own culture and in some case in their own language. Julie had talked to Joe about this and asked if he would mind if she spoke to Mary Evans about a possible funding stream to ensure success. She would bring it up to Kate first to see if there would be an interest.

Daylight savings came and went on March 13th and the days were getting longer. The science says that you gain one minute of daylight for every day after the first day of winter, starting on December 21st. Dusk was around 4:30 p.m. on December 21st, so you would gain 54 minutes in 54 days and gain an hour back for day light savings time. Now, dusk began around 6:24 p.m. and kept gaining one minute per day until summer began. Games that were normally started early because of the setting sun could now either begin later or at least the game wouldn't be called due to darkness. At 1:00 p.m. in December it got dark very early but in the beginning of April, all the games started at 1:00 p.m. and could be played without worry.

It was now Saturday, April 2nd and Joe's big day had finally arrived. The men's baseball team would be playing Joe's old team MIT or the Massachusetts Institute of Technology. It was funny that a university, always ranked in the very top of universities internationally would play sports at a Division III level. Sports were important to the students but no one could keep up academically at MIT or for that matter the Coast Guard Academy if they had to follow a rigorous Division I schedule, travelling across the country with little class attendance. Division I athletes had visions of playing professionally while MIT and Coast Guard Academy students had visions of curing cancer or saving lives like with Hurricane Katrina. There was a big difference. The biggest difference was that Division III athletes weren't on a par with Division I athletes physically, but academically and intelligence, they had a better understanding of what they were doing, not by rote but by study and learning the game. Picking off someone would be equally challenging at any level though.

Joe was there around 11:00 a.m. in uniform. Julie would be there at game time with Bella and Annie and Samantha would bring Emma. Sean was tied up off campus that day and wouldn't make the game but had wished Joe well earlier on Friday before he left for his off-campus meeting.

The game started right at 1:00 p.m., and the Coast Guard scored four runs in the bottom of the first inning, starting with back-to-back homeruns. They were cruising and were ahead 6-2 by the top of the 6th inning. MIT had two outs and runners on first and third base. A left-handed batter was coming to the plate. He was one of their best hitters so it was crucial to pitch around him if possible. Joe always dreamed about his 7-6 win for MIT against the Coast Guard Academy in the bottom of the 7th inning, when he came in for relief and picked off the runner at first and didn't have to throw home.

Coach Brian Casey called time and signaled for the bullpen for his lefty. Frankie Santiago, a freshman from the south Bronx, came running in and took the ball from Coach Casey. The coach said to him, "Remember what Joe taught you. It's all good. No pressure. Let's see what you learned."

That last thought spurred on Frankie and as he took the ball, he nodded toward Joe standing by the dugout. Frankie took his eight warm up tosses in the stretch and not a full windup. Joe loved Frankie. Frankie was as cool as a cucumber. He grew up two blocks from Yankee Stadium, which was Mecca as far as Joe Traynor was concerned. Joe looked into the stands and saw Julie who waved to him and then saw Frankie's parents sitting down a row from Julie. This was their first game that they attended at the Academy. There was a buzz in the air.

The left-handed batter came into the right side of the batter's box. A hit would score a run. A homerun would make the game close at 6-5 instead of 6-2. Joe thought that he remembered being very nervous before his first pitch. Joe hoped that Frankie wouldn't need a first pitch to home plate. With two outs, Frankie knew that the coach called him in not to pitch to the batter but to see if he could pick off the runner on first. Just like Joe, way back when, the first pitch wouldn't be to home but to first base.

Frankie had practiced the move the most and this was his time to shine. The runner was off the base about 12 feet near the cut out in the grass. Everyone thought Frankie would go right after the batter with a strike down the middle to get ahead. The left-handed batter loved to hit left-handers and was crowding the plate. Joe thought for sure if he did go home, he would hit the batter being as wild as he was. They were working on that as well. The umpire gave him the go ahead to start after throwing his warm-up pitches. Frankie walked around the mound and looked at the two runners and his infielders. He stared into the dugout and nodded to Joe. Joe smiled. He knew what was coming.

Frankie took his time staring into home and moved his bodyweight toward home, turned sideways and then whipped the ball to first after immediately turning and was diagonal to first. In less than Joe's calculated .69 seconds at 60 miles an hour. It was more in the 70 miles an hour range. The runner at first hesitated for a split second and dove back into first but was too late. He was out by a foot and a half, clearly. The umpire rung him up and Frankie pounded his glove and yelled at the top of his lungs. He did it. His parents started hooting and hollering. Joe was smiling from ear to ear. Frankie ended the inning without a throw home, just like Joe once did a long time ago.

That pickoff move took the wind right out of MIT's sails. The final score was 9-4. Frankie didn't throw one pitch home. He didn't get the win nor did he get a save. All he got was the eternal gratitude of the Assistant Superintendent of the Coast Guard Academy, otherwise known as the pitching coach. Coach Brian Casey just shook his head and smiled. Joe made his point in spades. Joe looked over into the MIT dugout and saw the coach shake his head as the runner walked back after getting picked off. After the game, Joe walked over to the MIT bench and saw his old coach. Smitty, as he was affectionately called, looked up at Joe and smiled. He said,

"I should have known it was you." He got up and shook Joe's hand. "How long has it been, Joe, about twenty years?"

"Just about," said Joe. "I can't believe you remembered."

"Not remember the only pitcher to get a recorded save without getting a called ball or strike? Those are things you remember. As soon as your pitcher threw over without a second thought, it all came back to me. What the hell are you doing here?"

Joe went on to explain that he was now Assistant Superintendent at the Academy and Captain in the Coast Guard. Joe said, as always, his first love is baseball, and he has been working with the left-handed pitchers to perfect their pickoff move.

"It is obviously working," he said.

Coach Casey came over and said to Smitty, "Do you want him back or do I get to keep him?"

Smitty said, "You can keep him but he can't show up for our next game with you. Fool me once shame on you, fool me twice shame on me. I'll be looking for it, Traynor," he said and laughed.

Joe told him whenever he was in town to stop in and Joe would treat him to dinner. All kidding aside, Smitty was quite proud of that 18-year-old kid from Troy, New York who pitched for him for only one semester and still held the record for pickoff moves.

Walking back after cleaning up after the game, Brian said to Joe that he would remember that play forever. He couldn't believe that it worked so perfectly. He also couldn't believe that Joe figured out mathematically a game that no one could figure out mathematically. He asked Joe to go over the data again with him during the week. Joe said sure and Brian thanked him for being part of the team. It was clear that Joe was a lot more than an administrator.

Joe and Julie walked home with Annie and Bella in tow. Several of the women from the softball team came over to say hello to Bella and Julie and congratulate Joe on the win. Annie was sound asleep in her stroller. Joe waved to Ensign Meg Olson and Captain Laura Chavez on the way home. They both gave thumbs up to Joe. Since Sean was away, Sam and Emma came with them to their house. It looked like another pizza and wing night for the family. Julie smiled at Joe and asked him if his wish finally came true. Joe smiled and said to have Frankie, a left-handed 18-year-old freshman from the south Bronx, near Yankee Stadium, perfect his pick-off move was more than he could ever ask for. The problem was once it got out of the bag, they would have to try the other two left-handers and couldn't just pitch to a left-handed batter. It made it more complicated said Joe but he said the mathematics stayed the same. If the runner was ten feet or more away from first base, then they always had a chance to pick off the runner.

It was bright and early Monday morning. It was almost three weeks to Easter on April 17th this year. Tillie would be flying in on Good Friday and staying for two weeks. Julie wanted her to stay longer but didn't want to impose on her. Tillie was almost seventy now and it crossed Julie's mind that she may not have Tillie forever. She wanted to make sure that they continued their loving relationship and always would error on the side of Tillie's feelings. After all, Tillie took care of her since she was eight years old. Julie owed her everything. Joe felt the same way.

Joe entered his office at 8:00 a.m., punctual as usual. Meg Olson stopped him in the hallway as he was heading for coffee. "Joe, what a great game yesterday. A little bird told me you were working with the pitchers especially

Frankie and the other two. That pickoff move was a thing of beauty. They had no idea that it was coming. He never even threw home."

"That was the plan," said Joe. "If he threw home, I was afraid he'd throw the ball over the backstop," he said and laughed. "Left-handers are kind of wild. I should know, pitching in the same spot, almost twenty years ago for MIT."

"So, I heard from Brian," said Meg. "Congratulations. It looks like we'll have a good season if we can get this Covid behind us and don't cancel any games."

"That's for sure," said Joe. "Is the Rear Admiral in yet?" he asked Meg.

"Just came in the backdoor. Give him fifteen minutes to start his day and get his coffee."

Joe nodded and walked back to his office. He called Laura about setting up a meeting on Thursday, one of the longer class days. He wanted to meet the professor teaching Russian and the president and then would come down to her classroom as it was going on. She said fine and she too congratulated him on the win. She said she hoped nothing else would happen this spring that would pull him away from the baseball schedule. She said they have not had a winning record in years and at 8-1 so far this spring, and in first place in the NEWMAC, they could win the conference if they got by the proverbial favorite, Babson College. They haven't beaten Babson College in ten years so this would be the year. The conference winner would represent the New England states in the NCAA Division III championships. Babson College, like Ithaca, Union College, and RPI had great sports programs as well as academics. Coast Guard cadets were more oriented toward serving in the military and those schools produced "jocks." Beating them all would be quite the achievement for Coach Casey but they could do it.

The Rear Admiral knocked on Joe's door and said he was ready. Joe got his notes together and walked down to his office.

"Glad I was there for the win Saturday, Joe." He said. "Couldn't believe the pickoff move from Frankie Santiago. Is that your doing?" he asked with a smile.

"It was all Frankie after I pointed out to all three left-handers that if they wanted to graduate on time from the Coast Guard Academy, they better be pretty good at mathematics."

"How so?" said Kelly.

Joe explained the entire process to him about going to first base and the calculations required making that move effectively and the body movements needed to pull it off. The Rear Admiral's eyes just lit up and shook his head.

"You mean they actually understood what the hell you were talking about? That must be a new first," he said.

"Evidently, Frankie did or he wouldn't have nailed that guy at first. My job is officially done," Joe said and laughed.

"I guess you're a pretty damn good coach according to Brian."

"Well, that's good news," said Joe.

"Joe, I need to call on you once again about a universal problem that appears to be in the making. Our intelligence from Washington just came in and it looks like someone is targeting military academies for harm. The Admiral knows all about your role in solving our bombing at the Academy but there are other issues, and I need you to be part of a team that represents all the academies including West Point, Annapolis, the Air Force Academy, us and the Merchant Marine Academy in Kings Point, New York. Intelligence is pointing to domestic terrorists including white supremacist and paramilitary groups formed over the last few years. They seem to hate our military academies since we produce officers. Most of these militia type groups are formed by non officers or noncoms as we say," said the Rear Admiral.

Joe said he would be honored to be part of the group. The Rear Admiral told him that there would be a meeting a week before Easter at Kings Point for Joe, West Point personnel and the Merchant Marine administrators. Annapolis and the Air Force Academy would attend the meeting by Zoom. The other three are close enough to get together in person. The Rear Admiral told him the types of people who would be attending. Joe reminded him that not only that he's a Captain in the Coast Guard but he also serves as a FBI Special Agent and Homeland Security officer as well. As far as the Coast Guard, Joe reminded him that he commanded an MSRT or Maritime Security Response Team, a tactical unit that specializes in maritime counter terrorism and high-risk law enforcement. MSRT are trained to board and secure vessels including those held by terrorists holding hostages. He said that's why he knew what to do immediately about the bombs planted on campus. He said there are several MSRT teams across the country at various ports including New York City and Boston that could be called on for immediate help. A terrorist is a terrorist he said. Joe also said that when they went to West Point, he studied the various military academies and their physical locations. The Coast Guard Academy was the only military academy that had another college right across the street from its front gate. This caused additional problems because most of the Academy cadets wound up taking courses at Connecticut College, especially since there were no language requirements at the Academy. He said that's one reason he wanted to look into moving some foreign language courses back onto the Academy campus to increase safety and security. He reminded the Rear Admiral that he would fund the Connecticut College safety and security systems to be compatible with the new upgraded systems that were installed at the Academy with the grants from Mary Evan's Teresa Trust Fund.

They came together and did an outline of what they both believed the Academy needed to get out of the committee to benefit their cadets and their facilities. It appeared that Joe and West Point were both way ahead of the other academies and Joe had the funds to upgrade almost anything they needed. They were in a very good position he told the Rear Admiral. Kelly said he was very grateful for being the beneficiary of those funds. It made the Coast Guard Academy safer and more secure but there never was enough security if intentions were bad. Anyone could get to anyone, at anytime, anywhere. That was just the way it was in 2022.

Chapter

Chapter **23**

Julie met Ellen Kelly and her daughter Grace at Connecticut College for lunch. There was a nice sandwich shop around the corner that catered to students and faculty. The owner was a friend of Ellen's so she had called ahead and her friend set aside a table in the back where they could dine unobstructed. Grace's class ended at 11:45 a.m. so she met them at the restaurant. Julie walked in and saw Ellen in the back, waved and walked to her table. Julie was sure that Ellen remembered who she was because they had met at the restaurant a few weeks ago when Julie's best friend Maddie was in town. Ellen got up and gave Julie a hug, clearing up that she was well aware of who she was. Grace came in and waved to her mother and made her way to the back. She had another class at 2:00 p.m. so Ellen ordered both their sandwiches and immediately asked Julie what she would like. She had the same as them making it easy.

Julie said, "I have a two hour window and then I have to get back to the babysitter watching Annie."

"Who is your babysitter, Julie?" asked Ellen.

"I have a very reliable caring sitter named Joe," she said

and laughed. "The price is right too," she added.

Ellen laughed as did Grace. Julie said, "Joe wanted a 50/50 marriage and this is what he got," she smiled. "I make more than him anyway."

"Does he know that?" asked Ellen laughing.

"He's well aware," she said.

Julie turned to Grace and asked her to tell her all about herself since Julie had never met her before. Grace was a junior at Connecticut College. She lived on campus only two blocks from her parents. Obviously, her father was Joe's commanding officer and the Superintendent of the Coast Guard Academy to Joe's Assistant Superintendent position. Grace was an English major and wanted to find out if she could fit into Julie's upcoming class in the fall and would it count toward her major.

Grace said, "Please don't hold it against me being named Grace Kelly. My parents had a wonderful sense of humor," as she turned to her mother.

Grace Kelly was a very famous Hollywood actress in the 1950s. She married Prince Rainier III of Monaco in 1956 and was the darling of society for years. She was also drop dead gorgeous as was this current version of Grace, now staring at Julie.

"Joe and I are very close to the Talbots down in Islamorada. Joan is in charge of the facility and is an officer in the Coast Guard. Her daughter is Lucy, short for Lucille, being named after her maternal grandmother. She hates both Lucille and Lucy so I started calling her Luce when she was a child. She likes the name Luce better. You can meet her early this summer. She is transferring to the Coast Guard Academy from a full cross-country scholarship at the University of Miami. We are thrilled to death. Maybe she can start being our kids' babysitter just like I was for her."

"Wow, that's great," said Grace. "So, you know where I'm coming from?" said Grace.

"I could have been named after my grandmother who raised me, Matilda, or Tillie for short. Joe thought I would name Annie after her but I said I wouldn't do that to my kid," said Julie. "Instead, Annie is named after my mother who passed away a number of years ago. My grandmother raised me since I was eight years old. I met Joe when I was in 5th grade at Key Largo Elementary School at age eleven. Joe walked in as a rookie first year sailor at eighteen years old, turning nineteen, with Joan Talbot as his first boss. They were there for career day, selling the Coast Guard as a career. Talk about wet behind the years," she said. "Want to hear the story or do you want to discuss my class? All my books are based on this experience growing up poor in the Florida Keys as a livelong Conch. Those lessons are in my books, the trilogy, *A Girl's Story.*"

Both Ellen and Grace were shocked to hear Julie tell her story, unabashed and unashamed of how she grew up, went to Brown University on full scholarship, with an MFA degree and a published first book before graduation. At the end of the conversation, Julie said, "Now I want to hear about you Grace and then you Ellen. This sisterhood is just beginning. I'll bring in Luce and we can be the *Four Musketeers*," she said and laughed.

Ellen said, "Julie, that is quite a remarkable story. I can see why you are married to Joe and no other. I can see how your determination informed all your decisions and helped you through the tough times. Now that you are successful, do you look back and think about anything you might change?" asked Ellen.

"Well the only thing I would change is growing up poor. That really sucks. You don't know it as a kid. You don't know you're poor because you have the love of your grandmother and then Joe but yes, poverty sucks. That's why I'm doing this course in hope that I can help some other poor young ladies who are here on scholarship because of poverty but have so much more to offer." She added, "Joe is doing the exact same thing at the Academy as we speak."

They ended their lunch and both Ellen and Grace asked if they could do it again and Julie said of course. "I have to get back to my babysitter so he can go back to work and save the world," Julie said with a laugh. She meant it though. Both Ellen and Grace understood the bond between Joe and Julie that would never be broken.

Julie got back a little before 1:30 p.m. to relieve Joe. He had a few meetings and then had to go to a Russian class at Connecticut College to see how they interacted just like the Spanish classes that he had already attended. He was concerned about the lack of Chechen in the Russian classroom. There were a growing population of Chechen people arriving in the United States, landing in the greater Boston area, Miami, and Orlando and of course, New York City that had a large Russian population already.

Joe got to the classroom just before the bell rang. He walked up to the back of the amphitheater and sat down. No one was near him for several rows. He felt kind of inconspicuous at the moment. He had spoken to the Chair of the Slavic Studies program at Connecticut College but had never met him. As class began, Joe was reading the college brochure outlining Slavic Studies. It basically stated, "Welcome to Slavic Studies! Our department is known for its innovative course offerings, close mentoring relationships between students and faculty, active co-curricular programming, frequent engagement with community partners, and excursions to nearby cities and sites abroad. We take pride in our faculty's reputation for excellence in teaching, and we are especially proud of our outstanding, accomplished students." It went on, "Anchored in a rigorous Russian language program, our curriculum is designed to bring students to advanced-level of proficiency in Russian over four years. Students and faculty work together for campus-wide events that showcase our passion for the cultures and cuisines of the Slavic world."

Joe was very attentive to Dr. Peter Ivanoff, chair of the department, and senior lecturer as he began his class. He was a graduate of the University of Sofia, and held advanced degrees from the University of Chicago, including an A.B.D. in Slavic Studies. The University of Chicago was one of the most premier institutions in the country.

The professor noticed Joe in the back and nodded to him. He asked Joe if he was the guest for the day and he asked him in Russian. Everyone turned around to see Joe. He was dressed casually and wouldn't be mistaken as the Assistant Superintendent of the Academy. Joe looked around the classroom before speaking. He noticed that half the class was made up of Academy cadets in their uniforms. Joe answered in Russian without any hesitation. It kind of surprised the professor who smiled at Joe and welcomed him. He asked Joe if he would mind speaking to the class since he now knew his status at the Academy. They went back and forth with introductions and Joe walked down to the front and began to sit on the desk with his feet dangling down. They carried on a long conversation and the students looked spellbound.

Every one of the cadets had heard about Joe Traynor but to see him in person, like this, in a classroom, answering questions in Russian, was truly amazing. The professor asked Joe if he would mind telling the class how he learned Russian. Joe went through his initiation into the language by explaining that by arresting Russian gangsters in Miami, all belonging to the Russian mob, he picked up the language. He told the students about the large population of Russian and Chechen immigrants in the region. Joe went into a dialogue in Chechen, which was similar to Russian but was not exactly the same. The words were similar but the expressions were as different as that Alabama man talking to someone from Brooklyn. Joe explained that difference. He said he had to learn Russian because of the long-term connection of Russian mafia members with Cuban drug runners.

He explained that he was fluent in Spanish but in many cases, drug interventions were between Russian mafia types and Cuban drug runners coming into the shores of Miami and further south into the Florida Keys. Joe asked the professor if he could share a story in Russian with the students on how he needed to converse with Russian mafia types in order to protect this country. The professor waved his hand and sat down giving Joe the floor. Joe spoke for about fifteen minutes and by the time he was done everyone was focused, attentive and mesmerized that they too could be in his shoes in a few short years. Joe mentioned for the non-cadets, they could certainly transfer to the Coast Guard Academy, get 100% room, board and tuition and be sitting right in this same seat, next year for free.

Joe smiled and apologized for the recruitment effort but they knew he was very sincere. The students clapped and told him thank you in Russian. When the bell sounded to end class, Joe shook hands with the professor and the students started to surround him and ask questions. Joe said he had a meeting to attend but would be glad to come back any time to talk to them, either in class or in the student union at their convenience. He gave them all his cards and ran out of them. He said, "Call me."

Dr. Ivanoff was very pleased to meet Joe and said so. He couldn't believe how down to earth Joe was. He said he had met Rear Admiral Kelly at a meet and greet at Connecticut College and he was 100% military all the way. Joe told him that he was 100% military all the way but handled situations differently. Joe never commanded anyone to do anything that he wouldn't do himself and that was a fact.

On the way back, Joe thought he got enough information from Captain Chavez for Spanish and from Dr. Ivanoff for Russian. He didn't need to visit the class in Chinese. He wasn't as fluent as he needed to be. If he attended that class, he wanted to be in charge of what he was willing to share in that language. He just wasn't ready yet. Joe did tell Dr. Ivanoff that he needed to bone up on Chechen because this was the new immigration wave into the country from Eastern Europe. The Russian and Chechen gangs tried to get them as soon as they landed but to Joe's thinking, if they were there first, welcoming them in their own language while warning them of the dangers of these gangs, there would be far less violence and danger within these communities. He also wanted to recruit them into the Coast Guard as speakers of other languages before they entered the Academy.

Joe headed home. He cancelled the meeting that he was going to attend right after class because he wouldn't have enough time to pack and prepare for the next day. He left for his meeting at the Merchant Marine Academy in Kings Point, New York, the following morning. The trip was only 125 miles and a little over two hours away. He would head west toward New York, getting on I-95S in Waterford, Connecticut for 118 miles getting off at South

Service Road in Lake Success, New York. He would take exit 33 from I-495E on the Long Island Expressway for about 2 miles, following Community Drive and East Shore Road to Wildwood Drive in Kings Point. He would check in at the gate and then head to the designated meeting area. Unlike the Coast Guard Academy, they had overnight accommodations because they were at the water's edge of the Long Island Sound with nothing else around them for miles. Joe would be meeting with Vice Admiral, Jim Bonesteel, the Superintendent of the U.S. Merchant Marine Academy. He was another lifer, spending forty years in the Merchant Marines and was a 1978 graduate of the Merchant Marine Academy. They would also meet with Colonel Keenan Smith, head of security for West Point along with his assistant, Lieutenant Gloria Samuels, of the strategy and planning department. Joe had already spent several days with Colonel Smith but didn't know Lieutenant Samuels. He thought the meeting should be interesting but as he was well aware, the Coast Guard Academy was the only military academy that had another college right across the street from their institution. The Army, Navy, Air Force and Merchant Marines could simply plan for their own facilities but Joe's cadets were running back and forth between classes at both institutions.

Joe left around 9:00 a.m. after seeing Bella off to school, eating breakfast and holding Annie while Julie got ready for her day. She would be fine for the three days while Joe was gone. He did ask Meg Olson if she could check on Julie once in a while and see if she needed anything. He asked Kim Matz to do the same since they became friends. Kim said she would come by that night with an Italian meal for everyone. Her husband was busy at tax time. Mid-April would prove to be very busy. Joe asked Kim's husband if he would handle their taxes this year because it became very complicated very quickly with the move to the Academy, Joe's increase in pay and a check just handed to Julie as an advance on her book. In addition, Tillie would be coming for Easter on April 17th this year. She would arrive on Good Friday and Joe's birthday was April 16th as well. He had a game that day at home. They were playing their rival, Babson College, who won every game against the Academy over the last several years. It would be a big present for Joe if the Academy won. Easter was Sunday, April 17th. The Easter bunny had to show up for Bella. She was worried because they had moved from Tavernier and she wasn't sure that the Easter bunny got the change of address card that Julie mailed to the Easter bunny, with Joe's office address. Joe had laughed when he got it.

Joe settled in after meeting everyone. They had lunch and he went to his assigned room for a while to make calls. They would have a short meeting from 2:00 p.m. to 5:00 p.m. and then dinner would be brought in for the guests. Everyone got the same intelligence that Joe got from Rear Admiral Kelly. It was believed that white supremacist militia groups would target all five academies over the next year. Joe already solved one targeting issue with the bombing. They also attended a simulation at West Point and installed millions of dollars into the safety and security of the Coast Guard Academy. Joe had also allocated special systems to upgrade security at Connecticut College. He needed to discuss this with the group to see if they had anything to add. Yes, their students attended other colleges to take specific courses not offered by their own academy but these institutions were miles away from the academies, not right across the street.

Dinner went well. Everyone seemed to like each other, which went a long way when forming an alliance and group to combat anything. After all the talk, Joe felt that the intelligence was a little weak. Just saying that they heard they would be targeted meant nothing in the way of trying to protect each academy. Joe felt that the Merchant Marine Academy was in the most vulnerable position due to its location on the Long Island Sound. It could basically be attacked by land or sea. The Coast Guard Academy was in the same position but every foot of the Thames River leading up to the Academy and the Navy Submarine Base was fully protected because there were nuclear submarines in the base. The firepower of the Navy alone should have been a detriment. Now that the Coast Guard Academy got its act together, Joe felt secure, at least on campus. He wasn't in charge of Connecticut College's security even though he upgraded the college's systems and attached those systems to the Academy. Paying for those systems out of his largesse from Mary Evans didn't mean he had any say over the college. It did worry him, especially with Academy students on their campus every day, only feet away across the street.

Joe shared all his upgrades with the Merchant Marine Academy staff and was assisted by the Colonel from the Army at West Point. Unless they got substantial funding to increase protection at their institution, there wasn't much they could do to upgrade their systems. If Joe had more funds, he would have mentioned it but he remained quiet on the topic. He had enough on his plate at the Coast Guard Academy. He would inform Rear Admiral Kelly that the meeting was informative but too general to react to at this time. They already knew about white supremacist militia groups in Connecticut. Joe made sure of that during the bombing and immediately after, shipping his arrestees to the CIA. However, the four that were arrested as terrorists had no idea about the funding of their group.

They appeared to be mid-level at best. They were the muscle for the group it appeared but they were still dangerous and could have killed many cadets and personnel if the bombs were not found and set off to do harm.

Joe drove home late Friday morning, arriving around 1:30 p.m. meeting Julie and Annie at the door. Julie said that the time went by very rapidly and she was closing in on almost 60% of her new book. Between naps and walks with Annie on the campus at the Academy, she dove into her book without interruption and she was pleased. They made plans for dinner out as a special treat. Bella loved seafood, so it was back to the New London seafood restaurant that they took her to before, *On The Waterfront Restaurant and Bar*.

Chapter 24

"Joe, we'll take the SUV to pick up Tillie at the airport so we all can go. Is that all right?" asked Julie.

"Sure, either that or my Coast Guard vehicle which probably won't have enough room with Tillie's luggage," said Joe.

Tillie was flying into the Groton-New London airport, arriving at 1:15 p.m. It was Good Friday, April 15th. She'd be staying for about two weeks, going home at the end of April. Both Julie and Joe missed Tillie. Tillie was Julie's grandmother but was her real mother since she was eight years old. Tillie semi-adopted Joe after meeting him when he was eighteen years old and had invited Julie for a tour of his Coast Guard ship with her guardian. At the time, Julie was in 5th grade and eleven years old. Joe took them to dinner after the tour to the nicest restaurant in Key Largo on his last dime. Tillie was well aware of this and Tillie and Julie became his second family away from home, next to the Talbots. Even though Tillie didn't speak Spanish, she and Bella were closer than close. Bella loved Tillie and only spoke English when Tillie was around. That was quite an accomplishment. Joe was fluent in Spanish and Julie was trying but whenever Tillie appeared, Bella only spoke English to her. Tillie hasn't seen the baby, Annie, since her baptism a few months ago.

Joe pulled up and parked in the lot. It was actually smaller than the Albany International Airport that Joe was so familiar with. Joe had laughed at the international part since internationally, its planes only flew to Montreal out of the country. They all got out of Julie's SUV and she placed Annie in a larger stroller that actually fit her now. She was so tiny they had to pad the seat with blankets so she wouldn't roll around. They met Tillie at the baggage carousel. To be funny, Joe pulled out a small sign from his jacket that had in large print "Mrs. Tillie Carpenter." As she came down the stairs to the baggage area, she saw the family and started to laugh at Joe's sign.

"I guess I really am a bigwig, huh?" she said and laughed. Joe handed her the sign and went over with her to pick out her two bags. She didn't bring a lot but it was always easier just to check her luggage in at the curb rather than carry it on and jam it into the overhead compartment. Someone always opened the overhead luggage compartment and things went flying. She sat in her seat and waited for the luggage onslaught to end before she even tried to walk down the aisle of the plane. She pointed out her bags and Joe grabbed them and they headed back to the SUV. Julie had her arm tightly around her and Bella was grabbing her legs. Joe had the stroller but couldn't handle Annie and the luggage so he gave the stroller back to Julie and picked up the bags. They'd be home by 2:00 p.m. Julie would help Tillie unpack while Joe watched television with Bella and Annie took her nap. Julie wanted to stay in instead of going out to dinner because it was Good Friday. So, Julie had already made macaroni and cheese, garlic bread and a salad, all meatless for Good

Friday.

Tillie went to bed early now that she was nearing seventy and travel took its toll on her. They only had three bedrooms so Tillie slept with Bella in a regular size bed in her room. It was a small double bed but it would do since Bella got lost in it anyway. They wanted her to be treated like a big girl and got her the bigger brand-new bed when they moved to New London. Bella was thrilled she said as long as Grammy didn't snore. Everyone laughed.

Tillie knew the next two days would be a strain so she wanted a good night's rest. Joe's birthday was Saturday and he had to be at his game against Babson College by noon. Julie, Tillie and the kids would get down to the game for a 1:00 p.m. start. Bella and Annie would wear their "Bat Girl" uniforms. Julie would pick up Joe's birthday cake in the morning and put up some birthday decorations. Joe loved steak and the grill was all set for the season so she stopped at the butcher shop and picked up some T-bone steaks, Joe's favorite. She'd make mashed potatoes and asparagus another of his favorites. She invited a few friends over after an early 5:00 p.m. dinner for drinks, cake and snacks for Joe's birthday. If they won that day it would make his day complete. If they didn't Joe probably wouldn't want to celebrate. She'd play it by ear. After all, the next day, Sunday, was Easter, and that would be another full day running around for Easter eggs and finding the Easter baskets from the Easter bunny. Julie had already planned to go out for Easter to their favorite restaurant, *On The Waterfront Restaurant and Bar*. The restaurant had a traditional Easter buffet with ham and all the fixings and you could order off the menu as well. Joe would appreciate the gesture. Tillie had never been there but Julie had already told her the plans and she thought that would be great, especially since Julie was treating everyone. He would have an excellent weekend, an excellent birthday, and no bills.

Joe was up bright and early. Julie said she had a few errands and took Tillie and Bella with her. Joe watched Annie until they got back. He made breakfast and watched the news. Annie was restless so he put her down on the carpet and played with her. She kept throwing every toy that Joe gave her back at him. He smiled and figured out that she was going to be right-handed. There goes his plans for the best left-handed softball pitcher to ever play the game. Bella is right-handed as well as every nine out of ten human beings. *Oh well,* he thought.

Julie left everything in the car so Joe wouldn't see the decorations or the steaks that Julie picked up. The cake was on the floor of the back seat, so she hoped Joe walked to the game. She would tell him to walk if he decided to take her car. He usually left his military vehicle in the Academy parking lot on the weekends so it wouldn't tie up their driveway. Joe opened the door when they got back around 11:30 a.m. He was already dressed in his baseball uniform and had his equipment bag on the front porch ready to go. He told her that he was getting anxious and she knew how he was when he has something planned. He has to do it right away or God forbid something terrible would happen. She kissed him and said, "Happy Birthday" and told him that she had a surprise for him later that night. He smiled and winked at her and asked if he could get his surprise right now. His mind wandered from baseball to something else. She smiled and shook her head as she turned around and saw Tillie and Bella gathering near the stairs. She laughed and so did he. He said goodbye and he would see them at the game.

Joe walked over to the campus which took him less than five minutes. As he walked by the front gate, he nodded at the guard on duty. The guard wished him well and told him to beat Babson. Joe smiled and waved and walked down the road to the baseball field. It was now 11:45 a.m. and most of the players were either on the field or getting ready in the field house. The Babson College bus had just pulled in and parked over in the visitor's bus lot. The players and coaches were getting off the bus and walking toward the field house. Most of them were already dressed for the game. They probably needed a bathroom break. The trip was just over one hundred miles and about an hour and a half. Joe waved at the coaches and they waved back.

Sean O'Neil was walking down toward Joe and said hello. He said his wife, Sam, and daughter, Emma, would be down for the start of the game. Before Joe even asked, Sean said Emma was all decked out in her uniform. He laughed. Joe walked into the field house to talk to Brian Casey before the game. This game was important. They hadn't beaten Babson since forever and if they did today, they would be in first place in the NEWMAC and would be the favorite in the tournament that would start in late April. The Academy's record was the best in many years and they were tied with Babson for the lead of all nine teams in the league. It was now about 12:30 p.m. and they started out to the field.

Julie just got there with Tillie and the girls and they were sitting with Sam and Emma. Most of the women's softball team was there as well to cheer on the men. Their game against Babson would take place on Tuesday. It would have been tomorrow but it was Easter so it was rescheduled. The men supported the women as well since they all would be the same rank of Ensign upon graduation and would work together equally. There was no better way to show that loyalty than right at the ball field. Julie looked around and saw Frankie's family back up to the Academy from the Bronx. They waved to Julie and she waved back. Frankie had pitched several games in relief and actually started two games and won both. However, he didn't have to pick off anyone since the scores were rather lopsided on the Academy's side.

It looked like it was going to be a tough game. Babson scored two runs in the first and the Academy was shut out. At the bottom of the fourth, the Academy tied the game on a two-run homerun. It went back and forth for quite a while and in the bottom of the 8th inning, the Academy had a single, a sacrifice bunt for an out, a strikeout and with two outs, the catcher got a line drive single up the middle bring the runner home to take the lead 3-2. In the top of the 9th inning, the Academy made one fantastic play after the other in the field and Babson went down one, two, three, to end the game for the Academy. Everyone was thrilled but they knew they would wind up probably playing Babson in the NEWMAC tournament for an invitation for the NCAA Division III national championships. They all lined up and shook hands with their opponents. As usual around home plate, the players sang the Coast Guard Academy song with most of the fans in the stands singing along. Joe was thrilled. What a season so far. He only missed a handful of away games and he really felt like he was part of the team. He harkened back to his old MIT days and had the same feeling after a win even though he didn't play a second.

They walked back together to home. Joe was all smiles. The Rear Admiral waved and was happy. Kim Matz showed up and was smiling. Her husband was in the midst of tax time. Meg Olson and Laura Chavez both came by to congratulate his team. Sam and Emma came along with them and they walked to their house to meet Sean. Little did Joe know that he was getting a mini-surprise birthday party later that evening. Joe started the grill while Julie only needed to heat the mashed potatoes that she'd made earlier. The asparagus went on the grill as well. Joe was a happy camper as they say. Dinner was great and they quickly cleared their plates around 6:00 p.m. The doorbell first rang right around 7:00 p.m. with Sean, Sam, Emma and her little brother showing up with a case of Sam Adams *Octoberfest* beer, Joe's favorite. Joe looked perplexed but it suddenly hit him that he was having a surprise party. Brian Casey and family, Kim and Eric Matz came waltzing in. Meg Olson and Laura Chavez knocked. Dave Simon and family showed up as well. Tillie and Sam helped Julie cut the cake and put out the snacks. They knew it had to be quick because the kids had to be home for baths and bed and sleep before the Easter bunny arrived. Joe was just glad that the entire baseball team didn't come and sing happy birthday on his front porch that night. He never told anyone that it was his birthday but it seems the cat was let out of the bag, by Julie. She was great, he thought. What a nice time.

Bella was up at the crack of dawn. She raced into the living room to find two large Easter baskets, one labeled "Bella" and one labeled "Annie." She was jumping around yelling, "The Easter bunny came. The Easter bunny came. Mommy, Daddy, the Easter bunny came." All of a sudden you could hear Annie starting to cry in her crib. "Looks like it's time to get up," said Julie. "Don't want to be late for the Easter bunny."

Tillie was in her pajamas and bathrobe, strolling down the hallway. Joe rolled over and wanted to get back to sleep. Evidently, he had a few too many beers last night celebrating his thirty-eighth birthday. "I'm coming. I'm coming. Put the coffee on, please," he shouted out. He hit the bathroom and then walked in to see Bella all over the place. Her basket was overloaded with candy and stuffed animals. Next to her basket was a new Easter outfit that the Easter bunny dropped off. She sat there and was looking at the new dress, shoes, socks, and a hat and said to no one in particular, "I'm wearing this today. It's my new Easter outfit."

She looked over at Annie's basket to see what she got and then said, "Annie, you got a new outfit too." She added, "Both look the same but yours is way smaller."

Julie just smiled. Tillie sat next to Bella to see all her presents and said not to eat too much candy before Mass or she would get sick. Bella didn't hear a word of it as she unwrapped a small chocolate Easter bunny and started eating it. Julie just looked at her and told her that one is enough. Joe put out coffee cups for Tillie and Julie and grabbed a cup. He needed a few aspirin to get through the morning. Please don't ever put a birthday, a winning game and Easter all on the same weekend, he said to himself. He took his coffee and Sunday paper and headed for the bathroom. Hopefully after his shower and breakfast, he would be good to go.

They went to Easter Sunday Mass at their church, St. Mary Star of the Sea, for the noon Hispanic Mass. The pastor, Father Henry DiMarco, would say the Mass in Spanish and they had several small gifts for the children after Mass and a quick Easter egg hunt right outside of church. No matter how successful every child was in picking up eggs, those not so successful, got the same amount at the end of the event so there were no hard feelings. Tillie helped out with the Easter egg hunt and had a wonderful time. Her faith was her life, especially back in Key Largo, where she was a life-long member of St. Justin, Martyr parish. She helped run the food bank and secondhand clothing store as well as special events like funerals and weddings. The gift they gave the parish several years ago from the found money in their attic went a long way to helping those most destitute in the town. Joe and Julie's wedding at the Church, after their big wedding at St. Patrick's Cathedral in New York City, produced $50,000.00 in contributions to the church's projects. They were one of the few Catholic Churches in the Florida Keys that were self-sustaining because of Tillie, Joe, and Julie. Tillie would only be here a few weeks but she would attend morning Mass at church after walking Bella to school in the morning. Bella didn't mind Grammy walking her but put a stop to her parents doing the same. It wasn't the same as per Bella.

After finally getting back, everyone hit the bathroom and they were off to the restaurant for the buffet. In minutes they were in the parking lot, which was starting to fill up. They had reservations with a special booster seat for Bella, with a highchair for Annie. Tillie got the Easter buffet along with Julie. Joe ordered a seafood platter, his favorite. Bella didn't want the children's menu items because she was getting older now at age seven soon to be eight. She had two appetizers of her favorites, fried shrimp and fried calamari with tomato sauce on the side. She also ordered a Shirley Temple. Joe couldn't believe they were still serving these to kids after fifty years or so. The ladies had dessert from the buffet and Bella had chocolate cake, her favorite. Joe had another Sam Adams *Octoberfest* instead. They were home by 4:30 p.m. with everyone completely wiped out. They all went in for naps and would have sandwiches for later and the rest of the enormous birthday cake she bought for Joe's get together. She made a turkey breast and a small ham for sandwiches, which Joe personally loved for that night and the next night. He would cut up the ham and fry it for breakfast until it was gone. *Waste not want not*, he was told growing up.

He certainly didn't feel like going to work on Monday but had to because he had a meeting with the Rear Admiral, his security team to keep in touch with all the changes, and a meeting with Dr. Kate Ballenger about the status of Connecticut College's security systems. They were testing it out this week to make sure that both the Academy and Connecticut College systems were tied together for emergencies, student identification and notification of important issues, as well as traffic control throughout the campus. They needed to know who was coming and going as importantly as the Academy needed to know. He didn't think Kate was up to speed on the importance. He was going to tell her step by step how they found the bombs and what they needed to do flying by the seat of their pants. Now, they had systems in place that gave them an early alert to potential problems. They also were testing artificial intelligence into the system to see if it could provide its own cognitive response and pick up on potential harmful activities.

Chapter 25

Joe got up bright and early Monday morning to help Julie with the kids before he headed to his office and the meeting with the Rear Admiral. He held Annie while watching television and drinking coffee while Julie got Bella all set for school. Her lunch was made, breakfast was done and she said goodbye and walked out the front door for school. It was only a few short blocks to her school but it still made Joe and Julie nervous watching her leave. Julie always hung by the front door to see as far as she could before Bella turned the corner to head to school. Bella didn't want her walking with her to school so Julie put on a happy face even though she was nervous about it. She took Annie from Joe and he ate his breakfast and got dressed in his full uniform. He knew he didn't have to dress up but thought it was only appropriate when he had a meeting with the head of the Academy, his boss, Rear Admiral Kelly. At other times, he would only wear his Coast Guard work attire similar to what he wore when he was knocking down doors in south Florida and in the Keys.

Most of the administrators didn't even wear a work uniform or even own one. Joe said goodbye. Julie had very little to do today so she said she was going to work on her book. It was hard she said to get back into it every few days for only a few hours at a time. After stopping for any length of time, she had to reread several chapters before she started again on the one she was working on before she was able to understand where she was and where she was going in the book. This was time consuming but as she memorized the text, she was able to pick it up more quickly, thus saving her time to actually write.

Joe's meeting was always scheduled for 10:00 a.m., which he didn't mind. Joe was not a morning person. He would work well into the night if he could and then sleep late as he could. This schedule worked well with Joe but sometimes Bella and Annie's schedules clashed so he would get up earlier, which he hated but did to help out Julie. Walking to work was a luxury. When he was at The College of the Florida Keys, he had an hour drive every day up and down the one lane highway in the Keys. He would try to take back roads whenever he could but depending on the time of day, he just had to bite the bullet. Walking a few blocks to work was a luxury that he was very glad to have.

He came in the front door, climbed the steps and dropped off his coat in his office. He grabbed his cup for coffee and walked down the hall to the break room, saying hello to everyone. Everyone talked about having a nice Easter and several were thrilled about the outcome of the baseball game against Babson College. They asked Joe if he was going to the women's softball game on Tuesday afternoon and he said he would be right there for practice with the baseball team. He said Julie would meet him there with the girls in their uniforms for a 3:00 p.m. game as soon as Bella got home from school.

Meg Olson said she loved the girl's tiny uniforms and

was glad that they were involved with both teams. Laura Sanchez saw him in the hall and asked if they could meet this week. She said she got quite a bit of feedback from his visits to her class and to the Russian class as well. She thought they could build a program around both languages and have some kind of project jointly. Joe told her that would be great and to let him know. She also congratulated him on the latest win against Babson College and wanted to know how far he thought they could go. He told her that the team was good but had no experience in conference championship playoffs let alone a shot at the NCAA Division III tournament. He said if they played well, they would do well.

Joe walked into the Rear Admiral's office exactly at 10:00 a.m. If Rear Admiral Kelly was anything it was punctual to say the least. They greeted each other and started right in on an agenda. Joe had his and the Rear Admiral had his. Both agendas were pretty much the same except Joe had a few ideas he wanted to bounce off his boss. He told him all about the meeting at the Merchant Marine Academy and went through the intelligence that they were given. Joe told him that most of it was nebulous. The intelligence was that known militia groups and white supremacist organizations, throughout the country, were targeting all the academies. Obviously, local groups would target the Coast Guard Academy, while the other academies would be targeted regionally as well. Their understanding was that several of these groups got together to form an alliance and a common plan to look bigger than each group would look individually.

Joe told the Rear Admiral that when they arrested the four individuals for the bombing attempt at the Academy that the ones arrested were not the ones in charge of the group. The FBI and CIA had not gotten back to him yet on anything further but Joe was uneasy. He asked permission to do his own follow-up with his former team that included Jack Forest and Mark Silva. It would also include his FBI friends in charge of the Albany, New York office, the Miami office and Kim Matz at the local New London office. He said he wanted to reach out to his good friend, Mike Hanley, with the CIA in Miami. Together, they had the resources to find out information that the FBI alone could not. He also wanted to reach out to his Homeland Security partners of which he was also a member to see if there was any movement on that front.

This made the Rear Admiral a little nervous so before setting up his team, he said he wanted them both to head to Washington, D.C. to talk to the Admiral in charge of the Coast Guard. This was not a normal Coast Guard Academy operation. Joe also brought up the continuing topic of safety and security at the Academy. Joe believed that the Academy campus was now locked down sufficiently to protect it from any further bombing attempts or other attempt at sabotage to the campus. He said the bigger problem now lies with the fact that only cadets are housed on campus, nor regular service men and women, not administrators nor professors. When they leave campus, they are all on their own, going home to their loved ones. If any group wanted to target the Academy now, it could attack where they are most vulnerable, at the homes of their staff.

Joe gave the Rear Admiral the outline of a plan. He wanted to pay, out of his grant funds, to provide security systems for every employee at the Academy, all one hundred plus members, so they would feel safer and more secure in their own homes. Each house would have a complete security system, monitored 24/7 by the Academy security office. Each vehicle, either personal or military, would have security attached so that with the push of a button, the Academy security team would know if there is a problem and exactly where the vehicle is located. For all adults in the homes, they would be issued the same security GPS tabs to wear on their clothes, shoes, or pocketbooks to ensure their safety. Children would be left untouched as not to raise fear and alarm to the children. Joe did not want a police state but he was very concerned about another potential attack.

The Rear Admiral said to Joe, "Joe, is this overkill? I don't know how necessary this is. It's been this way for a very long time. Let's think about it before we put in Draconian measures."

Joe said, "Sir, maybe we can do it in several steps. How about this? Instead of that level of security, can we designate two security officers in a patrol car to drive by all our member houses, twice a day, mostly at night, to make sure that no one is under surveillance?" He added, "If they see a problem, we can use our new state-of-the-art security equipment to take pictures of cars that are parked along the way or of people who may be sitting outside a home for some time?"

"Joe, let's do that. Let's set up a meeting with Dave Simon and bounce it off of him. We know where everyone lives in the immediate area. It would be too tough for those living outside the confines of New London. Some live on farms or even in apartment buildings but we can look at it anyway. Sound like a plan?" he asked. He added, "Don't take this the wrong way, but we should always be steadfast in protecting our people. That's a given. Thank you for thinking of this."

Joe was not thrilled but he understood that change is tough especially when there was less than nothing implemented before he came here. He added, "Sir, I would also suggest that we add a few key members of the Connecticut College administration to the list. If they don't need, or want, the protection then that's fine. However, I keep reiterating that as close as they are to the Academy, it's hard not to want to make them part of our campus for safety and security, especially since most of our cadets take classes there every day."

"Joe, I'll call Dr. Ballenger this morning and ask her opinion. I won't try to sell her on it but I will sell the cost free portion and see what she says."

"That's all we can do, Sir," said Joe. With that, they ended their weekly meeting. Joe wasn't quite sure what he had accomplished today but he thought it was better than what they had. He would meet with the Chief of Police of New London as soon as he could. He would also mention to the Chief that he and a team would be looking into local Connecticut hate groups but not before getting approval from Washington. He was looking forward to traveling to Washington to meet with the Admiral along with Rear Admiral Kelly.

It's been a long time since he met the Admiral and started thinking about his long-term plans for the future. He wasn't sure he always wanted to stay in the Coast Guard. He was thinking about attending law school, maybe at the University of Miami or at Yale University, an hour away from the Academy if he stayed. He wanted to stay but a lot is riding on Julie's success as well as his own. He also needed to think about Julie, Bella and Annie and their safety, living in a normal house only a few blocks from the Academy. If anyone wanted to get to Joe, they certainly could get to him through his family. He needed to think about that. He was thinking about them when he mentioned the patrols by homes of staff and other safety measures. He didn't want to look like it was self-serving to the Rear Admiral but he knew it was personal and couldn't stop thinking about it. *If he retired, would it all go away? He wondered.*

Joe could retire in one more year with twenty-years of service, starting at age eighteen but turning nineteen that first spring that he joined. Then at age thirty-nine, nearing forty, with his background and experience he knew he could always get a job with Homeland Security or the FBI or even be on tenure track at the Clyne, Roberts and Lynch law firm in Miami. After all, it was he and Julie who set the firm up, first with Julie and then with their multi-millionaire friends Mary Evans and Jack Manning. It was both of them who recommended Jane Swanson, to handle all their accounts for the Teresa Trust Fund for Florida. Joe also thought back to the surprise 40th birthday party for Mark Silva back in Fort Lauderdale at the Hard Rock Café so many years ago, when he was working at the Albany Coalition for Families, his first and only real job as a civilian, before returning to the Coast Guard. Joe couldn't believe how time had flown by and the changes made in his and Julie's lives. God, he would be forty very soon. *He thought he would be in a new target-marketing group for middle age adults. What a thought. He could only imagine the extra mail he would be getting for senior discounts.*

Joe got home by 5:30 p.m. Dinner would be ready at 6:00 p.m. as always so he had time to shower, change his clothes and pop open a beer. He would sit down by the television and start to read the daily paper. It was the one thing that kept him sane. By the end of the day, he was tired of iPads and computers, and cell phones and the news. He immediately went to the sports page to see what happened the night before and who was playing tonight. The Yankees had just started the season and only had about ten games under their belt. They had two rainouts and one quick snow out as well. At 8-2, it was a good start to the season. The only problem Joe had was that he couldn't get the *YES* channel in New London, right on the border between teams. He would not watch the Red Sox channel unless they were playing the Yankees. He had his shortwave radio right by his chair on the end table and could pick up the games that way. He actually enjoyed listening to the games on the radio rather than on television. There were less commercials and he liked John Sterling and Suzyn Waldman. There was less talk and more action because they actually had to describe what was going on in real time rather than watch television announcers shouting over the top of the play that you see on the screen. Games started at 7:30 p.m. so well after dinner, Joe would sit with the two girls in his lap, waiting for the game to start. He would help get them dressed for bed, make them a snack and hand them off to Julie so she could read to Bella before going to sleep. He never thought he would be part of a *Father Knows Best* scenario but here he was at thirty-eight years old, falling into place like it was 1960 all over again. He laughed to himself.

As he was handing over the kids to Julie for her nightly routine, the phone rang and it was Lucy Talbot on the line. "Hello," said Joe.

"Hello, Joe. How are you? It's Luce. Is Julie free?" she asked.

"She's with the kids right now and should be free in a half hour," he said.

"Well, I wanted to tell her first, after telling my mom and dad, but I'll tell you, I got accepted to the Coast Guard Academy for the fall semester. I can either be a junior or a sophomore depending on what I want to do. If I take a duel major and ease into my schedule, I can be a full sophomore with either three or all four years of eligibility for cross-country, even if I get a master's degree. If I become a junior, I am only eligible for two years or three years and only have one major. If I decide to go for three years, I would have to continue in the Coast Guard Academy in order to compete as a student. So it becomes complicated and I want to talk to Julie about it. However, thank you for everything. I think no matter what, this is a great move. I have to make up the outside non-classroom activities over the next few years to catch up as a transfer student but I can start in early June and then spend June, July, and August making up my time. Then, it will be mostly done. The problem is that by August 15th, the cross-country team starts practice for the fall schedule and I need to be there for that," she said.

"That's great," said Joe. "No matter what you decide, you will be well ahead of the game. Did you talk to your Miami coach yet?" he asked.

"I walked into his office even before I told my mom and dad. He said he was not surprised and if anything changed, he would welcome me back with open arms. He smiled and said he would see me at the 2024 Olympic trials during the 2023 season. He was asked to be an assistant for the Paris summer games and would do everything he could to help me. You can't ask for more than that. It's a shame he didn't come across that way before all this happened. He said the same thing," she said.

"Well that's great. I'm really happy for you and your parents. Just remember on top of this free ride, Mary Evans is giving you a stipend that will continue to take care of all the incidentals that would now occur. You won't be fifty miles from home. It's more like 1,500," he said. "Keep track of all your expenses and either I or Julie will forward the list to Mary."

Julie just finished putting the girls to bed and Joe said,

"Julie, it's Luce, she has some great news to tell you."

She took the phone and walked into their bedroom and closed the door so Joe could listen to the game on the radio. Julie was very excited and after talking to Luce, she spoke to Joan and Jeff. She told them to all come together the week before she had to start and they could stay at their house and if too cramped, Luce could stay here and Julie would book a suite at the hotel close by in downtown. In any case, plans would be made. Joe knew that he would have to have a hands-off approach to Luce's wellbeing while at the Academy but he felt like Luce was their own daughter. Hell, Joan practically raised Joe for ten years after he started as a first-year sailor at eighteen-years-old, with her serving the role as mother and boss. He guessed that everything was coming back full circle. This was a good thing and he knew that Julie certainly felt the same.

Chapter 26

Since Rear Admiral Kelly was the Rear Admiral and Superintendent of the Coast Guard Academy he was entitled to certain perks such as taking one of the Air Force private jets down to Washington, D.C. For Joe, it was like getting a lift from Mary Evans and Jack Manning up to Troy, New York to visit at Christmas time in a private jet. The Air Force operates multiple Gulfstream jets, some are painted in the blue-and-white livery and others are painted more low profile such as the one picking them up. While most branches of the military use the Gulfstream jets to fly officials within the branch, the Air Force uses its Gulfstream airplanes to fly officials throughout the US government including cabinet secretaries and others in the presidential line of succession, as well as high ranking military officials that includes Rear Admiral Kelly. Joe was just along for the ride so he thought.

The Gulfstream picked them up at the Groton-New London commercial wing after flying in from Washington, D.C. They would stay for two days and nights and be back by the end of the week. The Rear Admiral was kidding with Joe that he couldn't miss a weekend baseball game even if world peace was involved. Julie talked Tillie in to staying an extra week to help out with the kids while Joe was away. It was working out fine. The Rear Admiral and Joe were chauffeured to the airport and grabbed their bags. There was no waiting in line. They hopped on the Gulfstream and would be in Washington, D.C. in less than an hour. It was 350 miles door to door and at 600 miles an hour an hour, it wouldn't take long. With landing instructions it would take another half hour to forty-five minutes to get to their designated driver whom would be picking them up at the gate.

Their driver was parked right outside the door in a military parking spot. After all, it was Washington, D.C., and this was an ongoing routine for visiting guests. The trip from the airport to Coast Guard headquarters was less than five miles away. Depending on traffic, it could take fifteen minutes to an hour going across town. They started out going north on National Airport Access Road toward Smith Boulevard. They took the George Washington Memorial Parkway North for less than a mile and merged onto I-395 N/Southwest Freeway North toward Washington, crossing into the District of Columbia. They stayed straight and got onto I-695 S/Southwest Freeway North and merged onto South Capitol Street SW toward Nationals Park. They quickly turned right onto Potomac Avenue SW and then slightly right onto R Street SW. They finally turned left onto Second Street SW, which required gate access. They immediately pulled up in front of 2100 Second Street SW, which was on the left.

When they arrived at Coast Guard headquarters, Joe thanked the driver and walked up the stairs to security with Rear Admiral Kelly. They would be meeting Admiral Kenneth T. Hartnagle in a few minutes. Evidently, the Rear Admiral had put together a full itinerary for two days.

They would return to New London once again on a private jet on Friday, arriving around 5:00 p.m. They would be back home no later than 6:00 p.m. depending on traffic on a Friday night. Today they were meeting all day with the Admiral. Over the next two days they would also be meeting with the deputy director of the FBI and deputy secretary of Homeland Security. Joe was having dinner with Mike Hanley, his CIA friend from Miami who was in town, at Joe's request, to discuss what happened to his arrestees from the bombing at the Academy. No one has heard from them since they left in the hands of the FBI and handed over to Mike's agency, the CIA.

Joe didn't know if Rear Admiral Kelly was aware of his meeting a few years ago with the Admiral while he was in the middle of the Chechen investigation in Orlando. Joe was getting married to Julie and his time was coming to an end in the Coast Guard and he was leaning toward leaving the service and getting a job down in the Florida Keys so Julie could concentrate on her new books and affiliation with Disney Studios, bringing to life her trilogy on a new television series to be filmed at the Hollywood Studios in Orlando. At that time, Rear Admiral Barnes had set up the meeting with the Admiral and Joe so that the Admiral would see Joe's qualities and the reasons Jake didn't want him to leave the service. That meeting led to Joe becoming the Interim President of The College of the Florida Keys for one year and receiving his Ph.D. from Barry University. This ultimately led to his new position as Assistant Superintendent of the Coast Guard Academy.

As soon as they arrived, the Admiral met both Rear Admiral Kelly and Joe as soon as they came in the front door. He waved them through all the normal security checks and up the stairs to his office. "Welcome aboard," said Admiral Hartnagle. "Bill, Joe, it's good to see you both together. Thanks for coming down to give me an update on what's going on. I'm particularly interested in the bombing attempt and Joe's easy access to funds," he said and smiled. "Thanks Joe, for the ten-million-dollar largesse from your good friend, Mary Evans. Please tell her it's appreciated," he said.

"I will, Sir," said Joe as they sat down in the open sitting area of his office. It was as big as some of the cutters Joe had been on while still in the ranks.

The Admiral took Rear Admiral Kelly's agenda and read it and then passed out his own. At least in substance they looked very much the same. "Before we go any further, Bill are you aware that I have met Captain Traynor a few years ago at the request of Jake Barnes? Joe was thinking of leaving the service and both of us didn't want that to happen. Now with this bombing attempt, I can see where Joe's expertise has come into play. Bill, are you aware of his past background? Most of it has been redacted because of national security reasons."

"Sir, I am aware of many things about Joe Traynor but mostly from watching his daily activity which never ceases to amaze me. But, no I am unaware of some of his past efforts. I know about his past Interim Presidency at the college and his Ph.D. and MBA from RPI and his language skills but I'm unaware of how those skills have been used in the past," he said.

Admiral Hartnagle pulled out his notes from the meeting they had a few years ago and started to read line by line to the Rear Admiral. "I went over his dossier, Bill, and as I'm now reading I'm still quite impressed. I forgot that he's fluent in Spanish and Russian and now Chechen, written and verbally, and with cultural and historical background in all three and he's learning Chinese. That's quite impressive. May I summarize some of his efforts on our behalf, and you can correct me if I'm wrong, Joe."

Joe was a little frazzled at this point. He didn't know why this was being brought up. He knew he had one year left and could leave if he wanted or was this to explain his real value to Rear Admiral Kelly? Somewhere he'd read that someone might think that you are dumb so don't open your mouth and prove it. He simply sat there and listened as the Admiral continued.

"During your first tour from when you were eighteen to twenty-eight, you served with honor and decided to leave the service to obtain your MBA, which you did with honors from Rensselaer Polytechnic Institute. From there, everything seemed to have started clicking with you. You stopped a national money-laundering scheme that included the Mexican Mafia. It ended with the death of the son of the Mexican Mafia general and three gangbangers in the offices of the president of the Albany Coalition for Families. You received the second highest honor given by the Coast Guard, the Coast Guard Commendation Medal with a Ribbon. It's the highest award issued for heroism, not involving combat with an enemy outside the country, by the United States Coast Guard."

He went on, "Then after you rejoined the Coast Guard, you took down the Russian Mafia in Miami and the Florida Keys, the so-called Dixie meth distributors in Nashville, the Columbian cocaine cartel in Miami, and our own Coast Guard crooks. Then you caught the Haitian sex traffickers in Miami, and then helped take down Chechen terrorists in Orlando. Plus, you solved the murder of Tom Jones, one of our own."

"Bill, what Joe did was more in those few years than most officers have done during a thirty-year career. Now you stopped a bombing attempt at the Academy in the first few weeks you were there. Am I right?"

Joe answered, "Sir, it was a group effort and as you remember I have credentials from the Coast Guard, the FBI, and Homeland Security. I am also involved with the CIA when we find terrorists on our turf, as you are well aware. As you now know, the bombing came from a domestic terrorist group right in Connecticut. We were lucky. With the help of my team including, and especially including Jack Forest, we nailed them in one day and found them up in West Hartford. If I didn't make a deal with one of them, we would have had two bombs go off in the field house that we would never have known about. I know it looks risky but as I explained to Rear Admiral Kelly, we are allowed to lie to terrorists to save lives. It's that simple and then we hand them off to our friends in the FBI and the CIA."

"Bill, did you know of any of Joe's background that I just told you about?"

"No, Sir. I did not," he said.

The Admiral said, "I forgot to mention that your ten-million-dollar endowment from Mary Evans, that came through Joe, was in large part because he saved her after being kidnapped in the Keys by white supremacists. I may add they won't be around for a while and two of them are gone permanently," he added.

"Gone permanently?" asked the Rear Admiral.

"Yes, they were shot dead by Joe's SMRT team that provided the rescue for Mary Evans," said the Admiral.

The Admiral went on, "So, please tell me all the specifics of the bombing and your agenda item that you want to discuss taking on a project that would attempt to eliminate terrorists that come in contact or could potentially comer in contact with the Academy. That I find very interesting," the Admiral said. "By the way, Joe we are meeting once again with two people you met before when I met with you a few years ago. We are having lunch with the Deputy Secretary of Homeland Security, Martin Sutherland, and Deputy Director of the FBI, Stephen Sandberg. Joe, they want to hear about your task force meeting at the Merchant Marine Academy with all the other security teams at all the Academies on the intelligence that was picked up. I can't believe that these militia and white supremacist groups are now targeting the military academies. Perhaps, Joe, you can tell us why," he said.

They took a bathroom break and Rear Admiral Kelly spoke to Joe as they walked down the hall. "Joe, I didn't know any of that stuff he was talking about. I wish I did know. That's unbelievable. No wonder you were able to pick up the pieces immediately and then know exactly what to do and proceed accordingly. I'm kind of glad you're on our side. You are one dangerous dude, Joe," he said and laughed. "Your mild disposition and friendly banter is the complete opposite of you in these situations. Where does that come from, Joe?" he asked.

"It comes from picking off runners at first base, Sir. If you have the nerves to do that in the bottom of the inning with two outs and two on, only leading by a run, then you can do anything. To me playing baseball and playing it well is a leading indicator of how you will handle adversity in real life, Sir. And, Sir, I do believe that," said Joe.

The Rear Admiral simply nodded and really began to understand Joe Traynor and his personal makeup. He needed to find out how Joe grew up. It had to be independent and he must have taken charge at a very early age in life. It also must have something to do with his wife, Julie, because as different as they are in personality, they seem to be as one in spirit.

On the way back from the break, Rear Admiral Kelly

asked Joe point blank, "Joe do you have any desire to be Superintendent of the Coast Guard Academy?"

It took Joe by surprise but he answered honestly, "No, Sir. Not at all."

"Really, not at all?" He asked Joe. "You know I am considering retire at the end of the year. Perhaps you have heard the whispers in the hallways. I think it's my time. When Grace graduates next year from Connecticut College, I'm going to turn in my paperwork. It's time, Joe. I've been in the Coast Guard since I started at the Academy in 1978, that's 44 years. To run this Academy now takes a bunch of different skills, especially in the areas of technology of which I am ill prepared. You are prepared Joe. So please think about it. You have one year left on your enlistment and you will be 39 years old. You would be the youngest Superintendent in history that I know of, Joe. With the backing of the Admiral, Jake Barnes and me, I think you would be a winning candidate for the position. I just wanted to throw that out to you, Joe. You have all the credentials including a Ph.D. and advanced language skills, which is a lot more than I have ever been equipped with. Just saying, Joe."

"Thank you, Sir. I appreciate your support and your compliments. It is appreciated. However, I have to think about Julie, our beautiful, adopted daughter, Bella, and of course little Annie and maybe a few more additions to the family. Time is running out to have kids and I'm not sure I want to run around like I have for the last almost twenty years. However, I will keep it in mind and talk to Julie about it. Thank you again, Sir."

"Thank you, Joe, for listening to me about it. And no, I have not spoken to the Admiral or to Jake about this yet. I would only do so if and when you might think the time is right."

They had lunch with the Deputy Secretary of Homeland Security, Martin Sutherland, and Deputy Director of the FBI, Stephen Sandberg and a few high-ranking officers and members of the Admiral's administrative staff. Joe barely got a chance to eat after answering question after question only to be broken up by Rear Admiral Kelly's plea to please let him finish his lunch. They hadn't eaten since early morning before flying out of Groton-New London airport. At that point, the Rear Admiral jumped in and entertained the group for about twenty minutes letting Joe eat, which he appreciated.

Joe made it clear to everyone that the joint Academies Task Force was fine in concept but the Coast Guard Academy had different issues than the other four. He explained that they had to make sure two college campuses were safe, even if the second one, namely Connecticut College, was not very alarmed about any safety or security issues. He did explain that he had installed a million-dollar fix to their systems that tied it to the Academy but they still didn't have a sufficient force on campus to provide maximum security. They asked Joe what percentage was protected and he looked them in the eye and told them less than 50%. Anyone could walk on that campus and cause harm. That is no longer the case at the Academy. They were also intrigued about Joe's access to a ten-million-dollar fund and that he has liberally started to spend that dollar amount down on the most recent state-of-the-art security systems recommended to him by West Point. Joe thought they were more interested in how he got the funds rather than what he was doing with the funds. He said that he had invited Mary Evans and her husband, Jack Manning back to meet with Rear Admiral Kelly and the president of Connecticut College. He explained how their relationship grew, especially with Julie and Joe's friends in the Keys.

He said it led to a multi-million dollar investment in The College of the Florida Keys and a several million-dollar investment into a fund to recruit minorities and women into the Coast Guard from the Florida Keys. He also mentioned that Joe's father and brother still live in Troy, New York and were the general contractors on their new Career Center in Troy. At the end of this conversation, there was no doubt about Joe's access to funds.

Joe then brought up what he really wanted to discuss, which was shutting down hate groups, starting with those near the Academy in Connecticut. He handed out his cheat-sheet that he downloaded from the internet about every group, the size of the group, finances and crimes they have perpetrated but no one has gone to prison because there is no definition of domestic terrorism. Joe wanted to use his Coast Guard team and his connections to both the FBI and Homeland Security, over the next year, to do a full and complete evaluation of these groups and then start to shut them down one by one.

He told the assembled lunch group all about the kidnapping of Mary Evans and what they did subsequent to saving her life. They shut down the National Alliance, a white supremacy group originally from Mississippi but now outside of Miami. Not only were they arrested but sent to the CIA for interrogation but through some pretty detailed technology, closed all their accounts in the Cayman Islands and had the funds sent to the CIA's account. The account would start in the Cayman Islands and be transferred through several international drops before heading back to Jack Forest. The money was sent directly to Joe's CIA contact, that he did not name, and used the money process the leader of the National Alliance and anyone else they found. Joe told him prior to this, the Miami FBI Director, Paul Philips and Joe's CIA contact met Joe in Miami and they hammered out the plan that was implemented. So as Joe said, they could accomplish almost anything by working together.

Deputy Secretary of Homeland Security, Martin Sutherland, and Deputy Director of the FBI, Stephen Sandberg, both fully attentive now, were listening intently now as Joe was speaking. They looked at him like he was the one in charge, making all the deals, and putting together all the plans, because he was. The Admiral's two staff officers, who were equal in rank to Joe, simply shook their heads as if to say, *"Are we all in the same Coast Guard together? Really? You wouldn't know it."* It was like they never heard about any of these situations that were happening in real time in this country.

After the meeting, on the way back to the Admiral's office, he told both Rear Admiral Kelly and Joe that he would support any effort to address potential harm to the Academy both foreign and domestic. He didn't need to say any more. Joe had his marching orders. They asked Joe to go to dinner but he apologized and said he was meeting a friend that came to Washington to specifically meet with him over dinner. Both got the gist of what Joe was saying.

The Admiral, being very sharp, said, "Joe, would this friend be coming from Miami to see you tonight?" He smiled.

"Why, yes, Sir, he would be coming from Miami." He didn't need to say any more. "Rear Admiral, I'll see you for breakfast tomorrow at the hotel around 7:00 a.m. Is that all right?" Joe asked.

"Joe, I know you hate mornings. Let's meet at 8:30 a.m. for breakfast and we'll be back here for 10:00 a.m. Is that better?" Joe nodded and said his goodbyes and took a taxi back to the hotel and then on to his dinner meeting with Mike Hanley.

Chapter 27

Joe took a taxi from his hotel right around the corner from the Coast Guard headquarters to the restaurant in Dupont Circle, about four miles away and twenty minutes by cab. He was meeting Mike Hanley at Hank's Oyster Bar at 6:00 p.m. Their favorite seafood place used to be Phillips Seafood on Water Street in southwest Washington but it closed a number of years ago. Hank's took its place as one of the best in town. The last time Joe met Mike Hanley was in Miami in conversation with Paul Philips, the head of the Miami FBI office. There they planned the capture of the head of the National Alliance into the hands of the CIA. Ken Meggs, the founder and head of the National Alliance white supremacist group, was taken from his headquarters in Hialeah and is now in the hands of the CIA. This was right after Joe and his team rescued Mary Evans from being kidnapped in Big Pine Key in the Florida Keys. Meggs was the brain trust using three of his men to take Mary. It didn't work out and Meggs and his crew paid the price.

Just recently, after arresting the bombers in West Hartford, one call to Mike from Joe, brought in a team from the CIA to pick up the four members of the Sovereign Citizens of Connecticut to be interrogated. Thank God one of those captured gave up the other two bombs that were in the laundry room of the field house at the Academy. Joe did make a call to ease the pain for that individual.

Tonight, Joe wanted to discuss with Mike on how he could legally disrupt those militia and white supremacists' groups that were growing exponentially in the United States but specifically in Connecticut, near the Coast Guard Academy. A repeat of the bombing incident would not be tolerated and that's why Joe finally got the Admiral's approval to do research on these organizations to see what they can do about them and to prevent any further activity. Joe wanted to discuss the World Church of the Creator (WCOTC), the Sovereign Citizens of Connecticut, and the Ku Klux Klan, which is alive and well in Connecticut.

The WCOTC is one of the most publicized white supremacist groups in the United States in recent years led by Matt Hale. Over the years, Church members have also been linked to a number of violent crimes around the country. The WCOTC entered the new century with a deserved reputation for hate and violence. Just as Connecticut Klansmen engaged in illegal acts, members or supporters of the Connecticut WCOTC chapter committed several crimes during the group's brief history in the state.

The next group is one that Joe is very familiar with, the Sovereign Citizens of Connecticut who planted the bombs at the Academy. The "sovereign citizen" movement is a network of groups and individuals who have adopted a right wing, essentially anarchist ideology that has its origins in the beliefs of a group called the Posse Comitatus, which first emerged in the 1970s. Often those people who have suffered financial or other personal reverses are most susceptible to the lure of extreme antigovernment ideology. This has proven true for many of Connecticut's anti- government extremists. Finally Joe wants to know more about the Klansmen. It is difficult to estimate accurately the membership of the Connecticut Klansmen in 2022, but total numbers are probably no more than a few dozen. Yet while their numbers are small, the threat posed by the Klan remains real. What bothers Joe the most is that all extremist groups, including Klansmen, can get publicity in Connecticut by staging rallies and other public events, suggests that the Klan will continue to make its presence felt in Connecticut for years to come as well as the other groups. The more publicity they get, the more vocal they get and the more dangerous they get.

As Joe walked into Hank's, he was met at the door by the staff. He pointed to Mike at the bar and she waved him through. Although it was the middle of the week, this place was always hopping. Joe walked over to the bar, sat down on the stool next to Mike, and without even saying hello, ordered a Sam Adams. *It was Winter Ale not Octoberfest but what the hell,* he thought.

"And hello to you too," said Mike. "You need a beer that badly?" he asked.

"No, I just needed to avoid talking to you," said Joe. "Let's go get our table or we'll lose it. Hi, Mike how are you?"

"Just fine, thanks for asking," he said sarcastically. "Two Irishmen walked into a bar," he continued and smiled. Hanley is a very common southern Ireland name while Joe's is as well.

At last, Joe could relax. He could see that Mike was starting to unwind as well. He didn't travel well. It was probably because when he did, it was with terrorists being relocated out of the country. Mike was about the same age as Joe and they got along fine, like longtime friends usually do. He looked tired. Like Joe, he was married with two children, both in their early teens, an older daughter and a younger son, who didn't see their dad a whole lot. He too was starting to think about his time in the CIA and what he wanted to do with the remainder of his life. Joe knew this CIA gig wasn't it. Maybe together they could knock down a few white supremacists as they both headed to the door for an early retirement.

"How did you make out with the two million dollars that Mary sent you?" he asked.

"Still holding on to it. I'm now using the National Alliance money to house Meggs and his partner. Tell Jack Forest thank you for the deposit. It is appreciated. I wouldn't be able to do anything with the budget we have currently," he said.

"I hear you, Mike. Let's order." They did.

They got the famous Hank's Oyster House signature and award-winning plateau (served cold on a platter on a bed of ice) featuring oysters on the half shell, middle neck clams on the half shell, chilled jumbo shrimp, seafood ceviche, mussels escabeche, and chilled Maine lobster. They split the large order that serves two to four for $99.00. This was Joe's treat because the last time they were here, Mike treated Joe as a wedding gift, right before he got married. At that time, Joe was in town to visit the Admiral while working on the Chechen terrorists in Orlando. The Admiral knew Joe was putting in his papers to leave the Coast Guard. Jake Barnes asked the Admiral to meet Joe to give him other options. That option turned out to be the interim presidency of The College of the Florida Keys, a Ph.D. from Barry University and his new job at the Academy. At the time, Joe was meeting Mike to take care of the terrorists in Orlando but it ended up that the main terrorist was shot dead in an alley by Trinity Hightower, an Orlando detective friend of Joe's working on the case. While chasing the subject together, Joe was knocked cold by a chunk of cement that hit his head after a ricocheting bullet hit the wall behind him and dropped him. Trinity ended the confrontation, ending the terrorist's life.

Joe and Mike talked about everything other than terrorists. Joe told him about his newfound fame as a pitching coach for the Academy and his artful instruction on the Andy Pettitte pickoff move. Mike said maybe he'd fly up to meet him for a game if they got involved again with those groups in Connecticut. Joe said he was more than welcome to stay at his house. Joe told Mike he could give them pointers on raising two teenagers. Mike smiled and said it was all his wife's doing, not his. That's why he needed to get out soon before they left the nest. Mike knew he could get a job in security anywhere he wanted. At forty years old, he was becoming fluent in Spanish and had twenty years in the CIA coupled with a bachelor's degree from Vanderbilt. Of course, he could never say he was in the CIA but Joe could certainly get him moved over to Homeland Security to continue his service and retirement years. Mike said he would think about it and it sounded promising. Toward the end of dinner, Mike said he would meet Joe up in New London in the near future. In the meantime, he would gather all the information he needed, so they would have something to discuss. He would come alone the first time and his group was only a phone call away and could be there within a day's time. Joe was on the same wavelength.

Joe could get his MSRT team together immediately since they are now on campus but his real team, made up of all those friends over the years, might prove to be as valuable in a pinch. He would discuss everything with the Admiral and Rear Admiral Kelly tomorrow. Hopefully, they could leave tomorrow night and not the following day so he could get home earlier. He didn't need or want to meet with anyone else down here in Washington, D.C. It was all politics and he hated it. He watched the Admiral's staff at lunch and saw that they hung on every word the Admiral said. He wasn't sure that he'd want them in a foxhole next to him in an emergency. That's the difference in Joe's Coast Guard career and most of the other officers. Joe sees things from the bottom up and then down again. These entitled officers are sometimes a one-way street. Well, at least a lot of them anyway, he thought. He'd have to work on fine-tuning his prejudices about noncombat military officers.

Joe made it back to the hotel a little after 9:00 p.m. He had a nice dinner with Mike. Mike was a very good friend for a very long time. Mike was now speaking Spanish but it took him forever to learn the language but he was getting there. He still was not good enough for interrogations. Joe had continued to help him out and that's why whenever Mike had an interrogation, in Spanish, Russian or even now in Chechen, he didn't hesitate to call Joe for translation as long as it was close to stateside. Joe wouldn't go on any renditions, beyond the international water line. He wasn't allowed. It wasn't his jurisdiction.

If anything, the pandemic brought them even closer with Zoom calls. Joe could be anywhere to translate for Mike as well as watch the body language of the person being interrogated. Joe understood that the body language of different cultures meant different things. He learned a long time ago when speaking to an Asian about an event that the nodding of the head, up and down, didn't necessarily mean "yes" to that person. In fact in a lot of cases it meant the exact opposite so the translation was only half of the interview. Mike started to understand this technique a lot more with Joe around. They became good friends and helped each other out whenever asked.

Joe was now asking him for help. After Joe's final day in Washington, he would invite Mike up to the Academy and together they would start the investigation in person, not just develop the background needed to figure out the next steps. By nature, Joe was very suspicious of people until proven otherwise. Both Mike and Joe thought that the Sovereign Citizens arrested were only telling half-truths when confronted after their arrest. They would take this information and see what else they could add to it.

Joe called Julie. She had just put the kids to bed and she and Tillie were just having a glass of wine in front of the fireplace. It's been a while since Tillie had been back after Annie's baptism and they were catching up. Julie wanted to know more about Tillie's friend, Ed Lansing, but didn't want to ask her outright. She had called him several times during the last few weeks she was up at their house and she would be heading back after Joe got back from Washington, D.C. Mary Evans and Jack Manning were coming over next week and would meet with Rear Admiral Kelly and take a tour of Connecticut College with Julie and Joe. They were flying over to New London from Albany and then heading for Key West the following day. They asked Tillie if she would stay another few days and head back with them and she would then get a ride to Key Largo from one of their security team members. Mary thought Tillie's input into the Teresa Trust Fund South was as important as Julie's because Tillie represented all the seniors in South Florida and the Keys as far as intentions concerning funding were concerned. At Tillie's request, the fund spent several hundred thousands of dollars on seniors residing in nursing homes on cleaning and facemasks during the pandemic. She was also instrumental in pointing out the increase in homeless mothers with young children that suffered from the last hurricane that drove them from what little shelter they had. Tillie'd earned every dime she ever had and that toughness came through with affection for those who are now suffering the same issues that she had when she raised Julie all by herself.

Joe said that they should be coming tomorrow night and be back around 6:00 p.m. in New London. If they could leave earlier they would. It all depended on the Admiral's agenda for tomorrow. Joe started to pull his notes together for the day and add what he wanted to discuss tomorrow with the Rear Admiral. He hoped they could get out of headquarters early in the afternoon and get home earlier. He really hated meetings and he was the one that had to really participate. The Admiral's administrative team was not made up of combat trained officers like Joe. They usually came directly out of the Academy and then took the administrative side as a career. Very few officers started like Joe at eighteen years old working his way to a Captain position, now nearing twenty years in the service.

Joe met the Rear Admiral for breakfast and they talked about their pending meeting. They both remarked that they would like to get home earlier and avoid rush hour traffic if possible. The Rear Admiral had some academic issues to discuss and Joe wanted to reconfirm with both of them that he could start an investigation into the white supremacists groups in Connecticut. He would keep in mind his task force meeting at the Merchant Marine Academy but it was not on the front burner. He had additional worries with another college right across the street in which most of his cadets attended to take courses not offered by the Academy. As soon as they stepped off the now very secure Academy campus, they would walk over to the not as secure Connecticut College campus. It bothered Joe.

They met the Admiral right at 10:00 a.m. in his boardroom. They checked out of the hotel and brought their one carry-on bag with them. If noticed, it might end the meeting sooner. The Admiral said that they didn't need the Homeland Security or FBI staff there today because that was more of the general discussion brought on by the task force meeting. The Admiral also knew that Joe was affiliated with the FBI and Homeland Security and if needed, he could get what he wanted at any time. The Admiral asked Joe to summarize again the security issues for the newly assembled team and he did so in one hour. They all took notes but Joe didn't believe that if push came to shove that anyone of the subordinates would have any idea on how to handle a crisis like a bombing on campus. The meeting ended around noon so they got a quick bite to eat. During lunch the Admiral mentioned to Joe that when his time was up next year that if he was thinking of leaving for an early retirement at age thirty-nine that he should call him to discuss it because he wants Joe to stay on. The Rear Admiral mentioned the same thing. He asked Joe if he was thinking about another career choice and Joe mentioned that he was looking into going to law school, either at Yale, right down the road from the Academy or the University of Miami in Coral Gables if he and Julie decided to head back to Florida. The Admiral said to call Jake Barnes and discuss it with him as well. He said Jake would stay on the board of the Academy as a new member but was thinking about retiring as well and his slot might be open sooner than later. Joe told him he owed the Rear Admiral a call.

The Admiral walked them to the door as the same driver

that dropped them off previously in the military vehicle picked them up. They made the Gulfstream by 2:30 p.m. and taxied right out. They would be in New London no later than 4:00 p.m. after landing and Joe would be home by 5:00 p.m., an hour earlier than planned. On the way home, the Rear Admiral and Joe had a beer and started talking. It was becoming clear that the two of them were becoming friends as much as boss and subordinate. The Rear Admiral appreciated Joe's honesty and drive to be the best that he could be. Joe appreciated the old school approach that the Rear Admiral had to his job but it was clear that time might just be passing him by with the new state-of-the-art technologies that were required to keep everyone up to date, safe and secure as well as ease cadets into the 21st century. The next warfare will not be military and on the ground with competing armies. Knocking off the other country's electrical grid and the stock exchange, and messing with the treasury and financial systems will win it. One attack could kill the economy of its adversary.

They made it home safely. Joe and the Rear Admiral were picked up in a Coast Guard vehicle and both were dropped off at their homes. It was a good trip. Joe got to talk to his boss on a more level playing field without all the attending pressures of rank. The Admiral was a very good negotiator and understood those in his command. He wouldn't let Joe go without a fight.

Chapter 28

Joe made it back for the weekend baseball games against Wheaton College from Norton, Massachusetts. Norton was right down the road from the New England Patriots, Gillette Stadium, in nearby Foxborough, only fifteen miles away up I495N. The college was about eighty miles up I95N from New London. This was the first away game that Joe could attend. They were playing a double header on Saturday and a final game on Sunday. The team would stay over and Joe would go home and come back for Sunday's game. The Coast Guard was now 26-7, the best year they ever had. If they beat Wheaton College two out of three games this weekend, they will take first place in the NEWMAC, and be seeded first in the tournament. That's a bonus for the Academy because then Babson College has to play Wheaton to get to the Academy and Wheaton has beaten them twice this year. It was a close race for the title but the Academy has remained strong and has come from behind several times to win. The new coach, Brian Casey, has made a world of difference in changing the team's perception to one of a winner.

Julie and the kids would stay home with Tillie who would be leaving next week to go back home to Key Largo. Mary and Jack would fly in on Tuesday and spend all day Wednesday with Julie and Joe touring both the Academy and Connecticut College. They were here for Annie's baptism but came with Joe's family and they stayed at the Mohican Sun, just up the road. So, they didn't get to see a lot of the Academy's campus and none of Connecticut College. Joe would also introduce them to the administrators of the Coast Guard Academy Alumni Association, housed on the campus.

Tillie would spend her last day with Bella and Annie before her trip. She would walk Bella to school in the morning, pushing Annie in her stroller. Then at 11:30 a.m. the day before leaving while they did the tour, she and Annie would head back to Bella's school and eat lunch with her. The lunch for that day was all set up by Bella's teacher, and the cafeteria staff, along with the principal. They all knew who Tillie was and treated her like royalty. Being Julie Chapman Traynor's grandmother carried some weight. Unbeknownst to Bella, Julia has had several meetings with the administrators and staff at the New London school district, not only at Bella's school but at the district level as well. They had set up author's day in a few weeks and Julie would speak to the students about writing. The district was thrilled to have an international best-selling author in his or her own PTA, and did everything they could to make sure the kids knew who she was. It hadn't hit Bella's age level yet but when they started reading the first book in the Trilogy, *A Girl's Story*, they would soon find out. That day, and after lunch, when Bella got home, they would snuggle up in front of the television and Julie would bring home dinner for everyone after their tour. Julie was certainly going to miss Tillie, big time.

Joe had a lot on his plate. He thought the meetings in Washington went well. He congratulated himself on the fact that he either was now more mature or didn't let his temper get to him like it did several years ago when he had several meetings with the Admiral and his staff. The Admiral was pushing for Joe to stay in the Coast Guard and Joe was far from making a decision. However, he thought back to the one lunch where he really got mad at another officer. The Admiral brought Joe to lunch with his staff and he barely ate between questions. It was like they had no idea what it was like out in the field. The only time he showed his temper was when one of the officers laughed about Katrina and New Orleans. Joe almost bit his head off and told him in no uncertain terms how poorly the African American citizens of New Orleans were treated by American military forces. The Admiral noticed Joe's temper and was not surprised. Evidently, Jake Barnes told him directly about it and he said Joe would tell you exactly what was on his mind. The staff member will long remember the short but to the point confrontation at lunch with Joe. The Admiral admired Joe's passion, and at that point, knew that headquarters would be a waste of his talents.

Now Joe was still wondering if his administrative post at the Coast Guard Academy was becoming a waste of time. Rear Admiral Kelly was much more suited for the day-to-day mundane operations that took up most of the Rear Admiral's time and now was being passed down to Joe who took on more and more responsibility out of sheer boredom. He thought that time would tell. He still wanted to make changes at the Academy to make it better and make the cadets stronger with a sense of the real world outside the Academy.

Joe left with the team bright and early Saturday

morning. He took his own vehicle so he could head home after the double header and then back the next day for the third and final game in the series. It was well worth the trip. The Academy won both games handily, the first game was 6-1 and the second game was 5-0. Both games went quickly and the Academy was in sole possession of first place and would be seeded first regardless of the next day's game because Babson lost to Clark University in a squeaker 4-3 in ten innings. Now the Academy was 28-7 regardless of tomorrow's game so Joe bowed out to Brian who understood that Tillie was leaving soon and he wanted to be home for her last few days. He headed out and was home by 7:30 p.m. and the pizza was still hot and ready for him.

Joe picked up Mary Evans and Jack Manning at the airport. They finally broke down and bought a used $3.5 million dollar used Cessna M2, a bargain at that price. They put in another half million dollars into upgrades in technology for safety. Maintenance at the Albany International Airport and the Key West International Airport was extra as was picking up a flight crew whenever they needed it. But in lieu of getting kidnapped again, Jack put his foot down and bought the plane. Now, when leaving Albany, his two retired FBI agents could fly down with them at no extra cost since they were paying them anyway for security. If they were staying longer, then the Coast Guard team would kick in and his Albany security could head home with the plane. They wouldn't need it anyway when in the Keys and when they did need it, they could make a call and have it ready that day. Mary and Jack were still frugal, even after winning two national lotteries but circumstances made them see the light. Life had changed and they needed to recognize their vulnerability and deal with it. They didn't want to spend money on security but had to because of the celebrity it caused.

Joe went to the commercial private jet area and met Mary and Jack when they got off the plane. They only took overnight bags for tonight and tomorrow and left the rest on the plane. They never needed to bring a lot back to Key West since they had their Florida clothes already there. It was getting warm up north in late spring so they didn't need all their winter gear, which took up a lot of space. Now with the convenience of having their own plane and crew, they could simply do as they pleased and leave everything that they didn't need, right on the plane.

"Welcome," said Joe. "Nice plane. Sure beats travelling by Southwest and switching planes in Tampa to head to Key West."

"It does," said Jack. "I still can't get over how much it costs instead of flying Southwest. But you know our situation and we don't ever want a repeat of it."

Joe gave Mary a hug and a kiss on the cheek. They loaded up Joe's larger Coast Guard vehicle that could hold the three flight crewmembers, Mary and Jack, and their overnight luggage. Joe dropped them off at the hotel and gave them time to shower and relax before picking them up for dinner. Joe went home and helped Tillie and Julie prepare for dinner. It was spaghetti and meatballs night with fresh salad and garlic bread. Joe asked Bella if she wanted to go with him to pick up Mary and Jack and she shot to her room to get her coat. She had a great time at Christmas at their house up in Troy. It was the first time she ever saw snow in person. Jack bought her a complete snow outfit from head to toe and sleds. He also gave all of them on rides on their snowmobiles. Living near the top of the mountain on ten acres gave them plenty of room to move around and a really nice hill for Bella's adventures.

Joe has wanted to reciprocate ever since that trip. Hopefully, he would do them justice tomorrow. They would meet and greet and then have lunch in the officer's club at the Academy before heading to Connecticut College.

Joe also wanted to introduce them to the staff at the Coast Guard Alumni Association. They were in the midst of a massive fundraiser to build a new state-of-the-art facility right in the middle of the campus near the Thames River. Joe had downloaded documents from the Alumni website which started with a bold vision for the Maritime Center of Excellence. The new Center would complete the transformation of the Academy's waterfront by providing a centerpiece befitting the nation's premier maritime service academy.

Hopefully, the new Center would impress visitors by creating a beautiful space to host events during seminal Academy experiences such as Swearing-In Day, Academy Introductory Mission, Bears Day, Parents Weekend, and Homecoming. Joe was quite impressed with what they have done to date. To date, the goal was $23.0 million dollars and they have pledges totaling $21.5 million dollars, so they were at 91% of their goal. The association fundraisers seemed to have plateaued and were stuck at that level for the last several months. Joe thought that perhaps Mary and Jack would have an interest in closing the gap if the association included room for minority recruitment and visitation for students from Florida, especially women of color. If they could actually come to the campus and see what they would be doing for the next four years it might just inspire them to attend. They would also emphasize that they would receive a 100% free education, no tuition and no room and board. However, even the cost of trips home were out of reach for many of these poor students. Joe thought he could tie the pledge for recruitment into the Coast Guard, now headed up by Joan Talbot, could include the cost of getting these students back and forth to home all four years in addition to the recruitment effort.

Joe picked up Mary and Jack and the hotel with Bella in tow. They met them in the lobby and Bella ran up to them and gave them both a hug. Joe was very proud of Bella. She has come a very long way in a very short time. Showing love and affection to others meant that she was adjusting and thriving. Bella showed the same affection to Annie but especially to Tillie. Tillie told her that she was the best hugger ever. Bella laughed and hugged even harder.

Joe pulled up in their driveway and was met by Julie holding Annie in her arms and Tillie. Mary immediately reached out and Julie handed Annie to her.

"How beautiful she is. She is growing so fast," Mary said. "You have two beautiful daughters."

She walked in and sat down on the couch holding Annie. Joe immediately gave Jack a Sam Adam's *Octoberfest*. "How the hell do you get this out of season?" asked Jack.

"Pull. I got pull, Jack," said Joe and smiled. They clinked bottles and Jack gave both Tillie and Julie a hug. Julie took Annie from Mary's arms and Bella started to pull Mary to show her to her room and how it was set up. She said, "Grammy and I sleep in this bed. I'll miss her when she goes home." That brought a small tear to both Tillie and Julie's eyes.

They all sat down and enjoyed a wonderful home cooked meal. Tillie's meatballs were the best and the pledge sauce was made from scratch. No one wanted dessert, not even Bella. They sat around the living room and talked for a few hours. Joe told them what he and Julie had planned for them for tomorrow. Joe was in charge of the Academy tour while Julie would do the honors at Connecticut College. Around 9:00 p.m. after the kids were in bed, Joe and Julie took Mary and Jack back to the hotel. It was still a blessing having Tillie around to babysit. They had a drink at the hotel bar and Jack put the bill on his room tab. They would be picked up by Joe at 8:30 a.m. in the morning and would meet the Rear Admiral and his staff at 9:00 a.m. From there, Joe would give them the tour starting with the chapel, where Annie was baptized. It was the only building that they actually toured the last time. The Rear Admiral would meet them for lunch at the officer's club and then Joe would introduce them to the Alumni Association staff. From there, they would walk over to Connecticut College and meet the president, Dr. Kate Ballenger and the new Dean, Dr. Erica Jones, the first African-American Dean at the college.

Joe picked them up precisely at 8:30 a.m. and pulled right up at the administrative offices fifteen minutes later. As they walked through the door, Joe, Julie, Mary and Jack were all greeted by Ensign Meg Olson, the Rear Admiral's assistant. "Welcome, everyone. Can I get anything for you to drink?" she asked. They all had breakfast and asked for coffee. "Coming right up," she said as she led them to the boardroom. She whispered to Joe, "We won Sunday too, in a squeaker 4-3. Guess who picked off a runner at first base in the 6th inning with a man on third as well?"

Joe wasn't aware of the game's outcome. He was so tied up with Mary and Jack that he forgot to ask. "Frankie came through?" he asked.

"Frankie came through," she said. "I made it to the game around the 4th inning. I wasn't going to go but I said the hell with it. I picked up Laura and we went together.

Joe, it was a thing of beauty. So now, they're 29-7 going into the tournament on a high note."

Jack was listening to the conversation and said to Joe, "Is that the world-famous Andy Pettitte pick-off move to first?" He laughed.

"It is and it works when done properly," he added. He smiled. He couldn't wait to talk to Frankie. That was great.

They sat in the boardroom and immediately the Rear Admiral came in and introduced himself to Mary and Jack. He thanked them for all they have done for the Academy and told them whenever they wanted to visit to please call him directly and he would personally set up the tour. He shook hands with Julie as well and then said to Joe, "The pick-off move is still alive and well, huh? We are now 29-7, that's unbelievable."

"It is, isn't it?" said Joe.

In walked Captain Laura Chavez. She introduced herself as a member of the Board of Trustees. Working so directly with her, Joe almost forgot that she was a Trustee at the Coast Guard Academy. They have become such good friends that he never thought about it but she was instrumental in helping Joe with security at the Academy as well as helping him study the language requirement and courses at Connecticut College. She said to Joe, "You missed Sunday. It was a thing of beauty, Captain."

Joe laughed and he said he would talk to her later. He wanted to know if she would like to take the tour with them and she said she had classes until 2:00 p.m. and asked if she could meet them at the president's office across the street. Joe thought that would be fine.

The tour went well. Lunch was even better with a corner table overlooking the Thames River attended by Rear Admiral Kelly. The food was first rate and it was a very pleasant time. From there, Joe took them to the Alumni offices on campus. He introduced them to the team and they told Mary and Jack all about the new Center. They had a replica set up right outside their office door where everyone could see the detail of the new facility. They mentioned that they were almost there to the total but needed an extra push to get over the top.

Mary was a very quick study. Joe never had to say a thing to her about what he was thinking. She knew right away. It was to close the gap in funding to complete the project. However, he also knew that neither Jack nor Mary were pushovers. As they sat there, Mary began to speak. She said she loved the idea of a new center but didn't hear a word about the recruitment of women of color or other minorities into the Academy. She then went on to explain the millions of dollars she has pumped in to District 7's recruitment efforts run by Lieutenant Joan Talbot at the Islamorada station and at The College of the Florida Keys. She turned to Jack and then said, "Both Jack and I will contribute one million dollars for the completion of the project, if matched by a half million dollars from other alumni members, that's a 2 to 1 match," she said. However, you will have to make room available at the new center for the recruitment of minority men and women and advertise its existence and push the recruitment effort. You can work out the details with Lieutenant Talbot."

"That's very generous of you," said the director.

"We will set up an account and deposit one million dollars as a good faith measure. We will leave the funds in the account and as soon as you have the actual new cash in hand, not just pledges, we will release the funds," she said.

"Can we advertise this?" asked the director.

"Of course, it will be the only way to get the matching funds. However, you must stress that the initiative is to recognize and recruit minorities into the Coast Guard but especially into the Coast Guard Academy."

"Thank you. It will be done," said the Director.

They got up and left and started to head across the street to see Dr. Ballenger. Joe said, "Mary, that didn't take long. I love your thinking about matching funds and tying it to Joan's efforts. That's great."

"When you gave us the brochures without saying anything, I didn't need to figure it out. Joe, as I told you and Julie, we need good projects to fund. We have three to five years to release all our trust funds into worthy projects. After that, I won't say we are done but we want it to end so we can enjoy the rest of our lives. My rescue by you from the kidnappers put everything into perspective. Thanks, Joe," she said.

They walked over to Kate's office. As they were walking across the street, Tillie pushing a stroller with Annie and with Bella by her side came down the street. They stopped and talked to them and told Tillie they wouldn't be that long at the college. Tillie said that she'd put Annie down for a nap, give Bella a snack and start packing for tomorrow's trip home.

As they were walking, Julie said, "I don't think you know yet but Lucy Talbot has just been accepted at the Academy starting in the fall. She is way ahead academically and could be a junior but she'll take a double major and be a sophomore with four years of eligibility to run Division III cross-country. She has to make up the physical and leadership requirements and she'll start in June and take care of most of the obligations. She'll start cross-country in mid-August and have her first meet in early September. She gave up her full scholarship at Division I University of Miami so we are very excited for her. She's like our daughter after all. I was her babysitter."

"That's awesome," said Mary. "Now if we can tie in the

trust fund down in the 7th Division to the Academy Joan can have more opportunity to come up her to help and see her daughter."

"That would be the plan. She'll stay with us for a week before starting. Joan and Jeff will be here as well staying at your hotel. I wish we could squeeze more in here but until we know exactly how long we will be here, we don't want to buy anything," said Joe.

They met Laura Chavez at the door to the president's office. They walked in and were greeted by both Kate and Erica and were guided into their boardroom. Mary and Jack have seen more boardrooms in the last few years than they thought was humanly possible. Kate thanked them for allowing Joe to take some of the endowment and helping Connecticut College upgrade its security systems and tie into the Coast Guard Academy. She said they were still in the process of upgrading but their systems were quite antiquated and needed complete replacement. She also admitted that her security staff needs additional support and up until now, everything has been fine. After a few minutes, Mary told Kate and Erica the story of her kidnapping and subsequent rescue by Joe and his friends. She was quite clear that without Joe's intervention, she wouldn't be here today. They were absolute friends but it went further than that, he saved her life. Both Kate and Erica were starting to understand what Joe Traynor was all about and by proxy what Julie Chapman Traynor was all about. They knew her story growing up through her books but this went well beyond a simple story of a poor girl. These two were exceptional people and Mary framed it perfectly that without them, she wouldn't be here.

Chapter 29

Tillie was all packed. Joe pulled the SVU up closer to the front door so he could load Tillie's luggage into the back of the vehicle. Mary and Jack would meet them at the plane at the airport to save them an extra trip. They would head out at 9:00 a.m. with the flight crew in the hotel van. It was only twenty minutes to the airport so they ate breakfast at the hotel and were ready to go. Julie put Annie in her car seat and buckled up Bella in the back to sit with Tillie. Julie would bring her to school after they dropped off Tillie and said their goodbyes.

They left a little after 9:00 a.m. because Bella didn't want Tillie to go so she was hiding in her room, under her bed. They knew where she was so Tillie went in to talk to her and that made it better. She put her in her arms and told her she would see her real soon. Julie made Tillie compromise and they would visit every four months at the least. It was easier for Tillie to come north than it was for Julie and Joe and the kids. They promised Bella that they would go see Tillie in Key Largo in early July when school was out. They also thought that Bella was now old enough to appreciate Disney World up in Orlando so they would rent a van and head from Key Largo to Orlando during the second week of their vacation. Tillie would come with them and then take the new *Brightline* high-speed train down to Miami where she would be met by Jane Swanson who volunteered to drive Tillie home to Key Largo. They could talk about their mutual roles on the board of the Teresa Trust Fund South on the way down. Jane would stay over, go to dinner with Tillie, and then head back to Miami. Jane's husband was now doing much better with the side effects of Covid-19 as a long-hauler. It completely upset his life but he was thankful to being on the side of recovery.

The plane was all ready geared up to go and as they pulled up, Jack popped open Joe's rear hatch and started to unload Tillie's bags. He mentioned that as soon as they landed in Key West, she would get a ride up to Key Largo. Tillie said that wasn't necessary because Ed Lansing would meet them at the airport and give her a ride home. That was something Julie didn't know anything about and nodded to Joe and smiled. She guessed Tillie missed Ed a lot, more than she let on. They all said their goodbyes with extra hugs and kisses. Tillie went down on one knee to say goodbye to Bella who was sniffling. She told her that they would have a wonderful time in Disney World and she would call her every day she could. That seemed to settle Bella. The plane closed and started to taxi to the runway. They waved through the windows and blew kisses. They got back into the SUV a little sadder but then had to drop off Bella at her school. Julie would walk in with her and Annie in the stroller. Joe had to head to work so Julie would walk home the few blocks. She wanted to make sure that Bella was all right. When Bella's mother died, Bella wasn't sure that anyone would come back for her and she felt despair even at that age. Julie and Joe were always well aware that things could go astray at any time so they were always on top of it. If Bella started talking in Spanish again, they knew there was a problem.

Joe made it to his office and called Larry Curtis at the Navy Submarine Base. Larry had already been to the Academy and walked around with Joe a short time ago. Joe pointed out all the changes. Larry made a few suggestions about the front gate, which made a lot of sense. They had a special piece of equipment that did a complete infrared scan on every vehicle coming into their campus and it took a picture as well for further evidence. Larry said he would order the equipment and see to its installation and send Joe a bill. Larry knew that Joe was sitting on a substantial amount of money and it didn't matter to him as long at it secured the safety of those in the Academy. Joe's call today was in regard to the newly installed Maritime Security Response Team or MSRT that was approved by both the Admiral and Rear Admiral. One new MSRT team would now be housed at the Coast Guard Academy. It would cost several hundred thousand dollars per year but Joe said his resources would fund the program for a minimum of four years. Before this MSRT team came on board, there were only a few across the country with most at major seaports like New York City, Los Angeles and Miami. Joe made the point that not only would the Academy be secure, but also it added a layer of protection for the Navy Submarine Base right down the river. Joe's new MSRT team was to meet the Navy Seal team already stationed at the Base. Joe thought it was a good idea to have both teams on the same page if and when there were emergencies. Having the teams coordinated not only doubled the coverage, but it made them stronger if they trained and worked together.

Larry Curtis thought that was a terrific idea and he

didn't need any approval since he was in charge of all 600 acres at the base. He would also tie in their own security police force, the size of a small town. This was a very well packed facility with families, children, visitors, and military personnel surrounded by nuclear submarines. There could be no infiltration that was acceptable. One attack that could ignite one nuclear submarine would ignite them all and blow away a large portion of the state of Connecticut.

"Larry, it's Joe," he said. "How are you? Can I see you today? I want to see about getting our two teams together, your Seals and our MSRTs. How about lunch?"

"Sounds good. Can you come over here? I have a lot of high-priced individuals and a few Congressmen knocking on my door today. They must think this is a nuclear Disney World or something," he added.

It was now around 11:30 a.m. "I'll see you in a half hour, Larry," he said. He hopped in his vehicle and he knew by the time he got through all the guard stations it would be closer to noon. He called Julie and told her where he would be if she needed anything. She got back from school and put Annie in for a nap. She was writing another chapter so he said he wouldn't bother her. If she wanted, she could call him and he would pick up Bella to bring her back to work. She thought that was great. They would bring their bat, ball, and gloves down to the field where the ladies were warming up for their softball tournament. They did pretty well and made the playoffs by the skin of their teeth and a .500 record. There were a lot of underclassmen on the team so they should be much improved next year. This year's graduation on May 18th wouldn't affect them at all.

It was now heading into early May. The baseball team did very well but got beat in the NCAA Division III

Regionals by Southern Maine from Portland, Maine. They lost the first game, won the second and lost the third in extra innings 3-2. Southern Maine was a top 25 powerhouse at the Division III level so the Academy did very well for themselves. Joe couldn't make the trip but saw it on ESPN 3. He was heartbroken but figured that this was their best year ever, going 30-9. They headed into the tournament at 29-7, after winning the NEWMAC. Joe's friend, Mike Hanley from the CIA was heading to town so it was too bad they lost. He wanted to see a game because he was a huge baseball fan as well. He'll have to come back next year, earlier in the season to see a NEWMAC game, preferably against MIT or Babson College.

Joe picked up Mike at the airport. Bella would share a room with Annie so Mike could use her room. He would be here for three days and then head back to Miami. Julie bought a rollaway bed for these times. They would store it against the wall in Annie's room. It was the perfect size for Bella.

"So you couldn't win one more game so I could watch, huh?" he said.

"Well it was in Portland anyway. It's 210 miles away and about three hours. The trip would take twice as long back and forth than the game would take," said Joe.

"The women are playing this afternoon right at our field at 3:00 p.m. Want to go? They're getting better every game. Their tournament ran later than the men's so this was the NEWMAC finals for softball and they won their first two games. Bella is their Bat Girl so she wants to go anyway," said Joe.

"Sounds like a plan," said Mike. "By the way, let's talk about our life after the service if we can. Like you, with kids, I'm a year away from retirement as well. All my trips are overseas not to Portland, Maine."

"I have my resume all polished. Let's look at yours. Vanderbilt University is a good start. Let's build on that. I'm meeting with Larry Curtis at the Navy Submarine Base tomorrow so I want you to come along and tell him all about our local white supremacist groups brewing in the state of Connecticut. It may open his eyes a little. Larry is a good guy. We can also ask him about openings associated with Navy contractors and those he deals with on a daily basis. It may be to your benefit. I'm sure you don't have to live in Connecticut."

"Great. Sounds good. I'm hungry let's get lunch and head to the softball game," said Mike. They did. They walked out the front door saying goodbye to Julie and Annie. They said they would be back after the game. Julie was making one of Joe's favorites, beef stew. Mike thought that was great too. Bella ran ahead of them in her uniform. Mike just laughed and said, "I can't believe you got away with that."

"Got away with what?" as Joe smiled.

"I'm surprised she doesn't have pinstripes on, Joe," said Mike.

"I was told directly that it was a firing offense by the Red Sox loving Rear Admiral Kelly, so this was as close as I could get without getting shot. At least the men had their best record ever."

"Must have been the coaching and cheering, huh?" Mike laughed.

They settled into the stands and sat by themselves. Rear Admiral Kelly came walking by wife and daughter and waved to Joe. He came over and Joe introduced them to Mike. Joe had set up a meeting with the Rear Admiral for Mike later tomorrow after meeting Larry Curtis at the Navy Submarine Base. So, the Rear Admiral knew who Mike was. He looked at him kind of funny. Joe thought he never met a member of the CIA before and was checking him out. Ellen took a picture of Bella and one with Bella and Grace together. Bella went back to the dugout to put all the bats away and sat next to the coach. She loved it. The ladies won very easily 10-3. It wasn't even that close. This win put them one win over .500, the best in years so everyone was thrilled. At .500 they probably wouldn't win the NEWMAC tournament, so they wouldn't get as far as the baseball team but next year looked promising. Joe and Mike helped Bella pick up all the equipment and put it on the golf cart to head back to the fieldhouse. Joe showed him around a little and Mike was very impressed. Joe told him that he would be shocked at the size of the Navy Submarine Base when they visit tomorrow. He said the security looked like it was the White House. Joe told him all about the problems that Connecticut College could create if they didn't spend more on security but there was nothing he could do about it, other than what he had already done and already expensed.

Joe and Mike met Larry the next day for a full-guided tour of the submarine base. Mike was very impressed and watched the Navy Seal team train in their separate facility. He told Joe that partnering his new MSRT team with the Seals was a great idea and could prove very beneficial in a crisis.

Joe mentioned that like him, Mike was coming up on twenty years in the CIA and was looking at opportunities outside the department. He mentioned that he had spent too much time out of the country and missed the kids growing up. Now, he thought he could transfer his skills to a commercial entity, preferably in Miami because the kids were in high school now and he wanted them settled until they graduated and off to college. Larry was very accommodating. He said all the submarines and subcontractors building the ships were located right in Groton, right at the base or in Newport News, Virginia. General Dynamics Electric Boat Company was the primary source for all nuclear submarines but they also had partnerships in other areas including a great relationship with Boeing Corporation, whom just moved its Boeing Space and Launch headquarters from Arlington, Virginia to Titusville, right next to Kennedy Space Center, Cape Canaveral Air Force Station and Patrick Air Force base. They also had a presence in cyber security in Miami, which would be right up Mike's alley. The Rear Admiral asked Mike if he spoke Spanish and he said yes and he was not as fluent as Joe but getting better every day.

Captain Larry Curtis put his military hat on as they say and made one phone call to his close friend down in Arlington, Virginia. He was on the phone in another room for a good ten minutes and then said thanks and hung up. He went in and smiled and said, Mike, "Can you attend a meeting in Miami next Thursday at 11:00 a.m. to meet the head of Boeing's cyber security team on Brickell?"

"Yes, sir. I can. Can you tell me anything about it?"

"I take it that you have clearances equal to Joe's?" said Larry.

"I do, but for the CIA, only. I do not have Joe's credentials for the FBI or Homeland Security. However, we have partnered together on many details and my clearance with the CIA carried the day," said Mike.

"Good enough, Mike. That's what I told them and they were fine with it. I'm glad I didn't have to lie," he said and smiled.

"How about the pay, Larry?" Joe asked.

"Probably two to three times your current salary right now with full family benefits, paid vacation, and a very generous retirement program. These people make a lot of money," said Larry.

Joe said, "Thank you, Larry. It is appreciated. We'll head out. We have to meet Rear Admiral Kelly at 2:30 p.m. Mike let Larry know how you make out," as Larry handed him his card.

"Call me anytime, Mike. I would love to find out how you made out. You never know, I could be with you next year as well. We're all getting a little too old for national security, you know?" said Larry. With that they left. Joe set up another meeting for the Seals and the MSRT to meet. Both teams needed to walk the campuses of both sites to familiarize themselves with the comings and goings so there would be no surprises if another crisis hit. On the way back, Mike thanked Joe profusely. He said his wife would be thrilled with the news of a potential job right in Miami with a large pay raise and no international travel, especially clandestine travel that he knew way too well. They talked about meeting the Rear Admiral and how they would handle the information that Mike developed on all the white supremacists' groups in Connecticut. The information was substantial but since the CIA was not able to work within the continental United States, they would need to involve at least the FBI if not Homeland Security.

Chapter 30

Joe and Mike were meeting with the Rear Admiral at 10:00 a.m. this morning. Joe reviewed with Mike exactly what he was going to tell him and what he wasn't going to tell him. Joe told him that the Rear Admiral got nervous when he found out that when the CIA took over, the accused were renditioned and then interrogated. Joe told him to downplay it. It has happened so many times that Mike was used to it when dealing with Joe. First it was the Russians in Miami. Then it was the Columbians in Miami. Then the Haitian sex traffickers in Miami Beach and the Chechens in Orlando were stopped by Joe and sent to Mike. The only ones that didn't involve Mike were the Dixie mafia drug dealers up in Nashville. Finally, it was only several months ago that Mike picked up the National Alliance white supremacists in Hialeah after Joe saved Mary from her kidnappers. They made a pretty good team but winning every time didn't seem possible. Terrorists were relentless and both Joe and Mike were getting tired of it. It was ongoing and would never stop. They just didn't want to be forty years old and completely burned out way before they retired.

Joe and Mike walked over to the Academy. Joe told him that they had a special Academy officer drive around the homes of those employed by the Academy who lived in New London. They did several trips a day and it took about two hours per trip to complete a run. Joe saw the vehicle go by but didn't wave so as not to point out the vehicle if anyone was following them. Joe wasn't paranoid but was very aware that taking down the bombers that came from the Sovereign Citizens of Connecticut might tick them off and he was very careful. It was one thing if they got them all but they only got those that committed the crime. It was very difficult to charge anyone with conspiracy especially if those arrested didn't cooperate.

They walked in the front door and Joe introduced Mike Hanley to everyone in the office. He only introduced him as his good friend from Miami. They didn't need to know that he was one of the top crook chasers for the CIA. Joe hung up his jacket and gave Mike a hanger for his. They walked down the hall and both grabbed a cup of coffee. Joe knocked on the Rear Admiral's door right at 10:00 a.m. As Joe knew Rear Admiral Kelly had great respect for punctuality and Joe obliged whenever he could. He couldn't all the time because of all the emergencies that popped up and needed to tell Rear Admiral Kelly about the various situations.

"Sir, this is my good friend, Mike Hanley, from Miami," said Joe. He then whispered, "No one knows why he's here, Sir, or who he is," said Joe.

"Got it," said the Rear Admiral. "Nice to meet you. May I call you Mike?" he asked.

"Of course, Sir," said Mike. Outside the CIA, no one knew what anyone's rank within the CIA actually is. Joe knew he was the Officer in Charge for the South Atlantic district, headquartered in Miami. He had the same equivalent rank as Paul Philips in charge of the Miami FBI office and probably closer to Jake Barnes' title of Rear Admiral. Joe was probably one step down but Mike never mentioned it and they worked as equal partners. Actually, Mike was in charge outside the twelve nautical miles that defined international waters but it became iffy and gray in many cases. Sometimes, renditioning included bringing suspects from land to the outside international waters where the CIA could ply its trade. Technically, a nautical mile is multiplied by 1.151 to equate to land miles. Thus, the international waters at 12.0 nautical miles are actually 13.8094 land miles. It may not seem like much of a difference but if you miss it, it could cause major headaches in law enforcement. You could miss by a mile if you didn't know the difference.

"Thanks for coming. It is appreciated," said Rear Admiral Kelly. "I understand that you are thinking of retiring when you get your twenty years in next year. Is that true?"

"I'm thinking about it, Sir. It been a long haul with the work we do and it wears on you. I have two children and I'd like to see them before they leave the nest for college. I would also like to be able to pay for their college. As you know, it isn't easy on our salaries. The salaries are fine but we will have to borrow enough to pay for their colleges and it will be more than our mortgage. I'm forty, Rear Admiral. I'd like to enjoy life a little more," said Mike.

"I don't blame you. I know you are well acquainted with Joe and Rear Admiral Barnes and you met Captain Curtis yesterday. Joe told me that he was very helpful to you calling a few chips in from his friends in Miami," said Kelly.

"He did and I'm grateful. I am meeting someone from Boeing next week to discuss various options. I'll let you and Joe know what happens and of course I'll call Captain Curtis as well," said Mike.

"Great," said the Rear Admiral. "Now tell me everything you know about our white supremacist groups in Connecticut. Joe told me he asked you to work on it and he said you have some information for us," said Kelly.

Mike started off by naming the three largest white supremacist groups in Connecticut that included the Sovereign Citizens of Connecticut, the KKK, and the World Church of the Creator. None of these three are very far from the Academy. The Sovereign Citizens are in Windsor, Connecticut only 44 miles from here. The Klan is in both Orange and Milford, Connecticut, 56 miles west of New London. The World Church of the Creator is in Wallingford, Connecticut, 60 miles northwest of the Academy and near to Hartford. All three together account for perhaps a little over 300 members and a majority of those members have been incarcerated at both Connecticut and out-of-state prisons. They are some very scary dudes," he said.

He continued, "They all need money. They are not getting donations from their members because they are felons without resources. They are self-funding through kidnapping, murder, theft, and filing false documents for property ownership. They need funding. That's what happened in Florida with the kidnapping of Mary Evans. They were low on funds and thought they could kidnap Mary and get a $10.0 million dollar ransom for her. It's too bad they didn't know that they were dealing with Joe and his own MSRT team who squashed them within hours. Evidently, Joe's good friend Jack Forest took care of whatever funding they had in the Cayman Islands. He forwarded $2.0 million dollars to us to help defray the cost of their incarceration that was unfunded. Mary Evans was so grateful that she also sent us $2.0 million dollars to spend as needed. I've tried to figure out their resources using several steps. I know where they are located and I have checked all the financial transactions with Jack Forest, coming out of those areas that went south to the Caymans. We found several and we are keeping an eye on the funds. We don't want them to know what we're doing yet because we don't want to alert them and have them disappear into other groups in the region or nationally."

"You did a lot in such a short time," said Kelly.

"We try, Sir. That's what Joe and I do as a team in cooperation with the FBI and Homeland Security. We also know various members of each group. We have undercover officers at their rallies. They are free to move around and we can't do anything about it. However, we have a video of every person attending these rallies. We have used state-of-the-art facial recognition software to find out who they are. We have received names and criminal jackets on almost 125 members so far and we are still working. It's a long process. We have looked at every person's accounts and by the balances we can see what level any one individual seems to be. Just like in real life, the top dog has the most money and those we will watch like a hawk. At any time, we can shut them down financially but we cannot have them arrested or treated like the terrorists they are because there is no recognition of domestic terrorism or even a definition to hang our hats on. We have to go after each person, one at a time," said Mike.

"And that makes it difficult," said Joe as he jumped into the conversation. "We also don't have the manpower to watch all 300 or even those 125 that we have identified as bad guys. That's why we need to remain vigilant at the Academy and the surrounding area. Our watch, going house to house, several times a day, has shown that in fact there are some individuals who drive by certain houses, including mine, from time to time. We have taken pictures of three cars so far that looked to be suspicious. We are running those cars through DMV and we will find out if there is anything going on. Larry Curtis and I are on top of this. Our MSRT team and their Seals are working together as a team, just in case. They can be called in within minutes of any major crisis. Just having them work together gives me great confidence," said Joe

Joe summarized where they are right now and what he planned to do to continue to upgrade the facilities. They shook hands and Joe and Mike headed back to his house. Joe would take him to the airport where he would get a flight that would get him to Miami after a quick stop in Charlotte, North Carolina. They planned on continuing to talk every week about watching and listening to see if there was any new information coming down the pike. That is the best they can do for now, other than continue to be vigilant. There was so much more that Joe wanted to accomplish before his time was up. Unfortunately, this took up most of his time. He wanted to work with Laura Chavez to develop a project with both the Russian and Spanish classes at Connecticut College. He wanted to develop additional curriculum that reflected the "street" rather than academics. He wanted them to be aware of what they will actually be doing as newly appointed Ensigns in the Coast Guard. He wanted them to be proud of who they are and what they represent. He wants to make the Academy more reflective of the communities they serve and that includes a very large increase in minority participation and speakers of other languages before they even get to the Academy.

The following day, Joe got a call from Mike thanking him for the introductions and he said he got home on time.

He talked to his wife and he said she was thrilled about the potential of a new career right in Miami where they have made their home for years. He said he had a year to go for a decent retirement so that was still in front of him but he wasn't going to go on long renditions anymore. When he got back, he talked to his boss from Washington, D.C. who asked him to talk to him before he decided anything. Of course, he said he would. He's reported to him for the last ten years and they had great respect for each other. He too said that Mike could work for any government contractor he wanted or stay in government in a less provocative position. He told him he earned it and deserved it. Joe knew that he had the same rapport with his bosses as well.

The next day, Joe met again with Rear Admiral Kelly. He seemed unnerved by what was said yesterday. He told Joe that he was starting to understand the current security situation of his cadets but had totally underestimated what that really meant. He said both Joe and Mike and Larry Curtis has opened his eyes wider and he wanted to make sure they did all they could to fix whatever problems they had before it became bigger. Joe gave him the detailed list and plan that was already implemented with notations on upcoming projects and the costs associated with those plans. If anything, Joe was meticulous and accounted for every penny that was spent year to date. He never wanted anyone to ever question his integrity or call in to question his ability to manage all these interlocking activities. The Rear Admiral thanked Joe for giving his all. He knew deep down that Joe had no long-range plans to stay at the Academy after he did everything he thought he could to help. Joe wasn't sure what he wanted but going on forty years old meant honing in on what is important to his family and himself.

When Joe got home, Julie had just finished three

chapters of her book. She would FedEx it to her publisher to continue to edit the book well before it was scheduled for release. She was planning a trip to New York City in early October and wanted to be back with Joe for her birthday on October 17th. It was her 30th birthday and she thought it was a big deal and that she had crossed another milestone in her life. Unknown to Julie, Tillie was coming back for a party for Julie. Tillie tried to get her to come back to Key Largo but it wasn't in the cards. They did make plans to go down for Christmas though and spend two weeks with Tillie and their friends. Bella would make sure that Santa Claus knew where they would be staying just like last year when they were up in Troy at Mary Evan's and Jack Manning's place in Brunswick. Bella had two Santa sightings, one in Brunswick and one when they got back to Tavernier, Florida. Their next-door neighbor hid Bella's presents and put them under their tree when they came back and opened the door. Now, Bella said she wants to make sure it would happen again for both her and her new baby sister, Annie. That made Joe and Julie smile. They were a family.

Chapter 31

Graduation at the Academy was coming up on May 18th this year. It was Joe's first graduation ceremony since his own graduation from the Academy. He started at MIT for one semester. He got his Associates, two-year degree from Miami Dade College, and then finished up at the Academy as a gift from his Rear Admiral before leaving the service to attend Rensselaer Polytechnic Institute. At the time he was still a Chief Warrant Officer on his way out. His time at the Academy was not as enriching as most. He was there on an accelerated basis to simply get his degree so he could get his MBA at Rensselaer Polytechnic Institute. Joe remembered the kindness after all the difficulty serving as an enlisted man for all those years. To come back to the Coast Guard, they gave Joe back his time as if he never left. Taking down the Mexican Mafia in Albany and across the country in one swell swoop opened a lot of eyes earning him a medal for valor. It allowed Joe to return to Florida to help Julie and her grandmother who was injured in a car hit and run at the time. Somehow, it all worked out. Now, Joe will be second in command at the graduation, next to the Rear Admiral and the Admiral, who will be a guest along with the other dignitaries. Last year, President Biden spoke. Julie would attend a lot of the ceremonies held from Sunday, May 15rh until the actual graduation on May 18th.

They were planning on heading to Key Largo in July and then north to Disney World for Bella and for Julie to meet her contacts for the series now being filmed at the Hollywood Studios. Julie had a surprise for Bella and told Joe quietly and not to let Bella know. Bella would have a small part in one of the episodes. It was the beginning of a *Girl's Story* when Julie was very young. The audience for the new series would not only be for American girls that were English speakers only but for speakers of other languages as well. Bella would have a small role as an interpreter for young girls her age that only spoke Spanish. She would be in the episode and have speaking lines. When she got back to New London, whatever hesitation she had in making friends because she was different, would go away in a minute because of her newfound fame. If she did well as expected, they said they could feature her again up in New London along with her mother, Julie.

On Sunday, May 15th, Joe, Julie, and the kids attended the Catholic Baccalaureate Mass, at *Roland Hall.* At 12:30 p.m., they would head down to the Class of 2022 picnic at the lower athletic field. At 7:30 p.m., after their dinner and naps for the kids, they would attend the Sunset Drill Review Parade, at the *Washington Parade Ground.* After that, the kids would be wiped out. On Tuesday morning, Joe would skip the family golf outing. Joe hated golf. At 10:00 a.m. he would head out by himself and be a guest speaker at the Society for Policy and International Affairs Government Majors Brunch, at the Alumni Center. At 11:30 a.m. he would head with the Rear Admiral to the luncheon for cadets, guests, and academic awards in the Cadet War Room. At 4:30 p.m. he was invited not only as the second in command but as the pitching coach of the baseball team to the Athletic Awards Reception & Ceremony, *Reception: 3rd Deck Roland Hall/Ceremony: Billard Hall.* He was told to be there by Coach Brian Casey because everyone on the team, including the coaches, would receive their NEWMAC championship rings and a plaque for making the NCAA Division III finals.

Finally it would be graduation day. Julie was invited and Sam O'Neil would babysit for them all day. Sean O'Neil's main function was at the athletic events to hand out honors. Joe and Julie had to be at the Academy for a 9:30 a.m. reception and at 11:0 a.m. began the One Hundred Thirty Seventh Commencement Exercises. Julie was very proud that the Rear Admiral asked her, along with his wife, Ellen, to hand out the individual graduation diplomas at Cadet Memorial Field. They were prepared in case of rain to head to Leamy Hall Auditorium. After graduation, there was a special late luncheon in the officer's club for the Board of Trustees including Rear Admiral Jake Barnes who flew up for the occasion, Admiral Hartnagle from Washington, D.C. and staff, the guest speaker, and other dignitaries including Dr. Kate Ballenger and Dr. Erica Jones from Connecticut College. Joe personally invited Larry Curtis, Captain and head of the U. S. Navy Submarine Base.

It was a very nice day and one that reflected what Joe believed to be what the Coast Guard was all about. Walking out of the ceremony were over 200 new Ensigns in the United States Coast Guard ready to defend the Constitution of the United States of America. This was a very proud moment for Joe and Julie recognized that and gave him a hug and told him how proud she was of him. It was finally his day. The rest of May going into June was slow.

Cadets got only three weeks vacation per year and usually took those days right after graduation. Incoming first year cadets had a lot to do. Swab Summer is the beginning of swab (freshman) year, the first part of the journey taken by new cadets. It is the most difficult and demanding period of military training they will experience as a cadet, taking place over a period of eight weeks, one of which is aboard the tall ship *Eagle*. At the end of Swab Summer they are expected to understand cadet life and what it takes to prepare and to work as a team. For other cadets, moving up, less than 12 months after reporting to the Academy, they will be involved in their first Coast Guard mission. Second year cadets and above are trained aboard operational Coast Guard units during the summer. These units are located on the east and west coast, Alaska, Hawaii, Puerto Rico and aboard ships that deploy to the Pacific Ocean, Atlantic Ocean and Caribbean Sea. Some cadets head to Coast Guard Air Stations to learn more about life as a pilot, while others work at Sectors, Stations and specialized units like the Marine Safety Center in Washington, D.C.

As a transfer student, Lucy Talbot would join Swab Summer and not only spend eight weeks at the Academy but will make up other hands-on training going into the fall semester. In addition, her women's cross-country team will start practice in early August so she will have to manage her time very carefully. She will be in a group of twenty-five transfer students, all coming in as second year cadets. Lucy had the choice to be a double major second year cadet or a third year single major cadet. She chose the second year so she would get more time on the cross-country team with eligibility bringing her right up to the start of the 2024 Olympics in Paris.

Joan, Jeff, and Lucy arrived at the airport in a Coast Guard transport from Miami, saving them a small fortune in costs. Joan is now a Lieutenant and commander of the Islamorada Coast Guard Station, and as such, had clearance for this. A call from Rear Admiral Kelly certainly didn't hurt as well as a ride to the airport by Rear Admiral Barnes personal assistant. Joan and Jeff were staying in town for a week and then heading back on another transport plane to Miami. She parked her Coast Guard vehicle at headquarters and would drive home from there after meeting with Rear Admiral Barnes, making it an official trip.

Joe and the family would be heading down to Key Largo for the July 4th weekend, starting July 1st on a Friday. They would return on Saturday, July 23rd, giving them three nice vacation weeks to see friends, enjoy the beach, and then head up to Disney World and stay at the Hollywood Studios guest rooms already set up by Marshall Tillman, president of the studio. Claire Murphy set up everything with Julie so there would be no missed steps especially with young children. Julie made all the plans with Claire because she had time and was just about finished with her new book. When they get back from vacation, she would fully review and edit and then send it to her publisher in New York City, Sarah Atwood.

They decided on a nice Airbnb in Key Largo. It was right on Moon Bay, on the beach. It had three bedrooms so Tillie could stay all two weeks whenever she wanted. It was $6,078.00 for two weeks, which seems like a lot until she looked up Airbnb in New London, right down the road from them. In Florida it was offseason but up in New London it was full price. They even threw in a new crib for Annie so that Tillie could have her own room and Bella and Annie could bunk together. A three-bedroom ranch near the ocean and beach in Waterford, Connecticut beach was $11,040.00 for two weeks. The condo in Key Largo was less than a mile from Tillie's apartment in town. When Julie was looking up places to stay she found that the condo was right down the street from the Caribbean Club, where the famous movie *Key Largo* was filmed starring Humphrey Bogart and Lauren Bacall. The Club opened in 1938 and was still going strong.

As a gift to Joe and Julie, Rear Admiral Kelly booked a flight for him and his wife, Ellen, to Miami for that weekend. They would all fly in together. Kelly would tour the District 7 offices and meet with Jake Barnes to make it official. He would only stay a week. When Joe was ready to fly out, Hollywood Studios booked a private plane for Joe and the family to head home. After all, she was the author and original screenwriter for the series and was treated like royalty because the show was doing very well. When they landed in Miami, Joe would be given a Coast Guard SUV to drive down to Key Largo. Coming back, they would hitch a ride up to Orlando with Mark Silva and be dropped off at the Hollywood Studios or Joe would simply drive them. Tillie would go with them and then take the *Brightline* high speed train down to Miami and get a ride from Jane Swanson back to Key Largo. Joe was eternally grateful not to have to book rooms and plan vacations because he was lousy at it. Julie knew this and just did her thing.

They were all packed and ready to go. The Rear Admiral and his wife, Ellen, in a large vehicle used to transfer guests to the airport from the Academy, met them. Joe and Julie thanked them profusely. It was difficult enough flying with a seven-year-old but with a seven-month-old baby it would be a hassle. They had a nice chat on the plane and had lunch right before landing in Miami. They flew into the military section of the airport and were met by one of Jake Barnes' staff. They were driven right to Brickell Avenue where the hotel and Coast Guard headquarters were located. The Kellys would be staying at the SLS Brickell Hotel & Residence at 1300 South Miami Avenue, right in the Brickell Plaza, near the Coast Guard 7th Division headquarters. The driver got out and carried their luggage. Joe and the family stayed in the vehicle and Joe drove it down to Key Largo. It was early enough that they would make it to Tillie's apartment in the afternoon and then head right over to the Airbnb condo. Annie was out like a light and Bella's head was nodding back and forth, ready to fall asleep. It took about an hour and a half, not bad for a Friday afternoon heading down to the Keys. Thank God it was July and not January.

Chapter 32

As Joe pulled up to the condo to park, it was clear that Julie loved being home. Home was the Florida Keys since birth. Moving to New London, Connecticut was fine just as attending Brown University for five years for her MFA was fine. As soon as she stepped out of the SUV, she grabbed a handful of sand and smiled. Joe saw her and he didn't need to say a thing. This was her moment. He really felt bad about his career taking Julie out of her comfort zone. It wasn't if she hated New London. In fact, she loved her new home. She loved making new friends and she especially loved her new connection to Connecticut College. She missed her Florida Keys winters and didn't even mind the heat and humidity of July in Key Largo. She was home. Once they unpacked, they would head for dinner with Tillie and Ed Lansing. As soon as they got there, Bella asked if they could head to the beach. Julie asked Joe and he nodded and said he would do the unpacking and to have fun. He said let him know if Annie needed a nap and he would bring her into the bedroom with the new crib. They both had cell phones so Julie would just text him to come get her.

As stated on-line, this condo had everything they needed for the next two weeks. As soon as they booked it, they gave Joe the exact address so Tillie could go over and look for herself. She called them and told them the location and the place looked great. She spoke to the owner who was surprised that Tillie lived in Key Largo. When she told her that her granddaughter was an author, she recognized the name and thought that's great. When she found out that Joe was in the Coast Guard, she was very pleased.

The condo is at Moon Bay with two bedrooms, and a flex room with a pull-out bed. It had a bath and a half and was located on the 5th floor with no one above them to make noise. It's a 950 square feet condo that can accommodate six guests. It has an open living, dining, and well-equipped tidy kitchen. It has a king-size bed in the primary suite and a queen in the second bedroom. Amenities include two heated pools, an outdoor common area kitchen, tennis courts and a Keys type beach area with chairs, community room with games, kitchen and televisions, a marina and a gated entrance. It had everything they needed. It was also less than a mile to Tillie's apartment.

It took them a few nights to settle in. They went to breakfast at the Waffle House where Tillie worked all those years. It had changed quite a bit and she didn't recognize anyone. Julie used to have dinner there every night as a child, doing her homework while Tillie waited tables. It was the only way Tillie could support them both. The owners at the time were lifelong friends of Tillie's so they made it work.

Their unit has a direct view to the west and of the gorgeous Blackwater Sound. Nightly sunsets are some of the best in the Keys and they watched the sun go down right from their balcony right after the kids went to bed.

With that much sun and surf, Bella was out like a light by 8:00 p.m. It was a blessing as they sat on the balcony by themselves. Julie had a glass of wine and Joe drank his beer and simply sat there without saying a word. Joe knew that Julie was thinking about being home and he didn't want to interfere with her thoughts. It was the most relaxed they have been in some time.

"Julie, I won't try to guess what you're thinking but I probably know already," said Joe.

"So, you're a mind reader, huh?" Asked Julie and laughed.

"Actually, no," he said. "But, it's very clear that you are very glad to be back in your own hometown. I miss it too, if you're asking," he added.

"Do you think we will ever get back here to live permanently," she asked.

"I've been doing a lot of thinking lately, Julie. I know it's been hard on you living up north. I know you miss the Keys very much. I do too. My twenty years are up next year. Remember they gave me back my time when I left the service to rejoin? Well, that time has passed and it will be twenty years next April on my birthday. I like being at the Academy. It's too bad they can't move it to the Florida Keys. However, I'm not suited to be an administrator on a daily basis. I like changing things, setting them in motion, and then watching it progress and take hold. After that, I want someone else who is good in operations to take over and maintain and improve what we implemented. I'm not good at that. I like action as you know and I'm kind of bored to tell you the truth," he added. "I was actually thinking about going to law school, either at Yale near us in New London or at the University of Miami in Coral Gables. Either law school would be a good choice. I already inquired at both at it looks like with my education, background and status, I could do it in two years going in the summer as well. That would only put me one year over my retirement date and it would be paid for if I asked," he said.

"How about the LSAT law boards?" she asked.

"I can take the LSAT in October when we get back. There are several online tests that you can use as a study guide. I already took the online tests and I think I did pretty well. The scores are from 120 to 180. You need at least a 173-175 to get into Yale and a little less to get into the University of Miami Law School. I have talked to the Dean at both schools and they said if I was ready, and still a member of the Coast Guard, they would review my case beforehand and let me know. They already did that and told me to take the LSAT exam."

"I didn't even know. You've been a busy little beaver, haven't you," Julie said and laughed. "What did you get on the online tests?"

"I took the online tests four times just in case and scored 175 to 178 in all four. I think where I excelled was in my experience and analytical skills. My mathematics memory skills certainly helped. I can memorize passage after passage for a test, which is helpful but immediately forget it after the test." He went on, "I wanted to talk to Jake while we're down here to get his opinion. With a law degree, and passing both the Connecticut and Florida law boards, I could stay in the Coast Guard or go to the Justice Department but it would be in Washington, D.C. where I don't think we want to go. Or, I can simply open a law practice in Key Largo. I could hook up with Clyne, Roberts and Lynch, with Sidney Clyne and Jane Swanson, and have a branch office down here in Key Largo and go to the main office in Brickell when necessary. Remember, we also could have Mary Evans and Jack Manning as clients.

I would never poach business from the Clyne law firm though. I don't think that would be right," he offered.

"I agree with you. Why don't you ask Jake his opinion and then take it from there. I know you don't want to be the Superintendent of the Coast Guard Academy. That's just not you. However, if they offered you a full-time baseball coaching position, you'd probably jump on it," she laughed.

"You know me so well," said Joe and smiled. They hit the bed early. They never got enough time to themselves and this was one of those times they needed. Julie mentioned that she wanted another child but not for a while. Maybe in a year or two, they could try. She wanted to get her book behind her. She wanted to bond with Bella and Annie at the same time and she wanted to see how she would do teaching her English course starting in the fall.

Mary Evans and Jack Manning drove up from Key West for the day. They stayed on the beach and had DoorDash deliver everyone's lunch down in the common area. They could continue to watch Bella in the pool and bay area. Julie and Mary took Annie up for her nap and sat on the balcony drinking wine. It was a good day. Jack and Joe had a few beers sitting watching Bella. Joe completely cleared his mind and was just grateful to sit and mellow out. He and Jack talked about everything but work and nonprofit business.

They both loved the Yankees. Joe told Jack all about this year's Coast Guard Academy baseball team doing well in the NEWMAC league and going to the NCAA Division III championships for the first time. He told him about Frankie's perfection of the Andy Pettitte pick-off move to first base. Jack thought that was great because he was a big fan of Andy Pettitte as well.

They got up and walked the beach with Bella. Joe told

him about looking into law school. He said if he didn't do it now, he probably never would. Jack reminded Joe that Mary just got her Ph.D. at Barry University just like Joe got but she had turned fifty. Joe said he forgot and it was a good reminder. Jack told him that he and Mary would never compromise the Clyne firm but he had many more projects down in the Keys that would keep everyone busy for some time. He reminded Joe that they would be done with their giving within the next five years but would still be sitting on over $120.0 million dollars between the two of them and they would need help managing their own personal fortunes as well. Joe said that he would keep that in mind when making his decision.

Mary asked Julie all about her new book. She said she was getting there and only had a few chapters left and then needed to buckle down and review and edit what she has done. She said she would never hand in her manuscript until she thought it was as good as she could make it. She told Mary about the surprise for Bella to be in an episode of The *Girl's Story* up in Hollywood Studios where they would be heading the last week of their vacation. She thought that was great. Mary said that everything at The College of the Florida Keys was going well under the new president and her funding resources were being used wisely for the college and all the various projects they started down in the Keys. Her projects also included Covid-19 relief and supplies, the new homeless shelter in Key West, and the repairs and upgrades to the Catholic Church, school and convent. Mary said Linda and Jamie Lennon have been a big help in that regard. She also praised Tillie for jumping in and finding out all the needs of the various senior centers and nursing homes in the area.

They had a nice dinner and Mary and Jack headed out about 7:00 p.m. It was a long day. They had a few more days to themselves and then Mark and Louise Silva would come down in their boat and spend the day with them along with their daughter, Jennifer, and their son, MJ. Jennifer was blossoming and now a junior in High School. MJ was still in grammar school. Jennifer was their flower girl and MJ was the ring bearer for the wedding at St. Patrick's Cathedral. If they were back here, Joe and Julie couldn't think of a better babysitter than Jennifer or Luce Talbot. Maybe, someday it will happen thought Julie.

Joe met them at the marina attached to the property. Julie was near the dock with the two girls. Mark and Louise couldn't believe how big Annie was getting and they got a hug from Bella as well. It made their day. Mark and Louise, along with Tillie, were Bella's godparents and she was baptized right after their wedding. They were unsure if Bella had been baptized before her mother died. Jennifer and MJ hadn't seen Bella since that day and never met Annie.

It was a fun day. They decided to stay overnight on the boat and have breakfast the next day before heading back to Fort Lauderdale. It was quite a trip but Mark always loved the water. They stayed up late into the night and they walked them down to their boat at the dock and said goodnight. Julie and Joe had their breakfast ready by 7:30 a.m. so they could leave no later than 8:30 a.m. It would take them a good five hours to get home by boat. Julie said they would see them again soon. They would invite the whole family up to New London and see them again when they came down. They promised Tillie that, if they could get the time, they would spend Christmas with her in Key Largo.

That afternoon, Audrey and Mike Kenny stopped by quickly to say hello. Mike worked for the Monroe County Sheriff's Department and they both were instrumental in getting Bella back to them after being taken by an overzealous social worker after Bella's mother's death. Audrey was the head nurse at the hospital for both Tillie's hit and run and Juanita's death. She knew Juanita's desire for Julie and Joe to raise Bella and made it known to everyone. Until that time, Joe and Mike didn't always see eye-to-eye but became very close friends. When Mary Evans was kidnapped, Mike was one of the first people he called to make sure that the Monroe County officers didn't interfere with their rescue effort. Mike was well aware of Joe's capabilities as a leader of an MSRT team.

The next day, Joe took off to see Jake Barnes. By that time, his own boss, Rear Admiral Kelly and his wife, Ellen, would have headed back to New London. They met with Jake but the main focus was having a good time in Miami. Ellen had been there only once and he kept promising her another trip. When she found out that Joe and Julie were having a tough time booking flights with a baby, she put her foot down and insisted that they go down with him in his chartered plane. Joe smiled at Ellen, knowing what she did and mouthed "thank you" to her. Julie did the same when they went out to lunch the week before they left for Miami.

Joe was dressed in his full uniform heading up to District 7 Coast Guard headquarters on Brickell. He didn't want to show any disrespect to Jake, especially after showing respect to his current boss. On a good day, Joe could make the eighty miles in a little over an hour and a half. He wondered to himself that if they did come back to Key Largo and then commute to Miami, would he want to. He did that for quite a while heading to The College of the Florida Keys in Key West from his home in Tavernier, every day. It was fun but the drive got to him after a while. He was now officially spoiled up in New London living two blocks from his office.

He got there a little after 9:30 a.m. As soon as he hit the front door, he was greeted by security. Evidently, Jake told them to watch out for Joe and let him through quickly. Joe went up the steps and met his staff once again. They congratulated him on his new position as Assistant Superintendent of the Coast Guard Academy. He thanked them as he was ushered into Jake's office.

"Welcome back, Joe," Jake said. "How are you, Julie and the kids? Having fun in Key Largo with Tillie?" he asked.

"I'm afraid that Julie wants to stay there permanently. Once a Conch always a Conch," he said.

"Maybe, we can fix it then," the Rear Admiral said.

Joe smiled. "Speaking of that, do you have time this morning so I can bounce something off you?"

"Oh, oh. Bill was afraid this was coming," he said

"Well, my twenty years are up next April, sir. I was talking to Julie and we discussed next steps. Can I talk to you about them?" he added.

"Sure," said Jake.

They talked for two hours straight and then went to lunch. The gist was that Joe liked the Academy but was not an operations guy. Jake knew this and finally realized it. But then Jake threw Joe a curveball and asked him if he would be interested in taking over District 7 when he retired next year. Joe was blown away and didn't know what to say. He would be the youngest Rear Admiral in history as he was told, next year at 39 or the following year at age 40. Joe told him about his plans for law school and Jake said he could probably still do it if he was in Miami and do it part time. Jake knew that Joe was qualified to run this district. Hell, he's been Jake's go to guy since the beginning. Who else spoke four languages and now learning Chinese? English, Spanish, Russian and Chechen and he was still pursuing Chinese. He asked Joe if he has accomplished everything he needed to do at the Academy and Joe said no that he wanted to continue minority recruiting and bringing in speakers of other languages before they hit the Academy. Jake said as a new member of the Board of Trustees, he could champion that and Joe could still come up to the Academy and participate. Joe told him that Laura Chavez would push it as well and they were starting a project with Hispanic and Russian speakers to work together just as if it was Cuba.

Joe felt good about his meeting and told Jake that he would be pleased if he could push in that direction without being pushy. He still wanted to bounce it off Julie because without her okay, it would not happen. He got back to Key Largo later in the afternoon and he and Julie had a nice long conversation. To say that she was thrilled with the direction he could pursue would be an understatement. They could buy a house in the Key Largo area. Bella and Annie could attend the same schools that Julie attended and then attend Coral Shores High School, where Julie had tons of friends. It would put her in a good frame of mind to write more books. She would have to work it out with Connecticut College to be a visiting author or artist as opposed to being a teacher with defined classes. She was sure she could work it out.

Chapter 33

The two weeks seemed to end quickly. They packed their Coast Guard vehicle and left on Saturday, July 16th, heading for Disney World in Orlando. It was 290 miles away and would take almost five hours with a few rest stops. They would leave by 8:00 a.m. and be there before 2:00 p.m. Both Claire Murphy and Marshall Tillman would meet them at the front gate to Hollywood Studios. Their rooms would be ready. Joe and Julie would put Annie in their room in a portable crib and Tillie and Bella would once again share a room. There were no complaints from either Julie or Joe. Those rooms were $500.00 a night each for seven days. On top of that, they would be getting a private jet ride home to New London the following Saturday.

As soon as they arrived and stopped at the security gate to Hollywood Studios, Joe rolled down his window and the guards immediately knew who they were. They had stayed here before and the guards knew that Joe was in the Coast Guard. At the time, there were several different cartel and terrorist groups interested in bringing Joe down but they were there to smooth over a deal with Disney and kept it as quiet as possible. The Disney staff from California flew in just to meet Julie and work out a contract. The Orlando police department came up with a few detectives that shadowed them that weekend just to make sure they were safe. To say that Joe had contacts everywhere in Florida was an understatement. These two guards, today, recognized both Joe and Julie immediately. They showed Joe where to pull up to unload the Coast Guard vehicle, right at the entrance to where they were staying.

As Tillie and Bella got out of the back of the vehicle together, you could see Bella's eyes were wide open, looking around. She said, "We're really in Disney World?"

Tillie said, "Yes, Bella, we're really in Disney World. Let's get our bags into our rooms. Mrs. Murphy promised to give us a tour of the Hollywood Studios today and then of the whole place tomorrow. Isn't that exciting?"

"Yes, Grammy. I can't wait," said Bella as they walked up the stairs to their rooms. The guards helped Joe unload. Claire Murphy and Marshall Tillman had just come down to greet them. Julie gave Claire a hug and Joe shook Marshall's hand. Claire Murphy and Joe are very close because she is the daughter of Tom Jones, Joe's first boot camp instructor. It wasn't that long ago that Tom was murdered by one of the Orlando detectives, who had covered up drug dealing at the apartment complex where Tom lived at the time. Joe solved the murder and helped get rid of a bad cop. He made friends for life at the Orlando Police Department. Trinity Hightower, a rising detective in the department, was invited to the baptism but couldn't make it as duty called. She was now in line for Chief of Detectives and couldn't leave. Joe knew how that went. She said she would be able to have dinner with them in a few days.

Once settled, Julie and Joe met with Marshall about the

new series, *A Girl's Story*, now being filmed right at Disney World. It would be a surprise to Bella that she would be in the current episode now being filmed. Bella and Tillie went with Claire in her golf cart and took a quick tour of Hollywood Studios. They were meeting Marshall in their suite because Annie was taking her nap. They would all get together for a catered dinner right in headquarters so they wouldn't have to leave the building after Joe's long drive up from Key Largo.

Joe and Julie were in their room with Annie, sleeping in the crib. They looked around and remembered the first time they were here to sign a deal with Disney. Jane Swanson was here as well and she did an excellent job in negotiating a contract with Joe's input. After all, his MBA gave him a few hints as to what should and should not be in a contract. Both of them picked it apart at the same time and told Julie to walk away if those items were not deleted. All in all, it worked out fine.

Once again, both Joe and Julie looked out the window of their third-floor suite. The administrative offices were adjacent to the Streets of America and back lot. The area known as the Streets of America was probably one of the most overlooked attractions in Disney World. Most visitors didn't even realize that it was not just a few streets that got you from place to place. If you were standing in front of some of the areas that were supposed to represent the streets of New York City, you could hear the city noises, the traffic, pedestrians, and honking horns. Joe, once again, thought he was in Manhattan. It was that realistic.

He thought, *It's like New York City*. It reminded him of their wedding at St. Patrick's Cathedral and afterwards as they walked the two blocks to their reception. Looking out the window, you can hear the traffic and sounds. It is amazing. There was a brochure on the table explaining the scenes just outside their window. The brochure stated, *Take a look at the facades of the buildings—Chinese laundry and restaurant, complete with an old-fashioned telephone booth that's decorated with a little pagoda, just like you might see in Chinatown.* Julie was all smiles. They were here before to obtain a contract. Now with two children, they can visit all the sites for a week and marvel at Bella's delight. They would have never thought this possible a few years ago.

Joe remembers vividly the meeting with Marcia Manning, Vice President for Human Resources for Walt Disney Studios worldwide, Edward Bell, Assistant Vice President for Motion Picture Production, Ricardo Gomez, Assistant Vice President for Walt Disney Studios Marketing, and Deana Finkle, Vice President for Hollywood Records and Disney Music Publishing. The night before the official negotiations, as everyone ate and became acquainted, they seemed to loosen up. Joe watched Ed Bell and Ricardo Gomez speaking to each other at the end of the table. They spoke Spanish. From the gist of their conversation, Joe knew that Ricardo thought Julie was "one hot tomato," as he so eloquently put it. Ricardo made a few other blatant comments in Spanish as well and Joe kept those comments in the back of his mind. He smiled. Never would he give up his cover to them without a valid reason.

The next day at the meeting Riccardo said something, at length, to Ed in Spanish. Joe turned to him and said in Spanish, "Please keep your remarks to yourself or you'll blow this deal. Do you understand?" Ricardo appeared to be shocked, and Ed was wide-eyed. Joe said, again in Spanish, "Julie is beautiful and I believe your remarks yesterday were just off the cuff. Today, your remarks are unwarranted and, if I were you, I'd simply excuse myself from the table, Ricardo. Ed you can stay and let Ricardo know what happened after he leaves. Thank you." Ricardo excused himself from the table and closed the door behind him. Marcia turned to Joe and asked him if everything was all right.

Joe has a photographic memory or so he's been told. It's not so much photographic but like a lot of left-handers, he remembers multiple details in pictures and never, ever, forgets. He remembers that time exactly as it occurred. After Marcia asked him if he was all right, he said yes he was. When she asked why Ricardo left the room so suddenly, Joe told her to ask Ricardo.

After that quick confrontation, everyone at that time was a little on edge but, after a few minutes, they were back on target. They were down to negotiations and Jane stepped in for this discussion. They were just about ready to discuss the basis for a contract when Marcia said that perhaps they could eat lunch and start fresh this afternoon. As they were heading to the dining room, Marcia asked Joe if she could speak to him for a minute. He nodded and told Julie that he'd be right there. She asked for an explanation about Ricardo. Joe simply told her that Ricardo was out of line and made comments that he didn't appreciate, being Julie's fiancée. He then told Marcia about his background. He said he had an MBA from RPI but he is a lieutenant in the Coast Guard Intelligence Division, in charge of all investigations for South Florida and the Keys. He told her he speaks both Russian and Mexican-dialect Spanish. He said that Ricardo was very lucky that he didn't respond more directly to his remarks. Joe then mentioned that, in Julie's books, he was the lowly Coast Guard first year eighteen-year-old, who showed up at Julie's school for Career Day. He then went on to tell her that they had security because he just shot up a cartel down in Miami and had to get back because his partner was shot. Marcia was dumbfounded and told him how sorry she was for the incident and that it wouldn't happen again.

He remembered her saying as he smiled, "I think you scared him half to death with your Spanish remarks. We didn't understand the significance of what you do, and thank you for doing it. I mean that from the bottom of my heart. We want nothing but the best for Julie, and I believe we can do that and give her the success that she's entitled to after all these years. I promise you, I'll do everything I can to make this work. By the way, let me reiterate once again, you scared the living crap out of us with the banter in Spanish and the glare in your eyes. Our production team could never teach that to an actor. I guess you have to live it." She finally smiled. "Looking for a job?" Joe remembers everything.

"What are you thinking about?" asked Julie.

"Just the last time we were here and how well you did with the negotiations," Joe said.

"Nothing to do with Ricardo, huh?" she asked.

"No nothing," he said. "Let's get Annie up and head to dinner with Claire and Marshall. I'm sure that Tillie and Bella will be hungry too when they get back." Once again, they would have a full buffet dinner right at headquarters in their special guest dining room. The day went quickly and everyone was up early. Bella was jumping around with excitement. Tillie just shook her head and smiled and looked to say, "I hope I can keep up at almost seventy now, you guys."

For the next four days, they visited all the venues once again starting at Hollywood Studios, and then to Animal Kingdom, Epcot, and Magic Kingdom. As a special treat, they made reservations for lunch for Tillie, Bella, Julie, and Joe to the Fairytale Dining at Cinderella's Royal Table in the Grand Hall at the Magic Kingdom. Claire babysat for Annie and seemed to love every minute of it. This was the highlight of Bella's trip to Disney World and they didn't want it spoiled if Annie got restless. They entered the majestic Grand Hall and ascended a spiral staircase to the banquet hall above. They dined in a storybook setting surrounded by soaring stone archways, majestic medieval flags and spectacular stained-glass windows overlooking Fantasyland. Cinderella came down and hugged Bella, who was now the center of attention. She was thrilled.

On the last two days, Bella was asked if she would like a role in her Mommy's new series, *A Girl's Story*. Bella knew that her mother was a well-known author but didn't really know what that meant. They went to the Hollywood Studio and to the area where they were shooting the scene in which Bella would participate. She had just turned eight in June and was not an actress by any means. They asked her to sit around a group of young Hispanic girls, who only spoke Spanish and to translate their thoughts and words as they watched the production. She was just doing what she normally did talking to her father, Joe. She never even thought that she was being filmed doing her translation to an actress playing a part in the episode. She was very comfortable with these girls, all around her own age. It was like she just made new friends that were just like her in every way. Bella was Cuban and most of these young girls were either Cuban or were from a similar Caribbean background. She understood every young girl and when she had questions, she simply asked the girl what she meant. That was also translated to the actress. The episode and her small part took the better part of two days. They were near the end and would be having dinner with Trinity

Hightower that night at the Epcot Mexican restaurant. From there, they would get a ride back and Trinity would pick up her police cruiser and head back to Orlando.

"So, Trinity, how are you?" asked Julie. They became very good friends and she attended their wedding in Key Largo, the second wedding for all her friends, who lived in the Keys. Their wedding in New York City at St. Patrick's Cathedral was very small and only for family and a few friends from college and her publisher in New York City. When they got back, they had a large wedding for all their friends and all monetary gifts were given to the Church's food bank and secondhand store. They raised over $50,000.00 that day after everyone in the community found out about the donations. Their wedding picture on the steps of St. Justin Martyr in Key Largo with over 200 guests included in the picture is something they will cherish forever. Trinity remembered it well and even helped out at the cookout and was in the center of the picture. She's doing well she said. She will be the Chief of Detectives of the Orlando police department soon and is being groomed to take over as the full Chief when her boss retires. She has come a long way. They had a great time and made plans for later in the fall for Trinity to come up and visit at the Academy. Joe said he could take care of all her expenses if he could have her make a presentation to all the cadets on her career in law enforcement and how she and her team work very closely with the Coast Guard. Joe said he would work it out.

It was the final day. They got up and packed. Tillie would get a ride to the train and one of the security guards would make sure she got on the train and settled safely before leaving. Whenever she went anywhere, she never had more than a carry-on bag anyway so she could manage more easily. Jane Swanson would meet her at her stop in

Miami and Jane would drive her straight home. Jane would stay over and come back the next day. They needed to work out a few kinks in her senior programs for Mary Evan's Teresa Trust Fund South.

Claire Murphy gave Joe, Julie, Bella, and Annie a ride to the Orlando International Airport's private plane commercial area and then dropped them off right at the Disney hanger. From there, it was about a three-hour flight directly to the Groton-New London Airport. Sean O'Neil was picking them up and bringing them home. As soon as they arrived, they were met at their front door by Samantha, Emma, and her little brother. They exchanged keys just to make sure that everything was okay. Joe made sure that the security team driving around checking houses would make a few extra passes by their home while they were away. You could never be too cautious, thought Joe. They ordered pizza and wings and Sean made sure that Joe had a few cold ones waiting for him. Samantha popped open a bottle of bubbly and handed Julie a glass of champagne. "Welcome home," said Samantha.

"Thank you for doing this. It is greatly appreciated," said Joe. "Any sausage?" he asked Sam.

Julie just looked at him and he said, "What? I like sausage."

She just shook her head and made a toast to great friends. Julie's heart was still in Key Largo but she had great new friends here as well. She knew that when the time came, they would have a very hard decision to make about their future.

Chapter 34

It's now Sunday so they went to noon Mass and out to lunch afterwards. The weather was beautiful. Today reminded Julie of almost every day in the Florida Keys. That is every day except for hurricane season. It was now approaching this time of year from July through late September and evidently there were a few percolating out in the ocean near the Bahamas. Hurricanes in the northeast were few and far between. *Winter more than made up for a few hurricanes, she thought.*

Joe and Julie had talked about joining the Sponsor Family Program several months ago. The initial meeting for the incoming transfer students and freshman, first year, class is this week. There were forms to fill out and families sponsoring cadets had to live within a twenty-five mile range from the Academy. They lived two blocks away. They wanted to sponsor Luce Talbot but they wanted to clear it first with the organization because of their close relationship with the Talbot family and with Joe being second in command at the Academy. The organization didn't find any issues with it. In addition, they found another student from the Florida Keys who would be attending the Academy in the fall.

There was one student, Maria Estevez, from Key West. Joe already knew about Maria for several reasons. The first reason was that Joan Talbot was now running the military side of The College of the Florida Keys as well as the recruiting arm for the Coast Guard and the Academy. Maria just turned eighteen and is a new graduate from Key West High School. Her family attends the Basilica of St. Mary Star of the Sea and they are good friends with Linda and Skip Lennon. As a matter of fact, their daughter, Jamie, used to babysit Maria when she was younger. It was Linda who talked Maria into attending The College of the Florida Keys senior high school computer program and she became certified even before she entered college. She actually was paid to work part time in the spring before entering the Academy. Linda told Joan Talbot all about her. She was Hispanic, bilingual, extremely bright, certified in computer languages, and came from a relatively modest family. The 100% four-year scholarship to the Coast Guard Academy was a way out of financial burden for this young girl. Julie and Joe signed up to sponsor her as well.

The only issue they had was if Joe left the service and retired next year. Both Luce and Maria would be left without a family sponsor. So, Julie spoke to Samantha and Sean O'Neil and they said they would be glad to serve as a secondary sponsor for both cadets. With that assurance, they went ahead and were approved by the committee. The meeting this week was the first of several training sessions on what was expected for both the families and the cadets.

Luce already met Maria in the spring before coming up. She went down to the college to visit her mother and met Maria Estevez. They went to lunch and talked about all their plans. Joe made sure that Maria was funded for all her personal trips back and forth through Mary Evan's Teresa Trust Fund South. Luce was already taken care of and even stayed at Joe and Julie's house before entering the Academy. Joe met Maria coming off the plane. He made sure that Julie was with him so as not to alarm her that some older guy was meeting her. The whole family went to pick her up. She stayed with them for two nights along with Luce before their summer program began. Maria was a true freshman with a handful of credit hours unlike Luce who entered with tons of AP courses already credited to her, making her almost two years advanced over Maria.

Maria was also impressed that the Catholic Church in New London had the same names as her family church in Key West, St. Mary Star of the Sea, and had a Hispanic Mass at noon. Maria was also surprised that Bella was obviously Hispanic and Cuban and spoke fluent Spanish. She was also shocked that Joe was fluent in Spanish and that Julie was getting there. Julie told Maria all about Bella and her adoption and the death of Bella's mother Juanita. Maria felt very much at home, so far away from Key West.

Summer was moving along quite quickly. Bella was entering third grade in the fall. Annie was now almost nine months old and starting to babble. She was feeling her way around, trying to walk but crawling most of the time. When they put her on the floor, she would roll from one place to the other and only crawl when she wanted to be picked up. She was now the bell of the ball with three girls fawning all over her, Bella, Luce, and Maria. They didn't see much of Luce or Maria while they were doing their Swab Summer activities but as Labor Day was coming around, they got a few days off and would spend it at the Traynors. The O'Neil's were there a lot as well to make sure that if a hand-off may be pending, then they would all feel comfortable in doing so.

Luce was given time off from the Swab Summer because cross-country practice started in early August. While she was running, her practices counted toward her Swab Summer training. You couldn't train any harder than running 6K every day in the heat of the summer in New London. Ethan Brown, Luce's head coach for the Coast Guard Academy women's cross-country team, was extremely pleased at the hard work and dedication that Luce has shown even in this short amount of time. It was clear that she was there to win and prove that the University of Miami should have never red-shirted her or let her go. Again, in cross-country, it doesn't matter what NCAA division you run in, it matters what your time is in every race. Already Luce was running at least twenty to thirty seconds faster than her next six teammates. There was little jealousy at the Coast Guard Academy. Yes, they were there to compete, but first, they were taught to have each other's back as a new graduate, as an Ensign in the United States Coast Guard. That was first and foremost. Luce agreed with that and it took a lot of pressure off the young women. Last year, they ran 8th nationally at the NCAA Division III finals, without a single runner in the top ten. Luce would be qualified to be in that top ten at the end of the year. She wasn't just thinking of this year, she was thinking about the 2024 Olympics in Paris. That is what she was training for and Coach Brown knew it and supported it. The problem is that cross-country was not an Olympic event for 2024. They were hoping that it would be but the Olympic committee left it out. So, Luce would have to run the 10,000 meters which is a little over six miles compared to the three and three quarters miles she now runs. Luce has run a 10,000-meter event before and has the stamina and speed to compete at this level.

Their first 6K meet would be Saturday, September 10th at the Vassar Run Stonitsch Invitational, followed by the UMass Dartmouth Invitational the following Saturday. This year the NCAA Division III Women's Cross Country Championship would be held in Lansing, Michigan on Saturday, November 19th. If they made it to the championship, Joe and Julie would fly out and meet the Talbots in Lansing before the meet. They were sure that Bella and Annie would be fine with the O'Neil's and perhaps Maria could help out as well.

Joe spoke to Coach Brown earlier when they got back from Florida. He said that Luce right now was at the top level for Division III. He smiled at told Joe that Miami was out of their minds in letting her go. He said last year's winner, Kassie Rosenbum, from Loras College in Dubuque, Iowa ran the final 6K in 20.11.1. The next best was 20.28.6. He said that to go to the Olympics, Luce would have to compete with the Division I runners at the same 6K events. The 2021 Division I winner was Whittni Orton from BYU who ran 19.25.4. The real competition though was the top ten in Division 1. The 10th place runner came in at 19.37.7 or 33.4 seconds faster than the Division III winner. The Division I winner was 45.7 seconds faster than the Division III winner. Luce would have a ways to go to get into the top ten in her first year of eligibility. She would then have to start practice at the 10,000-meter level to keep up her stamina. This would also help her at the 6K level.

Coach Brown said it was not impossible but she would need a lot of determination. At that level it was who wanted it the most. Coach Brown said that Luce was already ahead of the Division III winner, coming in around 20.01.1. She would need to make up 23.4 seconds just to make the top 10 in Division1. However, the Division I 6K

NCAA winner would not make the top ten trying out for the Olympics. These women run into their thirties and are considered professionals and are financially supported through sponsorships.

Joe told him that he would explain that to Luce. It was nothing but pure math. It was no different than counting the tenth of a second in a pick-off move to first base. This would be great for her first year but they only take the top three or four with the fastest time. She needs to make up a half a minute over the 6K to even get a shot at the Olympics. Joe thought explaining that would give her a competitive edge. Every time she ran, she knew what she had to do to make her goal. It was right in front of her. The worst that can happen is that everyone calls her Ensign when she graduates.

Joe did his research before speaking to Luce. She was very mathematics oriented so he wanted to tell her exactly what her times needed to be to qualify for the 10,000 meter USA Olympic team. They only took the top three women and several alternates in case of issues before the games began. There have been situations where someone was hurt and replaced by an alternate but that was few and far between. In 2020, the women's gold medal winner ran the 10,000 meters in 29.17.45, or twenty-nine minutes, seventeen seconds and forty-five hundredths of a second. To equate that to 6K, Luce would have to run a 17.52.47, to match the gold winner. She would have to lose 2.47.13 off her best time at 6K. She thought that probably wouldn't happen. However, to qualify for the top three spots, she would have to run a 31.25.0, 10,000-meter or an equivalent of 18.51.0 at the 6K level. In other words, Luce would have to only shave off one-minute and nine seconds from her current time to at least qualify. She also has two more years to get better. So, not only does she need to lower her time from 20.01.0 to at least 19.25.4 to equal the NCAA Division I championship cross-country winner but would have to go even lower to 18.51.0 to at least qualify for consideration.

Joe knew that this was a process or one step at a time. He wasn't her coach but he was a hell of a lot better than almost anyone at mathematics. He proved that to the baseball coach with his pickoff moves theory. So he sat down with Coach Brown and Luce and explained the mathematical process that she would have to adhere to even have a chance at consideration. There has never been a NCAA Division III woman selected for the team, not ever. Coach Brown said he would be happy if they won the Division III championship this year after being ranked 8th last year.

They never had a runner of Luce's caliber before so his expectations were not even close to Luce's objectives. Joe could see it in her eyes. She now knew exactly what she had to do to make the team. She thought that one-minute and ten seconds off her 6K and then run at a 10,000-meter level was very possible. Doing the mathematics helped especially when she said it was only a 5% improvement from her twenty-minute time. That gave her the incentive she needed. She also knew that there was more to being a Coast Guard officer than winning the Olympics. She wanted to prove to everyone that she could do both.

Julie had multiple meetings at Connecticut College for her new fall semester novel course. When the students found out that she would be teaching this course, both men and women signed up. There were quite a few men who were in the English Department who wanted to become authors just as the women did. They had to cut off the class size to fifteen. They would meet two nights a week instead of days to accommodate her family schedule. Every

Tuesday and Thursday, she would walk over to the campus after dinner with the family.

Joe was very accommodating and would babysit, every chance he could. If he was out of town, which wasn't often, then she could get help from her friends. If not, she was perfectly willing to hold class in her living room with the kids watching television in Bella's room.

Julie got her schedule and the names of the students who would be attending her class. She was not surprised to find the name Grace Kelly among the students. She said she wanted to be in her class and it looks like she made it happen. Julie spoke to Ellen, Grace's mother and mentioned it. Ellen asked if it was all right and Julie said of course. She said she hoped that it would help her in her career decision to become a writer or work in the publishing industry. Julie mentioned to Ellen how hard it was to get a job in the industry but she did mention that if Grace did well, she would recommend her for an internship with her friend and publisher, Sarah Atwood in New York City. She knew that Grace could spend the summers in New York City before graduation and stay at the condo that she stayed at when in New York. Julie, like Joe, made very decisive decisions very quickly and stayed with those decisions unless proven wrong. She thought Grace probably had what it takes to be successful.

It was Labor Day weekend and Joe and Julie decided to stay home and relax. They would go to the town beach on Saturday, church on Sunday and then just mellow out through Labor Day. The weather was warm and sunny. Maria was able to go home for a week and Luce decided to stay around because of practice.

Classes started that Wednesday, right after Labor Day. The O'Neil's came over and went to the beach with them. They cooked out at Sean and Sam's on Saturday and they came over Sunday. They simply slept late on Monday and did absolutely nothing all day. Joe's favorite holiday meal came in the form of pizza, wings, and beer. They even had it delivered so as to not get out of their pajamas.

A new school year for Bella came early Tuesday morning. She was now in 3rd grade and feeling her oats especially after everyone found out that she appeared in a Disney episode at Hollywood Studios in Disney World. Everyone asked her when the episode would air and she told everyone that it would be sometime in October but wasn't sure. Her mother told her to say that so she wouldn't be hounded to death.

Annie took her first step that morning, walked three feet and fell. She looked up surprised and laughed and got up again and held on to the coffee table and started to walk around it. Joe had left for work already so she did a video on her phone and sent it to him saying, "See what you missed?" He was delighted and passed it around the room before his meeting with the Rear Admiral. It was a very slow Tuesday. Everyone was feeling the letdown after a holiday and just wanted to get through the day.

Chapter 35

S ir, I'm sorry to call you but our system just picked up some disturbance at the administration building over across the street at Connecticut College," said Dave Simon the director for safety and security at the Academy. "I was just notified by our security desk at the center."

"Do we have any information at all?" asked Joe. He had just walked into his office when he picked up the phone. It was just an ordinary Wednesday morning.

"Our cameras show that there are three SUVs that pulled up in front of the building. It looked like there were at least fifteen individuals that got out and several ran into the building and several others scattered across campus. My guess is at least ten, two at the front door and the back door and two on each of the three floors. There is one guy standing next to the vehicles in a tactical outfit, holding what looks like an AR-15. As you know, the AR-15 is the civilian equivalent of the M-16 military rifle, which is basically the same thing. I think we have another domestic terrorist attack on our hands. Since they couldn't get to the Academy again, this must be the next best thing. What do you want to do, Joe?"

Joe said, "That makes eleven at the administration building with four from the SUVs scattered. Our cameras are very well placed at each entry point and in all the hallways on all three floors. The system we just installed is crystal clear. However, we didn't put any in the classrooms or offices because of privacy issues. As you remember when we did the installation the president of the college was very clear about privacy issues." He continued, "We need a quick plan of attack and I need to inform Rear Admiral Kelly on what's happening. I hope his daughter isn't in that building this morning. I hope to God she isn't," Joe said. "I'm heading to his office right now. Dave, we're all in. Get the drones out immediately. We need to identify the vehicles first. Also, fly the drones around campus, specifically near the front gate and the security center. See what's happening. I just called both places and no one picks up. I'm afraid who is ever in those buildings isn't available now."

Joe ran down the hall and quickly opened the Rear Admiral's door, bypassing Meg Olson's desk. "Rear Admiral, I need you right now. We have a major problem on the campus of Connecticut College, sir."

"What's happening, Joe?" he asked.

"I believe there is a terrorist action going on at the administration building at Connecticut College. Sir, I need permission to start a strike team immediately. Dave Simon called me and saw what was happening in real time thanks to our new systems at both campuses. It's not pretty sir. It looks like it will be a hostage situation. I need to get our MSRT team together ASAP and I need to call Kim Matz at the local FBI and get a Navy Seal team here ASAP as well from the sub base. Do I have your permission, sir? We don't have time for a Board of Trustees vote, sir."

"I got that, Joe. Are you sure about all this? I don't want us to be wrong," he said.

"There is no way we're wrong, sir. It's happening right now. Let's call Kate Ballenger's office and Dean Erica Jones as well. If there is no answer right now, I kind of know why."

They called and there was no answer. Dave Simon came running up the hall and told them that the drones were in the air. They watched in real time as the drones flew over the campus. They immediately saw the three SUVs in front of the building being guarded by a guy in quasi-military dress, holding an AR-15. The drone picked up two more at both the front and back doors. The drones took all their pictures and then went around the building, floor by floor, to see what other activity was taking place. The drone settled on the three windows of the president's office. It snapped pictures of two armed men standing over the president sitting at her desk. They had no masks and their faces were very clear for facial recognition. One of the drones was only programmed for infrared identification of numbers of heat sources in the building by floor, meaning bodies. There were forty-eight heat sources in three classrooms on the first floor. That could mean fifteen per class and one teacher for each room. There were two in the hallway in addition to two at each front and back door. The second floor had ten heat sources in six rooms and the hallway. There should be eight staff and two gunmen in the hall. Heading to the third floor, there were only six that probably included the president, the dean, two administrative assistants and two armed men in the president's office. In all, it was a guess but Joe suspected that there were ten armed terrorists either in or in front of the building, one with the SUVs and forty-five students, three teachers, eight staff on the second floor, and the president, the dean and two administrative assistants on the third floor. In all, there were sixty potential hostages in the building.

Immediately, they checked the class schedule and found that of the forty-five students, twenty-five were 3rd and 4th year cadets. So, to their thinking, this was a direct attack on a U.S. military facility and would be handled appropriately. Joe knew that his MSRT team, the FBI and the Navy Seals will deal with this with maximum force and hopefully no one will get hurt except for the aftereffects of a few flash-bang grenades that could leave people disoriented, and confused with massive headaches. This was better than dying of course. When Joe originally installed the new security systems at both the Academy and Connecticut College, he also asked the Rear Admiral to support a new MSRT team to be housed at the Academy. Joe's grant would pay the annual cost for the next several years. Joe also pointed out that the team consisted of both men and women and would be a good thing to have this high level, highly trained, attack force walking the campus. It would also show equality in the ranks for women at the Academy and for recruitment efforts. It was a win-win all around and thank God they were now at Joe's immediate disposal for this emergency.

They watched the drones fly over the guardhouse and security center. There were two more militia-type individuals standing outside each of the two facilities, holding rifles. The drones focused in and it could see one guard in each building lying face down on the floor. It didn't look good.

Within the hour, Joe had called Kim Matz at the FBI. She would assemble her special agents in full gear. Joe's MSRT, the Maritime Security Response Team, to be led by him, were now assembled behind the Academy's administration building. Captain Larry Curtis, the commanding officer of the Navy Submarine Base down the road, had quickly become a good friend to Joe and they had several meetings after the initial walk through a while ago. Joe told him what was happening and asked for his onsite Seal team to participate in the takedown with his MSRT team and the FBI. Captain Curtis said the more the merrier and he would come with the Seal team, being a former retired member of the Seals before becoming an officer. The MSRT team and the Seals have been working together already.

Captain Curtis was well aware that this wasn't a drill but the real deal. He also knew how good the Coast Guard MSRT teams were since he had attended meetings where Coast Guard MSRT teams were present along with Navy Seals. He knew the equivalency between these teams and the Seals. Obviously, the Seals were active combat veterans while the MSRT were active hostage and domestic terrorist oriented but they have always worked well together. Also, the Seals were extremely valuable in rappelling down buildings and entering through whatever egress they found. To free the president and the dean and the staff on the second floor as well, from the throws of these terrorists, Joe thought this might have to happen. As the Seal team began its assault through the windows, Joe would enter the third floor, from the roof with two MSRT team members and head to the president's office, hopefully in time as the Seals flew through the third floor windows right into the president's office.

The first item on the agenda was to see whom the SUVs belonged to and it didn't take long. After taking the pictures of the license plates by the drone, it came back from Connecticut DMV that these three vehicles were stolen recently. *Well that explains everything,* thought Joe.

The next pictures of the faces of those they immediately took at the front and back of the building and standing by the SUVs explained it even more. Three of the five had records in the state of Connecticut. Three were ex-military, all Army. The three with records served time at Cheshire Correctional Institution with Fred Elliott, the leader of the bombing attack, who was captured with three others in West Hartford and sent to a secure CIA site. Joe was now sure that this just might be retaliation by the Sovereign Citizens of Connecticut. However, this seemed bigger and there were obviously trained militiamen involved. Maybe they joined forces with others for this direct assault across the street from the Academy. Whatever they think they would prove was not going to happen on Joe's watch. *Those sons of bitches will pay for this in full so it won't ever happen again,* he thought. They thought the indirect approach would take down the Academy but they were unaware of the strides Joe made in beefing up security at both places and sources he had at his fingertips now after the bombing attempt.

The next step was to take down the militia at the front gate and security office. They would use darts and if necessary suppressed weapons so there would be very little noise to alert the militia at the administration building. The MSRT and Seal teams went around to the back of Connecticut College. *Thank God it was an old campus with large mature trees everywhere.* It gave them coverage as they headed toward the buildings. Both teams had snipers and they were lined up to take out the militiamen if the darts didn't work. They had to get extremely close to both buildings to hit them with the darts. These were professional men and women on these two teams so they understood that this effort was crucial to free up the rest of the campus so students could leave. Students on campus were notified through their cell phones to stay in their rooms or not come to campus today for those commuting. Hopefully that would cut down traffic until this siege ended. At the Academy, every cadet received a flashing notice by the new individual GPS contact tracing devices attached to their uniforms. Cadets knew to head to a specific location on the Academy campus immediately.

Four members of both teams let the darts go after getting as close as they could. All four militiamen went down at the same time without a peep. The teams rushed the buildings only to find both Connecticut College security officers severely beaten and unconscious on the floor. They were quickly removed and brought off campus to be picked up by ambulance to the Coast Guard Hospital down the road. They called Joe and Larry and let them know that the two outposts were secured. They would leave two team members at both facilities and would wait for a call if needed to enter the administration building. They needed to make sure no one else came on to the campus.

The next step was to take down the terrorists at the administration building. Joe had the armed drone programmed to shoot darts at the militia guard by the SUVs. He wouldn't know what hit him if done right. Both the MSRT and Seal teams were moving away from the doors to the back south side area so the Seals could climb the back of the building to rappel into the windows from the roof. But, they had to get to the roof unseen before they could rappel. They needed special protection from flying glass so they wouldn't get cut or bleed to death before they even got to the floor. Joe took the plans of the building and saw that there was a door to the roof at the back end of the building. Joe wasn't that good at climbing. He knew what he was good at and what he wasn't. However, the Coast

Guard helicopter was ready and Joe and two MSRT members would hop on the helicopter and be in the air and then on the roof by the time the first two floors were taken down. If the door were unlocked, they would have no problem getting to the third floor. If it were locked, Joe would use his weapon, still silenced from before, to take off the lock and head to the president's office, which was near the roof entrance door.

It was unfortunate but there was no way that the teams could get close enough to hit the militia at the front and back doors immediately after the drone took out the SUV watcher. They used their sniper rifles with silencers and took out all four of them at the same time. Now all they had to worry about were the militia on the three floors, two per floor. The first floor held the students so that would be the priority to get them all out unharmed. If the gunmen were in the hall it would be easier. If they were in a classroom or two or moved everyone into one, they would have a major problem. Joe prayed to God that they weren't that smart. He prayed that they were of the same caliber as those four they took down in West Hartford. However, these guys were obviously trained in military tactics but maybe, hopefully, at a much lower level, and would panic when attacked.

Taking out the militia guards at the door and at the SUVs didn't seem to raise any inside activity. They were as quiet as they could be but one false move and there could be a tragedy in the making. The Seals rappelled up the back south side of the building. They walked across the roof and saw the roof door. It was unlocked. The Seal team leader called Joe at the helicopter and told him it was a go for the door to the third floor. The Seals walked quietly across the roof and positioned themselves above the three windows on the third floor and two windows on the second. The third floor windows were all in the president's office so the two hostages will be in shock when they come flying through the windows but it should only take seconds, especially with Joe Traynor and two others coming from the roof stairs to the third floor into the president's office.

In the meantime, Kim Matz had her FBI team standing by to arrest anyone still alive. They were in constant contact with the New London police department and told them this was a federal terrorist attack on a military facility that extended to Connecticut College since it served cadets from the Academy. The police also knew this was a very big deal when they caught sight of the Navy Seals pulling up with Captain Curtis in charge. The police chief met Joe Traynor just once but he knew about the bombing attack and knew they were in good hands for this situation. The FBI went from building to building moving out students that were close to the administration building. The other were made safe with an FBI Special Agent in full tactical gear standing at the front entrance of each building housing students. Kim prayed that Joe was able to get this situation under control without loss of life. Of course she didn't know about the two unconscious guards sent to the hospital or the four militia men shot dead by the snipers at the front and back doors of the administration building.

At the count of three, there was a full force invasion by the MSRT and Seals into the building. The team first breached the front door quietly and were able to see the two gunmen in the hallway, outside the classrooms. Evidently, they were simply on guard duty and were not harassing the students. As the teams rushed in, the two on the first floor raised their hands in surrender. The teams cuffed the two men and dragged them into a corner and were guarded by team members. They didn't want to bring them outside in case someone saw them from the second and third floors. The MSRT team knocked on each classroom and showed their IDs telling them to open up and to get out of the building as quickly as possible and to head south where there were no windows from the upper floors. They told them that there was a full-on assault on these terrorists and they wanted the students out ASAP. In the third classroom emerged Grace Kelly, Rear Admiral Kelly and Ellen Kelly's daughter. She was tearing up but composed and ran as fast as she could out the front door to the waiting FBI agents who sent them to the student union with full FBI protection.

Thirty seconds after the assault on the first floor, two Seals came flying through the glass windows in the hallways at the south end of the building into the second floor. One of the militia was in the hall and started to raise his gun but was shot dead. The other man tried to run in to an office but fortunately it was locked and boarded with chairs with the staff lying by the walls near the floor. He didn't have a chance. He was dead by the time he hit the floor.

The third part of the assault started as soon as they heard the crash into the second floor windows. Joe had hopped off the helicopter and landed on the roof with the other two MSRT team members. They ran to the door, opened it and ran down the stairs to the third floor. As they kicked in the door to the president's office there were screams and flying glass as the Seals came through three separate windows all at the same time. The two guys in charge of the attack blinked but were aiming their guns at the two women, Kate and Erica, who were in shock. Their assistants were tied up in the boardroom. By the time the Seals got off the floor to raise their guns, Joe and his two MSRT team members shot the two intruders as they turned in Joe's direction as they came through the door. Joe didn't wait a split second. He knew if he waited, the invaders could very easily pull the trigger and murder both women. He learned a long time ago, if he was still alive it was easier to answer questions than if he were dead. The two fully dressed in military garb, with military grade weapons, were shot dead, right in front of Kate and Erica. As they hit the floor, Joe ran over and kicked their guns away from them. He had no way of knowing if they were dead or alive. They were dead. The Seals got up and dusted themselves off.

"You know, you could have waited a split second so we could do our thing, you know," said one of the lead Seals as he smiled.

"I could have waited for you but you know us MSRT guys, we're just glory hounds," said Joe with a grin.

"Hi ladies, how are you doing?" said one of the Seals.

Joe didn't think Kate or Erica saw any humor in any of this but they didn't know about combat and the adrenalin that came racing out after a firefight. He took them both by the hands and walked them across the room, over the two dead bodies, and out the door of Kate's office. They took the elevator down to the first floor because he was afraid they would both fall down the stairs. The team took care of the two administrative assistants that were tied up and placed in the boardroom. They were lucky they didn't witness the excitement.

Kate asked Joe, "Is everyone all right, Joe?"

"Unfortunately your two guards at the front gate and the security office are in very rough shape. We got them quickly to the hospital. They will live but they took a very severe beating and it will take some time to recover. None of the students or your staff is harmed. We counted sixty hostages including you two and all are accounted for and well. Rear Admiral Kelly can rest easy as well since his daughter, Grace, was a hostage down in one of the first floor classrooms. It could have been much worse, Kate. I won't lie to you. We killed eight terrorists in this building, four at the doors, two on the second floor and two on the third. In addition, we used our dart guns not to kill but to paralyze, one by drone at the SUVs and four at the gate at security office, and two surrendered on the first floor of this building, accounting for all fifteen."

Joe continued, "We believe they're members of the terrorist group, the Sovereign Citizens of Connecticut. They were involved in the first bombing and were probably trying to seek revenge by attacking our cadets at Connecticut College but they could have just as easily been attacking you alone and our cadets were just handy. Until we get an interrogation going, we won't know for sure. What we do know is this is 2022, and this is the way it's going to be from now on, until we get a handle on white supremacists and domestic terrorists in this country. I'm sorry it happened but you are lucky to have fine people willing to give their lives to provide safety and security to all the citizens of the United States. You can thank the FBI, the Coast Guard and the Navy for stopping this attack. Eventually, they will be handed off to the CIA and I won't ever be able to discuss that with you."

"Joe, words can't express our thanks. I saw your eyes when you shot those two men. I have no idea how you do what you do but thank you. You are a blessing. When all is said and done, I believe I know who organized this rescue. It was you, Joe and we are eternally grateful. I need to get myself together. I'm sure there will be a few long days ahead. Can we call you when we need you and I believe we will need you?"

"Of course," he said. "Did they tell you why they

invaded your campus? I have my theories but I want to see if they said anything."

"Yes, as soon as they broke in and shut the building down, the leader said they wanted ten million dollars wired to their account in the Cayman Islands. He seemed to know everything about us and about the Academy. He did say that this time, the Academy wouldn't know what hit them and they would pay for taking their men," said Kate.

"Just as I thought. They thought it would be easier to get to us by going through you. It didn't work. It wouldn't work and it will never work. I'm sorry you're across the street but everyone knows about our mutual commitment to each other. Our assets are your assets. You have our students in your classrooms and that may never change but we need to look at protecting you as much as we look at ourselves. You are vulnerable because of your location. We will fix that," said Joe.

As they walked out the front door, Rear Admiral Kelly came over to Joe and had tears in his eyes. "Joe, I don't know how to thank you. You saved Grace's life and the lives of all these students and workers. I will never forget this as long as I live. Grace is home and completely shaken up, Joe. She said she never saw anything like this, not even in the movies. Just looking at the broken windowpanes, I can't believe that none of our team members were hurt."

"Well, they'll be a little sore for a while. It's been a while since I jumped out of a helicopter going into action but you remember damn quickly, I'll tell you that much," said Joe.

Larry Curtis came over and shook everyone's hands. Kim said thanks to everyone and she hoped the two guards would recover. The militiamen left alive were bundled up and this time, the white supremacist group in Connecticut will not survive. Joe had a call to make to Jack Forest down in Virginia. Joe will have him empty every piggy bank owned by the group and every asset will be forfeited before the end of the week. Jack would know to start in the Cayman Islands just like before.

Joe planned on going after every group these guys came in contact with and shut them all down as well. As long as Joe was at the Academy he swore that he would take down every known group by using every credential he had. He was also sure that he would have a lot of explaining to do as to why the MSRT and Seals and the FBI were contacted along with the local police and they all deferred to Joe and there was no infighting. It might be because Joe was all three in one.

Joe was beat. He walked home the three blocks and met Julie at the door. He called her as soon as he got out of the building to let her know that he was safe and that it was over. She heard the ambulances and the police sirens going off for the last hour. She was scared she said but knew he would be all right. He had no intention of telling her he jumped out of a helicopter onto the roof and down the stairs to shoot dead two homegrown white supremacist terrorists. Maybe someday, he would tell her, maybe when he retired.

He got to his office the following morning. There were national headlines about the attack on Connecticut College and how it was broken up by the Coast Guard, FBI, and the Navy, all working together. There were reporters at the front of the main building at the Academy so Joe simply slipped past them and went through the back door. As he went up the stairs, Meg Olson grabbed Joe by the shoulder and gave him a hug and said what they just did was almost as big as beating MIT with a pickoff move. Joe couldn't help but laugh as he shook his head.

"Word has it you jumped out of the helicopter to the

roof and down the stairs to the third floor and shot the two leaders. Is that right?" she asked in awe.

"I have no comment, Ensign Olson. Shouldn't you be doing some filing or something productive?" he asked.

"I'm telling Julie you said that, you chauvinist," she smirked. "By the way, Joe, we are very proud of you."

"Thanks Meg, that really means a lot," he said. He grabbed a coffee and a donut and walked down to his office. As soon as he sat down, the Rear Admiral came to his door. He walked in and sat in the visitor's chair in front of his desk. Joe was wide eyed. "Did I do something?" he asked.

"Do something? What the hell do you think? Do something? You saved my daughter's life, Joe. You saved sixty people. You took down a group of domestic terrorists for the second time since you've been here. That's what you've done, Joe," he said.

"First, sir. It wasn't me. It was both the MSRT team and the Navy Seals that saved the day. I told you the MSRT team would make a huge difference someday. I didn't think it would be this soon. Sir, you should have seen the Seals flying down a rope and crashing through the windows, two on the second floor and three on the third. It was unbelievable. If the Seals didn't tell me the door was open on the roof, I would have never made it down the stairs on time. Those guys went flying through the windows. It was unbelievable. I don't know how they do it but we got to thank Larry Curtis for lending them to us."

"You're right, Joe. We will thank everyone in due time. However, I personally want to thank you for making a huge difference here at the Academy. I'm afraid that after this adventure, I'll never be able to keep you at the Academy as Assistant Superintendent. The Coast Guard will probably fly you all over to secure facilities everywhere. I don't want to lose you," he said.

"Well, I don't plan on going anywhere for now. Julie likes it here. She's comfortable. She's found a new home and new friends and an assignment at Connecticut College that she loves and she found peace here and is finishing her book. Bella has made friends and I can't uproot her again. She had a terrible time losing her mother and being adopted by us. I don't want her to get hurt. So, no, I don't plan on going anywhere even if they tell me to. We have what we need here or it's back to Julie's beloved Florida Keys and I'll teach mathematics at Coral Shores High School along with Julie. She only took a leave of absence and it's coming up soon."

"Don't get ahead of yourself," the Rear Admiral said. Knocking on the door was Kelly's wife, Ellen, and their daughter, Grace. "Grace has something to say to you, Joe," he said.

"Captain, Sir, Joe, I don't know what to call you. All I can say is I was scared to death and saw my life flashing in front of me yesterday. Thank you for saving our lives. I know now what you do. It's not academics, you serve and protect and I now know what that really means. When I heard those guys flying through the windows on both floors, I thought our lives were over. What you and they did was unbelievable. The two guys holding us in the classroom were overwhelmed and gave up. I heard what happened on the top two floors. To throw yourself in harms way to save us, and people you don't even know, says everything. I will remember yesterday, every day of my life, followed by a prayer to thank you and protect your family. Thank you, Joe," she said.

"Grace, thank you. You have no idea what that means to me and to everyone on the rescue team. We don't ever hear anything after the fact. We just do our jobs and move on. It's nice to be appreciated," said Joe.

He got up from behind his desk and gave both Ellen and Grace a big hug. He had tears in his eyes. Grace told him how she and her mother had lunch with Julie and wanted to be in her class in the fall. She thanked both Joe and Julie for being here at the Academy and giving her a chance to meet them and gain from them. Joe nodded and nodded to the Rear Admiral. He took the hint and moved Grace and Ellen back to his office. He whispered to them on the way back to his office, "He doesn't like praise and doesn't want to accept it. He says it's simply his job, but don't believe it."

Both Dave and Kim showed up as well. It was like homecoming week. He got a call from Kate and Erica at the college and they asked if they could see him. He told them he would be over in a little while. He couldn't wait to get out of his office. He walked over to his house, picked up Julie and Annie and they walked to the campus. Bella was in school. The lockdown at the elementary school came to an end and they simply said there were some other issues that were resolved and now everything was back to normal. They wanted to play it down for the little kids including Bella so they wouldn't be stressed out. It worked.

They walked up to the administration building. Whomever they called had now fixed all five windows on the second and third floors like nothing happened. A cleaning team came in overnight and sanitized the entire place, cleaning up the blood from the front and back entrances and on the second and third floors. It was like it never happened.

Joe, Julie, and Annie took the elevator and got off at the third floor. They were repainting the window trim as they got off. Joe walked up to the administrative assistant's desk and she got up and simply gave Joe a hug and said thank you. Kate and Erica walked out of Kate's office and went to Joe and gave both him and Julie a hug and brought them into the boardroom that was unaffected from yesterday's assault.

"Joe, thank you. I don't know what else to say to someone who just saved sixty lives including mine, Erica's and our two assistants. I still think I was watching a movie. It was unreal. It's still playing in my head. I'm sure you don't want to relive the moment with Julie here. Maybe on another day we can talk. I just wanted to see if we are missing any steps we need to take to get this behind us," she said. "And I will never fight you on any suggestion you ever make to me to keep this college safe. That's a promise," Kate said. "In my mind, I'm still watching you come in and the windows crashing with three armed Seals coming through. It was unbelievable," she said.

Joe was in for a long week. It looked like he would be on a speaking engagement for quite a while. He had to address the Academy's Board of Trustees. He was asked to speak at Connecticut College to their board. Joe called a meeting of all the cadets and would speak to all of them at once in the field house tomorrow. He still had to head to the Maritime Marine Academy and he thought he would get a call from his old Rear Admiral Jake Barnes and probably would meet him with the Admiral in Washington. He had too much to do. If they didn't follow up the money link to the terrorists, it could be lost forever. He had already called Jack Forest and he was working on it with the hint from their leader about wiring funds to the Cayman Islands.

As usual, Joe sat down for a half hour and wrote out his To Do List. If it were not on the list, it wouldn't get done. Joe never understood how anyone could ever get anything done or remember anything without writing it down and committing it to memory. Finally, as requested, Joe came up, step by step, on how he wanted Kate to handle the public relations, the board and the students. Everyone was shook up. After his address to the cadets, Joe asked if he could speak to the non-cadet students at the college to ease their minds and tell them that they were under the full protection from now on by the United States Coast Guard and the Navy. He would bring along Larry Curtis to make that point at both addresses this week.

Joe thought Rear Admiral Kelly should be doing this but the Rear Admiral wanted it to come from Joe, being younger and more adaptable to current student needs. Joe could see it on the Rear Admiral's face that his time in the Coast Guard was coming to an end. Joe wanted no part in being the next Superintendent of the Coast Guard Academy. Joe would not be the youngest college president of all time. That would have been Leon Botstein, president of Bard College at age 23. Joe would lose that by a mile at age 38.

Joe got calls from a ton of people and could hardly keep up. Joan Talbot called. Mark Silva called. Several of his FBI friends heard through the grapevine and Jake Barnes gave him a buzz as well. He was grateful to have such friends but he simply wanted it over with so he could move on and do what he wanted. He thought he owed Mary Evans and her husband, Jack Manning, a call to thank them for funding the MSRT unit on campus. He told them what happened and how they rescued sixty lives at Connecticut College yesterday. He also wanted them to come back over and meet Kate at the college. Julie wanted to talk to them as well about special funding opportunities for minority women and Joe wanted to discuss way to help students achieve whose parents never attended college. These students were both vulnerable and naïve in dealing with academic pressure. The federal government funds a program called TRIO but didn't have sufficient funding to serve everyone's needs. It worked miracles for many students. Both he and Julie wanted to see if they could revitalize the program. The Federal TRIO Programs are federal outreach and student services programs in the United States designed to identify and provide services for individuals from disadvantaged backgrounds. They are administered, funded, and implemented by the United States Department of Education. Unfortunately, too many students fall through the cracks including cadets at the Academy and minority students at the very prestigious Connecticut College.

Chapter 36

Joe didn't do it often but today he took the day off. The attack on Connecticut College was actually an attack by the Sovereign Citizens of Connecticut on the Coast Guard Academy itself. Joe needed to get his head around that. This was the second attack this year. He attended the meeting of all the military academies because there was intelligence about targeting United States military academies. Perhaps he should have expected more after the first bombing attempt that was thwarted. It wasn't thwarted because of a massive security system. It was thwarted because of quick action and understanding of procedures for these kinds of crisis. They solved the bombing quickly and arrested four members of this terrorist group but it left behind others to retaliate, which they did.

However, it did point out that they didn't attack the Academy directly because of the new systems and methods installed recently with millions of dollars spent on that effort from his fund set up by Mary Evans and Jack Manning. Maybe the terrorists went to the gate to see if they could tour the campus and were stopped. Maybe that was sufficient to let them know that there were significant changes to security at the Academy. No one enters without permission anymore. They were pretty smart in picking up the fact that cadets attended classes at Connecticut College on a daily basis and this is where they put their efforts. The backdoor was always easier to enter than the front. Before anything else, Joe needs to make sure that Connecticut College is as safe and secure as the Academy. When Jack Forest gets through his financial and technology investigation, any money found would go into a fund to vastly improve security at the college and add security staff that was evident to the world as to new improved security. For one day, Joe just wanted to take his mind off of everything that happened.

On Thursday morning, Joe was up bright and early. Julie made his coffee and a bowl of cereal knowing he had a full day ahead. At 11:00 a.m. in full uniform, Joe spoke to all the cadets, who were gathered at the athletic field. Rear Admiral Kelly accompanied Joe, many members of the Board of Trustees, and Captain Larry Curtis, head of the Navy Submarine Base.

Joe said, "You are protected by the United States Coast Guard, the FBI, Homeland Security, and the Navy Seals from now on. When completed, your safety and security will be second to none from now on." He took it one step further and said, "If you don't believe me, here is my cell phone number. Call me any time of day or night if you're not feeling safe. If I'm here, I will be at your place within fifteen minutes to where you are. I live two blocks from here. I am making that pledge to you. If I'm away on duty, here is the second number for Captain Larry Curtis, superintendent of the Navy Submarine Base, right down the street. I have a complete MSRT team available within minutes of contact and Captain Curtis has his Navy Seals on call 24/7. This is our pledge to you. We will take this as seriously as we did during the attack. Those individuals are now gone for good as well as those that helped them. Their financial backing has and will continue to be drained as soon as possible and Homeland Security has taken this attack as priority number one. Are there any questions?" he asked.

A few cadets raised their hands and asked what had been done to improve security and Joe gave them very specific answers. The cadets were impressed by Joe's sincerity. Both Marie Estevez and Luce Talbot stood mesmerized in thinking that this was their own Joe who was speaking to the entire corps. Luce never really realized the position that Joe held at the Academy and in the Coast Guard itself. No matter how many times her mother told her about Joe and his position, it never really registered until now. She was also amazed as well as the rest of the cadets after they found out that Captain Joe Traynor led the charge onto the campus of Connecticut College and jumped out of a helicopter down to the president's office and shot dead two terrorists holding them hostage. They couldn't wrap their heads around it. Luce thought that when Joe talked to her about mathematics and cross-country and what it takes to win, she never envisioned Joe Traynor as a superhero. Maybe he wasn't but he certainly was that day as they looked around and saw everyone nodding their heads.

At the end of the presentation, everyone gave Joe a standing ovation, even though they were standing anyway in the athletic field. Joe wanted this outdoors, in the sunshine, in the good weather to reconfirm that they were in charge not the terrorists. After the presentation, Joe and Larry went to Joe's house for lunch before trotting over to

Connecticut College to make the same presentation. The Rear Admiral would be coming to the Academy that afternoon so the Rear Admiral and the Board of Trustees would be tied up for some time.

Both Joe and Larry figured that they didn't need them for this so they invited Kim Matz from the local FBI office, a friend to both Joe and Larry. They walked over to the president's office. Kate Ballinger greeted both Joe and Larry at the door coming in. Kim was already there. Kate had her board assembled and they would all walk over to the Charles B. Luce Fieldhouse overlooking Silfen Field and the Thames River. This new addition provides spectator seating for the turf field and track, a refurbished lobby and campus function room, renovated squash courts, an expanded sports medicine facility, team rooms and athlete support spaces and coaches' offices, as well as all the Division III sports that need indoor facilities. Yesterday, Kate sent out a text message to everyone involved with the college to please attend this most important meeting at 2:00 p.m. There are about 1,900 students and with faculty, there were over 2,000 people in attendance. It was the biggest meeting they ever had at the college open to all for this important discussion. At this point, Joe was unaffected by large crowds. He has done it enough to know that all he had to do was look at one or two individuals in a crowd on all sides of the auditorium and that gave him confidence. He was introduced by Dr. Ballinger and as he looked around, he saw Julie in the front row, next to other professors. She never let on who she was or that she was married to Joe. Samantha picked up the kids so she could attend. She would reciprocate down the road. Sitting next to Joe was Kim Matz and Larry Curtis, along with their board and administration staff.

They were all introduced and then Joe went to the

podium and began speaking. He started with the winter bombing incident and how it was solved. He went on to discuss all the measures they took at the Academy and the gifts made to Connecticut College from the trust fund. He went on to say, if someone wants to harm you enough, it might happen regardless of the precautions put in place. He went on to apologize that the original target was the Coast Guard Academy itself and they went through Connecticut College to get to them. He went on to say that he couldn't say it wouldn't happen again but he did say he was giving the college several million dollars more from the trust fund to hire additional security staff and increase the technology at the campus for earlier detection.

He told the students that every cadet has his or her own warning signal attached to their clothing so if you get to know the cadets and hang around them long enough, you will always be the first to know as soon as the Academy knows of any crisis. If they want their own GPS pins, they will be given to any student free of charge and become a part of the Academy alert system. At the end of the presentation, Kim Matz and Larry Curtis spoke for only a minute but assured everyone that the phone numbers Joe gave out were real and to call as soon as you see a problem or don't feel safe.

At the end, they received a loud round of applause from the crowded center. It was clear that the cooperation between all these institutions is real moving forward. Joe shook hands with the board, with Kate, and Erica Jones and left the podium to walk home with Julie and Larry.

"What do you think?" Joe asked her.

"I think it went very well. I don't know if it has sunk into everyone's head yet but it certainly has sunk into Kate's and the board's brains. Can you image the lawsuits that would happen if you didn't stop this assault from happening? Can you imagine if one student died because of these terrorists? Can you image how Rear Admiral Kelly and Ellen would feel if anything ever happened to Grace?" she asked.

"Yes to all of it," he said. At that, people started to come up to Joe and thank him for the heroism shown by everyone involved. Students especially crowded around and thanked Joe. He vocalized what he said and asked everyone if they wrote down those two phone numbers. They all said yes so Joe simply nodded. On the way out, he met with Kate briefly and gave her a list of added security that was needed by the college and it totaled well over two million dollars above what was already spent for security at the college. She said she would review the list with her board that also included ten new additional armed security personnel including two administrators to always have backup. That alone was over $600,000.00 a year. He would pay the price for two years and they needed to raise the rest. This was not paying farmers not to plant tobacco like the old days. If it's handed to them they would continue to expect it every year. Joe knew he could only do so much.

He walked back with Julie and Larry and gave her a kiss at the door. He and Larry were meeting with Admiral Hartnagle and the Board of Trustees at 5:00 p.m. along with Rear Admiral Kelly. He hoped he didn't have to go away again for a while. He and Julie and the kids were going to Luce's first meet this Saturday, September 10th at the Vassar Run Stonitsch Invitational in Poughkeepsie, New York, about 130 miles away and about two hours in time. The meet begins at 11:20 a.m. on the campus. They would leave from New London around 8:00 a.m. just to make sure they get there on time. They asked Maria if she wanted to go and she was delighted. She asked permission and it was granted. The administration was not about to turn down a request from Joe and Julie Traynor.

Joe and Larry walked through the front door of the administration building like they were joined at the hip. They have become good friends because they were thrown in together to sink or swim and they swam well together. Joe came to the door with Larry and he was introduced to Admiral Hartnagle by the Rear Admiral. The full board had been assembled because it was an emergency meeting. *Maybe now they'll take this way more seriously,* Joe thought. They walked into the boardroom and took a seat. As soon as they did, the clapping began and seemed to go on forever. The Admiral stood up and congratulated both of them for a job well done above and beyond the call of duty. Larry looked around and smiled and saw his boss from Washington, D.C. as well. They were both given medals of honor. This was Joe's second, winning one back in Troy, New York for taking down the Mexican Mafia. Everyone smiled so Joe didn't say a word. He winked at Larry and he got the message to simply keep his mouth shut and roll with the tide. The meeting ended and the Admiral asked if he could meet with Joe, Rear Admiral Kelly and Rear Admiral Jake Barnes, Joe's mentor, who is now part of the board of trustees. Joe was leery about what they wanted. He would find out tomorrow. Joe went to bed when the kids did. Julie had a few calls to make to her publisher, as her book would soon be ready for editing. It seemed like their vacation was long gone and she missed going home to Key Largo already. At least they would head back for Christmas and a nice visit with Tillie and her friends. After Christmas, Tillie would come back with them for a few weeks. The planning was done and the waiting would seem long.

Joe was dressed in his full uniform and shoes shined so

you could see your face in the leather. As soon as Bella was leaving for school, Joe walked her to the corner and watched her head down the next block on her way to school. She was growing like a weed. You couldn't stop Annie from walking all over the house now. It took two days for her to figure out she could walk and then never stopped from morning to night. It was becoming obvious that Julie was getting worn down. He would pick up the slack as soon as he got home from work. He would cook, do the dishes and tuck the kids into bed. At least that would help a little. Julie needed time to finish her own edits and time to prepare for her class at the college. Class was cancelled that first week of the onslaught so she had to make up the classes. Since there were only 15 and the classes were in the evening, Joe helped free her up to go teach.

Joe walked in to the administration building, taking two steps at a time, until he hit the front door. He headed for his office and then grabbed a cup of coffee. His meeting was at 9:15 a.m. because Jake and the Admiral were heading out by noon in their private plane at the airport. The Admiral and a few staff would be dropped off in Washington, D.C. and Jake would continue on to Miami. As soon as Joe sat down, Jake knocked on his door.

"Joe, do you have a minute before the meeting?" he asked.

"Of course, Sir," said Joe. He was becoming more and more curious.

"I just want to personally congratulate you on a remarkable job you did taking down the terrorists once more. The scuttlebutt is that you jumped from a helicopter with two of your team and ran down the stairs from the roof and personally took out the two terrorists as the Seals were crashing through the windows. Is that true?" he asked.

"Most of it, Sir. I had two MSRT team members right along for the ride and the terrorists were distracted by the flying broken glass but I did shoot both of them. They were far enough removed from Kate and Erica that I didn't think they would be harmed if we went in quickly, which we did," said Joe.

"Well that settles that," he said. "By the way, I'm retiring in the spring of next year. The Admiral wants to talk to you about your next move in or out of the Coast Guard. You have done a fantastic job here and everyone I spoke to including all the Trustees want you to stay. However, I have recommended that you take my place as Rear Admiral for the Miami District 7. I believe the job is yours if you want it. It obviously means a move back to Florida and perhaps Julie would like that. It also means uprooting Bella once again. However, this would be a long-term placement of at least eight years. That would mean Bella who's almost eight will be almost sixteen and sophomore in high school. It's something to think about, Joe," Jake said. "I'll leave you with that. I'm hitting the head before the meeting. Kelly will be there too," he said.

Joe walked into the boardroom and met with Jake, Rear Admiral Kelly and Admiral Hartnagle. They all congratulated Joe on his accomplishments and said that word from the cadets is that Joe's a rock star. Several board members from Connecticut College called Rear Admiral Kelly and asked him when his time was up at the Academy so he could move over to their college. Joe laughed and said no thank you. The Admiral brought up that Jake was retiring and asked Joe point blank if he wanted the job and to move back to Miami. He said Joe could take all the time he needed. All three wanted him back as a member of the Board of Trustees if he took Jake's position when he retired. They made it sound like it was a win-win situation. Joe was torn. He really liked being at the Academy but he was bored with his assignments here. He did the jobs that Kelly didn't want. It was like being Vice President of the United States, ceremonial at best and in charge of not much. As head of a District, he got to make all the changes he thought were relevant to meet the needs of the 21st century. He could strengthen recruitment to reflect the community. He could probably get as much funding as he needed from Jack and Mary to fight white supremacy, which was a major priority. He could make Julie happy, truly happy.

Joe thanked all of them for their confidence in his ability and told them that he and Julie had a lot to think about. He also quickly mentioned that Jack Forest just uncovered $6.2 million dollars in accounts in the Cayman Islands in the names of the individuals shot dead at Connecticut College. All the money was in their personal name, not in the name of the organization. If and when the Sovereign Citizens of Connecticut wanted to make a withdrawal, they would be unpleasantly surprised. Joe gave the Admiral the new account number and passwords necessary to transfer into any accounts he wanted. The funds were now safely stored in a secret Coast Guard Account. It was the same account that stored Mike Hanley's CIA funds to pay to house the Nationalist Alliance captives in Florida. Joe told them that the bill for the newest upgrade to Connecticut College would be in the $2.0 to $3.0 million dollar range. With that, Joe thanked them and took his leave. He had a lot to discuss with Julie tonight. She would probably be pleased in the long run. He just needed to think long term. Eight years more in the Coast Guard was probably six years more than he wanted to give.

Chapter 37

After talking to Joe at great length, Luce has a much better understanding of what she needs to accomplish to make the 2024 United States Women's Olympic team for the 10,000-meter run. The cross-country event that was presented to the Paris committee was rejected even though many expected it to be accepted. Luce thought there was a better chance in 2028. So, Luce did the mathematics with Joe to see what she needed to do this fall to be on track to be invited for tryouts for the 10,000-meter event in late 2023 for the 2024 Olympics in Paris. Her last best time was 20.01.1 for the 6K, which is 60% of a 10,000-meter run.

She really didn't know what that 6K time even meant in light of the fact that it was her high school record for Florida and her practice time at Miami. There was no incentive to beat that time since she won every event she was in at high school and didn't compete at Miami because she was redshirted. Now she had something to shoot for and had actual numbers to reach to meet that goal. She never had a coach, or anyone, tell her exactly what she needed to do until Joe proved his point mathematically. So, in her first meet at Vassar, she needed to get her time down considerably to make heads turn in her direction that she was someone to watch. First things first, she thought. She needed to go for the Women's Division I NCAA championship time for the 6K and then she would be noticed, even as she ran Division III. Last year's Division III winner ran a 20.11.1, which was slower by ten seconds than what Luce was running now. So, in the meantime, Luce would also concentrate on being the Division III winner. If she could run at the Division I winner's rate, it would blow the Division III record away.

As both Joe and her coach said, it's the time not the division she runs in. She needs to meet or exceed 19.25.4 this Saturday to be even with last year's Division I winner. Regardless of how any of the women run today, she needs to win by a wide margin. She has to cut her time by 35.6 seconds to tie last year's Division I winner. She would think about wearing a stopwatch on her wrist and develop a time to do this pace over the course of the 6K. However, she also thought it might be a distraction and every second counted. She would just go all out for this race.

Joe, Julie, Bella and Annie were all in the SUV and Maria just got there on time. She had some morning duties and couldn't leave until they were done. With some help from her friends, who knew she was going to see Luce with the Traynors, they pitched in and made sure she made it in time. She did. They left right at 8:00 a.m. as planned. It was 130 miles away and about two hours. They wanted to get there and park and see Luce before the 11:20 a.m. start. They got there right at 10:30 a.m. Parking was no problem. Division III cross-country meets didn't attract a lot of attention from students or the public. Joe hoped that after this run, Luce's first as a college student, that would change. They found the bleachers where the race would start and end. This was quite a big race. There were students from the Coast Guard Academy, Vassar, RPI, Ithaca College, SUNY New Paltz, Sage Colleges, Ramapo College, SUNY Delhi, Bard and Farleigh Dickinson University, which is large enough to be a Division I school. Joe thought if it weren't for Luce and the Coast Guard Academy, he would root for RPI, his Alma Mater.

They started out in order by their best times with the slowest runners in the back of the pack. Luce was in the third row because she didn't have a college time to her credit, other than her submitted practices, which were accepted. They all started to cheer when the gun went off and Luce was near the head of the pack within a minute. Joe wished they could follow the runners around but that was impossible with the ins and outs all through the campus. They simply had to wait. Twenty minutes was not a long time but a lifetime when waiting to see who would be in front of the pack. It was now very clear that Luce Talbot was running like her hair was on fire. As they turned the corner, she was all alone by herself. There was no one even close to her as she broke through the finish line. She simply trotted over immediately to see her time. It appeared that the closest runner to her was a minute longer, coming in second. Luce looked up and her time was posted at 19.24.8, a new tournament record. Not only did she shatter the women's Division III record of 20.11.1 and the second runner up at 20.28.6, but also she beat the Division I 2021 winner by a fraction. Last year's winner was at 19.25.4 and Luce just ran a 19.24.8. That's 6/10th of a second better than last year's Division I winner. She knocked off 35.3 seconds from her previous best time, which obviously was not her best time. She never needed to compete this hard before.

Joe looked at Julie and Maria and said, "She just beat

the 2021 Division I winner's time by 6/10th of a second in her first Division III event. I think she's on her way. Maybe she can't get down to a 17.52.47 equivalent from the 10,000-meter winner but she could make the top three invitees with an 18.51.0 within the next year and a half. She now has something to shoot for," he said.

Julie has never seen Joe this excited. Luce came over and thanked them for being there for the event. Julie had the beginning and the ending of the race on video and would ship it off to Luce's parents as soon as she could. Julie told her that she was family and of course they would be there. Luce hugged Maria as well who was all excited. She couldn't believe what Luce just did.

Last year, the Coast Guard Academy was ranked 8th nationally at the Division III level. They never won an event and never had anyone come in first, especially by such a large margin. They won this event going away with 39 points, versus RPI's second place 69 points, Vassar at 77 points and SUNY New Paltz at coming in 4th with 112. You add up the runner placements and when you only have to add a "1," you are well on your way to winning. Ribbons were handed out and a plaque went to Coach Brown who was grinning from ear to ear. He spoke to Joe and told him he couldn't believe that Luce had over a full one-minute lead over the 2nd place finisher. The first four runners for The Coast Guard Academy came in 1 (never happened before), 8 (never happened before), 10 (never happened before, and 20th, equaling 39 points. It was also announced that Cadet Luce Talbot of the Coast Guard Academy shattered the Division III record and also beat the Division I record by 6/10 of a second. Everyone on the team went nuts. Bella didn't understand what was happening until Julie told her that Luce came in first and beat 40 other women in the race. Bella cheered while Annie was sound asleep in her stroller. It was a little after 1:30 p.m. when they headed back to their SUV and the ride home. It was pizza and wing night again. Joe would never get sick of it. Julie already was.

Luce was the talk of the Academy the next day. The local sports reporter on WNPX-TV came on and at the end of the broadcast mentioned that Luce Talbot of the Coast Guard Academy, in her first college event broke the Division III women's cross-country record and beat last year's Division I winner by 6/10th of a second. She said that they better keep an eye on her next Saturday at her next event. If she wins again by such a wide margin, it means she's the real deal. Luce simply smiled throughout the day and said thank you to everyone. Her own teammates said that her dedication to running made them better and it showed with their finishes with two others in the top 10. It was amazing how one event could light up an entire campus but it happened. Most of the administrators knew that Luce came up from the Florida Keys and they knew about her relationship with Joe and Julie Traynor. They even laughed when they found out that Julie was Luce's babysitter and that Luce was Bella's babysitter.

Things were going pretty well with Julie's author class at Connecticut College. Her Tuesday and Thursday evening classes were well attended and there was a waiting list for next semester. That night that Joe got back from speaking to Jake Barnes and Admiral Hartnagle proved to be very interesting. Julie didn't know what to make of it. She kept asking Joe if they really want him to take Jake's position as Rear Admiral of District 7 in Miami. She couldn't believe it. He said he couldn't either. They went back and forth and wound up not knowing what to do. There was a lot to consider. Julie vividly remembers picking up sand in her hand outside the condo in Key

Largo, wishing they were there permanently. If they went back and lived in Key Largo, Joe would have an eighty-mile drive back and forth every day, five days a week. That's a little much at 800 miles a week or over 40,000 miles a year with vacations.

They could live in Coral Gables or even a little south and cut it by two thirds but then they would have to commute to see Tillie almost every week as she got older. At least they would be in Florida. She thought about her new career as a college professor, which she liked very much. She could write her books anywhere and visit her publisher anytime he wanted by plane. Annie would not be a problem because she is just a baby. Uprooting Bella could be an issue since she had settled in so nicely here in New London. She has made great new friends as well. It was a flip of a coin but ultimately what did Joe want to do?

Did he want to stay at the Academy, coach baseball which he loved, watch Luce become a national story or lead the 7th District in routing out white supremacy and those who wanted to destroy this country. He had a very hard decision to make and soon. They would head to Florida for Christmas. She needed to go to New York City to finish her edits and get her new book released before Christmas. Her 30th birthday was coming up on October 17th and Bella would make her first appearance in a Disney episode from Hollywood Studios in Orlando, Florida. Once again, everything was starting to pile up on both Joe and Julie and they decided that the best thing to do before the end of the year was nothing. They would let everything play out. Joe was still deciding if he wanted to retire on his birthday next April 16th and attend law school either at Yale down the road from New London or back at the University of Miami, in Coral Gables. Julie would ask Tillie what she thought and wanted to ask Mary Evans the same questions. No one has had their lives uprooted as much as Mary Evans and Jack Manning. She was sure they both could offer Joe and her good advice.

Chapter 38

Epilogue

Julie took the Amtrak train to New York City. She would be there for one full workweek, Monday through Friday, coming home late Friday night. Joe dropped her off at the New London Amtrak station at 27 Water Street, only a mile and a half from their house. Her train for New York City leaves at 9:48 a.m. and arrives at Penn Station in New York City at 12:22 p.m. She only had a single carry-on bag and her computer bag, along with her largest pocketbook. She would be coming home from Penn Station on Friday, leaving at 5:38 p.m., with an arrival time of 8:13 p.m. Joe and the kids would be waiting for her at the New London station.

Julie arrived right on time and as she headed up the stairs, Sarah told her that she would meet her right under the large main concourse clock. As Julie came up the stairs, Sarah called out her name and waved. With her was Catherine, her assistant, that Julie had met in New London when they came to give her a very large check for her new book.

"Julie how was your trip? How's Joe and the kids?" she asked. Catherine just nodded. She had the secondary role down pat. Julie could only imagine working in New York City for a well-known publisher and all that entails.

"Everyone is doing fine. Annie is growing like a weed. Bella started third grade and Joe took down another bunch of criminals that were attacking the Academy. Just another day's work, Joe said," said Julie and smiled.

"We heard about it on the national news. I was sure that Joe was in the middle of it," said Sarah. "After you get settled, you have to tell us all about it. We're walking to the apartment first so you can drop your things off. Then we can head over to the office, a block away. Everyone is excited to see you. They haven't seen you since your wedding at St. Patrick's Cathedral. They want baby pictures too and pictures of Bella. She is getting so grown up," said Sarah.

They walked out of Penn Station and down the two blocks to the apartment. The same security team was seated at the front desk and they were very pleased to see Julie. She and Joe made quite an impression on them the last time they were here. Julie dropped off her stuff and went to the bathroom. She washed up a little and then they headed back out. From there, they went to Sarah's publishing office to meet the team that has worked so hard on her trilogy. They were waiting for her to give an overview of her new book. She shook hands with everyone and those she knew she gave hugs. They went into the boardroom, which was a catch all for about every kind of meeting they ever had. Julie hadn't eaten since breakfast so she had a cup of coffee and a New York City style bagel with cream cheese. She said she couldn't wait to get a bagel, a real bagel once again. As she sat there, she aimed her iPhone and connected it to the overhead screen and started to show all her pictures since they came to New London including a picture of her in the hospital holding her newborn. They were amazed at how big Bella had grown. They saw pictures of Joe in his dress uniform and most of the women simply shook their head as if to say, "How do I snag one of those?"

They all wanted to know about the latest attack at Connecticut College so Julie very lightly went over what happened. They just couldn't believe that Joe was the Assistant Superintendent of the Academy at thirty-eight years old. They also couldn't believe that in only a few weeks, Julie would turn thirty. They remember her as the new graduate with an MFA from Brown University, signing a contract for her trilogy. They all said that time simply flew. At that point, Julie handed her manuscript to Sarah, who asked Catherine to make several copies so they all could read it first and then review it together during the week. They knew that Julie was on a time schedule, especially with a newborn. Julie had made it easier for them all along by sending in a few chapters at a time after she edited it herself. She was an excellent editor and it showed.

Julie was getting tired and wanted to head to the apartment. From there, Sarah and her husband, Bennett, would pick up Julie and walk over to Luigi's on West 29th Street. It is the place that Julie loved after finding it on her own when she was first here to promote her trilogy. She ate there every night for a week and actually made friends with the owners. She wondered if they would remember her. They had the best northern Italian cuisine in the area. As they walked in, the owners came out and welcomed Julie back. She was shocked that they remembered her from so long ago. "Your exploits in New York City remain legendary," they said. "A bride, in her full wedding gown, walking to the Waldorf Astoria, from St. Patrick's Cathedral along 5th Avenue in New York City attracted quite a crowd," they said. She laughed. The food was excellent and she said she was here all week and would be back if they didn't drag her someplace else.

Joe planned on working from home all week to take care of Annie and to make sure that Bella made it to and from school safely. It wasn't but a few weeks ago that her school was locked down because of the attack at Connecticut College. Julie had made spaghetti and meatballs to have during the week. She told Joe that man did not live alone on pizza and wings. He complied. Samantha brought over beef stew one night and Joe made pancakes and bacon. He could eat breakfast anytime. Bella would eat anything that had maple syrup on it. Annie was restless at first because she missed Julie but she started to settle in. Joe took her for walks several times a day and they walked to his office to see everyone. They knew that Julie was in New York City for her final edits and they all helped Joe out. Luce and Maria came over one evening to sit with them and make sure the wash was done and the dishes and general clean up. As meticulous as Joe was, he couldn't keep up with the whirlwind of two daughters.

Joe couldn't make Luce's second meet at UMASS Dartmouth, which is south of Boston and only thirty miles to the beginning of Cape Cod. It's a little over eighty miles southeast from the Academy. Luce made another splash, getting her name better known after each event. She dropped her time again by 20 seconds from 19.24.8 to 19.04.2. That put her well ahead of the previous Division I winner from 2021. She needs to get to 18.51.0 to be invited for tryouts. She's now documented only 13.2 seconds short for an invitation.

She knew that Joe and her coach were right, all that counted was her time not her Division. She told Joe that she heard from her old coach from the University of Miami. The fastest Hurricane last year ran a 21.05.06 and now Luce was already down to 19.04.2, almost two minutes faster. Coach Deem said he would pick her up tomorrow and bring her back to Miami. She knew he was kidding but was he really? She was confident in her own abilities and he never even knew she existed until she left to head to the Coast Guard Academy.

Julie spent all week with Sarah and Catherine and the rest of the staff. She thought she would be done by Thursday but Sarah wanted her to attend a few meetings she set up with other national reviewers to get a few words on the cover of the new book recommending it to young women everywhere. Julie went along with it because she just got a check for an advance for a lot of money. She needed to sell books if she wanted this to continue. Writing a book was arduous but certainly not any harder than waiting tables at the Waffle House like her grandmother did to support her. This was a piece of cake compared to that. It was also easier than jumping out of helicopters to save hostages. She found that out when Dr. Ballenger let it out of the bag when they went to visit her the next day after the attack. She certainly hoped that Joe didn't have to do this again. Her work was done in New York City and she arrived back in New London on Friday night right on time. As soon as Bella and Annie saw her, they both climbed all over her. Joe smiled and simply nodded welcome home and gave her a big kiss.

When Julie was gone, he was free to talk about her upcoming 30th birthday. He wanted a celebration because he thought it was a big deal. He mentioned it to his Rear Admiral and he asked if he could rent the Officer's Club for Monday, October 17th for her birthday. He smiled and told him that if it was approved, the Rear Admiral, Ellen and Grace were invited. The Rear Admiral smiled and said what a great guy Joe was. Joe laughed. He wanted about 30 people there including Tillie and Ed Lansing. Joe would fly them up and put them in a hotel in town as a surprise. Tillie should not miss Julie's 30th birthday party. He invited all her local friends including Maddy and Jim White, Kim and Eric Matz, Sean and Samantha O'Neil, Larry Curtis and his wife, Brian Casey and his wife, along with several in his office. He called Kate Ballenger and Erica Jones and they would make it as well.

He called Mary Evans to ask her a special favor. They spoke for a while and they would come with Joe's father, his brother Pete, and Tanya, his wife. He told Mary that he wanted to get both Julie and Tillie special gifts commemorating the event. He was hesitant but she readily agreed to help get the presents and bring the gifts with her to the party. She knew the birthdays and gemstones for Bella, Annie and Julie and knew that Tillie would be 70 in November. Joe and Julie and the kids would be down there for Christmas but would miss her birthday. So, Joe wanted to get her something special and give it to her at Julie's party. Tillie had been a surrogate mother to him since he was eighteen years old. Both Luce and Maria asked special permission to stay at their house to watch the girls during the party. It would be from 7:00 p.m. until 10:00 p.m. and Joe would get them back to their dorm room. He doubted that anyone would give him a hard time especially now.

Joe told Julie that he was taking her to the Officer's Club for her birthday. He didn't want to make it a big deal so it would blow the surprise but he did dress up in his full uniform. Julie dressed to the nines as well. Luce and Maria showed up at 6:30 p.m., right on time. Bella was thrilled and Annie was running around the coffee table playing catch me if you can. Joe and Julie bent down to give them each a kiss and a hug and told them to mind Luce and Maria and to go to bed on time. If they were good, Julie said she would get them a special treat the next day.

They walked hand in hand through the front gate to the Academy and the guards at the gate saluted Joe. He returned the salute and they walked to the Officer's Club. The Club was rather dark and Julie wondered if Joe even asked if they were open on Monday night. She thought they could then go to their favorite seafood place but Joe would be disappointed. They walked up the steps and entered through the front door. All you could hear was, "HAPPY BIRTHDAY TO YOU until the song ended. Julie was in shock. She looked around at all her friends and then saw Tillie and started to cry. Tillie came over and gave her a big hug.

"You don't think I'd forget your 30th birthday, do you? I love you. Ed's here too," she said. Julie gave Ed a big hug and thanked him for coming.

She then hugged everyone in the place. After getting her composure, she turned to Joe and said, "I can't believe you kept this a secret. There is no way you could do that. I've known you since forever. There's no way," said Julie and then gave him a big kiss.

Dinner was a great success. The food was as always exceptional, especially with the Rear Admiral and his family attending. Julie was embarrassed about getting gifts but opened them all and thanked everyone. At the end, Joe gave her a small wrapped jewelry box. Joe turned to Mary Evans and mouthed, "Thank you." Julie opened her gift. It was a mother's ring with two large stones representing her two daughters. Bella's birth month is June so there was a perfect pearl. Annie's birth month was January, which is

Garnet, which looks like a large pomegranate. She read off the inscription in the box that stated that a pearl was for purity and the Garnet stood for a seed. She tried the ring on the traditional right-hand ring finger and it fit perfectly. She just kept staring at it and had a glow about her.

Joe called over Tillie and said he had a gift for her as well. Her birthday would be coming up in November and they wouldn't be able to make it down until Christmas, so he had something for her. Again, he looked at Mary and nodded. He handed the box to Tillie who opened it cautiously. She lightly lifted up a gold Grandmother's necklace. On the necklace were three large charms, all in gold. On the charms were the names Julie, with an opal attached, Bella with a pearl, and Annie with a garnet stone. On Julie's it was written granddaughter and on Bella's and Annie's, it was written great-granddaughter. Tillie didn't know what to say. There wasn't a dry eye among any of the women attending. A few of the guys were tearing up as well as Rear Admiral Kelly. It was a wonderful moment that they could share with friends and family.

They said their goodbyes. Everyone would stop at the house on Tuesday to say goodbye. Tillie and Ed would stay a few more days and then heads back to Key Largo. Joe thanked Mary for helping him out. She thought it was a wonderful present for both Julie and Tillie and a moment to remember. They said they would be back in Key West for Christmas and they would get together. Joe told them about the condo where they would be staying again. Joe drove the two young ladies back to the dorm and thanked them for watching the kids. They loved Julie's ring.

On Wednesday night, Bella would be making her debut on the Disney channel from the Hollywood Studios in Disney World. The show would start at 7:00 p.m. and was the 4th in the trilogy series, *A Girl's Story*. It was the first of the three books, capturing Julie's life as a preteen. They all sat around the television with Bella right in the middle. Bella's part came on about twenty minutes into the episode and she sat with young girls who only spoke Spanish. She did a wonderful job interpreting the Spanish into English for the actress playing the role of a teacher. During the filming, the teacher asked Bella how she had come to learn Spanish. Being so young and honest, she simply said, "My mother came from Cuba and I was born in Florida. We only spoke Spanish at home so I had a hard time in school. Julie was a good friend of my mommy and Julie helped both of us with English. My mommy died of a brain tumor when I was in kindergarten. Before she died, she asked Julie if she would be my mommy and for Joe to be my daddy. They both said yes. When she died, I came to live with them and I am their daughter. I now have a baby sister that I love and I am very happy. I love my mommy and daddy."

The actress was taken aback a little and you could see that they had cut to a break. Bella asked how she did and both Joe and Julie gave her a big hug. Tillie and Ed had wet eyes but held it in. No one knew what to say but they were together as one family. Wherever they go or whatever they do, they'll do it together. Joe and Julie had a lot to think about in the next few months. The decision they make will affect all of them for the rest of their lives. To Joe and Julie, family comes first.

THE END

About the Author

Daniel J. Barrett was born in Rutland, Vermont and has lived his entire life in Troy, New York, ten miles north of Albany. He is a graduate of both Siena College in Loudonville, N.Y. with a BS in Finance, and from Rensselaer Polytechnic Institute in Troy, NY, with an MBA in Management. He has had a varied career, first as a commercial banker, then as the chief accountant and manager of financial and strategic planning for a large division of a major international corporation. He has extensive international experience, traveling worldwide.

Barrett has also served as the first executive director for economic development for a county in New York State, and as the first lay director for a Catholic shrine in Massachusetts. For the last thirty years, he has served as a financial, strategic planning, and educational consultant to corporations, non-profit organizations, colleges and universities, and government agencies.

Barrett continues to live in Troy and has been married to his wife, Sandy, for 53 years this year. They have three children, Sean, Eileen, and Ryan, and four grandchildren, Shannon, Caden, Megan, and Declan.

An avid reader, and inspired by numerous authors, Barrett has read almost 3,400 books in the last fifteen years which has helped him craft his two series and eight books.